DRAWER #7

Jeff Wade

CHAPTER ONE

WHO

-Born on Stage-

B lankets of smoke hung like fog in a cemetery; the mirror was clouded with layers of nicotine. But this much was certain: *That was not her face!*

Not her eyes staring back at her but then, what did her eyes look like anyway? She cocked her head, anticipating amusement when she realized what was happening.

No revelation enlightened her.

She inched forward for a closer look. No, definitely not her face.

Assess: I'd been . . .

Been doing what, exactly? And where?

Her memory was as blank as the eyes in the glass.

Well, what do *I remember?*

No farther back than maybe sixty seconds ago.

Spinning. She found herself spinning, woke up spinning, was seemingly *born* spinning, centripetal force flinging her hair wildly. Scenery passing in a blur. Her skull rattled with rhythmic pulses over which Rod Stewart husked something about being sexy and wanting his body. Her circling created a recurring Doppler effect, the pitch of the music rising and falling, rising and falling.

Motion sickness. A lump balled in her belly, exacerbated by the smell of . . . What was that *smell?*

Spinning.

She realized the pivot point was a thick brass pole, to which she was tethered by her own grip. Disoriented, she lost purchase on the metal—and tumbled to the floor like a discarded ventriloquist dummy. She sucked a hiss through her teeth and flipped her hair out of her face.

Spinning, now only in her head, eyes swimming, she propped herself on one elbow. Pin spots cut through a fetid haze like searchlights seeking an escaped convict. She squinted, shading her eyes from the slashing colored beams. Her nostrils stung with the overwhelming tang of cigarette smoke.

Still spinning, slower now, her eyes began to lock on images. Above her, suspended speakers. A distorted voice, torn to rags by the pounding beat, competed with the music. Beside her, the brass pole from which she'd just fallen. Beyond that, jeering faces shouted. Some waved . . . dollar bills? Why just faces and arms? Were they standing in a pit?

No. She herself was elevated somehow.

A *stage?*

A stage. With a brass pole. Before an audience.

She struggled to her feet and shaded her eyes from the blinding lights. Beyond the line of bellowing masks, a throng of silhouettes gestured wildly. *That* was the smell.

She grimaced at the pungency of oversexed bodies in unwashed clothes, all ripe with alcohol sweat—all men. Most were yelling, or maybe cheering, hands cupped to their mouths. Some whistled through circled fingers. A few doubled over with laughter.

The distorted voice vying for attention again: "Let's give it up for Star!"

She turned, tottered, nearly tripped. Emergency exit. Backdoor. Doggy door. *Anything.*

Instead, floor-to-ceiling mirrors presented other, more urgent concerns.

As expected, the glass revealed the usual mirror world, where right was left and front was back. There was the reversed stage on which she stood; backwards patrons jeered from deeper beyond the surface.

But what she saw within *this* fantasy world suggested other, more troubling opposites. Perhaps good was evil there. Perhaps people grew to infancy as they aged, for they were born dead.

It was the image of herself that disturbed her, that conjured the darkness. She saw her reflection, yes—but seeing in no way meant believing.

She was topless. A black leather g-string barely covered her in a studded triangle. The elastic straps holding it in place disappeared around her hips. She felt them now, meeting just below the dimples at the small of her back, turning south, disappearing into her gluteal cleft. Her ass, then, would be exposed to the fetid air of the club.

For the scrutiny of all.

Her feet were wedged into open-toed, chic black corset heels. Their leather straps wound almost to her knees. She struggled to maintain balance, teetering as she wriggled her toes.

(I said, let's give it up for Star! Hey! Star!)

The face.

This had to be a ruse of some sort. A wall-mounted screen? Some digital version of a funhouse mirror? Except even the peripherally visible shapes of her nose and lips were all wrong.

Like with anyone, the outermost aspects of her face were apparent. Accustomed to them, they remained beyond conscious notice. In the case of blemishes, makeup, or sometimes with certain wounds, the changed topography is quite apparent until we acclimate ourselves to it.

She could undoubtedly discern facial alterations in her peripheral, but no blemishes or irregularities of any kind marred the countenance in the glass. Injury free, the face was healthy and normal enough, except for the purple dyed tips of its brown hair. Just that, it wasn't *her* hair. Not her nose, not her lips, not her *face*.

Flummoxed, confused, she gently ran the fingers of her right hand over her eyes, nose, lips, throat . . .

(Star!)

A glance down at her real body proved the mirror 100% accurate in its assessment—if not brutal in its indifferent presentation.

She shifted her eyes back to the glass. In fact, she realized, that was not her body, either Not her breasts, not her legs, not even her toes peeking from the ends of the heels. As her focus shifted to the fingers tracing her body, the mirror revealed chipped red polish on bitten nails as if they belonged to a twelve-year-old.

Those were not even her hands!

Pursing her lips, wriggling her eyebrows, blinking—the face mimicked her every expression.

"JULES!"

She was snapped out of her reverie not by the DJ but by the more insistent, acoustic voice booming for attention from behind her—and by the enormous body of the voice bumbling up onto the stage.

"What's wrong, baby girl?"

Assess: Black male. Maybe six-six, 300 pounds.

Instinctively, she crossed her arms to cover herself, right over left. Just as his right hand fell on her left shoulder, she seized the first three fingers of it in her right hand.

Adrenaline flooded her bloodstream. She ducked under his arm, twisting it as she skittered into place. Changing hands as she wound up behind him, she hyper-extended his fingers in her left fist, shooting his elbow skyward.

The refrigerator grimaced and teetered. She yanked down and body-checked him, *hard.*

Wind-milling his arms for balance, his size working against him, he careened into the brass pole, vibrating the entire stage. He slipped off the platform and onto a front-row table. Glass shattered and patrons scattered like cockroaches.

She confirmed his neutralization only peripherally, for her focus was on escape—getting *out,* waking *up,* getting *gone,* flying *free.*

Leaping from the stage, stumbling on the heels, dizzied by the dancing colored pin spots, dodging a drunk, colliding with a topless waitress balancing a tray of drinks *(Goddamn it, Star!),* she jostled her way toward the glowing exit sign, hands protecting her breasts.

Her left ankle turned painfully on the heels. She managed to catch herself on a baby-faced frat brother. His t-shirt exclaimed, *No means Yes and Yes means TRAIN!*

The punk took advantage of the moment for a quick grope. So she broke the left spike-heel off on his foot, chambering her knee nearly all the way to her collarbone. Her ankle screamed with the impact.

The boy crumbled to the floor. The pounding music swallowed his shouts of pain. She stomped the other heel off on the floor and shot into the crowd.

A man's suit jacket draped over the back of a chair. Grab it. Twirl it over her shoulders. That's it, faster now, picking up momentum, toward the exit, toward sanity.

Pushing and shoving her way through the crowd, she puzzled over her combat instincts. How had she done those things? Of what else was she capable?

She was dreaming. Had to be.

She slammed that square peg against the round hole of what her five senses were telling her, but it refused to penetrate.

A dead-eyed waitress stepped aside, barricading drunks with one hand, raising her tray above the path with the other.

But if not a dream, what was it? Who was *she?* Where had she come from?

Stop it!

Focus. Get the hell out of here.

Dodging another drunk, stepping over a spill, she worked her way through the maze of bodies and then—

"Where you think you going, *Cat?*" Another bouncer, a black Arnold Schwarzenegger, blocked the doorway with his bulk. *BT's,* apparently the name of this hellhole, was embroidered over his left pec. His massive chest stretched the letters like Play-Doh. Hands on his hips, he was a mountain, immovable. She glanced left, then right—then snapped her head left again.

Another mirrored wall. Panicked expression, slender arms, ivory skin stretched taut over thin legs, again she gawked at herself.

That's not me, damn it!

Why the amnesia? Was she in shock? Maybe on drugs? She felt sober. Lucid. She'd never taken an illegal substance in her life. *(And how do I know this?)* But perhaps she'd been slipped something?

By whom? And for what purpose?

Perhaps she'd suffered a head injury. She felt no pain or dizziness, save for the effects of the dancing lights and second-hand smoke, which was no doubt laced with weed.

Or maybe this was a nightmare after all, and she'd soon wake up.

But wake up *where?* If it wasn't a dream, where was she *now? Who* was she?

Reality intruded when the bouncer's fist clamped around her left upper arm. She spied another topless waitress with a tray of drinks. Just within reach.

In one quick motion, she seized the neck of a frosty Corona, hand flipped thumb-side down, and arced it over her shoulder. The container shattered over the bouncer's head.

Blinded by suds and shards of glass, he released her, more concerned now with swiping slivers from his face without further lacerating himself.

She slipped past and slammed into the push-bar of the front door.

She stumbled to a stop. The door eased shut behind her, muting the chaos and Rod Stewart's husky crooning. Incongruously, a cool breeze lightly caressed her hair. Halogen lights provided a glowing blanket for the cars dozing in the lot. She took a deep breath. Released it slowly. The fresh air calmed her, but she knew better than to relax.

Silence, save for the sound of her breathing.

Hugging the jacket tightly around her, she desperately surveyed the lot. Heart pounding. She felt like a damn Dutch milkmaid in the broken-heel footwear, toes turned skyward ridiculously. She was ready to bolt, *yearning* to run.

But to *where?* Her mind offered no memories of a home—no car, no pet, no friends, no past.

She stood frozen, shackled by indecision. Behind her the strip joint. To her left a six-foot wooden fence. Straight ahead a dumpster. Hide behind it? Burrow into the garbage? No, they'd find her.

Somewhere in the distance, a dog barked.

To her right, a four-lane roadway divided by a median. The susurration of light traffic was somehow comforting, but she fought its lulling effects.

Hotwire a car?

Now how did she know she could do that? Or *could* she do it? Maybe the ability to steal a car was part of her nightmare. No, she knew she could do it, in too much detail to be a dream. Still, she couldn't do it fast enough to avoid apprehension. Countless questions bombarded her, threatening to bury her in unwanted distractions.

The door burst open, behind it surely the beer-soaked bouncer, thoroughly pissed. Shouts from deeper inside the club edging closer *(Little shit stole my jacket!)*, Rod Stewart now un-muted, blasting something about letting him know—smoke roiled out, engulfing her in a malignant cloud.

Without risking even a moment to glance back, she bolted for the highway, jacket billowing, just as fast as her Dutch milkmaid clogs would carry her.

-Yacht-

There was no rhyme or reason for it—no correlation to sleep, caffeine or anything else he could figure. It just came and went as it pleased, and to hell with whatever he happened to be doing at the time.

Sometimes it felt as if the storm had finally passed, almost as if it had never happened at all—not really. And even if it had, the memories were nothing more than the stuff of dreams long forgotten. He fell for it every time, allowed himself to believe only better days lay ahead, that he was finally through it.

Those were the good days.

Other days were not so good. On bad days—days like today—the memories roiled like storm clouds, the promise of the nightmare pelting him like sheets of frozen rain.

On "hail days," he focused on his work.

The Tiger Saw was a bronco, crazy with panic, plaster shrapnel flying like foam from its bladed mouth. The tool bucked and gyrated, desperate to throw its rider and gallop free. Freddie "the Fixer" Schaeffer clung stubbornly to the molded plastic. Teeth clenched, forearms bulging. Refusing to relinquish his mount.

He knelt in a sweltering attic, bent to his task. The glow from a dangling forty-watt bulb cut through abandoned cobwebs and cast agitated shadows in the growing cloud of dust. Through drywall and rafters alike, he inched along the two-by three-foot rectangle he'd drawn, careful to maintain his tenuous balance and death grip on the saw. The noise was horrendous.

After what seemed an eternity, the section of ceiling finally gave way. It crashed to the kitchen floor below, sucking much of the dust along with it. Freddie rose with a grimace and balanced on parallel rafters. After a moment, he removed his safety goggles. At six-four, it was necessary to contort himself to stretch his back. He stood staring down through the dust.

(Subsonic vibrations)

What was the next step? Framing? Fine adjustments to the opening?

(Creeping through his feet, into his legs)

Prep the shelving unit? Set up the saw horses? Take a break? Come on, think!

(Rumbling, so low it registered only in his spine)

Frame. Springs. Tools. Fasteners. What was the next step?

(Lift the beam somehow. Quick! What could serve as a lever? A fulcrum? Come on, think!)

His legs trembled and his hands shook. The square hole he'd just cut morphed into a jagged maw, the drywall massive plates of ravaged concrete. Stray slivers of rafter were mangled fingers of rebar. The eight-foot drop to the kitchen floor yawned to a bottomless chasm, at the bottom of which lay—

"What the hell are you doing to my *house?*" Joe Zaydon laughed, peering up from below. Joe was the owner of the house. He waived away dust and repositioned himself to locate Freddie in the gloom.

"You think this is a shock, wait 'til you see my final bill."

The banter dissipated the daydream, rumble receding like dying thunder. Freddie lowered the Tiger Saw by the cord.

By unspoken agreement, Joe retrieved the tool and eased it to the kitchen floor. "We're headed out. If we're not back before you're done for the day, just lock up behind yourself."

Hands on his knees, Freddie leaned over the hole and smiled. "Say, where do you keep the valuables?"

Joe chuckled as he walked away. "Under a tarp in the yacht out back," he called over his shoulder.

The front door opened . . . closed . . . then all was silent.

Only Joe Zaydon could coax a chuckle from Freddie on a hail day. There was no yacht. Probably nothing more than a swim noodle back there. The Zaydons had five daughters, all home-schooled by their mother Dymphna. Joe owned a flower shop downtown and did okay. Still, with one income and seven mouths to feed, they struggled. Freddie was doing the job at cost.

No other handyman would have even attempted the project regardless of the price. Freddie was a solid craftsman, no genius but smarter than most. While he could tackle any run-of-the-mill repairs and construction, his specialty lay in solving unorthodox problems. Building a loft with no ground support. Erecting a tree house. Creating a waterproof hole in the ground for the drop-pin of a chain link fence gate.

He'd once installed a backyard firing range for a cop in Pinecrest. The code department had told him, *You show us blueprints for a structure that will A, be soundproof, and B, contain stray rounds fired in any direction, we'll approve the permit.* In other words, no.

The next day, Freddie had shown up with plans for an underground range, complete with sump-pump drainage and ventilation system. The city had reluctantly granted the permit.

His uncanny ability to resolve seemingly impossible problems was not only a source of income but an effective distraction from thoughts of the past. Usually.

Today, he was adding storage space to an already crowded kitchen. Most times, conventional wisdom generated the answer, *It can't be done.* So Freddie avoided conventional wisdom, gently easing it from his thoughts as he assessed the issue. His clever solutions always began with an objective assessment of the problem, then proceeded with a completely open mind as to the solution. He allowed his imagination to roam free, much farther astray than most were comfortable.

With the storage space puzzle, when his mind had concluded there was utterly no space in the kitchen in which to start, he'd simply refused to accept it. Instead, he posed a question: *Where is space available?*

As he'd peered around the counters and cabinets with Joe, his gaze had wandered upward. "Do you have much head-room in the attic?"

"Sure. But I don't want to climb the folding ladder every time we need a frying pan!"

"You won't have to."

Construction of any kind works only as well as the parts from which it's created. Loathe to let his mind wander, Freddie climbed down from the attic and headed to his van for the stainless-steel shelving system he'd recommended.

The unit weighed ninety pounds. Printed on the side of the box, within a green circle, was a simple graphic of a man carting a box on a hand truck, crescent smile under dot eyes. Beside it, within a red slashed circle, the same figure strained to lift the box. Droplets of cartoon sweat squirted from his head, a lightning bolt at his lower back.

Freddie hefted the box and threw it over one shoulder. At six-four, 250 pounds, he could lift a bag of Quikrete, or a stainless-steel shelving unit, as if it were a sack of sugar. His size made him clumsy in enclosed spaces. But outside in his element, he thrived.

This genetic strength did not automatically come with a lean and cut physique. He was solidly built but by no means a bodybuilder. Nor was he a model. Though far from homely, his mug was that of a boxer—like a beating with an ax handle would leave his face no worse for the wear, the wielder of the weapon spent.

He cut his own hair, and only "when it needed it." When it got out of control, he'd buzz it down to a bur with dog shears, after which he'd dedicate about as much thought to the matter as a bear did to table manners. After a year or so, his mane would morph back into what it was now: a boyish, shoulder length, disheveled mop.

Style concerned him not in the least. He had no business meetings to attend. Nor was he plagued by thoughts of courting. He'd carefully constructed for himself a life of simplicity. His friends were more acquaintances, consisting for the most part of satisfied clients. He was content with his loneliness, or pretended to be.

He plugged in his saws and set up wooden horses on the patio. Over the next several hours, he framed out the hole, being sure to include firm support for the garage door springs. He ran cables and measured space for the counterweights. When he realized the sun was going down, he picked up the pace, careful to compensate for his growing fatigue. His desire to see the solution work was stronger than his need for rest.

Nearing completion, his excitement grew. He wrestled the stainless-steel shelving unit up the folding ladder to the attic. He attached the cables, springs and folding arms.

Back down in the kitchen, he stared up at the new door on the ceiling. He reached up, grasped the handle and pulled gently. With a yawning of springs not unlike those of the attic door, the unit coasted down.

Freddie smiled.

Life should be so simple.

He swept the kitchen and patio, wound his cords, collected his tools and blew his saws free of dust. He loaded it all into the van.

Freddie loved the old bucket, a 1992 Dodge Ram. Old but reliable, he'd named her "Mable." Old Mable. White paint long since dulled, it featured faded logos on the sides, hood, and rear cargo doors: *Freddie the Fixer*.

Back in the day, he'd picked her up at a Bellsouth auction. A steal of a deal, of course, meant it needed some work, but hey—that's what Freddie did. He'd replaced the seals, dropped in a new transmission and lubed her up good. After a shot of gloss white paint, she was ready to roll.

He was pleased with his cargo compartment design, a system of roll out shelves installed on gate rollers, the tracks welded to the interior bed. Heading for Old Mable at the end of the day was almost as sweet as heading for home.

The sun had long since retreated over the horizon. He locked up the house, chuckled at the non-existent yacht and hopped in the van. He keyed the ignition, and Old Mable rumbled to life. Switching on the headlights, he threw her in gear and swung out onto the open road.

Freedom at last. The day the earth yawned beneath him had not so much as crossed his mind. Nor had Stevie. What had started as a hail day had turned out sunny.

He was content with a good day's work and proud of a job well done.

-Hit n Run-

She'd been making it, damn it. Outta there, into the blue, history. Then the van.

Determined footsteps on her heels, assaulted by incensed shouts of anger, she'd cut through traffic in the northbound lanes.

Under threat, attack what's attacking you.

Where had she heard that?

Across the northbound lane, she'd vaulted the curb of the median. She'd bolted through the grass, arms tucked tightly to her sides, over the left curb of the southbound traffic—then *WHAM!*

Two more inches and she'd have made it. It was the damn heels. Or what was left of them.

Tires screeching, the jalopy had struck her right buttock. She'd gone sailing through the air spinning clockwise but managed to somehow "cat-twist" as she flew. She'd relaxed into it—then tucked her head and rolled when she landed. *What was that?*

Now she stood facing the van, owl-eyed driver gawking through the windshield. Glaring angry mob to her right across the highway. They shouted and gestured rabidly, waiting for traffic to clear.

She looked at the driver. He was taking in the scene across the highway.

She jerked her head right to the mini-mob.

Then straight ahead to the driver (he now returned her glance).

Then back to the mob.

The bouncer and leader of the gang took the first steps of a head start across the road, emphatically waving a car past. *(Hurry up, fool!)* With an angry honk, the car swerved to miss him—and the way was clear.

She cut her eyes back to the van. The driver leaned quickly over and unlocked the passenger door.

Keep running or hop in the van? She didn't know the driver but could safely assume he was "Freddie the Fixer," since it was emblazoned mirror image across the front of the hood.

The mob was almost upon her.

She bolted for the passenger door, yanked it open and vaulted inside.

"Go. *GO!*" she yelled, just as the bouncer flashed across the headlight beams and scrambled around to her side.

"*Go!*"

Tires peeling rubber, they surged forward.

She tried to shut the door. Something obstructed it. The bouncer, shredded face, snarling in rage. His left hand gripped the doorpost, his right the door itself. Hanging on stubbornly. The smell of Corona and cologne-sweat flooded the cab as he strained to keep up.

She hopped onto her left knee. Braced her right hand on the dash. She stomped her broken right heel into his face. Once, twice, then the third kick hit nothing but air when the bouncer finally let go. He stumbled to the pavement. Shouts indiscernible as he faded, kneeling on the road behind them, he swung his fists wildly in the air.

She slammed the door shut.

-Awkward Ride-

Now, why had he done this?

He'd had a choice: Avoid the introduction of drama into his life—or mire himself in it. Very simple.

The door had been locked. Why hadn't he left it that way? Why hadn't he taken off the moment she'd stood up? She'd been fine, dazzling in the headlights, crouched and poised to fight—or to jet into the night like a damn panther.

But no, he'd done it.

Thinking it was one thing. Anyone would. But doing it was quite another. By taking action—with his *volition*—by leaning over and unlocking that door, he'd sealed his fate.

Now he'd chosen sides; now he was committed.

She was trouble. How much more obvious could that have been? Dashing across the street in the middle of the night? Wearing nothing but a suit jacket and purple hair dye? Angry mob in hot pursuit? What the hell else *could* she be?

Well, maybe something. Despite her bizarre getup, he thought he'd seen in her something more—something that outweighed the risk she posed. How he could determine this in but a few seconds—from fifteen feet away, the woman bathed in the glow of his headlights—was beyond him. But he was convinced he'd seen it. Her determined posture, set of jaw, fire in her eyes—they somehow didn't line up with her haggard appearance. Or her predicament.

Attackers, it seemed, boiled down to two types: those with whom a woman was familiar (abusive husbands or bosses) and total strangers (muggers or rapists). While undoubtedly similar, surely there were subtle differences in a victim's reaction depending on which type of attacker she was addressing.

Freddie felt all but certain this woman was dealing with the latter. Despite her clothing, or lack thereof, she'd given the impression of being not a disaffected member of the gang, but an outsider. Perhaps a patron of the club. Or an escaped captive. It was strange. It was . . .

Something.

Or maybe wishful thinking. Probably wishful thinking.

Whatever the case, here he was. And there she sat.

"Thank you," she said breathlessly, then again, "Thank you," as she glanced in the rearview on her side, panting, then over him through the driver's side window. One more careful look at the mirror and she finally sat back with a sigh. She closed her eyes and laced her fingers in her hair.

Freddie said, "You okay?"

She bolted upright and slid forward on the seat. Right hand braced on the dash, she jammed her left pointer at his face. "I appreciate your help. But if you try anything . . . if you *touch* me . . ."

"Hey. Take it easy. You don't even know me."

"Ex-*actly!*" She punctuated with another jab of her finger.

"Okay, I get it." He shook his head, raised his right hand in surrender. "I'm friendly; not going to try anything."

"Well good. Because if you do . . . I can take care of myself." It was clear she meant business, although her walls seemed to be crumbling. A little.

"If you like, you could zip-tie my hands to the steering wheel. Or blindfold me with that dirty bandana." He jutted his chin at the soiled blue rag stuffed between the dash and windshield. "Although in that case, I may need a little assistance navigating." His intent was to lighten the air, and he hoped he didn't sound patronizing.

She allowed a pained chuckle, still not smiling, then shook her head and bent to her legs. After a moment of struggling with the complicated straps, she glanced up at Freddie's thigh. She snared the clip-on jackknife from his right cargo pocket.

A moment of panic seized him when she flipped open the blade one-handed, then he relaxed as she bent once more to her task and began cutting at the windings. As she finished each side, she slapped the bird's nest of sole and straps into the floorboard.

Job completed, she folded the knife and tossed it into the accessory compartment.

"Thanks," she said, then finally sat back. After a minute staring out the windshield, she turned to the window of her door, pensive.

Freddie's mind filled with questions as the blocks rolled past. Who was she? What was with the strange garb? Who were those men? Why were they chasing her? At each traffic light, he'd steal a peek at her, furtively, wondering. But she never returned his glances. Her mind was elsewhere, elbow propped on the windowsill, rolling her lower lip between her fingers.

The more they sat together, even in the absence of conversation, the more he became convinced she was indeed more than she appeared. Although her bizarre presentation screamed *Trouble! Drama!* something in her posture, her knitted brow, even just her vibe, belied that assumption. What had happened? Who was she, exactly? It nagged at him, but he felt he should remain silent. When she was ready, she'd let him know.

Then it dawned on him the house was getting close. A few more blocks and they'd be there. What then? Ask her inside? No doubt that would result in his having to extract the jackknife from his thigh. So, should he drop her at her place? Was it anywhere near? Maybe the police station? Had she thought of this? What would she think if he just rolled into his driveway? Would she stop to realize she'd offered him no other destination? He could bring it up, but again felt her need for silence outweighed his desire for direction.

He decided to pass the turn to his house and just drive on down the highway. Give her some time to think. They'd resolve it soon enough, then he'd get his life back.

Finally, she spoke. "I'm sorry. I shouldn't have gotten you involved." She'd looked away from her window, though not at him. She faced straight ahead through the windshield. "You can drop me here."

"Where?"

"Just . . . anywhere."

"I'm happy to take you home. Or wherever you need to go."

"That's okay I just . . . " her jaw kept moving, but no words came forth.

"I'm done for the day. Nothing on my calendar until tomorrow morning. And I can cancel that too if you need me to drive you, like, to Alaska or something."

The van swayed with the contours of the road. A motorcycle buzzed past, then a minivan full of laughing kids.

"Why are you helping me?"

He shrugged. "It's just the right thing to do. Anyone would."

"It may be the right thing, but 'anyone' wouldn't." She scoffed. "*I* wouldn't."

He somehow doubted that but didn't argue with her.

An idea occurred to him. Despite the continued socializing it would cost him, he decided to suggest it. "Listen. There's a

McDonald's up ahead. Why don't we stop there, get some food and maybe some coffee in you? Give you a chance to clear your head a little." He shrugged. "It's a public place. Safe. I definitely couldn't try anything there."

She laughed a little, this time allowing a half smile. "Sorry I accused you of being an ax murderer."

"Well, you didn't really accuse me of being an ax murderer. Not in those exact words."

"Yeah well, I implied it. No offense."

"None taken."

The Golden Arches grew steadily in the distance, half a mile or so up the road.

She said, "So. This McDonald's. Think they'd allow a half-dressed stripper with bare feet in the joint?"

"I think not only would they allow it, they'd encourage it."

She shook her head and offered a pained smile, but didn't laugh.

"Sorry. That was tacky. I know you're—"

"This is not me." She shook her head. "I don't . . . I mean, I'm not . . ."

"It's okay."

"No. I mean it. I'm not . . . This is not me."

He gave her a little space. What did she mean, *this is not me?* Turning over a new leaf, was she? Despite his misgivings about her appearance, surely she was employed at the strip club. Perhaps she was ashamed of that. Maybe he'd stumbled upon the very night she was turning her life around, quitting the flesh business for good. Stranger things had happened.

Yeah right.

"Hey, I don't judge. What people do for a living is their own busin—"

"This is not me!" Not yelling but more emphatic.

He tested several responses in his head but rejected all of them.

"This is not me," she repeated.

He nodded, decided to just let it go. "I've got some paint-er's coveralls that may fit you. They belonged to a temp I hired a few weeks ago. You can change in the back—"

She started to object, got as far as opening her mouth.

"—and I will *stand outside,* lock and guard the door." He gave it a beat, then added, "And I promise not to peek."

She turned back to the window, rolling her lip between her fingers again.

Freddie caught himself watching her. He'd come to the conclusion that he'd long since stopped producing the subtle hormones or pheromones or whatever was responsible for stirring attraction between the sexes. He turned his gaze back to the highway.

Admittedly, they were nice lips. He remembered a time when he may have been nagged by the thought of kissing them. He was comforted by the fact he was no longer bur-dened by such feelings, or the anxiety sure to follow any pur-suit of them. He realized he lived his life balanced on the precipice between comfortable solitude and paranoid isola-tion, but he didn't care. That was just the way he liked it.

Then why are you watching her again?

He turned his gaze back to the highway.

We're from different worlds, he assured himself.

But something told him their worlds were perhaps simi-lar—if not one and the same. Once again, he got the notion she was something very different from what she presented.

"Okay." She nodded. "McDonald's in coveralls it is. Won't be the greatest fashion statement ever made, but at least I won't be wearing—" She airbrushed her fingers down the front of her body. "—whatever this is."

Whatever this is? What was that supposed to mean? She acted as if someone else had dressed her while she'd been asleep or something. Again his curiosity nagged at him, but again he chose to let it go.

-Not Me-

She pushed through the women's room door, scanning the restaurant subtly. Though she hid it well, he was certain her eyes missed nothing. Despite being barefoot, draped in a drop cloth, and no more than five-four, she carried herself like a superhero.

As she approached the table, he realized she'd rinsed out the purple dye and scrubbed her face and hands. She'd bound her hair in a rubber band for which she'd asked him earlier. The interior lights of McDonald's revealed light beige striations in her brown eyes, something he'd missed entirely up to now.

"Thank you for this." She took her seat, examined the cheeseburger and fries before her, then dug in.

For a full minute he watched, fascinated. Before she'd finish one bite, she'd wolf down another then wash it all down with Coke, nodding her head with the effort to get it swallowed. Then she'd start again, gorging herself shamelessly.

Finally, through a mouthful of food, she said, "Sorry . . . mmm . . ." She swallowed a little more. "I feel like I haven't eaten in days." She finally cleared her mouth.

"Well, *have* you eaten in days?"

She paused. Thought about it. "I don't know, Freddie."

He nodded, wondering what that meant. "Okay, let's back up. You know my name, obviously from my shoddy logo, but you never told me yours."

She stared directly at him, first at his left eye, then his right, back and forth, as if she were flipping through the pages of his mind. While not exactly intimidating, it was more than a little disconcerting. He didn't know what to think of that.

She nodded almost imperceptibly. "I don't know that either."

She was not kidding. And he didn't feel she was being evasive. Apparently, she really meant what she said, actually had no recollection of her own name. But he was Freddie the Fixer. Helping people work puzzles was what he did. "Okay, so you really, literally don't remember your name. How about the accident? You could have struck your head without realizing it. So maybe you've got amnesia."

"It's amnesia alright, but not from the accident. I remember everything with clarity but only starting from that disgusting place. I don't know, I just—" She shrugged. "—woke up there. Like, *poof*. I was just *there*. I have no idea where I'd come from, and no idea where to go from here. It's like, I was born on stage, and my entire life consists only of the last hour and change."

He stared back at her, perplexed, trying to get to the Non-Conventional-Wisdom root of the matter. There could only be so many causes of her condition.

Brain trauma, as he'd suggested. But there were no apparent head wounds, no bleeding, no pupil dilation. She showed no other symptoms of having suffered a skull impact.

Or drugs. Although she seemed clear-headed enough, maybe some drugs affected memory without symptoms of intoxication. That didn't seem right, but he'd keep it in mind.

So what about less conventional considerations?

Like maybe she was lying. Not that she was necessarily a stripper pretending to be something else. In fact, if anything, she may be something else, pretending to be a stripper. Like he was being set up. After all, his motivation to work had little to do with finances. The life insurance payout had set him up indefinitely. So maybe someone wanted to get at the pot.

No. He was a handyman, a nobody. He had no use for boats or fancy cars, so the money just sat in a bank somewhere, undisturbed. No one would know about it. And if they did, and wanted to take it, they'd simply hack the account. Or hold him at gunpoint. They wouldn't arrange a near fatal accident with a half-naked actress. That was not it.

So maybe she was just batshit crazy.

Due to her clarity and sharpness, he tended to reject that idea—although crazy and smart were not necessarily mutually exclusive. He scratched it off his mental list but left it for later consideration.

Still stumped, he decided just to gather more intel. "Okay, what *do* you remember? Assuming you're willing to share that with me."

She sighed. "Sure. You seem like a good enough guy and, besides—there's really not much to tell."

"Start from the beginning, wherever that happens to be right now. Try to recall every sight and sound. Every thought, everything."

She went through it all, from the murky mirror, not recognizing her own face or body, to the scuffle on the stage, the punk with the now broken foot, the jacket on the chair, the bouncer and the beer bottle— "And then someone hit me in his handy-van," she finished, deadpan.

"Sorry again. No offense." His face grew warm.

"None taken." Then she winked at him. It was not flirtatious—more of a platonic gesture, though she offered it with a half smile. Still, it set him aback. It was her eyes. Undeniably alluring, yet . . . they just bored right into you.

Masking his awkwardness, he focused on the amnesia. "Now, when you say you didn't recognize your face, what do you mean exactly? Even with amnesia, wouldn't you at least be able to recognize yourself?"

"I didn't say I didn't recognize my *own* face. I said I don't recognize *this* face. I don't have the skill to draw a self-portrait, not even mentally. But I do know for sure, this ain't me." She air-circled her face.

"Okay wait a minute. What are you saying? That you believe you look like someone other than yourself?"

"This is *not* 'myself.' I can't explain it, but I'm certain. I'm not a stripper, Freddie. And these are not my hands. Not my feet, not my body, not my face. *This is not me.*" She punctuated with an emphatic shrug of her shoulders.

This declaration so baffled him that he sat back in the booth and folded his arms. "Now, hold on. In order to solve anything here, we have to stay within the bounds of reality. You're sitting right there, in *that* body—" He pointed at her. "—talking to me with *that* face. So one thing we have to agree upon is, *you're you.* You may believe yourself to look differently, but you can't be anyone other than yourself, right?"

She shrugged again. "This is not me."

He nodded, eyes squinted. That was it for the time being; they'd just have to take it up later.

But of course there would be no "later." They were finished here; he'd done all he could do for her. Freddie was surprised at his slightest tinge of regret.

She loosed a sigh. "I'm out at sea here. I don't know where I live, don't know where to go . . ." She shrugged again.

Freddie slowly nodded, his mind unexpectedly atwirl. He longed for the smell of fresh cut lumber, the hypnotic buzz of his saws, the burn of blisters on his palms. That's what he told himself.

But a heretofore silent voice, or one he'd long ignored, whispered something that belied that notion—argued that what he'd been calling comfort was no more than cowardice, that the path down which he was headed could lead only to despair.

He told himself he did not know her.

He told himself he didn't care.

"You're welcome to crash at my place."

She glared at him. "Your place."

Even beaming through those angel eyes—perhaps because of it—her drill sergeant stare set his heart agallop. How could a woman half his size make him squirm like a kid in the principal's office?

What he wanted to say was, *Sorry, that was out of line.* That would put it back in the box; that would make it safe.

Instead, he heard himself saying, "I know it's awkward, but what else are you going to do? We can set things up however will make you feel comfortable."

He was on a precipice. He didn't know what he hoped she'd say.

She drilled into him again, paint-stained elbows of the coveralls resting on the table, forearms crossed.

Just when he took a breath to speak, she sat back, shook her head once and said, "Well alright, I suppose. Like you said, what the hell else am I going to do? Thank you. Thank you so much."

Freddie didn't feel the earth shift beneath him, but it did.

-Sleeping Arrangements-

He'd picked up a puppy from the pound for Stevie, long ago in another life. The animal's behavior upon entering the Schaeffer house had so fascinated him that he remembered the scene like it had happened yesterday.

As Stevie had carried it across the yard on the way in, the puppy's eyes had been like cameras, scanning this way and that, burning all they saw into its canine brain.

Once released on the living room floor, it had ignored the people watching it, focused solely on taking in its new surroundings. Glancing left and right, sniffing, floppy ears perked, the little dog had seemed to be making a mental recording of every bit of information its memory could hold.

It had occasionally glanced up at the humans and wagged its tiny tail briefly—but then returned immediately to its task.

To the entertainment center, around the couch, under the end table then down the hall to the bedrooms it had padded, absorbing it all like a furry sponge.

Tail tucked shyly between its legs, it had finally approached the boy.

Now the woman seemed to be doing the same thing. Again he saw that her eyes missed nothing. She practically ignored him, her focus on making a mental impression of this new environment. Fascinated, he'd watched her taking it all in as he'd locked up Mable and made his way to the front door. It was as if she'd never seen a house with a yard before. Of course, given the circumstances, her wariness made sense. Still, it was impressive. Apparently, she could indeed take care of herself.

Like the puppy, satisfied everything was in order, she finally relaxed and pulled out a chair at his table. She sat to the side, right arm resting on the tabletop.

"Would you like a drink?" Freddie offered from the kitchen. It was separated from the dining area by a counter, under which there were cabinets accessible only from the kitchen side.

She shot him a look. "Trying to get me drunk, Freddie?" She managed to keep him off balance, and he found that amusing. Comforting. Almost familiar somehow.

"Hey." He laughed it off and raised his hands in surrender. "Just being polite. I have water, orange juice ... nothing spiked with roofies if that's what you're thinking."

"Well, I'm thinking it *now*."

He couldn't resist a chuckle. "I'll get you some water. If you decide you want something else, let me know." He plucked a plastic cup from the drain pan and pressed it to the water dispenser on the fridge door.

"Sorry. I guess I'm still a little on edge." She shook her head. "This is crazy."

"In what sense?" Freddie smiled as he delivered the cup.

"Very funny. So, how are we going to work this? I mean, sleeping arrangements."

Freddie padded back to the kitchen counter and leaned his hands there. Sleeping arrangements. How long had it been since he'd slept under the same roof with a member of the opposite sex? Unavoidably, the memory of how it felt to share a bed with a woman rose like a zombie and shuffled toward him. He shoved the corpse back into the grave and offered the plan on which he'd been thinking. "Obviously, you can't trust me."

She opened her mouth to comment, but he raised his hands, cutting her off. "No, it's okay. You *shouldn't* trust me. It's only common sense."

She relaxed. Still beaming at him.

"There's an extra bedroom I use as an electronics room. It ain't pretty, but there's a futon in there. Currently stacked with buckets of electric components, but we could make it presentable in a few minutes. The interior doors have locks." He shrugged. "You could even lean a chair against the inside knob if that would make you feel safer."

"It would."

Freddie nodded approval. "Or, you could sleep on the couch?" He grimaced at the idea. "But that seems so . . . rude. Still, it's there if you want it. You'd be near the front door?"

She thought about it. "Okay the electronics room."

Freddie nodded agreement, patted his palms on the counter and said, "Okay then. Come on back and let's do it."

"Do it?" She cocked one eyebrow.

Was she serious? Embarrassed, Freddie shook his head and smiled. "I mean, let's set it up. Let's get going. Let's do *this*."

She nodded once and rose. "Fair enough."

-Looking Glass-

The bathroom was small but clean and tidy. She'd locked the door and checked it twice and was satisfied she was safe.

In the shower, she'd successfully resisted the urge to rip back the curtain at every imagined sound, doing her best to enjoy the steam and hot water as it sloughed off the rancid shroud of cigarette smoke. Now, Freddie's robe draped over her, hair in a turban towel, she wiped condensation from the mirror.

The fluorescent light revealed everything in stark clarity as she leaned on the sink. Staring into the looking glass. She knitted her brow in concentration, trying to *remember*.

Freddie had been right, of course. This was her body, her face—duh—yet she was convinced something was wrong somehow.

She concentrated harder still.

Freddie. Why had he gone out of his way like this? She'd have been foolish not to consider the possibility of ulterior motives. But once she'd gotten over his intimidating size, it was clear he was a big teddy bear with nothing but the best of intentions. He was without doubt a tortured man, struggling with demons either seen or unseen. She hated that, wished there was something she could say or do to help the guy. But she couldn't help anyone until she helped herself.

She stared at her reflection. Nope. Not her face.

Insanity. This is *my face!*

Plastic surgery? Maybe. But not even the slightest hint of scarring marred her jaw or hairline. Besides, why would someone go to the trouble and expense of knocking her out, changing her face (not to mention her body), then erasing her memory—only to bring her to consciousness on the stage of some sleazy nightclub?

"Come on, Zoe. *Focus.*"

She gasped.

She said the name aloud again, testing the feel as it crossed her lips. She had no recollection of a mother calling, *Zooo-eee. Dinner time*—or a first-grade teacher yelling, *Zoe! Simmer down!* Nonetheless, she felt confident that was her name.

Okay, great. Now the face. Concentrate. *What's the deal with my face?*

While she'd wiped away the steam, it still hung pleasantly in the air. It began to adhere to the glass again, distorting the woman therein. Rather than clear it, she allowed the image to dissolve, peering harder still into the wavering countenance.

Her efforts were rewarded. Her mind filled in the characteristics the condensation hid, and she gradually saw not brown eyes but blue. Not brunette hair but blonde. Harder face. *Her* face. Then suddenly she realized she should have been taller.

Or not.

She shook her head, casting off the fantasy. This was simply irrational and could not be. But yet . . .

That was enough for tonight. She was exhausted and desperately needed sleep.

When she opened the bathroom door, Freddie called out from the adjacent bedroom. "You decent?"

She paused for a beat. "Uh. Did you expect otherwise?"

"Just trying to be a gentleman," he said, appearing in the hallway.

"I'm Zoe." She extended her hand.

"So, finally decided to open up, huh?"

"Nope. I never kept my name from you. I just remembered it. I mean, I *just* remembered it. Moments ago."

"Well. Pleased to meet you, Zoe." Freddie took her hand.

Once joined, she somehow took over the handshake, *her* shaking *his* hand rather than a mutual gesture. It drew a smile from him.

"You're still dressed." The way she said it, she made it sound like he had plans to sharpen a machete while she slept.

He raised his eyebrows. "I figured you'd feel more comfortable if I waited until you were settled in before I changed?"

"Oh. Yes of course. Thanks." Their hands dropped to their sides.

"No problem," he said, barely avoiding the natural *My Pleasure,* an unintentional innuendo that surely would have opened the door to more banter.

She sighed and shook her head.

"What?"

"Here you are going out of your way—"

"It's not out of—"

"—for someone you don't even know—"

He opened his mouth to speak.

"—who by *all* evidence is nothing but trouble—"

He closed his mouth and let her finish.

"—and here I am being a total bitch."

"Hey. You're just watching out for yourself. I get it."

"Well, I get that you're a good guy, Freddie. You stuck your neck out for me where sure as hell no one else would have. So, I'm sorry. Okay?"

He nodded and smiled. "Okay."

"Truce?" She extended her hand again.

"Truce."

Again she took over the handshake, and again it drew a smile from him.

"Good night, Freddie."

"Good night, Zoe."

She spun on her heel, padded into the electronics room and turned to close herself in. The fact that she threw him one final glance—and an awkward smile—just before the door met the frame charmed him.

The lock engaged from the other side and he noted that she checked it twice. Then the clomping of the chair as she wedged it under the knob.

Then silence.

He shook off the spell and turned for his bedroom.

-Ceiling Fan-

An eternity later, hands laced between head and pillow, Freddie stared through the darkness at the ceiling fan. He'd tried closing his eyes, but that never worked. They had to fall shut on their own.

Lying alone with one's self is when the rubber hits the road. The wise heed these night voices; only a fool ignores them. He examined his judgment of the last few hours. He had no idea who the woman was laying twenty feet away in the other room, but he'd picked her up, literally off the street, and allowed her into his home.

She could be trouble. As in dangerous.

True, he outweighed her by more than double, but that counted for little when you were asleep. Maybe *he* should lock *his* door.

He made no move to get up and do it.

She'd been hit by a van (way to go, Fix-It man), which had to have hurt like hell. She had not complained in the least. He respected that toughness. And he'd been blown away at how she'd flown through the air then somehow rolled into the landing and ended up on her feet.

Impressive. Amazing, really. Maybe she was a gymnast or something. Or a martial arts expert.

Or a stripper.

"Come on, Freddie," he said, just louder than a whisper. Let's face it. Despite himself, and in mere hours, she'd worked her way pleasantly under his skin.

He resisted that thought. The best thing for him would be getting back to his old life. Caring involved risk. In the case of this woman, those risks may include his safety. If he was going to turn a page in his life, why not choose someone sensible with whom to turn it? Someone simple. Someone he knew.

Why was it that when he ran across a "nice girl," one with whom he could build a life, a turnkey relationship with no drama, his interest could be measured in micro-shits? But give him a half dressed, broken-heels wearing, purple-haired acrobat stripper with amnesia—and his "zing meter" rang off the charts.

His intrigue frustrated him but didn't surprise him. After all, the way he spent the hours of his life was helping people solve problems. God knew this fireball in the electronics room was full of them. On the one hand, his compulsion to repair and renew was undeniably an escape mechanism, a way to keep his mind busy. But on the other, it was simply a part of him.

He could have bought a new work van. With a warranty, he'd have had fewer repairs, less headache. But in Mable, he'd seen something worth saving—and he *had* saved her. That gave him satisfaction, a sense of self-worth. It also created a bond between man and machine, fostered in him a commitment to the old girl. He valued these intangibles beyond measure, and none would have been possible with a new vehicle and a warranty.

His computer was one he'd recovered from a trash pile. With a little tinkering, it was good as new. Again he felt that sense of worth, of care and commitment, even to a box of electronic components. Why add more junk to the world when there were things already in existence that worked just fine—if you were willing to commit the time and energy it took to rehabilitate them?

Perhaps this is why his relationship with Stevie ate at him so. Stevie was his *son,* and of course Freddie loved him. But there was "the thing" between them, and it ate at him like a cancer. Freddie was the father, so he ought to be the one to start the conversation. He longed for that sense of effort rewarded, of commitment, in this case to another human being—one of his own flesh and blood.

But what had he done about it? Nothing. Because—

Don't go there!

As always, thoughts of Stevie struck a kind of mental tripwire. A silent screaming alarm warned him of danger. And as always, he welcomed any distraction from addressing it.

So along comes this zany woman, obviously broken. Broken badly, worse than any busted vehicle or computer. Maybe it was time he came out from his emotional refuge and did something for someone else—something more than adding a bathroom to a vacation home.

In addition to her beauty and scrappy disposition, both of which charmed him, Zoe had guts and grit. A rare combination of virtues to find in a woman these days. She was worth saving, more so than any machine. She was the most uniquely fascinating—and uniquely broken—person he'd ever met. Far from perfect but perhaps perfect for him.

What are you thinking, Fix-It man? Expose your neck, lose your head.

Well, maybe it was time he stuck his neck out a little. Who knew? Maybe it would be just what the doctor ordered.

Or not. Surely not.

He comforted himself with the fact he'd be happy regardless, with an interesting friend or with the return of his old life. He'd just play it by ear, see what happened, expect the worst but hope for the best.

And just what, exactly, defines The Best, *Handyman?*

He chuffed once and shook his head. His eyelids grew heavy, fell once . . . then twice . . . then finally he slept.

-Something Inside-

Suffocation.

Distorted image . . . Someone hovering, working busily.
Working on *her*.
(Surgery)
Rippling like a ghost. Friend or foe?
Amber.
Everything amber. Odorless. Sterile.
Dead.
"Help me." *(no sound)*
HELP ME!
Can't catch my breath.
(Muted voices converse casually)
Can't breathe.
(Small tool clanks on metal tray)
Can't speak.
(A scalpel?)
Can't breathe . . . *Can't breathe . . . CAN'T BREATHE!*
Help me?

Nightmare. Electronics room. Freddie the Fixer. Okay to trust him in here, in my head. After all, anything goes in a dream.

But . . . not a dream.
Solid.
Substantive.

Zoe gasps—or tries to—but her airway is blocked. She lies on her back, submerged in . . . something . . . gazing into the amber light.

Try to blink.

Eyes somehow locked open . . . They work, yet—

Can't blink.

Body immobile, gagged by . . . "it" . . . this amber . . . what?

Choking her.

Helpless.

(Help me.)

The ghost ripples on her right, now joined by another on her left.

Can't breathe . . .

Not ghosts.

Doctors. *(Surgeons)*

Or something *like* doctors.

Or maybe Freddie is not what he appears, a wolf in sheep's clothing. But this is not the electronics room.

How could he have gotten me here? Where is here?

Nightmare. Has to be. So wake up. Call out.

WAKE UP!

Their faces are smudges, voices human. But muted, unintelligible. She can tell the first is younger, his tone almost adolescent. Nervous.

The second voice is deeper, authoritative.

(Help me!)

Yes, he's in charge.

(What are they saying?)

Her body jerks. They're jostling her.

(What are they *doing?*)

Jostling something *inside* her.

Nauseated, unable to resist, unable to move, gagged—her heart slams with panic.

"Help me Freddie!" *No sound.*

Their conversation has stopped. They're focused, bent over her . . . concentrating . . .

By his tone, she can tell the younger one asks a muted three syllable question, brief but pressing.

Then silence . . . Another muted metallic clanking . . .

The older one blurbs a one-word reply and then . . .

The younger one carefully lifts something.

Slowly lifts something in a . . . a spoon? A spatula? The tool looks like *(amber)* stainless steel, maybe the size of a saucer—long handle . . .

He hoists a jiggling . . . something . . . in the tool . . .

(Anything goes in a dream)

Lifts something *out.*

(Not a dream)

Out of *her.*

But still connected deep inside, tethered to her, trailed by something . . . ropey *(veiny?)* glistening *(amber)*

(HELP MEEEEE!)

Silence.

-Murmurs-

Someone was in the house. Heart leaping into his throat, Freddie rolled right, to the nightstand. He tore open the drawer. Shaking off the cobwebs, he groped desperately inside.

Book. Pencil. Cough drops. *Gun.*

He sat up, listening, doing his best to still his panicked breathing. The sound was coming from the electronics room. Zoe's room. Just across the hall from him. He adjusted his grip on the weapon, sure to keep his finger off the trigger to avoid blowing a hole in the damn wall. Or his foot. He threw his legs over the edge of the bed and honed in on the voices.

He rose, pistol in a two-hand grip, aimed at the ceiling. His skin turned to gooseflesh as he crept to the electronics room.

Further scrutiny revealed she was probably just talking in her sleep.

He breathed a sigh of relief and lowered the weapon.

More specifically, she seemed to be living a nightmare. He reached for the doorknob—but stopped. Yes, he could do her a kindness by waking her from her torment. But how would she react? Based on their short history, he had no trouble piecing together a few unpleasant scenarios. Who knew what might happen with a gun between them?

Besides, he remembered, she'd barricaded herself in there.

His hand retreated from the knob.

Her troubled murmurs continued. He leaned closer, could almost decipher the words. He turned his head sideways and leaned closer still. While muted, he could just make it out:

"Sea level. Desalt. Drawer number seven."

Groans punctuated her senseless rambling. Freddie pitied her—empathized with her—and wished he could do something to help. He marveled at how the subconscious dream-mind worked, wondered why our creator would curse us with these terrifying night jaunts. It seemed God had a twisted sense of humor.

"Sea level. Desalt. Drawer number seven."

Who knew what was happening inside her head? Maybe she was adrift at sea aboard a slowly deflating raft. Perhaps the sea level was plummeting, threatening to strand her on the ocean floor. Strange creatures would materialize, from jellyfish to whales, all flailing toward her, lifeless eyes rolling, teeth snapping.

And perhaps she was dying of thirst. Trillions of gallons of water would surround her—all salt infested, desalinization her only salvation. Or maybe salvation—or more threat?—somehow lied within drawer number seven. In a bureau? A file cabinet?

What file cabinet? On the shore? In the raft? It never made sense, of course.

"Sea level. Desalt. Drawer number seven."

Freddie himself traversed currents like these almost nightly. Rarely was it the actual event—*the* event—that plagued his sleep. But regardless of the mental metaphor—adrift at sea, running through syrup, monsters impervious to gunfire—it was always about the thing, the event, the death—the day his life fell through a hole in the earth.

Freddie rapped lightly on the door. "Zoe?" he whispered. "You okay?"

"Sea level. Desalt. Drawer number seven." The groans eased, words softened.

"You're having a nightmare." This time in full voice, although quietly.

Her murmurs faded to near silence.

He stood waiting . . . then decided it had passed. He padded back to his bed, stowed the piece, pulled up the covers and slept. He did not dream.

CHAPTER TWO

RHYME & REASON

-Feed the Fire-

Bruce Vega was so angry he could kill someone. In fact, that was precisely what he was here to do. While most everyone on occasion finds themselves angry enough to imagine killing someone, few actually do it. Even fewer make a living at it.

Bruce did.

He slid the blade silently against the latch and worked it free of the strike plate.

Most mediators (that's what the agency was calling them now) were thrilled by use of the latest gadgets. Bruce knew how to work all the high tech equipment, but why use it if you didn't have to? Why not employ a little resourcefulness using simpler, more easily accessible tools? What if you found yourself with none of the fancy stuff available when your life depended on it? He loathed the thought of being dependent on anything—or any*one*.

He opened the door only far enough to prevent the latch from falling back into place, then waited. Listening.

Most mediators worked with a cool head, too. While Bruce supported this mindset, anger is what drove him. Without anger, he wouldn't be here in the first place.

Satisfied the whisper of the blade had not betrayed him, he opened the door a little farther, just enough to make room for the tip of his mini tactical flashlight. The beam cleaved the darkness, revealing only a linoleum floor and the legs of a cheap kitchen table ensemble. He waited five seconds . . . ten . . .

The light revealed neither human presence nor animal eye-shine.

Bruce realized his motives were unhealthy. Not to mention useless. Tonight would make eighty-seven times he'd exacted revenge on extremist Islam, yet the anger remained, a fire within his soul. The blood he spilled in an attempt to quench those insatiable flames turned out to work not like water but gasoline. Once started, however, he was simply unable to stop pouring it on.

Feed the fire.

He eased the door open, slipped inside, then slowly closed it behind him—although not to the point of latching shut. Only a fool in this business failed to prepare a hasty retreat when possible.

His career had started in the infantry. He'd enlisted with one goal in mind: To put a bullet in as many towel heads as he possibly could. In the killing fields of Iraq, he'd done just that. Taking insane risks, he'd managed to do things no soldier could do, to survive what no one should survive.

When things get tight, attack what's attacking you.

After allowing his eyes to adjust to the gloom, he crept cautiously through the kitchen. Peripherally, he noted a ticking wall clock on the face of which was printed, *Alarm clocks: Because every morning should start with a heart attack.*

Eyes peeled, ears perked for even the faintest fall of sock feet on carpeted floor, he missed nothing. He was aware of every scent, every creak and groan of the old house, every dance of shadow from the trees outside—even as he crept forward, even as he drew the suppressed Springfield XD .45 from his shoulder rig.

Bruce Vega couldn't have cared less about the medals with which his uniform had become decorated. There were people, however, who did care. They took notice, and were not so dismissive of his valor—if you could even call it that. He had no particular feelings one way or the other about serving his country. His focus had been solely on feeding the fire.

His target tonight was Brennan Payne. Not exactly a member of the Taliban, but perhaps something worse.

A traitor.

According to Vega's briefing, this sack of shit had been selling information to jihadist groups. Enriching himself on the blood of innocents.

Not that you could tell by where he lived. Dirty money could not easily be spent without raising suspicion. The jerk probably had nicer digs under false identities. Or maybe he spent it on women and drugs. He probably owned a boat. Maybe an airplane.

Well, that would all be coming to an end here shortly.

He followed the sights of the .45, out of the kitchen, through the living room, then into the only hallway. According to the floor plan with which he'd been provided, Payne's bedroom was the last door on the right.

Bruce didn't like leaving un-cleared doors in his wake. You never knew. Behind any of them could lay sleeping an overnight guest or family member. Or an entire brigade of camel jockeys for that matter.

But the briefing had made no mention of family or roommates, and Payne had no known co-conspirators. Bruce trusted the intelligence; they'd never let him down before.

Besides, he wasn't exactly navigating an opium den in Afghanistan. If there were family or friends in the house, opening doors would only risk waking them—which would turn this into a complete shit-show. No, he'd proceed directly to the target, conclude his business and leave.

The fire beckoned.

After three tours in the desert, Vega had accepted a promotion to a new, recently militarized department: the DSA. Department of Scientific Alternatives. He accepted the job only because of his assignment to a special division within the agency, the Terrorism Task Force. He didn't give a damn about the increased salary or prestige, only that the position would provide him essentially a license to kill—and thus more fuel for the fire.

He froze at a faint creaking. He checked his six, scanned each door for movement.

Nothing.

The creaking came again. This time, he noted it occurred in conjunction with wind gusts from outside. Satisfied it was nothing more than complaints from the old house, he proceeded.

Bruce's appearance was ideal for the job. He stood just under six feet on an average frame. While deceptively strong, he was absent bulging muscles. His hair was straight and mousy blond, styled like your average weatherman or news anchor—unmemorable, virtually invisible in a crowd.

He took a full ten seconds turning the knob of the bedroom door. The mechanism made not the faintest squeak. He eased it slowly open with his left hand, pistol leading him in his right. While his eyes were accustomed to the dim light of the house, the target's quarters proved to be not dim but pitch black.

He turned on the red stealth light strapped to his forehead. He had access to night vision goggles, but fuck 'em. He didn't need their shit.

The light he wore could be purchased at any home improvement center or even Walmart. Bruce had selected a model with a silent switch. One advantage of this simpler solution was depth perception. NVGs were basically television screens mounted before your eyes, emitting two-dimensional moving pictures of what the front-mounted camera was receiving.

Another advantage of the headlamp was peripheral vision. To see something to either side of the goggles, you had to turn your head toward it—and be aware there was something to see in the first place. You could easily be flanked and ambushed.

The single redeeming feature of NVGs was the ability to see while not being seen in complete darkness. In a mission within a residence that posed little threat and was partially lighted anyway, this feature offered little or no advantage.

Besides, a target *seeing* the headlamp beam could also be expressed as being blinded by it. Against inexperienced combatants, this in itself could be considered an advantage of the simpler solution.

While the red light was indeed stealthier than plain white, and cast little residual glow, it was undoubtedly visible when seen directly—perhaps, if held close enough, even through eyelids. He'd have to avoid shining it straight in the sleeping man's face.

He cat-stepped five paces to the bed positioned head against the center of the wall on his far left. A man lay slumbering on his back, hands beside his head as if silently pleading, *Hands up don't shoot!*

Weapon now in a two-hand grip, sights trained on the target's chest, Vega took a moment to study the sleeping countenance in the ambient red light. Unruly auburn hair, sharp nose, patchy beard—the face was an exact match with the ID photo in the briefing. It was him. Brennan Payne.

The fire grew brighter, screaming in hunger.

Standard operating procedure in a sanction would have been to place a single bullet in the target's brain, quickly and quietly. In and out, mission complete.

Instead, Bruce leaned over, cupped his left hand over Payne's mouth, even as he braced his right shin across the man's torso.

Payne's eyes popped open and his body jumped. Startled from sleep, he made a feeble attempt at struggling.

Bruce pinned him effortlessly. "Sh sh sh. Be still." He showed Payne the gun in the full beam of the headlamp. "Can you see that?"

Eyes like saucers, Payne nodded and settled.

Bruce let the pistol hang there a moment anyway. Just to be sure. "I'm going to set it down for a minute. If you even so much as flinch, I will pick it up and shoot you in the head." He pressed the muzzle of the suppressor against Payne's right eye. "Do you believe me?"

Eyes squeezed shut, Payne nodded again.

Bruce slowly lifted the Springfield, let it hang there another beat, then set it on the bed. Left hand still clamped over the target's mouth, he reached inside his sport coat with his right. He produced a portrait photograph of a five-year-old girl and held it in the headlamp's beam. "Have you seen this girl?"

Payne's panicked eyes rolled to the photograph, shot back to Bruce. He shook his head under Bruce's hand.

"Take a close look now; I need you to be sure."

Payne's brow furled. Impossibly, his eyes gaped even wider.

"Now, don't go jumping to conclusions. Just take a good look at the photo."

Payne studied the face once more—this time for a few seconds. He turned back to Bruce and shook his head again.

"Yeah, that's about what I expected." Bruce sighed and returned the picture to his coat pocket. "Photo's fifteen years old, thereabouts." He chuckled as he picked up the gun. "She'd be in her twenties now."

Bruce shot him through the right eye. The left remained open, staring through gun smoke into the world beyond. "But it never hurts to try."

He stood, watching the growing blossom on the pillow. In the strange light, red on red, the blood appeared only as expanding wetness—a macabre halo. After a few post-mortem twitches and one last eruption of gore from mouth and nose, the corpse settled into its final resting position. Left eye wide open.

Sanction complete.

Bruce wiped the blood from his hand on the bedspread.

He had no fear of leaving DNA evidence or fingerprints, both of which were stored digitally nowadays. Data could be altered. Hard drives could fail.

Short of that, the data points must be read and interpreted by experts. Only human, these experts were vulnerable to certain pressures—pressures that may influence them to perhaps misread the information or declare it inadmissible in court. Or the data could be misfiled, the files inadvertently deleted.

If the pressures were ineffective, well, these experts might find themselves victims of unfortunate accidents, replaced by other, more sympathetic experts who grasped the treachery of digital evidence.

Less circumspect but still cautious, Bruce hastily made his way back down the hallway and through the living room. The fire burned brightly, raging from this last infusion of fuel.

It brought him no peace. He'd once heard a recovering addict say about cocaine, *That shit's good for nothing but the next bump.* That's how it was with killing. Not twenty seconds had passed since the last one, and already he yearned for the next.

Just as he drew near the threshold to the kitchen, an almost inaudible shuffle alerted him to someone—or some-*thing*—behind him. Into Bruce's head staggered the grinning corpse of Brennan Payne, brains dangling from the cavern once occupied by his right eye. Risen from the dead, it carried an AK-47. Trained on Bruce's back.

Not that a zombie would have need of a weapon.

-Thief in the Night-

Bruce turned to stone. He'd be dragged like fallen prey, bloody and broken over sharp terrain, to eternal torment in an underworld that did not exist. Even as the shambling corpse chuckled, Bruce spun on his heel, shattering the granite cast. He dropped to one knee, raised the .45 to center mass.

His sights found only a cheap painting on the living room wall.

Underneath the sites, however, in crimson shadows cast by his own arms, he sensed more than saw—a presence. Chills renewed, he lowered the pistol to the new target and squeezed the trigger. Except he never applied the final ounce of pressure necessary to fire the weapon.

In the red glow of his headlamp stood a tiny apparition. It clung tightly to a Lalaloopsie doll, the toy's head skewed impossibly sideways: A corpse embracing a corpse.

Bruce gasped. The ghost wore a pillowcase-sized gossamer nightgown. Having grown unchecked in the grave, her hair was a rat's nest. Or perhaps in life, the kid had been raised by wolves.

No, not a ghost.

A girl.

A real little girl, now shading her eyes from his headlamp. Complete with dolly and a severe case of bed-head, she looked to be around five. No zombie. Not a ghost.

But of course he'd have to make her one.

He tightened his grip on the pistol, clenching his jaws and renewing his aim.

Witnesses were frowned upon by the agency, regardless of age, gender, or innocence. After all, kids could kill you. With knives, guns, or vest bombs. Or as witnesses.

But he couldn't do it, was powerless to squeeze the trigger. Not because taking her out was imprudent. Most certainly not because the agency would grant an exception.

Just admit it. He was stuck because she was the girl in the photograph tucked away in his coat pocket. She was Amy.

He squeezed again. *(Not Amy!)* She was standing *right there,* unmoving, point blank range, centered in his sites.

Not. Amy.

So do it.

It was as if the safety was engaged—except the only thing locked was his mind.

The gears in his head spun out of control, the workings of a machine that served no purpose. Smoking, they began to clatter, wobbling dangerously. The entire assembly froze, broken teeth flying like missiles, embedding in the walls of his mind, this monkey wrench now tangled in the works.

He lowered the pistol. "Amy?" His voice cracked.

There was no reply.

He registered her breath, precious and sweet, no louder than the ticking of the kitchen clock. *(Because every morning should start with a heart attack.)*

He slowly stood, fumbling the pistol back into the shoulder rig. It required use of both hands. He realized sweat had formed on his palms.

"Who are *you?*" She glided her *R*s, pronouncing it, *Who ah you.*

Just like Amy.

Not Amy!

It was Bruce's turn to reply with silence.

Okay, focus. Amy would be in her twenties now.

Not if she'd died at 5.

Amy would have recognized him.

After all these years? Silhouetted in the headlamp?

There were no such things as ghosts.

Are you so sure about that?

Stop it. *Stop it!* What was the smart play, what was the safe bet, what was he going to do with her, whoever she was, *right now?*

She'd asked him something. What was it? *What had she asked him?*

Who are you.

Right. She'd said it calmly enough, but undeniably with a slight edge. This could have been apprehension—or at her age, the seeds of excitement may have been sown at the prospect of play. The hour wouldn't be an issue, not in her little mind. Or maybe it would be; you just couldn't tell with kids.

Come on, *think!* Who are you? What benign guest would even *possibly* come calling in the middle of the night?

"I'm Santa Claus." *Oh great. Where the hell can you possibly go with* that?

A thought stole a gasp from Bruce. Had blood backsplashed onto his face or clothing? If so, could she see it? Probably not. He'd be but a silhouette in the glow of the headlamp, the color of which would mask the gore. Hopefully.

What are you going to do?

"It's not Christmas *(Chwismas)*," the girl challenged. But she was smiling. Evidently—hopefully—her natural sense of mischief had been stirred.

Bruce had engaged in such childish banter on a daily basis, long ago in another life. He was familiar with its rhythms and found himself falling in step as if he'd played along only yesterday.

"It's *not?*" He shrugged dramatically, palms up. He struggled to stay in character, just a funny playmate, teasing and playing. He ignored the insanity knocking at the door.

She giggled. "*No,* silly!"

Bruce sighed. "I suppose you're not Amy, either." He kept his voice down. If the girl was unexpectedly present, who else might be in the house?

Up to now, agency policy had been one of mutual respect. Don't ask, don't tell. Indeed, the less he knew about a target, the better. If the wrong someone discovered he knew the wrong something, why, Bruce himself might wake up to a bullet in the eye one night. He was granted autonomy in the field, allowed to select his own methods of execution—unless a particular tableau was desired. He obeyed the rules of inattention, and they provided reliable intelligence and logistical cover. It was a workable arrangement. Up to now.

"Nope," she said.

"Nancy?"

"Nope"

"Abigail?"

"Nope."

"Leroy?" this time he let his voice crack in faux exasperation. Good. He was holding the line. Just a little longer.

"That's a *boy's* name!" Her giggles turned to bubbly laughter. "I'm *Kwisty!*"

Christie. Okay. "Do you like flowers, Christie?" Bruce slipped his left hand into his cargo pocket and eased out a Ziploc bag.

"Yay! I *love* flowers!"

He opened the bag at his side—careful to avoid getting it anywhere near his face—and removed a small damp cloth. "Well then, I have something you're going to like."

"You *do?*"

Bruce eased closer. "Something . . . magical."

"Magic?"

Almost there. "Yes, Christie. Close your eyes. I want to see if you can guess what it is, only by the smell."

She closed her eyes, bobbing on her toes. *"Flowers?"*

"You tell me." He held the cloth beneath her nose.

As the girl swooned, he pressed the rag firmly over her face. He scooped her up and held the cloth in place a few more seconds. When he was sure she was out, he laid her gently on the couch then bent to retrieve the doll.

The stringent fumes registered as a taste: apricots and turpentine. He turned his face away, blindly working the cloth back into the bag. After making certain it was thoroughly sealed, he stuffed it back in his cargo pocket.

He lifted her, brushed a strand of hair back from her brow. "Sweet dreams, little angel." Lalaloopsie lay peacefully on the girl's tummy. The plastic eyes stared up at him. He avoided meeting that accusing gaze.

He eased his way to the exit, using only his peripheral vision, eyes riveted to Christie's cherub face. He toed open the door and stole one final glance over his shoulder. You just never could be too cautious.

He slipped out, babe in his arms, a thief in the night.

-BT Boys-

"I still can't believe you let her do that shit to your face," Pokey said to Tank.

They called him *Pokey* not because he was slow. Quite the contrary. Of below average size and height, he loved knives, was in fact lightning quick with a blade.

Tank had once seen Pokey, on a bet, skewer a man's hand to a bar table. Dude had been giving Pokey shit all night. Thought he was all badass. So Pokey had teased him into a little game.

Each put up a hundred dollar bill. Pokey had agreed to wait, butterfly knife folded at his side, for this mother fucker to grab the money. If he snagged it, he was a hundred bucks richer. If Pokey successfully defended the pot by stabbing the invading hand, *he* would be up by a Benjamin—although the bills would probably need some cleaning.

Tank had been certain Pokey would lose. He remembered being mad at himself for failing to catch it on his phone. Then again, there hadn't been much to catch.

Flinch. Slam. Done.

The punk had screamed bloody murder, his hand stuck to the table. Pokey had held the blade firm until he'd taken a selfie.

Both car doors banged shut, the Plymouth listing to port with Tank's weight. *"Let* her do this? You heard what I told

Paxyl last night. Bitch went crazy. Threw Big Man off the stage, broke some rich kid foot." He shook his head. "Stole a jacket then did all this." Tank air-circled his face, one eye swollen nearly shut.

"Why didn't you bust her head?"

"Think I didn't try? She too fast. Got hit by a big van, too. *Bayam!* Didn't do *nothin'* to her. She just roll like a cat, land on her feet, then that motha fucker let her in and drove off."

"Musta been on some kind of drugs."

"Somethin'."

"Now Paxyl wanna talk to her." Pokey chuckled. "He gonna do more than talk." He shook his head, eyebrows raised.

"Better do more than talk."

They merged into the morning traffic on US-1 and headed south. At the first light, Tank added, "If he don't want me damaging his merchandise—" He looked over at Pokey. "—he better do some kind of damage his *self.*"

"Or what?"

"Sheeee-it . . ."

"You ain't gonna do shit!"

Both men laughed. They knew the score. No one crossed Paxyl Dread and lived to tell about it.

Tank said, "But you watch and see if I ain't smiling when we throw her narrow ass in this car."

"I know that's right." Pokey reached over and clicked on a CD.

They headed toward Julie's place.

-Sorry to Say-

Someone once said, "The fastest way to a man's heart is through his stomach." By Freddie's way of thinking, whoever said it—probably female—was off by about ten inches north. But he figured it might apply with women. Not that he was after anyone's heart.

He stood over the stove, cursing himself that his scrambled eggs were sticking to the pan. Sometimes, if he buttered the skillet good and got the temperature just right, they'd slip right off the surface. Fluffy as you please, no burnt marks on the bottom.

Not today.

He almost discarded the whole batch and started over. He stopped himself just short of a full-blown OCD air-raid siren that would have woken the whole neighborhood.

The coffee pot chuckled and the toast popped up.

Freddie felt certain a good night's sleep would prove to have been an effective remedy for Zoe's amnesia. He himself felt much more clear-headed, confident the morning would bring closure. They'd enjoy a hearty breakfast, marveling at the experience. They'd ooh and ah at the wonders of the human mind. She'd thank him, call an Uber and be on her way. He'd head to his next job and lose himself in the comfort of work. Maybe she'd turn out to be an interesting friend. Maybe they'd only meet occasionally in passing.

Or not. Probably not.

He called out, "Mornin' sunshine!"

She didn't answer, but that was no surprise. She'd been exhausted. Beat to a pulp. Hit by a van. His van.

No doubt she'd crashed hard, but it was ten in the morning—plenty of time for a good night's sleep—so he padded back to the electronics room.

He raised the back of his knuckles, intending to knock—but hesitated.

What are you afraid of? Just knock!

He drew back his knuckles again, even loosed two rapping gestures, but made no contact with the door.

What if her sleep had been fitful? That's what the nightmare seemed to indicate.

He eased his ear to the door and listened . . . waited . . .

He immediately drew his head back. What if she caught him with his ear to the door? She'd accuse him of spying—which of course he was.

To hell with it.

He knocked softly. "Hey. You up yet?"

Now that was stupid. What if she *weren't* up yet? No doubt she'd respond in her now familiar spicy tone, *Well, I am now!*

Silence.

He turned and traipsed back toward the kitchen—then stopped.

What if her injuries were worse than they'd thought? What if the nightmare had been a symptom of brain damage?

The numbing effects of adrenaline could mask a severe injury. All the glove compartment pamphlets said, *After an accident, proceed immediately to the hospital, even if you feel okay.* Of course, ladder manuals read, *Do not climb,* extension cord instructions warned, *Not for live current,* and emblazoned on microwave entrees was the admonition, *Warning! Cool to room temperature before serving!*

But still.

With a sigh, he returned to her door. Before he could chicken out again, he knocked and called out, "Hey. Zoe. Breakfast is ready."

Nothing.

Louder now: "Yo! Sleeping Beauty. You crawl out a window last night?"

He froze. What did he really know about this woman? When he stopped and thought about it, wasn't the notion she'd split on him really not so shocking?

He knocked again. "Hey Zoe. You okay?"

Silence.

"I mean, you *were* hit by a van last night." He chuckled . . . waited . . .

That did it. She may indeed be in need of medical attention. Or not there. At this point, Freddie got the distinct impression he was talking to himself. Just to be safe, he warned, "Heads up, coming in," then twisted the handle, forgetting that it should have been locked and that a chair should have blocked his way.

The door opened without resistance.

The room was empty.

Knowing it would be a waste of time, he took a few steps and peered into the closet.

A waste of time.

"Zoe?" He cocked his head, listening, not expecting an answer. A quick glance into his bedroom on the way out of course proved it vacant.

Back to the kitchen, into the adjacent living room . . .

Nothing.

He returned to the bathroom. Only silence awaited him. Just to be thorough, he drew back the shower curtain. No one squeezed into the corner, no one crouched hiding in the tub. He closed the curtain and turned to go—and stopped. He stood staring at the bathroom mirror. Scrawled in bubbly, girlish script, a poem awaited his discovery:

Stranger Danger

Sorry to say,
Did you such seed?
Full fill your need?

Sorry to say,
My intenchuns
Were your invenchuns

How did I get
You get me here?
You get me?

My dear face less stranger,
Is my life in danger?

Sorry to say,
My ivery flesh
is not for sell.

Sorry to say,
I bid the fair well.

What the hell? He read it again, then a third time.

This was not Zoe. Sure, he'd known her only a few hours, but he was confident this was utterly out of character for the woman he'd met last night.

She wouldn't have left a *poem*. Had she written anything at all, it would have been a brief note, direct, free of drama— and spelled correctly.

Yet here it was.

It could not have been written by anyone other than Zoe. If Zoe *was* her name. *He* sure as hell hadn't written it.

Suddenly her insistent *This is not me* rang in his ears. And the nightmare took on a disturbing new significance. Like some mythical monster, a new explanation for her amnesia swam gently through his mind, a muted shape clouded by fathoms of water. He tried to bring it into focus . . . almost had it . . . but lost it in the depths. Finally, he shook himself back to reality.

The woman was gone.

-Curbside Service-

"There she go there she go there she go!" Pokey practically leaped out of the seat, pointing across Tank to a woman shuffling down the sidewalk in painter coveralls. She was headed in the opposite direction across the highway from them.

Tank turned the volume down and followed Pokey's gyrating pointer. "What? Nah, that ain't her."

"Yeah it is yeah it is! Turn this shit around."

"That's just some homeless . . ." Tank squinted . . . "Whattha-fuck?"

"I done *told* you, man! Turn this shit around!"

"Last night her hair was *purple.*" Tank put on his left blinker and executed an illegal U-turn at the first break in the median. He shot the bird at but otherwise ignored a honking SUV. He changed lanes without looking, eyes locked on the painter's-coverall-wearing, barefoot bitch that was his quarry. "Be cool now. Last night she's a Tasmanian devil on crack cocaine."

"She don't look like no Tas-whatta-fuck-ever-you-said. She look like Star the stripper, all head-in-the-clouds 'n shit like always."

"Just be cool."

"Alright, alright." Pokey fished the Glock from the front of his pants. When they reached her, Tank bounced the Plymouth right over the curb then across the grass and onto the sidewalk. Blocking her way.

The girl stuffed her hands in the roomy pockets and shuffled nervously in place. Pokey stepped one foot out, making sure the door kept his pistol from plain view. He surveyed the terrain.

Tank unfolded from the other side with his 9 well-hidden at his waist.

She just stood there. Her left hand ventured from the safety of her pocket and began twirling her hair.

What Tank wanted to say was, *Get your ass in this car, bitch.* Instead, face injuries burning anew, he said, "Paxyl want a word with you."

-Cell B-

Colonel Taggart Creed stepped lively, enjoying his morning stroll to the office. In his imagination, he soaked up the rays of the sun and inhaled the crisp morning air. Birds flitted playfully in the trees as they watched him pass. He smiled up at them, these birds of his mind. "Thank you, Lord," he said, "for such a glorious day."

Of course he was bathed only in harsh fluorescent lighting. Any hint of the sun's rays was stopped well above him, blocked by a trillion tons of earth and stone, digested via photosynthesis by the forest over 300 feet above top level. The only breeze flowed from overhead vents along the hallway, the air having been forced through countless micron filters.

The screening of micro-particles was rated at one part per trillion. Far greater air filtration than was available to the general public, it would block virtually any contagion. The word *virtually* bothered Creed sometimes. Considering what they kept down here. There was HIV, weaponized smallpox, dengue and other well-known diseases. More troubling were strains like bubonic plague, Ebola and Trixie. Worst of all, however, were the abominations as of yet unnamed, referred to only as strings of letters and numbers: OXY34. DNZ9. Y2K44. Most were synthetic, some hybrid. All were lethal.

Then there were materials of . . . other origins.

Of course, pristine filtration would amount to cutting off the air flow entirely. As it was, massive pumps slaved tirelessly, working at over 10,000 PSI to supply the bunker with precious oxygen through the rigorous screening.

In the case of a catastrophic event—such as a terrorist attack—in which filtration was compromised, release to the outside world of anything housed in these caverns was simply unthinkable. Some would wipe out a population the size of a small town within days. Others could quite possibly render most mammals—including the human race—entirely extinct. With a few materials, the consequences of release were utterly unknowable. So a contingency plan had been established.

First, the entryway to the bunker would seal airtight.

Then decontamination would occur.

Spaced every two feet—embedded in granite behind the concrete walls—ran a massive network of over ten miles of two-inch diameter pipes. Completely hidden from view, they lined every wall of every room and walkway. The pipes contained a substance not referenced in any science journal or textbook. Created by the DSA, it amounted to a network of thermobaric weaponry without equal.

Within the first .01 seconds of detonation, the metal pipe would be vaporized along with the stone encasing it. In the next millisecond, the temperature would skyrocket to between eight and nine thousand degrees Fahrenheit, sufficient heat for momentary ignition of the atmospheric oxygen itself.

It set the air on fire.

No one was certain what would happen next. One hypothesis was that, once the oxygen was set aflame, the dominoes would continue to fall, incinerating cubic miles of atmosphere, possibly consuming every air molecule throughout the entire planet. This doomsday scenario was bandied about by only a paranoid few.

One thing, however, was certain. The mountain under which the bunker resided would react like a volcano, blasting the molten remains of everything (and every*one*) down here through the paths of least resistance in the granite outer-crust of the earth. It would spew forth in the form of man-made magma, vaporizing the peaceful forest above and every form of life it touched as it vomited down the mountainside.

Catastrophic, yes. But any threat of an extinction event would have been contained. No organism known to man would survive within a five mile radius of the bunker. Maybe farther. Creed tried not to worry, tried to have faith. He'd be fine. Or he wouldn't. In the end, it was the Lord's will, praise God Amen.

"Morning, Colonel." Gloria beamed as he entered the reception area. Her right hand was positioned inconspicuously beneath her desk where she gripped a bottom-mounted .50 caliber Desert Eagle pistol. She was well trained in its use.

"Morning, Glory." Glory was his personal nickname for his secretary.

As he placed his palm on the scanner, he gazed with pride at the six-foot diameter brass seal in relief on the wall behind her. Bedazzled in pin spots, it read, *The Great Seal of The Department of Scientific Alternatives.*

The DSA's origins had been strictly scientific, its duties confined to research of energy alternatives and other useless technologies. Under Colonel Creed's tutelage, it had become a militarized department charged with exploring heretofore unexamined conventions of warfare including innovative new concepts for weaponry. Their work being of a top-secret nature, only a select few in Congress were privy to what went on in these caverns. Creed had little concern of oversight, of pesky committees looking over his shoulder, hampering his efforts.

When the green light glowed on her desk display, Gloria resumed her work, pistol forgotten. "You'll want to check your morning briefings first thing."

"Uh oh. Highlights?"

"Better just read it for yourself." She buzzed him through.

Creed sighed. "Thanks, Gloria."

Moments later at his desk, he propped his elbows on the ink blotter, clasped his hands and peered not at the ceiling but through it, and through the floor above, his gaze penetrating the trillion tons of earth and stone, beyond the forest canopy and into the sky.

After the sanction he'd scheduled for last night, he didn't know what to pray. So he just sat there. Staring at the sky. Open to God's will. After a moment, he shook his head and sighed. "Have mercy on us, Amen."

He pulled up his briefings.

Monday, 22 June 2020, 800 hrs.

CONF REQ: Percy, Lyle
FOR: Today, A.M.
STATUS: Urgent
CONFIRM || DECLINE

He knew what Percy had to say; the kid had made his case a thousand times before. While Creed understood the sentiment, there was simply nothing he could do about it. He shook his head and clicked *DECLINE*. The next notification popped up.

```
------------------------------------
```
NOTICE: Delta sanction completed successfully
ACKNOWLEDGE
```
------------------------------------
```

Sad thing, Brennan Payne. He hated it, but in this business, unpleasantries were necessary to keep the buses running on time. He sent up a silent prayer of remorse and clicked *ACKNOWLEDGE.*

```
------------------------------------
```
UnDet: Payne, Christie
LOC: Cell B
ACKNOWLEDGE
```
------------------------------------
```

He sat staring at this last post. UnDet stood for *Unscheduled Detainee.* The detainee was Payne's daughter, Christie.

Here. Now. In cell B.

What in God's name was she doing *here?*

Vega.

Damn it all . . . The girl wasn't even supposed to have been there. She'd had a sleepover scheduled with a friend from school. This had been confirmed. Maybe there had been a last minute change of plans.

He made a mental note to find out who'd been monitoring Payne's phones and email. That unfortunate nitwit would soon find himself guarding diesel generators in the frozen plains of Alaska.

After careful consideration, Creed had decided to withhold all mention of the girl from Vega. In consideration of his unique sensitivities. And of course had Vega known the assignment did not exactly fall under Terrorism Task Force duties, he'd have refused it. Keeping that from him was a lie by omission, but Creed saw no harm in that. The job needed doing, and Vega had been the best man to do it. 300 million Americans were counting on them.

Besides, what you didn't know wouldn't hurt you.

Vega certainly had a gift, but lately he'd been . . . malfunctioning. Creed hated to lose him and wondered how much longer he could wait to retire the agent. He supposed God would give him a sign when the time came. Maybe this was it.

He sighed. In the worst case scenario—the unlikely event someone witnessed any part of a mission—SOP was to remove the threat. In the case of the girl, he realized Vega would have had a problem with it. But what were the odds? The intel was good. Or should have been.

Creed had serious problems sanctioning a child. In fact, he had personal reservations about most departmental policies, but he kept them to himself. His job was not to set policy but to enforce it.

He was good at his job. He hated the unavoidable ugliness, but that was just the cost of freedom.

300 hundred million Americans were counting on him.

The Bible instructs us to submit to authority, and maybe that was why. The big decisions were for the big decision makers, assigned to their positions by God Himself. That offered Creed at least some comfort.

But now the problem of the girl had been dumped into *his* lap. Resentment swelled in him. He needed to confront Vega, *now*.

He pressed a button on his desk console: "Vega still in the complex?"

"Sorry, sir. He popped in and right back out back out late last night."

The intercom system remained on standby at all times. It was as if invisible versions of Creed and Gloria were always standing right there, each in the other's office.

Creed felt cheated. Played. He tried to leave his emotions out of it, but humans were, after all, emotional creatures. He closed his eyes and took a deep breath. Maybe this was indeed the sign. He'd pray on it.

"Will there be anything else sir?"

He realized he was still holding the call button. "Sorry, Gloria. Just thinking."

"Sir?"

He released the button and leaned back in his chair.

Bruce Vega. What to do, what to do?

-Fish Food-

Knuckles white on the wheel, Freddie kept his eyes on the road—or on the Walmart sign across the street, or the two seagulls flying overhead—anything but the pink building wrapped in purple neon lights. There was nothing to do about it. Zoe, if Zoe was her name, had split on him.

He should have felt nothing but indifference. Even relief.

You wanted your life back, remember?

So why was resentment churning in him, threatening to render undiluted anger?

Because your feelings are hurt.

He rejected that notion. He *did* want his life back. He'd ventured out from the comfort of his solitude to help her. He'd taken a risk. Okay, perhaps even an emotional one. Then she'd left without even telling him, much less thanking him. Worse, that childish poem on the mirror had been outright insulting! *(Is my life in danger?)*

Yes, he was just pissed.

Keep telling yourself that.

Sighing, he stole a glance at the club.

Nothing happening over there—just a man in a necktie, slinking along the wall toward the entrance, trying to make himself invisible.

Why were strip clubs even open during the day? Did businessmen hold lunch meetings there? While gawking at naked girls begging for college tuition? Or grocery money? Strange world.

Why had he looked? Did he expect Zoe to be kneading her hands in the parking lot? Bobbing on her toes, waving as he sped past? Hell, she wouldn't even be there. Much less standing outside looking for him. In fact, the way she'd talked, she'd never darken the doors of that place again. Much less his place.

Just let it go.

He took a deep breath and guided his focus toward today's job: building a storage closet in a living room.

Adding a closet within an existing room was not difficult, but involved important differences from including one in the original structure. In order to fit between finished floor and ceiling—

("You stuck your neck out for me where I'm sure as hell no one else would have.")

—he'd need to cut the studs slightly shorter than that of new construction. And original walls were often not entirely square, in which case you had to—

("You're a good guy, Freddie. Truce?")

—split the difference with the new walls. He'd in all likelihood need anchors, so he made a mental note to drop by Home Depot at lunch. By that time, he'd be ready to—

Everything had seemed alright when they'd turned in. Did the nightmare mean anything? Was she okay?

Throughout the day and despite his resistance, thoughts of the woman fought for his attention. He forgot measurements, wasted lumber, and lost his place and had to backtrack. What should have taken but a few hours ended up taking all day. He managed to complete the framing but forgot to pre-drill channels for wiring. That would mean an unpleasant task for tomorrow morning.

Construction can be merciless.

Like life.

By the time he navigated the shadows of the client's yard for Old Mable, tool belt slung over his shoulder, he'd decided enough was enough. The infatuation of Freddie the Fixer with Zoe-If-That-Even-Is-Her-Name was *over*. He knew better, and wondered why he'd allowed himself to care. It was just childish.

Waste of time.

Unhealthy.

It was just a slip, he told himself, but he was over it. He breathed a sigh of relief as he headed for home, windows down, breeze caressing his hair.

He chuckled aloud and shook his head. He supposed everyone got lonely. That was no crime. Maybe he was lonelier than he'd realized. Maybe he'd gotten desperate, which had skewed his judgment. Messed with his emotions. This was nothing more than a wakeup call. Perhaps he did need to make some friends. Hell, go sit at a bar.

The strip club was up ahead on his left, but he wasn't worried about it. Hell, she most likely wouldn't be there anyway.

He'd just drive on past.

Simple.

No problemo.

Zip. Zero. Nada.

Freddie pulled the van into BT's parking lot. After finding a space, he killed the engine and laid his head on the steering wheel. He butted it there, gently, three times.

Bump. Bump. Bump.

"Freddie . . . *Freddie,*" he said quietly. He shook his head, rolling it on the wheel. "What are you doing, man?"

Well, for one thing, he really should make sure she was okay. What was the Chinese proverb? When you save a life, you're responsible for it forever? Something like that. He certainly hadn't saved her *life*—maybe saved her from a severe ass-kicking by the looks of it—but he did legitimately need to make sure she was okay.

Yeah.

Legitimately.

What about the staff? That bouncer had been a rabid dog, chasing the woman into traffic like he had. Would they recognize his van? Have a bone to pick with him?

Surely not. For them, that had to have been just another day at the office. Tonight would bring new drunks, more fights, another evening's door to collect. And if these guys *were* dangerous, why, that only justified his checking on Zoe. Chances were, they'd never see the van, much less recognize him. He'd be in and out of here before you knew it.

He slipped on the corduroy blazer with patches on the elbows he'd brought along "just in case." He opened the van door and stepped out, feeling like a Saint Bernard at a Chihuahua party. The blazer did little to disguise what he was: a big Shrek just off a job site in cargo pants and soiled t-shirt. As he walked toward the entrance, he felt a strong beat vibrating the walls of the place, though he could hear no music. The rhythm agitated him, upped his anxiety.

He couldn't remember the last time he'd been in a strip club. In his twenties, maybe—long ago—but he did remember he hadn't liked it. He hadn't liked it at all. He'd been burdened by a crushing pity for the working girls. He'd burned with scorn for the laughing, dollar-bill waving assholes who made such demeaning work possible by funding it.

He'd slip in and find Zoe. He'd make sure she was still breathing, do an about face, and leave.

Simple as that.

He wrenched open the steel fire door. Cigarette smoke engulfed him, and he was immediately nauseated. The music was deafening, a British-sounding woman rapping something about a pussy drop. He didn't think she referred to losing one's grip on a house pet.

Through the haze, a looming figure materialized.

A bouncer.

The bouncer.

The marks on his face left little doubt this was the same guy Zoe had kicked out the passenger door. Freddie doubted the man would recognize him, but he tensed just the same.

"Forty dollars."

Thinking he'd heard wrong, Freddie shouted over the music, *"What!?"*

"FORTY DOLLARS!"

"FORTY DOLLARS!?" Surely he was kidding.

"TWO DRINK MINIMUM!"

Freddie pulled his head back, incredulous. "FORTY DOLLARS, *AND* I HAVE TO BUY TWO DRINKS?"

"FIRST TWO FREE!" The guy was losing his patience. *"FORTY DOLLARS!"*

Freddie started to seek additional clarification—then realized the futility of further debate. He fished two twenties from his pants pocket, and they disappeared into the Goliath's fist.

"WELCOME TO BT'S ENJOY Y'SELF!" the bouncer quoted by rote, without even so much as a Mona Lisa smile.

Like fish to puke over the edge of a boat, they swarmed him. Most were average-looking, some beautiful, others downright ugly. But all were topless and had an eye for newbies, the most likely to be shocked by nudity and thus come forth with the almighty greenbacks.

"Hey baby, wanna table dance?"

"Whatchoo starin' at, honey? Wanna closer look?"

"I'm Ariel." *Fat chance.* "Ever see a mermaid dance?"

"No, no please," Freddie said. "No thank you, so sorry . . ."

His emotions were genuine, his words sincere. But the regrets he expressed were not about his unwillingness to offer a tip. It was about the fact he was powerless to help them find their ways, to elevate even a single one above this groveling cesspool into which they'd descended. On he went, looking into each set of eyes, finding nothing but desperation. Every girl here had a life and a history, a soul and a story—but he could offer them nothing more than a passing glance.

Helpless.

Then there she was.

Seeing Zoe like this stirred not the slightest hint of desire in him. Rather, it broke his heart. To Freddie, the body was one's "secret face." Infinitely more sacred than the one on your skull, the privacy of one's body was to be revealed only to self and soul mate—or life partner, or significant other—or whatever the hell had taken the place of husband and wife these days.

He had no rational claim to her heart, nor her to his. But damn it, there had been a little chemistry, hadn't there? He'd respected the way she'd defended her honor. It had touched him—more so than he'd allowed himself to believe, he reluctantly admitted. He'd taken a risk. Let her in. Into his home and, okay fine, at least across the threshold of his heart.

Unlikely as it was, if the day ever *did* come when they would share a life together, that pride in herself would have made this "revelation of secret faces" all the more hallowed.

Now here she was, flaunting her precious private secrets to every Tom Dick and Harry in this revolting den of iniquity. To him too, yes, but he didn't want it like this. He wanted it to be *just them;* he wanted it to be *special;* he wanted it to be *right.* Now any possibility of intimacy had been crushed.

Check on her and leave, remember?

She squirmed her way through the throng of weaving women to his side. She didn't recognize him, or pretended not to.

"Zoe!" he yelled over the cacophony.

"Hey, man." She slid her hands up and down the lapels of his blazer.

Despite himself, he quivered with pleasure. The dancing pin spots dizzied him; the music entranced. He felt disoriented. Confused. Even so, he could tell she was avoiding his eyes.

"Want a dance?" Apparently, she was accustomed to making herself heard through the racket. Unlike the others, she spoke quietly, right in his ear. Her warm breath raised goosebumps on his neck. Her hands never stopped moving—up and down his chest, around his waist, back up and into his hair. Though he tried to resist it, he found her touch intoxicating.

Her voice. Last night she'd been articulate and well-spoken. Her pronunciation had been perhaps mid-western, even non-regional. Now she spoke with a severe southern accent—pretty much what you'd call a drawl. *(Hey mayan.)*

Last night she'd been confident. Bordering on aggressive. At the very least assertive. Now she was tentative and meek as if constantly afraid of offending.

He needed some answers. "Can we talk?" He mimicked the same speaking technique but evidently overdid it. She backed off, grimaced and covered her ear—albeit with a flirty smile and light smacking motion of her hand. But she never quite met his eyes.

The other girls had disappeared, apparently drawn to another newbie sheep being sheered for two Andrew Jacksons by the Goliath.

"We can talk while I dance." She led him by one lapel across the crowded floor.

Maybe twins.

Except he noticed a sizable bruise on her right hip—although she'd done a fairly decent job of masking it with makeup.

It was her; they were one and the same person. Had to be. So then what was with the dummy act? What was she doing back here after so adamantly insisting she was not a stripper? At the very least, he'd have expected some awkwardness, if not for her to duck out before he even saw her.

Yet here she was.

As they passed a table of twenty-something loudmouths, one of the men yelled to another, "*Fucking bums with tits!*" Freddie almost confronted them—but realized the jerk's assessment was regretfully poignant. It just stung a little.

Before he turned away, he noted one of the men palmed a small camera. Pointed at them. When the punk realized he'd been busted, he smiled conspiratorially and raised a finger to his lips.

Before Freddie could protest, the girl pulled him away to a table near the corner and stuck out her hand. "I'm Star! Forty dollars!"

What *was* it with this place? Forty bucks to walk through the door, now forty bucks for . . . what? A dance?

Oh. A *private* dance.

He fished out two more twenties and forked them over. She took the bills and stuffed them in her g-string.

Someone tapped his shoulder. Freddie turned. A dead-faced waitress, eyes sagging as much as her boobs, handed him two plastic cups of almond-colored liquid on ice.

Ah. Two drink minimum.

And here were his drinks.

Evidently, you got the flavor of the night and were not offered a choice. Most likely, the clientele here didn't give a shit what was in the cups—only that they contained alcohol. However, Freddie got the impression it would require a team of NASA scientists and a celebrity star playing a high school chemistry teacher to detect even the faintest whiff of the substance.

Or perhaps they contained *pure* alcohol, so concocted to loosen the pockets of the gawkers. Regardless, he had no intentions of getting the rims of that plastic anywhere near his lips.

He set the drinks on a nearby table and turned to . . . what was it now? Star? to Star.

"Listen, I—" But she was already dancing. She gently pushed him down in the chair in front of which he'd been standing, then straddled him and sat. Her hair was a liquid hypnotist's pendulum, first hiding her face, then revealing it, eyes closed . . . Her body swayed and rippled, always moving, slow and calm, never stopping, circles and waves, her hair tickling his neck, now behind her, slowly . . . entrancing . . .

He raised his hands to stop her, but she grabbed his wrists— "Uh-uh. No touchin', sweetheart." —and gently placed them behind his head.

Insanity. He'd stepped off the brain train, one stop short of reality. What should he do? His emotions were pulled a dozen different directions, and he suddenly decided that, right now, he wanted *out*.

He was ready to just throw her off and bolt when from behind him rose a ruckus. Chairs screeched noisily, and he recognized the doorman's booming voice when he yelled, *"NO CAMERAS!"* Freddie turned despite the stripper's resistance. The bouncer was carrying the jerk with the camera, literally by the scruff of his neck. The smaller man's feet kicked for purchase, the floor a good ten inches below his shoes. In his other hand, the walking tank held the camera. He casually tossed it in the trash barrel by the exit. Then, using the punk's head, he banged open the door and tossed the guy out. Before the door had even eased shut completely, the bouncer was perched on his bar stool, arms folded over his bulk.

"Hey cowboy, show's over here." Her drawl gave the word *here* two syllables: "Hee-yer."

That was enough. He grabbed her wrists before she could stop him and yelled, "Stranger Danger? Bid the farewell? Ring a bell? What the hell are you doing, Zoe? *Why did you lie to me?*"

At first she looked perplexed, then her face brightened. "That was *you*?" She threw her head back and laughed. "Oh my God. Did we—"

"No. We didn't," he yelled over the deafening music. This was the same woman—yet utterly and completely different. Her hands hung limp over the wrists he held, and she sat slumped, smiling with nothing but amusement at the notion she'd woken up somewhere she hadn't remembered going.

Freddie was certain that if any man were to grab "Zoe's" (if that *was* her name) wrists like this, it would be like taking hold of two live fire hoses. He'd instantly get a very close look at her forehead as she slammed it into his face, along with a swift knee to the peaches.

"Man, this is *trippin' - me - out!* How did I—"

She was interrupted by another bouncer. Or maybe a floor manager? This giant wore a conservative black suit, evidently custom tailored by Omar the tent maker. He eased the girl out of his way and grasped one of Freddie's lapels. Not nearly as pleasant as when "Star" had caressed him minutes ago.

"NO TOUCHING!" he shouted, and tried to lift Freddie out of his seat.

Star said, "Come on, Big Man. I was only—"

"Hey. I'm just trying to look out for you, Jules. Ain't you been scratched enough for one day?"

Scratched? And now she's Jules?

Big Man was indeed a big man, but so was Freddie. He wasn't as easy to man-handle as the camera punk had been. But Freddie cooperated, raising his hands in surrender as he stood.

Apparently realizing Freddie would be a formidable opponent, and seeing he was compliant, the bouncer released him
and pointed over Freddie's shoulder toward the exit, raising
his eyebrows to make the message clear.

"Okay, I'm leaving," Freddie said, hands still raised.

He turned and began negotiating his way through the
crowd. He sensed Big Man at his back and had no intention of
starting anything.

Perhaps it was fortunate he was being escorted out, for his
tangled emotions were out of control. God only knows how
long he'd have wound up staying if this hadn't happened—and
time here seemed to be measured in twenty-dollar bills.

As he dodged waitresses and stepped over puddles of God-
knows-what, Freddie's mind worked the puzzle of
"Zoe/Star/Jules" like a Rubik's cube. It was heartbreaking,
yes, but also simply remarkable. Clearly the same woman, not
twins (he'd seen the bruise on her hip), and yet utterly and
completely different people, right down to the accent, facial
expressions, and body language.

Suddenly, the idea that had teased his imagination this
morning—that leviathan from the abyss of his mind—lunged
from the depths like the shark into Brody's face off the back of
the Orca.

And he thought of a plan.

As they approached the exit, Freddie slowed his pace,
gradually so as not to be obvious. Past the bar, through a
throng of jabbering dancers, then nudging past a staggering
businessman, tie unknotted to his chest, causing Freddie to
move slower still . . . he worried it wasn't going to work. Then
from behind him came the cue for which he'd been waiting.

"Let's go, now," said the bouncer with a gentle nudge.
Freddie turned to face Big Man, hands raised, walking backwards, just as the trash can came into view. Sometime during
their walk, the bouncer had produced a handkerchief from his

considerable suit jacket. He wiped sweat from his brow with one hand as he guided Freddie with the other.

"Sorry. I'm moving." Freddie adjusted his course ever so slightly. He turned back around facing the direction he was walking and—

Perfect.

He stumbled into the trash can. He didn't have to fake a moment of surprise as he tripped over it. Though he hadn't planned to go this far, he found himself sprawled in the garbage.

Even better.

"SORRY, SORRY!" he yelled over the music, picking up litter and tossing it back into the upturned barrel.

Above him, Big Man shouted for the doorman: "Tank! Help me out over here!"

Crawling through the rubbish, he searched . . . surreptitiously . . . desperately . . . *There!*

Just as he found—and palmed—what he was looking for, the other bouncer (The doorman. What was it? Tank?) came to Big Man's assistance. Together, they hoisted Freddie, one on each shoulder. "FORGET THE FUCKIN' TRASH, ASSHOLE!" Tank shouted, and shoved him rudely outside.

Freddie stutter-stepped into the parking lot.

That was all; it was over. He felt fortunate to have avoided a scuffle.

"Don't come back," Tank said over his shoulder.

The last thing he saw as the bouncers disappeared was Big Man wiping sweat from the back of his neck with his hanky.

Freddie smiled.

-It's Him-

As Freddie pulled out of the parking lot, he was unaware of Tank's having stepped back outside. The bouncer spoke into the edge of his phone as he watched the van turn the corner. "Yeah, I'm sure." His voice resonated as if from an oil drum. "Same one. Freddie the Fixer. Want me to follow him?"

A tinny voice responded through the phone's speaker. "Nah, that's alright. We know who that mutha fucker is and where to find him. He stay gone, forget him. He come back, *then* you follow him . . .

"And make sure *he* don't forget *us.*"

-What's the Word-

In a sparse trailer park in Colorado Springs, Bruce Vega lay staring at the ceiling, entranced by the soft rumble of a storm rolling in. The thin metal walls didn't offer much sound reduction. From outside his window, the rustle of branches were whispers from the graves he'd filled. It was about 8:00 p.m.

The cell phone hummed on the mattress. Normal in appearance, like an old flip phone, the device's sole function was the sending and receiving of coded text messages. Calls were not possible.

He smiled as he read the message:

WHY PACKAGE DROPPED HERE?

EXPLANATION REQUIRED ASAP.

He wanted to respond, *Why package not in briefing?* Instead, he typed, THERE IN THREE DAYS, and clicked send. That ought to give him enough time to figure things out, decide what he was going to do.

After a moment, he couldn't resist adding:

BEDTIME 8:00.

WARM MILK AND STORY.

Forestalling the onslaught of expletives, he flipped the phone shut and tossed it on the nightstand. To hell with them. Turnabout was fair play.

The first droplets patted gently on the roof, whispered promises of the storm to come.

As always when things were still, his mind drifted to Amy. Like never before, this led to thoughts of something new.

Christie.

The likeness was uncanny. Chilling. Indeed the idea of Christie's being Amy (*Not Amy!*) or Amy's ghost had been alluring. He'd resisted the temptation to linger on it.

Accompanying a more insistent rumble, the droplets crescendoed into hypnotic sheets.

Amy had worshipped the ground upon which her big brother tread. She'd believed in her heart there was nothing of which Bruce was incapable. He'd been only ten years old at the time, but to his sister, he'd been ten feet tall and bulletproof.

Her hero.

Bruce scoffed bitterly. *Some hero.*

The ceiling began to ripple. As if warning him of the abyss into which he was slipping, the thunder called out to him . . . followed him down . . . embracing him as he skimmed the surface, then pierced it . . . diving deep . . .

Amy had made it through her meatloaf. She sat grimacing at her broccoli, lips drawn up in a V by her supporting hands. Ten-year-old Bruce knelt on the floor nearby with a G.I. Joe.

"I'm setting the timer," Mom called from the kitchen.

"But Mommm!"

"Don't but *me, young lady. You finish that broccoli before the timer dings or no ice cream!"*

As Bruce narrated an Army adventure, he glanced up at Amy. Then to his mother in the kitchen. She and Dad were talking grownup talk.

When he looked back at Amy, she was looking back at him. Her breath hitched with a post-tears sob.

He winked at her.

G.I. Joe launched skyward, empowered now with the gift of flight. To a dramatic theme, the toy skimmed the couch—wobbled, nearly crashed—then soared across the den, over the table, and finally to Amy's side.

After shooting one last glance toward the kitchen, Bruce plucked a head of broccoli from her plate and stuffed it in his mouth. Then another, then a third. He kept cramming, dropped the GI-Joe so he could use both hands.

Amy's giggle broke through another sob-hitch.

Bruce drew his hands to his chest, jerked his head left, then right. Hamster-style.

Amy had to use both hands to mute her laughter.

A distant rumble stirred him. He rolled over and was transported to France, where his father had been stationed a year later.

"What was ya favorite part?" She glided her Rs.

"I don't know. What was yours?" Bruce tipped the popcorn bag toward his sister.

They were exiting one of the few theaters that played movies in English. Bright-colored awnings cast rainbow shadows on the sidewalk. The aroma of fresh baked pastries was intoxicating. They'd just seen Little Mermaid.

"I like the What's the Word *song." She took a handful of popcorn, spilling most of it.*

"What's the Word song? What are you talking about, knuckles?" Bruce called her knucklehead *sometimes, but only affectionately.* Knuckles *was for short.*

"You know, 'Dancin' around on those . . . What's the word? . . . legs.' Dat song."

Their parents had been there, but in the dream it was just the two of them.

"Oh yeah!" He broke into song, dancing dramatically. "What is a dog, and why do they . . . What's the word . . . POOOOP!"

Amy giggled and spanked Bruce on the rear. "No, silly! That wasn't part of the song!"

"Who is that Bruce, and why is he so . . . What's the word? . . . COOOOL!"

Amy shrieked with delight, chasing her brother for another butt slap. He easily evaded her, pirouetting, never breaking character.

Belching filth into the air, a beat up Honda bounced over the curb and blocked the sidewalk.

"No . . ." His chest heaved, eyes clenched shut, tossing his head on the pillow.

Bruce stands in a dusty village. Dissonant twangs from unseen sitars whisper ancient desert tales. Peering between passing tunics, enveloped in senseless words of foreign tongues, he slides slowly forward. The crowd parts, unaware of him.

He stares straight ahead, curious, yet knowing what he'll find.

A groom, his back turned. Ornamental cloak. Bejeweled crown.

Bride but a child. Draped in white. Blonde tresses flow down her back, adorned with flowers.

She slowly turns to face him.

He suddenly stares down a hallway. Dirt floor. Wall-mounted torches. A stucco-lined wormhole spiraling to eternity.

Dim light bleeds through a distant doorway. Motionless in the doorway, silhouetted by a candle's glow, the groom. He says to Bruce, "Privacy."

Behind the groom, the bride. Sitting motionless on the bed. Bare feet dangling.

"Privacy."

Inch by inch, the door is closing.

"Privacy."

The bride is trembling.

"Privacy."

Amy reaches for him. "Bruce!"

A blast of thunder brought him bolting upright in soaking sheets.

-Premise of Purity-

Deep in the bowels of the underground bunker, seventeen fathoms beneath the peaceful forest, Colonel Taggart Creed sprawled in his recliner, sock feet crossed on the ottoman. A pair of combat boots sat by the door, ready for service. His gunmetal-gray crew cut was nearly a perfect match for the Kimber 1911 holstered in a belt slung over the back of his chair. He never kept it far from reach.

His right hand draped over the armrest. From it dangled a glass of Merlot: the blood of Christ. Unlike many Christians, Creed was confident the Lord had no problem with drinking—as long as you didn't lose control, didn't allow alcohol to become an idol. After all, hadn't Jesus turned the water into wine?

Yes, he had.

He gazed beyond the wall ahead of him, face sagged, eyes in a thousand-yard stare. Had anyone been watching, the man would have appeared inebriated.

This was an illusion. Despite his limp posture, his mind was an industrious beehive, furry legs skittering, mandibles munching. Working busily.

Bruce Vega.

He'd clearly skirted policy. At best. At worst, he was guilty of DDO. Disobeying a Direct Order. Creed could easily justify a sanction, but he didn't want to resort to that unless he had to. Taking out a comrade in arms was no small thing. Necessary sometimes, yes, but not a decision to be made lightly.

He sniffed his Merlot, swirled the glass.

But there was more to it than that, wasn't there? They were not friends per se—but they had shared a little history.

"Hi! Taggart Creed," he said, hand extended hardily, teeth gleaming like a young fool.

They were both in their skivvies, towels draped around their necks, prepping for lights-out at twenty-one hundred hours. Other cadets swerved around them, carrying toiletry kits, focused on hitting the sack before the barracks went dark.

Vega accepted his hand warily. He did not return the introduction.

"I'd like to introduce you to someone." He handed Vega a pamphlet entitled, Give it to Jesus.

Vega took the booklet, examined it for a beat, then peered back at him without even so much as a smile.

They just stood there, Creed beaming, Vega's face an empty canvas. Finally, Creed gripped the ends of his towel and shrugged. "Listen. I don't know what it is—and it's none of my business—but something's eating you, brother. Something big. Or at least it seems big to you."

Vega just looked at him.

"But I don't care what it is, friend. Nothing is too big for Jesus." He nodded, grinning like a dolt. "Nothing."

Vega scowled.

Creed was unperturbed. "Listen. Could we . . . pray together?" He placed his hand gently on Vega's shoulder.

"What?" Vega scoffed, bristling at the touch. "Here?" He glanced around the barracks then back at Creed.

He thought the guy might be ready to punch him. That would be okay; he'd be happy to take one for Jesus. Maintaining his stupid grin, he shrugged. "Why not?"

They both just stood there, each waiting for the other to back down.

A voice barked over the intercom: "Lights out in three minutes."

"Yeah thanks. Maybe later." Vega did an about-face and headed for his bunk. Creed watched him go, brow furled. As Vega passed a trash barrel, he shot the pamphlet in and kept walking.

Even now, his heart bled for the guy. He'd reach out to him if he could, but Vega kept a low profile. He rarely used agency safe houses and, no surprise, hadn't checked into one today. When asked where he was going to be, his stock answer was, *Don't worry, I'll find you.*

He'd just last night been in the complex, so he was in all likelihood holed up somewhere in Colorado, perhaps right here in Cheyenne county. But it was a big world out there, and the agent could be anywhere.

If Creed were able to find him, he would not approach the man from a Christian platform. Creed had matured in Christ since that night in the barracks. He'd realized the hard-sell approach wasn't good for anyone. It made him look like a nut-job zealot. Drove away new converts. Better to serve silently as a Christian example and let those lost souls with the courage to reach out come to him.

Vega hadn't been the only soul he'd sought back then. God had blessed him with the power of persuasion, and he'd used it. Perhaps abused it.

Okay, yes. He'd abused it. He cringed at the memory.

The word *philanderer* had been whispered about. *Womanizer. Playboy.* He couldn't recall anyone saying it to his face; if they had he'd have punched their lights out. But they didn't have to. Their faces told him everything, revealed their contempt through plastic smiles.

The silent scorn had been painful. It still hurt, even today. They just hadn't understood. No one had bothered to hear his heart, to sit with him, listen to him, much less pray with him.

It was never about the sex.

It was about love. And life itself, really. He was convinced that, with the youngest girls, he somehow absorbed their youth, nudging his own time-clock back with each encounter. There was nothing wrong with self-preservation, was there? Holding on to his youth? Especially if it inflicted no harm on others.

He'd loved them, each and every one. He'd told them as much. That counted for something, didn't it?

Flashes of Liza danced before him, her luscious curves subtly softened by fading remnants of baby fat, lazy blue eyes under pale lashes. She'd been the sweetest little redhead, young and naïve, trying to convince herself she was rebelling—even as she'd desperately sought a father figure. And hadn't he been just that for her? In exchange for but a drop of her youth? Hadn't he looked out for her? Sheltered her? Even paved the way for her promotion?

Yes, he had.

Then there was Sheila. Sheila of the "magic touch." Yes, that girl could sneak up behind him, give him just a light goose and, doggone it, a concrete zucchini would sprout in his pants, just like that. Astounding, really—if not disconcerting. He'd never seen—or felt—anything like it. His embarrassment had only made it worse.

She'd either drag him into a deserted barracks or closet or something and take care of him—or give him a grope and a wink and just sashay away.

Good old Sheila. Protecting was the last thing she needed. She sought only a friends-with-benefits thing. Nothing wrong with that, was there?

In fact, when in the heat of passion he'd revealed his love for her, she'd said, "That is so much bullshit."

"I mean it, Sheila. I honestly—"

"Oh shut up and fuck me," she'd panted.

And he'd obliged.

There were others—so many others—and he'd loved them all, every single one. He genuinely cared, would have done anything to—

"Oh, come on," he said aloud.

What was the truth? What was the real, honest to goodness truth? God knew it, so who, exactly, did he think he was fooling?

Okay, the truth was, he'd discovered the power of purity. Or rather, the power of *premise* of purity. With a chaste Christian man, he'd realized, women would drop their guards.

Without hesitation.

He muttered aloud, "And when I played my cards right, they'd drop their drawers."

There. He said it. Owned it. Regardless of the love he'd so desperately sought, and regardless of what he'd offered in return, fornication was a sin. He'd selfishly led each of those girls to the spiritual slaughter. The choice to follow had been theirs, but he'd certainly cleared a path for them.

That is, except for Decker. She'd been something else entirely. With all the others, he'd been the pursuer. It had been Decker who pursued him—albeit unbeknownst to her. Uncanny, really. She'd attracted him like bees to honey. Racy thoughts of unbridled passion had plagued his mind, unbidden and unwanted. Intertwined with love, of course, but hot sex nonetheless. He hated remembering himself being so out of control—but there it was. The truth.

Creed gulped the last of his wine and blindly set the glass on the end table.

He'd made his bullshit play, extended one Jesus pamphlet or another with that casual Christian good-guy grin. Decker had just stood there looking at him, eyes burning under knitted brows. She'd drilled into him somehow. What had Constantine called her? A black swan? Yes, the woman possessed something alright—perhaps summoned entities unknowable and inaccessible to the rest of us—and he didn't need any lab tests to tell him that.

She'd been reading his mind; he was convinced of it. He shuddered even now at the memory. Like Dracula presented with the cross (and in retrospect, that's how he'd felt—like a spiritual vampire), he'd practically hissed in fear at the realization she was in there, poking around inside his head, riffling through his private memories—*knowing* him—perhaps better than even he knew his own self.

After but a moment, she'd disengaged. Her face neutralized. She was no longer interested and not in the least deceived. "I know who you are, Creed." Clearly, she'd meant, I know *what* you are—and now Creed saw himself through her eyes, recognized his rotting soul for what it truly had been. "You get that shit outta my face before I cram my fist down your throat and yank you inside out by the asshole."

Then she'd walked away.

Creed had stumbled back to his quarters and spent the rest of the day in prayer.

He'd never approached a woman in sin again, not one single time.

Decker had saved him. He'd never gathered the courage to thank her, nor had he worked up the nerve to even apologize.

But what *had* he done? Where was Decker now, on *his* orders?

"Put a lid on that shit!" he snarled. He had a job to do, and there were few if any other men with the stones to do it. Like those above him, he had tough decisions to make. With God's help, he'd made them. His chin quivered and his vision clouded. He quoted a line he'd once heard somewhere, maybe in a movie: "I have long feared my sins would return to haunt me, and that the cost would be more than I could bear."

He took a deep breath, let it slowly out. And in that moment, he made his decision about Bruce Vega.

He was clueless as to the agent's whereabouts, but had something perhaps even better. Creed knew where he *would* be.

"God forgive me."

-Better off Dead-

Bruce Vega staggered to the bedroom door, stubbed his toe on the facing, then stumbled down the hall to the kitchen. The trailer rocked with his movements. Hands trembling, he snared a glass from the cabinet and snatched a bottle of Jack from the counter. He popped the top with a single snap of his thumb. The cap spun across the scarred linoleum and disappeared under the stove.

He didn't care.

The bottle tinkled against the rim of the glass. Slopping whiskey on the counter, he slammed down the bottle with one hand, tossed back the shot with the other. Calmer now, he repeated the process then set down the glass.

He leaned his palms on the counter. Head hung low. Catching his breath. Gravity channeled the sweat on his face to his nose, from which a single drop fell to the floor. He braced himself, struggled to resist what he knew was coming. Five seconds . . . ten . . .

Sobs racked him. Tears merged with the sweat streaming down his face. The spatter on the floor grew into a blurry puddle. "God damn it," he blubbered, balling his fist on the counter.

Against his will, blinding block letters flashed before his mind's eye:

BETTER IF SHE WERE DEAD.

"No." He shook his head. "No, no no . . ." But his words had no conviction. In fact, death would have been over-whelmingly likely the better scenario for Amy. With that thought, another ghost from this mental haunt materialized before him like a relentless stalker:

WHAT HAS SHE ENDURED THE LAST FIFTEEN YEARS? WHAT IS HAPPENING TO HER, *RIGHT NOW*?

They had a thing about virgins. Eighteen was "too old to wed." So had they raised her like a veal calf until she turned twelve? Or even as young as five, had they—

He snatched the glass off the counter and chunked it aim-lessly into the den. It struck the back of the Lazy Boy and tumbled intact to the cheap carpet.

Better if she were dead.

Not knowing was the thing. His wounds were daily torn open anew, his anguish amplified by his helplessness. He'd been just a boy—but guilt ate at him, every hour, every mi-nute. He had been Amy's *hero*.

Some hero.

The best he could hope for was that she'd somehow escaped. But even if she had, she'd have been but a child in a foreign land. Wandering homeless, working as someone's slave, eking out an existence in the harsh desert . . . those would have been the best lives available to her. If she'd escaped.

Better if she were dead.

And how did *she* remember *him,* if in fact she was still alive today? Had she been instantly disillusioned with her hero even as she was whisked away? Was she disappointed? Did she hate him for failing her?

Or did she forgive him?

This last possibility disturbed him the most. He didn't want her forgiveness, because he didn't deserve it.

But the point was probably moot. When Bruce thought back to his own childhood, memories from his tenth year played like a badly worn VHS tape. Only the day at the theater could he recall with clarity. Besides that, he remembered only vague random moments.

But when he dug back as far as five, the people in those visions, even his parents, were nothing more than grainy still-lifes, the events—or single frame moments from just a few of them—like squinting at an out-of-focus slideshow through murky water.

In fact, maybe she didn't remember him at all. Maybe the inevitable violence she'd endured early on had overloaded her little mind to the point it was forced to delete permanently anything not essential for survival. Like her country. Her parents.

Her brother.

The sons of bitches.

The stinking savages.

"I'll find you," he whispered, as he had every day since the Little Mermaid. He'd committed himself to a lifetime of searching. But deep down, a still quiet voice echoed, *and never finding*.

But life had presented him something new, hadn't it? A chance for redemption. Perhaps even peace. He stared across the den at the blank screen of the old TV. "I'll save her."

Yes, saving Christie was something he could *do*. "For you, Amy. I'll save her for you." But would that redeem him in his sister's eyes? Make her proud of him? Or would she be hurt? Jealous? He shook his head and stared back down at the puddle.

A chuckle escaped him. *Damned if you do, damned if you don't.* This somehow struck him as funny, just the whole fucked up lot of it. He threw his head back and laughed. After a time, he realized this was the cackle of a man on the edge.

He calmed himself, drew a deep breath. He needed to get out of here. Out in the open. Shake it off.

Clear his head a little.

-D.I.D.-

Schizophrenia.
Split personality.

That had been the monster in the depths, the diagnosis Freddie couldn't see. But considering the introduction of "Star" into the equation, what the hell else *could* this be?

While he was excited about the prospects of exploring such an explosive possibility, he realized this also made the idea of pursuing the woman even more reckless. After all, who was she *really?* Was she Zoe, the sassy, hard-edged gymnast? Or was she the limp-wristed, semi-illiterate poet, Star the Stripper?

Or was she truly both?

His hope was that the "root" identity—if that's what you called it—the one with which the enigmatic woman had been born, was the former. Perhaps she had some psychological issue for which she'd created the meeker personality. If that were the case, maybe he could help her jettison the stripper identity. This seemed much more likely. That Zoe could conjure up a meek soul like Star to address some deep dark issue was entirely plausible. But Star conjuring up anything more than adolescent poetry—much less a confident, capable dynamo like Zoe—was simply too much of a stretch.

But what did he know?

Regardless, this would be fascinating. He told himself his fascination had nothing to do with the increasing complexity of his feelings for the woman.

Or was it . . . "these women?"

Jesus, handyman. Why don't you just bail out while you still have a chance?

He sighed as he sat down at his computer and fished from his pocket the mini-cam he'd palmed back at the strip club. He discovered a small door on the back. When he pried it open, it proved to be the cover of the SD card slot. He removed the card and inserted it into his computer. A prompt popped up inquiring as to how he wished to handle the files. He selected *Open folder and explore contents.* When the virtual hourglass completed its cycle, File Explorer displayed several subfolders.

VCDX. Evidently a system folder, it was populated by files with cryptic names. He backed out of it.

Jag F-Type imgs. Jaguar photos. Apparently, the jerk liked fast cars.

Shocker.

South Beach. This one contained selfies of the sleazeball partying with his beer-toting buds at the beach. None included any hint of Zoe. Again he returned to the main menu.

DCIM. On his cell phone, this was the folder in which photo and video media were stored. He hoped it was the same on all devices.

His assessment proved correct. He was rewarded with several icons indicating video files. They'd been titled automatically by the device, with numbers corresponding to the date trailed by the time of day in military format. The dates were all today. The times ranged from an hour to ninety minutes ago.

No thumbnail images were provided for the video files, so he dragged the icons to his desktop, waited a moment while they downloaded, then removed the card.

Before reviewing the videos, he opened a browser and typed the search string *Schizophrenia split personality.* Within a few clicks, he learned that these terms were often confused. In fact, they were completely different conditions.

According to one site, schizophrenia was characterized by the splitting, or breaking, of the mind's capacity to function. On the other hand, the condition for which he was seeking information was referred to as Dissociative Identity Disorder, or "DID," formerly known as Multiple Personality Disorder. DID was characterized by a severely dissociative, or separated, identity.

He refined his search to Dissociative Identity Disorder.

Jackpot.

He clicked on a Mayo Clinic post and dug in, fascinated:

SYMPTOMS:

Signs and symptoms depend on the type of dissociative disorders you have, but may include:

• Memory loss (amnesia) of certain time periods, events, people and personal information

Freddie's heart quickened.

> • A sense of being detached from yourself and your emotions

> • A perception of the people and things around you as distorted and unreal

> • A blurred sense of identity

Ya think? Zoe's sense of identity was much more than blurred. It was completely divided, right down the line, black and white.

He read on:

> • Significant stress or problems in your relationships, work or other important areas of your life

> • Inability to cope well with emotional or professional stress

> • Mental health problems, such as depression, anxiety, and suicidal thoughts and behaviors

Reading this made his heart sink. Good *God* what must she have gone through? Or maybe she was still going through it. Increasingly sympathetic to the woman's condition, he went on to the next section.

> There are three major dissociative disorders defined in the Diagnostic and Statistical Manual of Mental Disorders (DSM-5), published by the American Psychiatric Association:

> • **DISSOCIATIVE AMNESIA.** The main symptom is memory loss that's more severe than normal forgetfulness and that

can't be explained by a medical condition. You can't recall information about yourself or events and people in your life, especially from a traumatic time. Dissociative amnesia can be specific to events in a certain time, such as intense combat, or more rarely, can involve complete loss of memory about yourself. It may sometimes involve travel or confused wandering away from your life (dissociative fugue). An episode of amnesia usually occurs suddenly and may last minutes, hours, or rarely, months or even years.

• **DISSOCIATIVE IDENTITY DISORDER.** Formerly known as multiple personality disorder, this disorder is characterized by "switching" to alternate identities. You may feel the presence of two or more people talking or living inside your head, and you may feel as though you're possessed by other identities. Each identity may have a unique name, personal history, and characteristics, including obvious differences in voice, gender, mannerisms and even such physical qualities as the need for eyeglasses. There also are differences in how familiar each identity (often referred to as "splits") is with the others. People with Dissociative Identity Disorder typically also have dissociative amnesia and often have dissociative fugue.

• **DEPERSONALIZATION-DEREALIZATION DISORDER.** This involves an ongoing or episodic sense of detachment or being outside yourself — observing your actions, feelings, thoughts, and self from a distance as though watching a movie (depersonalization). Other people and things around you may feel detached and foggy or dreamlike, time may be slowed down or sped up, and the world may seem unreal (derealization). You may experience depersonalization, derealization or both. Symptoms, which can be pro-

foundly distressing, may last only a few moments or come
and go over many years.

The first two entries seemed to fit Zoe perfectly. The last
he would keep in mind, but it didn't apply—at least not at this
point.

CAUSES

Dissociative disorders usually develop as a way to cope
with trauma. The disorders most often form in children sub-
jected to long-term physical, sexual or emotional abuse or,
less often, a home environment that's frightening or highly
unpredictable. The stress of war or natural disasters also
can bring on dissociative disorders.

Personal identity is still forming during childhood. So a child
is more able than an adult to step outside him or herself
and observe trauma as though it's happening to a different
person. A child who learns to dissociate in order to endure
an extended period of youth may use this coping mechanism in response to stressful situations throughout life.

This *causes* section greatly disturbed Freddie. He was un-
nerved at the thought of a child—of Zoe as a child—having
experienced something horrible enough to resort to such a
bizarre escape mechanism. It was also a heads-up that he had
a lot of work ahead of him, if in fact he was going to allow
himself to pursue this further. Maybe it was time to just stop
while he was ahead.

He finished the post.

RISK FACTORS

People who experience long-term physical, sexual or emotional abuse during childhood are at greatest risk of developing dissociative disorders. Children and adults who experience other traumatic events, such as war, natural disasters, kidnapping, torture, or extended, traumatic, early-life medical procedures, also may develop these conditions.

The word *adults* caught his attention, along with the terrible experiences necessary to trigger DID after childhood. While tragic indeed, perhaps adult onset DID would be easier to ferret out and cure—or at least cope with—than when it was developed in the dawn of life.

There were of course the usual disclaimers, *When To Call A Doctor* (Immediately) and *Suicidal Thoughts And Behaviors* (If you have thoughts of hurting yourself or someone else, call 911 or contact the National Suicide Prevention Lifeline at 1-800-We're-Not-Liable).

He quickly scanned the disclaimer section then closed the browser.

He'd been at this for a while. He was surprised to find it was already 11:13 p.m. But the remainder of tonight's plans wouldn't need to be carried out for a few more hours. He had plenty of time to study the videos.

He began with the oldest of the five icons, recorded roughly an hour before he'd arrived at BT's. Nothing there, really—just one of the girls on the stage doing her thing. Still, he watched all two minutes and thirteen seconds of it in case Zoe—or "Star"—happened to show up on the periphery.

She remained absent.

The second, third and fourth videos were equally useless. He saved them anyway in case he may have overlooked some important detail or came up with a use for the footage later.

The fifth and final video contained precisely the material he was looking for. It started with Freddie himself. The men at the table had pegged him as a strip joint novice. They mocked him and made fun of his cluelessness as he debated the bouncer over the door fee. The video continued as the working girls swarmed him. He was astonished at his own awkwardness, his anguish at the plight of the women unnervingly obvious.

Then Star.
Zoe.

His emotions were torn between giddiness at having a recording of the woman and disappointment at seeing her like this. He watched as they spoke, then as she led him to a chair for the lap dance. *(Fucking bums with tits.)* Several moments offered clear shots of her face—exactly what he needed. Her voice rang out with clarity when she shouted, *"Forty Dollars,"* although the southern drawl was not as pronounced as he'd hoped.

Still, this would work just fine.

Next came the walking-dead waitress with the watered-down drinks. Then Star's dancing. Then pandemonium and the camera banging noisily as Tank hoisted the jerk.

The last several minutes were a recording of the inside of the trash barrel—then the cacophony of bottles and litter as it tipped over.

He watched the close up of himself searching desperately for the camera. He looked way more distraught than he'd felt. Then finally his hand covered the lens, and the recording ended. Evidently, he'd inadvertently pressed *stop* when he palmed the mini-cam.

He closed the file, hopped up and headed for the shower.

He still had a long night ahead of him.

-Barbie Doll-

Bruce Vega drove through the night, windows down, hair blowing in the desert air. He had no particular destination in mind. The Springfield in his shoulder rig comforted him.

The more he considered it, the more his conviction grew. Wherever Amy was, whatever had become of her, she'd approve of his looking out for Christie. Giving her a life. "For you, Amy." He watched the road slide beneath the car in front of him.

An oasis of light was approaching on his left. As it grew, the source of the luminance was revealed.

The block building was a lonely vessel on a sea of desert, beyond the glow of its lights only floating shadows of boulders and tumbleweed. No sign advertised the name of the joint— but curled tubes of neon revealed what they offered inside.

Sand and gravel pinged the undercarriage as he wheeled into the lot, a dust cloud in his wake.

Making his way to the entrance, always alert for trouble, he silently admired the iron parked alongside the building. A Harley Softail, customized classic Kawasaki Vulcan, flat-black Honda Rebel . . . Nice.

The door hung askew; dim blades of light cut through the cracks. The door side of the top hinge had long since broken free and was now permanently plastered to the frame.

When he pried the door open, he found himself immersed in cigar smoke overlaid with the sweet stink of cannabis.

Rob Halford was growling about breaking the law behind a wall of electric guitars. Several leather-coated, bandana-topped bikers racked colored balls on green velvet in the corner. Others hooped and hollered in small groups.

Scattered throughout were pedestal bar-tables, none quite level, topped with plastic red-and-white checked tablecloths.

A young woman in jeans and boots danced before the jukebox, studying song titles as she flailed her hair. He caught only glimpses of her ghostly face in the backsplash of the glass.

Bruce pulled up a barstool. A coaster spun to a halt before him.

"Whatdya have?" The bartender wore a red handlebar mustache with matching ponytail. His hands were Bigfoot's. Coppery hair somewhat obscured the freckled leathery skin beneath. Bruce thought the guy might hibernate in winter.

"Bud."

A bottle magically appeared in the furry hands. With a crack and a hiss, it was atop the coaster. Ice crystals slid down the glass.

"Start you a tab?"

"Please."

Bigfoot raised his eyebrows.

"Chuck."

Name locked in memory, the bartender turned and scooted down the bar to toss another coaster. *Whatdya have?*

Bruce took a swig from the bottle, over which he caught his own eye in the mirror behind the bar. He resisted the inclination to look away. Amazing, really. One moment, he was a knobby-kneed ten-year-old, best friends with his kid sister. The next, here he sat, hanging out in a biker bar listening to Judas Priest. In France, he'd survived staring down the barrel of an AK-47 and a blast that had killed twenty-three. Even that paled in comparison to what he'd survived since.

He'd survived his loss of Amy. For the most part.

His eyes drifted to the glass liquor shelves behind the bar, then to the counter beneath. A Denver Sentinel laid face up, folded on a blue jean jacket embroidered with eagle's wings. Apparently Bigfoot's.

He glanced at the bottles on the glowing shelves, then beyond the surface of the mirror to the bikers shooting pool behind him.

Live to ride, ride to live.

He smiled and took another swig. The scene comforted him. Just normal life, people being people. Alive and free. His eyes fell to the beer in front of him, the coaster, the cheap Formica on which it rested . . . then darted back to the newspaper. He squinted and leaned forward.

(Chuck?)

There on the front page was the man he'd shot in the eye just the night previous. Unruly hair, sharp nose, smiling through that scraggly beard, wearing a shirt and tie rather than pajamas in the photo, it looked like Brennan Payne.

(Hey. Chuck.)

But what really caught his eye was the headline. *Journalist Slain in Brutal Murder.*

Journalist.

Something touched his shoulder. "Chuck!"

Bruce jumped in his seat. A fifty-something woman with slicked back hair had nudged him with a wooden bowl. A dragon tattoo slithered from beneath her tank-top and wound around her neck. "Peanuts?"

Oh yeah. I'm Chuck. "Sure. Sorry." He glanced back to the Sentinel—then caught the bar-back before she faded. "Say, mind if I take a look at that?" He nodded toward the paper.

She looked at Bruce—then back to the Sentinel. She snatched it off the jacket and tossed it his way, already headed back down the bar.

Closer scrutiny of the photo verified his assessment. He scanned the copy:

> Journalist killed last night . . . brutal murder . . . worked at the Sentinel for two decades . . .

He found something of further interest:

> —known for his work exposing government corruption.

He looked up, checked his 6 in the mirror, then stared at himself. After a beat, he turned several pages to where the story continued.

> Last year, three were indicted when Payne rocked Washington with his Guns and Glory piece covering a scandal involving ICE and a Mexican drug cartel. The agency had conspired with Guzman himself to—

He skipped a few lines.

> In the late nineties, Payne uncovered a money laundering scheme at the Department of Education, resulting in two arrests and the conviction of state senator—

Not surprising was the absence of anything about Christie. No doubt, the agency was already on the case—revising records, bribing officials, deleting files. Applying their "pressures." Bruce knew how it worked. He knew *exactly* how it worked. Roughly two thousand kids went missing each day. Resources were limited. If a trail went cold, it was abandoned until further evidence came to light. Of course, they referred to the files as "open." They could refer to them however they wished. What they really were was dormant.

Dead.

He knew all the platitudes.

We will not rest until—

We're making every effort—

There's always hope—

How easy it would be to sweep a kid under the rug, especially with no hysterical parents pushing the agenda.

He lowered the paper and stared at the liquor bottles. He realized Charlie Daniels was on the jukebox, not askin' for nothin', if he couldn't get it on his own.

A nosy journalist would present considerable complications for a corrupt agency. So if said journalist dug too deep in the wrong field, why, his shovel was likely to wind up striking a landmine. Perhaps in this case, that landmine had been he himself, Bruce Vega.

He fidgeted in his seat.

The nagging feeling about the girl being left out of his briefing itched anew.

Following a resounding *crack,* a cue ball went sailing through the smoke to the delighted shrieks of observers.

While curious—perhaps even disconcerting—this didn't necessarily prove anything. A go-getter journalist could also be a traitor to his country, couldn't he? Besides, newspapers these days served more to influence than inform. Even giving them the benefit of the doubt when it came to honesty, what the news left out was as influential as what it chose to report.

So what, if anything, had been omitted here? Besides Christie? And did that even matter, considering what the article revealed? Could a journalist with such passion for accountability and honesty turn out to be one of the very people he sought to expose?

Had Brennan Payne been working with a terrorist cell, well, Christie would just have to get over it. But if Bruce had been used to do the agency's dirty work, that was different. That was *very* different. If that were the case, hadn't the agency done to the Payne family exactly what the towel-heads had done to the Vegas? But that wasn't exactly right, was it? More directly, the question was this:

Hadn't *Bruce Vega* done to the Payne family exactly what the terrorists had done to Bruce Vega?

Now *that* disturbed him. He was strictly TTF. Not sanitation. Not an assassin for hire.

He took a long pull from his Budweiser; killed it.

He laid down a ten, rose from the barstool and headed for the door.

Another thought occurred to him. If indeed the agency had used him as a foil, that not only made him a mindless tool— not to mention a murderer of fathers—but a loose end.

A target.

He froze in place. Fist glued to the knob. When crime bosses hired out a murder, it was common practice to later take out the hitman himself. This effectively erased the trail leading back to the commissioner of the crime. Especially if the slain hitman disappeared without a trace. Would the agency employ such a tactic? In fact, he realized, why *wouldn't* they?

Maybe. Maybe not. No doubt he'd watch his six for a while.

He shoved through to the dusty lot.

Gathered around the hood of an old Chevy sedan, all in jeans and boots, three men conversed as they passed a joint. A trucker cap sat loosely atop one guy's head, a shriveled, sallow man. Another's gut hung over his belt and wore a thick gray beard. The third and youngest of the group was smooth-faced and solidly built. Bruce surmised this guy would present the most trouble in a tussle. He subconsciously assigned them names: Trucker, Fatso, and Baby-face.

Only Fatso, his bulk rippling the hood, seemed to even notice Bruce as he walked by. Baby-Face, his back half turned, burst out in laugher at something and took a step sideways. He and Bruce collided. Their feet tangled.

Bruce managed to keep his balance—but the kid fell on his ass.

"I'm so sorry," Bruce said. He bent to help him up.

The kid slapped his hand away and scrambled to his feet. "Watch where you're going, asshole!" He lunged forward and took a swing.

Bruce sidestepped, not even bothering to raise his hands. "Hey, take it easy."

"Who you tellin' to take it easy?" Trucker. Bruce would have expected a shrill, wavering voice from this one. Rather, it resounded with the resonance of a gospel quartet bass.

Like a pack of wolves, the three formed a blockade. Obstructing Bruce's path to his car. Baby-Face was to his left. Trucker was to his right, and leaned over to spit a stream of syrupy liquid into the dust. Fatso in the middle took a last drag off the roach and tossed it aside.

"Look. I'm really sorry," Bruce said. "You're right, I should watch where I'm going."

"What are you, some kind of sissy?" Incongruously, Fatso spoke in melodic tones. Almost effeminate. He seemed to have traded voices with Trucker.

Baby-Face stepped forward and shoved Bruce's shoulder.

Bruce just took it, did nothing to retaliate. He gritted his teeth. A snarl flashed across his upper lip. "Put that hand on me again, I'll bend your arm backwards for you."

Baby-Face spat out a laugh. *"You?"* His smile vanished. He planted his fists on his hips. "Z'at a fact?"

"It is." Bruce smiled. "You'd look like a broken Barbie Doll." He said it playfully in an attempt to lighten the air while still making his point.

Baby-Face scoffed and shook his head. He looked back at his buddies. Fatso, evidently the leader, jutted his beard at Bruce.

Baby-Face turned and shoved Bruce again. Only his palm never reached its target.

Bruce stepped back, arcing his left hand counterclockwise. Baby-Face's right arm was suddenly twisted palm up, fingers firmly clamped in Bruce's left fist.

Bruce lifted. *Hard.*

Dancing en pointe, palm turned skyward, Baby-Face looked as if he were presenting a tithe. Except whatever gift he offered would have rolled off his downturned fingers.

Bruce lifted harder still.

Baby-Face shrieked in pain.

The other two just stood there, mouths agape. After a beat, they shared a glance—then lunged forward to assist.

Bruce had already drawn the Springfield.

With two coughs no louder than cat farts, he unceremoniously shot Fatso, then Trucker—both in the thigh. Each hit the dirt like a tripped-up rodeo calf. Wailing and clawing at their legs.

He was still holding Baby-Face in tithe position. "Oh hush," he said to the men on the ground. "They're flesh wounds. You'll be fine." He holstered the piece, shrugged and added, "Probably."

He casually fished from his inside coat pocket the photo of Amy. "Say. Baby-face."

The man was keening now. Perilously close to tears.

"You wouldn't happen to have seen this girl around, would you?"

"What?" He tried in vain to find a more comfortable position. Tiptoeing in his boots. The two on the ground moaned and kept making dust angels.

"Take a close look, now." Bruce shoved the photo closer.

Sweat trickling down his jawline, Baby-Face took a glance—then grimaced. "No!"

"How about you guys?" Bruce lowered the photograph to the leg-shot pair. They didn't even hear the question, much less see the photo.

Bruce sighed. "No matter. It's an old photograph anyway." His hand disappeared inside the sport coat as he tucked the snapshot away.

"Wh-wh-what are you gonna do?" Baby-Face whimpered.

"Oh now, don't go jumping to conclusions." Bruce removed his hand from the coat, showed it to him, front and back, gun-free. "But I did make you a promise, didn't I?"

"*What?*"

In one quick motion, Bruce slipped under the elevated arm and broke it backwards at the elbow over his left shoulder.

Hysterical shrieks behind him, he headed for the car. As he opened the door, he glanced back at the three stooges. Baby-Face was on his knees. Wailing to the heavens. Elbow askew, Bruce noted, he indeed looked like a broken Barbie Doll.

-Life is a Thief-

Driving down the highway toward BT's, choice words from the Mayo Clinic article haunted him.

Depression. Abuse. Torture.

Suicide.

Unbeckoned, morbid images flashed through his mind. Cigarette branding pristine skin. Shrapnel slicing flesh and bone. Razor slashing tender wrist.

Always the Fixer, he clung desperately to hope. Hope that he could help her, that he could make this right somehow. Anything could be fixed, and he could fix anything. Or at least he would try; indeed he felt a growing determination to exhaust every available resource in pursuit of her recovery.

At 1:00 a.m., Freddie parked at the Walmart across the deserted highway from BT's. He was prepared to be there awhile. He had no idea when Star's shift had begun, and was well aware that strip clubs remained open into the wee hours.

As it turned out, it wasn't nearly as long as he'd expected. At about 1:15 a.m., a red street-cruiser bicycle crept like a mouse from behind the club and made a right onto the sidewalk. Long brown hair, posture passive even from this distance, it had to be Star. She wore jeans, light tennis shoes and a chartreuse t-shirt under an unbuttoned black-and-white-checked shirt. Slung over her shoulders was a beige backpack.

Freddie eased from the parking lot onto the street that intersected the highway. He waited at the light as she rode past four lanes away. Her pace was slow and steady. Eyes down, head in the clouds. She had no idea he was there, and seemed as if she'd have remained oblivious even if he'd honked the horn—or stood in the middle of the road blowing a trumpet while waving a damn flag.

When the signal changed, he made a left, following her by a hundred feet or so.

And *kept* following her.

Two blocks . . . three . . .

It occurred to him that, while he'd planned it this far, he had no idea what to do next. Following was the easy part. But he wanted to speak with her—uninterrupted and undistracted by nudity, noise and Toyota-sized bouncers.

So. How would he make the transition from following to talking? He cursed himself for his lack of foresight and patiently maintained his hundred-foot gap. He prayed traffic wouldn't suddenly pick up.

Usually, fate plays with loaded dice. But as will happen from time to time, tonight she smiled on Freddie. The girl suddenly peered down at her pedals—first the left, then the right—shaken out of her reverie by what was apparently a problem with her bike. She lowered her feet and slowed the machine by scraping the toes of her shoes on the sidewalk. At her snail's pace, it didn't take much. She stopped in front of a Firestone.

Freddie eased Old Mable into the parking lot, still not arousing the girl's attention, much less alarm. He couldn't understand how she'd survived this sordid life of hers with no more street awareness than this. But there she was.

He cut the engine and stepped out. "Hey." He shut the door. "Need some help?"

"My chain come off." She was squatting by the bike, poking curiously at the front sprocket. She still hadn't looked up.

"Maybe you could write a poem about it," he said—and immediately regretted it. He'd meant it to sound lighthearted, and maybe cue her to the fact he was not a stranger—exactly. But it came off sounding sarcastic, although it did finally pique her curiosity.

She looked up at last, but failed to quite make eye contact. "Aw, hey!" She stood with a nervous laugh and began pulling at a strand of hair hanging near her left shoulder. "How'd you know I'z a poet?"

A *poet?* Well, he supposed that made sense. Anyone could call themselves a poet—although few were *good* poets. "My bathroom mirror? Sorry to Say?"

"Oh," she said. "Duh." She shrugged and rolled her eyes. Then that nervous half-laugh.

Freddie smiled sadly— "Let's see what the problem is." — and bent to her bike.

Then from above him, her meek voice took wing:

A link in a chain is a day in a life,
A husband, a wife.
Bound tightly together,
They steadfastly weather.

Happiness, sadness, Joy and grief.
Life is a thief.
Take solace in ink.
What do you think?

He'd looked up from the chain on *steadfastly weather,* eyebrows knitted. When she finished, he processed it for a moment. She'd taken literally his suggestion to write a poem.

And did it right on the spot.

While not earth-shattering, it nonetheless fit his sarcastic request, worked nicely for the moment. And she'd cleverly woven in the question at the end.

Not bad.

It was anyone's guess how she'd have *spelled* the words of the poem, but still. Her improvisation pointed to more intelligence than he'd given her credit for. He couldn't help but note (Or was he projecting?) the underlying theme of struggle in the verses. Steadfastly Weather, Sadness, Grief, Life is a Thief—the *Risk Factors* portion of the Mayo Clinic article flashed anew before his eyes and then—

"I'm Julie. Jula' V. Ayers," she said, and offered her hand.

Freddie shuddered.

-Conspiracy Theory-

Bruce climbed the rickety metal steps to the trailer and stepped inside. As he turned on the light, the cell hummed in his pocket. He fished it out and flipped it open. Surprisingly, there was no mention of the package. The coded message read only, *NOTIFICATIONS.*

He padded to the cramped bathroom, raised the plastic toilet seat and returned the beer he'd rented. The flush was pathetic, followed instantly by a trickling sound beneath the smashed-tin-can floor of the trailer. He tried not to think about that.

Sitting on the bed with his laptop, a wiggle of the mouse brought the computer to life. He entered the password then clicked on a tiny transparent folder in the upper right-hand corner of the desktop. If you didn't know it was there, you'd never find it.

He entered another password—carefully, because even one bad attempt would wipe the entire hard drive—and opened the only document in the folder. He entered a final password to view his next assignment.

An image materialized on the screen.

He sat frozen. Eyebrows furled.

He read the description, the intel and the dossier—but the ID photo was all he needed.

Because he knew her.

They'd attended training together. She'd been a gung-ho agent candidate, a decent marksman with any firearm and brutal competition in hand-to-hand combat, even for the toughest of men. A martial arts instructor in her pre-military life, she'd picked up a whole slew of dirty tricks. Biting, gouging, clawing, stomping, sneaky elbows to the most sensitive of targets—if you didn't cover your nuts, you'd end up singing soprano the rest of your life.

But she was straight down the line. She'd kick your ass, then help you off the mat. She'd enthusiastically work with anyone on anything—if you had the courage to ask.

She was honest to a fault, and never joined in the camaraderie of inebriation and hell-raising during leaves—even if she did have a mouth like a sailor. She always concocted some excuse for staying behind—and tortured herself with more training.

She was a straight nail, and he pitied the fool who tried to bend her. Bruce had trouble believing she was a turncoat.

Yet here she was. A terrorist sympathizer. Or so they said.

Looks like he'd be headed to Miami in the morning. And he may have to employ some of those latest gadgets after all, because this one would not go down without a fight.

Not Zoe Decker.

-Questions-

Her grip had been limp, control of the handshake forfeited to him. Talking her into coffee at Jongo's had been painfully simple. Julie, alias Star, seemed to just drift wherever the winds of life carried her.

Freddie offered to get them something to eat, but Julie claimed she was not hungry. He didn't know how this could be since she'd just gotten off work. Perhaps she'd snacked on something at BT's. The thought of putting anything in his mouth—even bubble gum—within a mile of that place sickened him. So he didn't think about it.

They both got coffee.

Julie sat hopping her foot, practically twirling a knot in her hair. She glanced around the place as if the minimalist décor interested her.

Freddie broke the silence. "So you're a poet."

The name of the coffee shop was actually Joe-n-Go, but people called it Joe-n-Go's, like they say Costco's. Joe-n-Go's evolved into Jongo's and that's what finally stuck. Open 24/7, they catered to waitstaff and musicians who, shifts completed, sought a little downtime before heading home for bed. They were often crowded into the wee hours. On other nights, like tonight, the place was deserted.

"Ink is where I find peace." She dug in her threadbare backpack for what turned out to be a composition notebook. She brightened, evidently relieved to have something for her hands to do. "Go on, take a look." She slid it over.

Freddie opened the dog-eared journal to a random page:

Questions:

Dreamed I walked by a sacred river,
Distint land in a past gone by.
Fishes there swam up with trezhure,
Naked children wondering by.

Questions?

Black horse, thundern hooves fill the landscape,
Hooded rider, sikle red.
Run for the moutins, run from the river.
Reeper hells from the land of dead.

Questions?

Run for the forest, run for the medows,
Run for your life from the man on the shor.
Run til you cant feel the legs beneeth you.
Run, for the children breeth no more.

Questions?

He flipped to another tattered page:

Johnny:

Johnny use to brang me flowers,
But he dont do that any more.
Johnny use to by me candy and trinkets,
But he fell threw a hole in the floor.

Or maybe he didnt fall at all.
Maybe sumthin dragged him down,
Kickin and fightin

Bone and boom,
Blue sage, lady, love,
And lightnin

All help me try to forget,
But I havnt yet.

Johnny use to brang me flowers.

Each verse was an expression of struggle, of something precious lost. Lamentations of an ideal candidate for DID—and a sentiment with which he could relate.

But here also was evidence that, while clearly uneducated, the girl had some native intelligence—perhaps enough that she may indeed have the capacity to conjure up the spicier Zoe. In fact, though he hated to admit it, this made more sense than Zoe inventing Julie. After all, why would Zoe need to create a mouse like Star, or anyone? Zoe was tough, quick-witted and, as she'd proclaimed, able to take care of herself. It made much more sense that the meek poet would have need of a protector and defender.

This disheartened him because his infatuation was with Zoe, not the stripper. But still. Weren't they one and the same person? It certainly appeared that way. And so maybe in guiding the woman through recovery, her personalities would merge: A feisty acrobat black belt poet on a bike—hopefully sans the public nudity.

"Wow, Julie. This is good stuff."

"You really like it?" She made eye contact for the first time, more buoyant than he'd seen her yet.

"Yes, I really do. So, who's this Johnny? Is he real or did you make him up?"

Her smile faded, and she lowered her eyes again. "He was my daddy—or I think maybe he was. I wasn't allowed to call him that, 'Daddy.' Victoria didn't like it."

Freddie almost asked who Victoria was, but noted the word *was* and remained silent.

"He really did brang me flowers though, almost ever' day after work." Her face brightened with the memory. "And candy and toys and stuff, too. I'z just a little girl . . ." Her eyes followed a moth that had flown into the coffee shop and now battered itself against the light above them. "But like the poem says, one day the world just opened up and swallowed him whole. Didn't say goodbye or nothin'. He just—" She shrugged. "—stopped comin' home one day." She smiled despite herself. An almost imperceptible quiver in her chin belied the dry eyes she maintained with some effort.

Moth forgotten, she looked back at Freddie—but not directly at him, as if meeting his eyes might open the floodgates of her emotions.

"We could find him, Julie. With the internet, you can find anyone. If you'll let me, I can—"

"I did find him. Years later. See Mama . . . Victoria," she corrected, "she never let me talk about him after he disappeared. I got a beatin' if I even said his name. We didn't have no friends, so I had no way of askin' what happened to him.

Much less finding him." She took a sip of her vanilla latte, seemingly bolstering her courage. "But I grew up, oh yes I did."

She laughed that nervous laugh and shook her head. "First thang I done when I left home was go lookin' for Johnny. He'z in prison, I found out. But I didn't care. I'z just excited to get to see him again. So I made a 'pointment to visit." Her head tilted slightly, like the iconic image of Jesus as he suffered on the cross. "I'z too late by a single day." She scoffed. "*One day, man!*"

She searched again for the moth, but it had disappeared—perhaps hidden atop the light fixture. "Stabbed to death, they said. Didn't get to see his body neither. He was cremated that mornin', I got there that afternoon. They didn't give a shit whether maybe somebody wanted to make their peace."

She lowered her eyes to him again—to perhaps a button on his shirt—always smiling, ever the trooper. "He was in for somethin' complicated; I don't even remember what it was. One the guards said Johnny got framed for it. Least that's what he thought. I got the idea maybe somehow Victoria done him in, but . . . what difference is it? He's just gone, and that's just that."

She sighed. Then again with the nervous laugh, she said, "It was that ole black cat, I guess. I just didn't know it at the time."

"Black cat?"

"Paxyl says bad luck sits on my head like a big ole black cat. Sucks the life right outta me ever' night while I sleep."

Freddie just looked at her, perplexed. *Paxyl?*

Evidence was mounting that Julie was indeed the root identity here, and that Zoe was her invented hero. This was discouraging but yet, if Julie could *create* Zoe, wouldn't that mean she also *was* Zoe?

"Who's Paxyl?"

"My boss. At BT's. Paxyl, he's funny. Not like funny ha-ha, funny like scary funny. Crazy funny. Don't nobody cross Paxyl." Then the awkward laugh as she took up the hair twirling again.

Whatever was going on with the DID, this Paxyl was an issue with which he could help, something he could sink his teeth into *now.*

"Julie. There is no 'black cat.' There is no such thing as bad luck. Luck is just—" He shrugged. "—life. Yeah, bad things happen sometimes, but we all get our share of it." Unbidden and unwelcome, into Freddie's mind rose a silhouette of Stevie. He eased it gently aside.

"Well, it happens to me a *lot.*" Then the laugh yet again, both sad and infuriating.

"So, is this Paxyl the one who talked you into becoming a stripper?"

"I prefer the term *dancer,"* she said. "And no, I just walked in there one day, desperate for money. I got to know him real quick though. He takes good care of us—"

Yeah, I'll bet he does.

"—but you gotta follow the rules."

Freddie didn't know what to think of *rules,* but he had a few unpleasant ideas. "Rules?"

"Yeah. Like, I had to get punished for what I done last night."

"Punished?" The word just erupted from him.

"Yeah, but he don't let nobody do it but him. He's careful, don't like his girls marked up." With her right hand, she reached over and pulled up the left side of her hair. "See?" She turned and leaned toward him.

Surrounded by a nasty bruise, visible even through the roots of her hair, a puncture wound about the diameter of a first-grade pencil. Though it was clotted with dried blood, he realized with some disgust it was curiously octagonal.

"His ring. I thank he wears it just for punishing us girls."

That word again, Freddie thought.

She released her hair. "He turns it around to the palm of his hand and *BAYAM!* Smacks ya *right* upside the head!" She said this with something like glee, laughing a little too hard, trying to downplay the cruelty.

"Julie. He's a *pimp!*"

"I ain't no whore," she snapped, more assertively than he'd have believed her to be capable. In fact, she almost sounded like Zoe. He found himself waiting for her to transition right before his eyes.

She remained Julie, Star the stripper.

"I just dance, that's all. And only 'cause I need the money. Paxyl wants me to lay down, pushes me about it all the time. But I won't. He can punish me all he likes. I won't do it. I ain't no whore." She pronounced the last word *hoe-er,* like she was referring to a gardener.

Who knew what all was going on in that place? Certainly prostitution, probably worse. "Do you even remember what you did last night, Julie?"

She raised her eyebrows. "I don't remember *nothin'.* They sure told me about it though. I don't know how I coulda done them things, but they seen me, so I guess I did."

"Do you remember how you got that bruise on your hip?"

"Like I said, I don't remember nothing. One minute I was dancin' like usual, the next I woke up in your bed." She blushed, tugged at her hair. "I mean, your house."

She laughed again, that pathetic laugh; it always sounded like she was one step from crying. "Man, that freaked me *out,* man! I woke up and said, 'What the *hell,* Jules!' I laid there a minute, thinkin'—then decided I best sneak on outta there. I seen the bathroom when I passed, decided to leave a poem on the mirror."

She suddenly brightened, sat up straight and looked him directly in the eyes—only the second time of the night. "Hey!

Did I tell you I can write a poem about anything? Any time, any place. Go ahead, try me."

"What do you mean?"

"Name anything, I can write a poem about it. Right off the top of my head. Go on, name somethin'."

Freddie looked around the coffee shop. "Okay, a cup of coffee." He immediately realized that was lame. Whatever this girl was, she was also an artist. A damn cup of coffee was about the lousiest subject for a poem he could think of. Hell, he'd have had to work hard to think of something *less* artistic.

I'd like to take a break today,
Just sit and sip the day away.
The chain is broken,
Words unspoken . . .

Frozen by night's cold embrace,
Warm shelter I find in his face.
With a cup, he sets me free,
My boy, who's come to rescue me.

Not Emily Dickenson, but astounding when he considered it was put together on the spot, right off the top of her head. There was no way she could have predicted these circumstances and pieced together ahead of time a verse that included allusions to the bicycle chain—or contained the romantic overtures.

Of course there was a certain artistic license that must be accounted for. Together with *rescue me, My boy* could be an innocent reference to anyone—any man—that stepped up to the plate and demonstrated some chivalry. Still, it was awkward.

"So, what do you think?"

And here again was the underlying hint of tragedy. *The chain is broken.* Indeed her bicycle chain had been the problem, but it had simply slipped off the sprocket. It wasn't broken. She'd used *broken*. That could imply a broken chain of bad experiences—or broken trust or love.

Then there was *night's cold embrace*. Summer was fading to fall outside, but it was still not in the least cold. In fact, here in Miami, temperatures below 50 degrees were rare. Even in the middle of winter. So why *cold embrace?* Clearly she sought warmth from some chilling aspect of her life.

Or he was just over-thinking it. He was neither a psychologist nor a poetry critic. Hell, maybe she just chose the words because they rhymed.

"It's wonderful, Julie."

"My friends call me Jules."

Freddie nodded. "It's wonderful, Jules. Are you going to write it down?"

"Heavens no!" She was so merry when it came to her writing. "I make 'em up all the time. If I wrote down ever' poem crossed my mind, I'd need a whole *library* o' tablets!"

A thought occurred to him. "Would you mind if I recorded you? I mean, reciting the poem?" His idea with nabbing the camera at BT's was that, eventually, he hoped to speak with Zoe again (he couldn't believe he was referring to her as two different people) and use the footage to perhaps jog her memory. This would be even better.

"Really? Why, that'd be just the cat's pajamas!"

He fished his cell from his pocket then glanced around the coffee shop. They were the only patrons at the moment. Good. Although Julie was ecstatic about this performance, Freddie was a little self-conscious. He guessed it would take a lot to embarrass "Star."

He pulled up the camera app as she stood and straightened her checkered shirt, getting into character.

"Okay," Freddie said. "Roll 'em!"

"'Cup o' Coffee,' by Jula' V. Ayers." She cleared her throat then recited the poem word-for-word, just as she'd composed it.

Freddie had a couple of thoughts on this. The first was that, while improvising a poem without so much as a stutter was impressive, it was outright extraordinary that she could repeat it word-for-word from memory. Then the second thought was that this was surely impossible.

So maybe she had written it beforehand after all. But then how could she have known he'd choose *Cup of Coffee* as the subject matter? Of course, the poem could also be said to be about a slipped bicycle chain, a cold night—or Freddie and Julie.

Or maybe she had a whole library of verses stored in her head: *Poems for Ever' Occasion, by Jula' V. Ayers*. But no, it felt like she'd indeed composed it spontaneously and pulled it once again from her short-term memory.

Impressive.

"Can I do another one?"

"Of course." Freddie felt good about providing the girl a respite from her unsavory life—but unaccountably guilty for his plans to share the videos with Zoe.

Why? Julie and Zoe were the *same person!* He was surprised at the perplexing ethical issues that surrounded dealing with a victim of DID.

Julie opened her notebook and chose a poem. When she finished, he kept the video rolling for the next, then several more. He was happy to see she was enthusiastically providing explanations for a few, offering a robust sampling of Julie's personality to show Zoe—if in fact he would ever see the feisty woman again.

The Mayo Clinic post had been vague about how often splits were revealed. Maybe it was every day—or maybe every week, or year—or maybe only once in a lifetime. He'd have to review the article.

Finally, and much to the girl's disappointment, Freddie had to beg exhaustion. He found it interesting that, while Zoe had kept her emotional distance, Julie was openly clingy. She was disappointed their "magical night" had come to an end. But it was 3:30 a.m. and Freddie was about to fall asleep standing.

He'd quickly fixed her chain back at the Firestone, even adjusted her back wheel tension so it wouldn't happen again. Her tires were in bad need of inflation, but a bicycle pump was one tool Old Mable didn't carry. The bike now rested between the roll out shelves in the bed of the van.

Julie directed him to a warehouse district about three miles from Jongo's. But it was really no longer a warehouse district at all. While there were a few industrial hold-overs, nestled into most of the spaces were more winsome establishments. Sandwich shops, a carved furniture store, a dance studio, an Ocaquatics swim gym, and a martial arts school bearing the slogan *Master Your Life.*

Yeah, I'm working on it, Freddie thought.

"Well, here it is. Home sweet home." She sighed as they pulled into the spacious parking lot.

The single-story warehouse was U-shaped, open toward the road, and as large as any Ikea. It was divided into smaller spaces, each with both a man-sized entrance and a roll-up garage door over which were mounted simple signs: *A-1 Plumbing, Stitching Around* (an embroidery shop), *Leo's Custom Frames,* one that simply read *Welding,* and finally Julie's door, over which no sign was mounted.

Freddie wrestled the Schwinn to the pavement.

"Thanks so much for this." Clearly she referred not only to the bike. "Will I see you agin?"

His heart sank at the girl's unveiled desperation for company. How long had it been since she'd spoken with anyone but bouncers and barflies?

"Of course you will." And she *would* see him again, although he had no intentions of returning to the strip club. "Why don't we trade numbers and I'll call you." Immediately he regretted the suggestion, because he suspected she had no phone.

She confirmed his suspicion. "I ain't got no phone. And best not to call BT's looking for me. Paxyl don't allow no boyfriends. I mean, like, 'course no lovey-dovey boyfriends, but no *boys* that's *friends* neither."

This fucking Paxyl!

"But I'm off Sundies," she announced hopefully. "I'll just be sittin' here waitin' on you." And here was the final laugh-that's-one-step-from-crying again.

An orange tabby, mercury in the halogen lights, darted from beneath a plumbing van and disappeared around the side of the building.

"Sunday it is then."

Freddie made sure she got to her door safely. She waited there, bike halfway inside, watching him until he'd rounded the corner.

He thought maybe she'd waved goodbye.

-Black Swan-

It was approaching the wee hours. Wide-eyed, as he had been for hours, Bruce struggled upright and rubbed his face in his hands—then looked over at the laptop.

With a sigh, he opened it, his face aglow in the blue light of the screen. He navigated to a special browser for which no icon existed. You had to enter the entire address in File Explorer.

This browser connected only to the DSA database, which was protected by numerous firewalls. In this case, entrance of an incorrect password would ensure a visit from a team of Navy Seals—or the less accountable agency equivalent.

Once inside, he navigated not to his own account but to Zoe Decker's personnel file, where he'd be able to study records of her movements, citations and other information kept under tight security. He had no clearance for viewing this area and had not been provided login credentials.

Bruce had educated himself well in college. Losing Amy had fostered in him a determination to learn all he could—in order to make sense of what had happened, to decipher how the world worked—to understand *why*.

Of course, there was no *why*. It was just life.

But what he *had* come to understand was computers. While mastering the legit side of things, he'd also slid into hacking. He'd come to realize any system could be invaded. For every security measure, there was a hack. For any firewall, there was a hammer that could break it or a drill that could breach it.

Even in this, he'd applied his propensity for low tech solutions.

All the complex passwords in the world were useless if you forgot them. If, in order to supplement one's memory, the password were written somewhere, all it would take to break in was locating the cheat sheet. Even a child could do it.

And thus more often than not, a complicated password was less secure than using a birthday or mother's maiden name.

In this case, he'd learned the password—the DSA congressional chairman's password—by sheer luck. The chairman, a bloated arrogant ass, had hurriedly entered it during a case review. Bruce had been standing to the side and just behind him, and caught the keystrokes. Thinking it may come in handy someday, he'd made a point of memorizing it.

Tonight it came in handy.

Decker's file revealed most of what he expected—and one thing he hadn't. She'd been assigned to a special project called simply "Amber."

Project Amber.

Most times, mediators and other operatives caught wind of other details, even if they'd not been assigned to them. Bruce had never heard mention of Project Amber.

It involved a physicist, Aldus Constantine. He was leading research on, of all things, telekinesis. National Inquirer mumbo jumbo, right up there with ESP, Bigfoot, and Mother Theresa's face appearing on a toasted bun. But the country's pit of corrupt money was bottomless, so why not? After all, an army of soldiers that could move things—and destroy them—using only their minds would be a juggernaut. Invincible.

But *telekinesis?* The money would have been better spent supplying each soldier with a slingshot.

More interesting, he discovered that Zoe Decker not only worked on the detail, but was also a subject. She'd been labeled a "Black Swan."

Bruce crinkled his brow.

Statements in the file seemed to suggest anyone with any contact whatsoever with Project Amber was tested for psi abilities. Apparently, Decker had scored off the charts.

Black Swan?

He wondered what such a "test" would even entail.

"Move this pencil with your mind."

"What am I thinking?"

"What would Elvis be doing if he were alive today?"

Probably trying to scratch his way out of that coffin, Bruce answered to himself, shaking his head with a chuckle.

Funny thing was, the citation for her involvement with Brennan Payne was nonexistent—as was the order for her sanction. In fact, mention of her was completely absent when he checked the TTF records.

These guys kept track of *everything,* and it should have been here. He did a quick search, for "Sanction," "Collaboration," "Terrorism," and several other keyphrases. Zero results. In both the TTF files and the DSA database as a whole.

His search for a file on the journalist also came up empty.

Nothing.

Perhaps the reason Christie Payne had been left out of the briefing on Brennan Payne was that the pencil neck geeks who authored the briefings had never been summoned. Perhaps the assignment indeed fell outside Terrorism Task Force jurisdiction. Perhaps the hit had been illegitimate, even by DSA standards, and so no records had been kept.

His hackles were raised anew, and his hand instinctively moved to the Springfield on the nightstand.

But this also stirred in him excitement at the prospect of making moves in his *own* mission, an endeavor that actually meant something.

He closed the computer lid, lay back down and shut his eyes. He had only a few hours before his flight to Miami, after which he was supposed to shoot Zoe Decker dead in her own kitchen. Dialogue now a priority in pursuit of his personal mission, he would avoid killing her.

If he could help it.

-Narcotic-

Friday came and went uneventfully. Freddie planned his work, worked his plan, and did a good job. Although weekend nights were likely BT's busiest—and thus presented the greatest likelihood for trouble—Freddie resisted the urge to drop in and check on Julie. Or Zoe.

He'd started mentally referring to her as "JZ" sometime on the job Friday. He'd shaken his head and chuckled inwardly at the predicament in which he'd allowed himself to become entangled.

Although worry gnawed like a rat at the thought of this Paxyl, he reminded himself that Julie had managed to survive this long without him. She would live through the weekend.

Saturday morning, he awoke with an idea. He fired up, wolfed down a banana and whipped together a cup of instant—then quickly showered and threw on some old cargo shorts and a t-shirt.

In the corner of his quarter-acre lot stood an air-conditioned, 12x24 workshop complete with stocked mini-fridge. Sporting the finest of tools, including a table saw and a metal lathe, the shop was lined with shelves containing most any fastener or hardware imaginable. He was more at home in the tricked out man-cave than the house.

Behind the workshop—under a tarp, deep in hibernation— slept an old Huffy 3-speed cruiser bicycle. He stripped away the dilapidated cover and found the bike tangled in pale vines, frozen serpents tunneling aimlessly for the sunlight above. A line of ants hauled tiny bits of food up the seat tube. A grayish tree frog hugged its legs tightly to its body along one of the forks, trying to make itself invisible. The tires were flat and it needed cleaning, but rust was surprisingly absent except in a few tight corners of the frame. If he started now, he'd have it up and running by day's end.

He only stood staring. The bike released an onslaught of memories, unbidden and unwelcome.

"Look at me, Daddy! I'm riding with one hand!"

Freddie had shown seven-year-old Stevie how to ride with no hands, and this was as close as the kid could get.

Freddie chuckled. "Careful now, that looks dangerous."

The snaggletooth boy beamed with pride, bike weaving precariously. "Not dangerous for me. This is cinchy!"

He was so proud of himself; there was no way on earth Freddie was going to burst his bubble by pointing out riding with one hand was as easy as with two.

The memories skipped through time like a flat stone violating the serenity of a placid pool.

Up until now, Stevie had ridden a rehabilitated bike, a trash-pile find. Ever patient, Freddie had allowed the boy to work the pliers and wrenches. Teaching his son the trade. He'd enveloped the kid's tender hand in his own whenever a task required electric tools.

Proud of his work, Stevie had ridden the bike everywhere, had worn the rubber off the tires. Three years later when he expressed interest in an upgrade—a new bicycle from the store—his parents had approved. But they made him earn it. Freddie had provided the boy various paid jobs around the house, tasks a kid could accomplish unassisted.

Freddie glanced at the shitty paint job on his workshop—a collage of dull colors in the strokes of a sloppy hand. It was the most beautiful thing he'd ever seen.

His throat seized up.

" . . . fifty-eight, fifty-niiiiine . . . SIXTY BUCKS! See Dad? I've got enough!"

From behind him, Stephanie wrapped her arms around Freddie's middle. "Yaaay! Way to go, Stevie!" She kissed Freddie's neck and shot him a wink when he glanced back at her.

"Can we go today? Huh? Can we, can we?"

"Well, I don't know," Freddie teased. "Old Mable's out of service. Putting a new alternator in her today."

He squeezed his eyes shut. Trying to make it stop.

Stephanie laughed when Stevie started jabbing his dad's gut. "We can (punch) take Mom's car (punch), dude!" The boy bounced like a boxer, head tucked behind bony fists. Just like Freddie had taught him.

"Watch it, tough guy!" Freddie parried and started sparring back.

Stephanie shook her head as she padded away. "Alright you two, get cleaned up while I find my purse."

"Mo-om, I am *cleaned up!"*

"Stevie . . ."

"Please . . ." Freddie realized he was trembling.

They pulled into the parking garage. It was crowded today, so they had to circle all the way to the top. Stephanie punched it as much as she dared, enjoying the boy's anti-gravity act as inertia stuck him to the back passenger door. "Whoooooa!"

He shook his head and his eyes popped open. They fell on the tree frog just as it shinnied to the opposite side of the fork tube.

Once inside, they had no need to shop. Stevie knew precisely which bike he wanted, the price, and the aisle on which it was parked. The clerk took the UPC number and started for the back.

"Uh-uh!" Stevie protested. "I want that *bike!" He pointed to the one on display. The adults tried to explain this was a floor model, but Stevie was having none of it. Freddie secured authorization for purchase of—even a discount on—the one and only bike on which his son's heart was set. Stevie nearly fidgeted out of his shoes waiting in line to check out.*

But before long, he was rolling his new best friend up to his mother's blue Cayenne.

Freddie remembered every detail of the day with stark clarity. The ocean breeze, the animated Solo cup rattling along the concrete floor of the parking garage, the surreptitious glances Steph had thrown him *(By golly, this may wind up getting me laid!),* even the motorcycle engine he'd heard echoing from several stories below.

One minute earlier or one minute later would have changed everything. Just one minute.

A chirp echoed through the cavernous space and the tailgate opened. Stevie was right there, poised to heft the bike.

That's when it started. Nothing noteworthy—not at first— just a subtle rumble like beneath an overpass when cars passed overhead. Sensed more than felt, it seemed to come from deeper—from the earth itself—the towering structure but a transmitter of the event.

"What was that?" Freddie had stopped ten paces back, bike forgotten, trying to determine the source of the vibrations.

Stephanie slammed the cargo door shut then ducked into the driver's seat.

Quiet. Listen. Feel . . .

"Hey! Open!" Stevie shouted from the rear passenger door. Then, "Coming, Dad?"

The clunk of the locks disengaging . . . Stevie opening the back door . . .

"Wait a minute," Freddie said, too quietly. He slowly held up his hand, head cocked, concentrating.

"Da-ad!"

Something's wrong . . . something's coming . . .

"Yo! Daddy! Let's go!"

Freddie wasn't paying attention. "Get out of the car."

They didn't hear him. They weren't listening! *He felt it first in his feet . . . then his legs . . . then in the marrow of his spine. "GET OUT OF THE—"*

"No!" he roared—but it was only a hoarse whisper. He realized he was panting. He took a deep breath, swallowed hard, closed his eyes—then opened them again. He surveyed the yard. Squirrels played in the trees, caprice silhouettes capering in the sunlight filtering through the canopy.

Relax.

His breathing slowed.

Listen.

No rumble. Music playing blocks away. Light traffic eased past, heard but not seen. A gentle breeze teased pleasantly at his face.

He shook his head, scattering the stones of his memory. He knew what he had to do—the only thing that ever eased the pain. Jaw set, he bent to his narcotic of choice.

Keep moving. Gotta stay busy.

Grasping the machine by handlebars and frame, he yanked it free of the weeds. The frog leaped gracefully for the ivy woven into the property line fence. Gone forever.

Okay, think. What's the first step in a bicycle rehab?

He plucked a few strands of vine from the frame as he headed for the side of the house, proceeding quickly, almost at a jog. Each idle moment offered his mind another opportunity to gather the stones and cast them once again across the settling waters.

Focus on the bike.

He arrived at the hose, leaned the Huffy against the wall and cranked the spigot.

Initial cleaning. Doesn't have to be perfect; just clear the worst of it.

He sprayed away the ants and debris, and the memories.

-Silent Alarm-

In a singular wooded neighborhood—an anomaly for Miami—on the outskirts of the Matheson Hammock nature reserve, a Global Broadcom van pulled into a pea gravel driveway.

Repair vehicles for Broadcom were held to strict standards as to make, model and appearance. If even one scratch was visible, if any part of the logo was faded enough to prevent passersby from seeing bright blue and yellow reflections of themselves, if even the smallest of gnats was squashed to the windshield—the van was snatched from the street and quarantined until maintenance could perform repairs or upgrades.

This van was freshly washed and fairly new, but it bore magnetic logos instead of images baked in with the paint job. The make was compliant, but the model was inferior by Broadcom standards.

Good thing most people were clueless about Broadcom standards.

Bruce Vega stepped out of the vehicle, feeling stupid in blue nylon work pants, bleached white polo shirt and navy windbreaker adorned with a gay blue and yellow logo. He almost lost the hat but decided to play it safe. Repairmen for the fastidious company were required to wear it at all times, even on lunch breaks.

It was funny how Hollywood portrayed "spies"—if that's even what he was—as living in mansions and lounging on leer jets, all the while decked out in lab-designed Armani suits featuring bulletproof lining. To the contrary, he'd been holed up in a trailer park. His ride had been a Toyota Corolla (the van would later be burned beyond recognition), and today he wore this blue and yellow clown suit through which a lead projectile could penetrate as easily as snot through wet tissue.

Invisibility was more readily achieved with unnoteworthy transportation and wardrobe, and with living arrangements not involving contracts.

Bruce had come to think of himself as "pauper rich." A dazzling house like the one before him would have been all but useless since he was rarely in one place for more than a few days. And of what use was a nice car when he may end up in a jungle, on the waterways of Venice, or posing as a drug dealer on the streets of New York City?

The agency shoveled out a lavish salary, but so what? He had no way of enjoying it. It was like being blessed with eternal life—then sentenced to life in prison. He had access to piles of cash and carried agency-provided credit cards with practically no limit. He could purchase anything he desired any time or place he chose. Jet skis, baseball gloves, computers, artwork, appliances, TV's—or a racecar for that matter—with the understanding he'd leave it all behind when the next assignment inevitably dragged him across the globe.

Baggage was something with which he'd never be burdened—and roots something with which he'd never be blessed.

Decker was currently shacking up in the backroom in-law quarters of this glorious home. As the briefing had provided, the main residence was a 40,000 square foot bungalow—a single story mansion tucked into a two-acre wooded lot. Luscious elephant ear ivy grew unchecked up the trunks of ancient pin oaks. Acorns crunched under his work boots with each step.

The yard was not really a yard at all, but more of a staged jungle. In fact, he could discern not a single blade of mown grass. Rather, gravel trails wound through vine-covered palms, patches of exotic ferns and other foliage. The entire lot was shaded.

Nice digs—and countless blind corners that offered concealment but little actual cover.

He proceeded down one of the quaint paths to the front door, clipboard in hand.

What was it about a clipboard? Without it, your employment as a midlevel laborer would be questioned, even with company uniform and name tag. But with it, people would walk right up and inquire about services, even if you wore nothing but a bathing suit. He hoped the whole charade would be enough to at least get him close without walking through a hail of lead.

He pressed the ornate doorbell, stood through a two-second delay—then listened as a muted mechanical bell choir loosed a Mozart cantata. He waited patiently, ten seconds . . . twenty . . . then tried knocking.

Renting in-laws quarters and backrooms to UM and FIU students was common practice in Miami—although not technically permitted by code. He considered the income stream this family and others like it would enjoy by renting out a portion of their property. For better or worse, only people with no need of this windfall were able to make it. That seemed ironic to Bruce, though he supposed it was only logical. Takes money to make money.

He decided no one was home. His plan had been to enter through the main residence then lie his way into Decker's apartment under the pretense of examining wires throughout the property.

This was better. He could now proceed directly to the back without involving the innocent homeowner's family.

Memorizing as much of the layout as he could, he navigated his way to Decker's efficiency.

A small screened-in porch partially concealed a sliding glass door. According to the lot and house plan in the briefing, that was the entryway to the rental space.

This would be tricky. Even now, Decker could be watching him over the sites of a rifle. He wondered if she could make out his face and, if she could, whether she'd recognize him after all this time.

If he chose to pull the pistol, while being more prepared for confrontation, he'd reveal his true intentions—or at least those assigned to him. At this point, that would mean being shot before he even saw the woman.

But if he left the weapon concealed, he'd be stuck relying on a quick-draw. When and if she recognized him, he'd have to either get the drop on her—unlikely—or let her know he only wanted to talk before she started shooting.

All this could be avoided if his disguise held. So his life depended on successfully pulling off the role of a hapless repairman, at least until he was close enough to talk.

He consulted the clipboard, hiding his face under the bill of the cap, studying the fake work order as he entered the patio. He approached the sliding glass door feeling both stupid and terrified.

He knocked. "Broadcom, anyone home?"

No answer.

He glanced around the yard. Figuring an innocent man would not be circumspect, he turned his hat around, pressed the edges of his palms against the glass and peered through.

The only occupants were a neatly made bed, two chests of drawers, a full-sized refrigerator and a countertop stove eye on a rolling cart. A door to the left opened to what appeared to be a changing room and sink. Beyond that probably the bathroom. A second door, to his right of the first, could have been a closet, a laundry room—or anything.

One more knock . . . another pause . . . and he decided he was alone.

Examining the top edge of the sliding glass door, he chuckled when he discovered that Zoe too had developed a propensity for low tech. Across the union of door and frame lay a human hair.

Decker's color.

All but invisible if you weren't looking for it, this served as a signal that someone had been here—or was hiding inside. One end of the hair was taped to the edge of the door, the other to the metal facing. When the barrier was slid open, one end of the hair would be pulled from the Scotch tape, or the hair would be severed.

Silently and permanently.

Every time she left, she would set this up. And every time she returned home, she would check it before entering. If it were intact, she was good to go. If not, her pistol would lead her over the threshold. If she found the apartment deserted, she'd know to check for evidence of theft, tampering, or searching.

Or explosives.

Even if this setup were discovered, it would be impossible to place it in "set" position without being outside the closed door. Ambushing her inside the apartment would not be possible.

An agent would not be expected to employ such a simple device, nor would most mediators look for it. Though simple, even common in some circles, it was beyond consideration by a professional.

This suggested Decker was indeed working against the agency.

Regardless, this now served *his* purposes. Unless there was a way to enter through the main dwelling—and there didn't appear to be—she herself would have been forced to disable the alarm when entering her own apartment.

He carefully unsecured the tape from the door and left it dangling by the thin filament. He'd have to be sure to remember to put it back when he left.

Sliding glass doors were rarely installed with anything other than the simplest locks. This one was no exception.

In under ten seconds, he was in.

-Slash n Stitch-

Sunday morning, Freddie the Fixer woke without need of the alarm he'd set. Sparkling in his memory, new tubes and tires (he'd made a trip to a nearby bike shop), freshly greased bearings and a de-rusted chain. He'd forgotten how much he loved the old bike. He could hardly wait to ride it.

With Julie.

Or Zoe if he got lucky.

After a quick breakfast, he showered and shaved, loaded the bike in Old Mable and headed for the warehouses. During the drive over, he wondered if she'd even be there. If she were, he wondered who she'd be today.

She opened the door and waived even as he pulled into a parking space. She was draped in a prairie skirt that fell just below the knees, simple and white with peach trim. She'd washed her hair and pulled it back in a wide headband adorned with a bright floral print. She wore short white socks trimmed in lace, and peach flats.

She looked like a young girl dressed for a church picnic. Her Sunday's finest.

He pitied her naïve fashion sense. But hell, who was he to criticize? Freddie himself was sporting khaki cargo shorts, tank top and crocks, in expectation of a bike ride. Of course, they'd made no arrangements as to what, exactly, they were going to do today.

Maybe a bike ride, maybe Sunday School.

In fact, he realized, they hadn't even set a time. He was touched that she was up early and ready for their . . . date?

She bobbed on her toes in the doorway Waiving excitedly. Then as Freddie exited the van, she seemed to remember her status as a mouse and withdrew. She fidgeted, twirled her hair nervously and stared into the space between her eyes and the pavement.

Freddie walked the distance from van to door. "Good morning."

Julie returned the greeting with a poem:

No rooster sits upon my sill.
At first light I awaken still,
In expectation of this day.
Oh please, fat black cat, stay away . . .
Today.

The black cat again. "Did you just make that up?"

In the scrubby trees eking out an existence in the gravel bordering the road, birds twittered and played—aviary promises of a beautiful day to come.

Julie swiveled her ankle like a shy schoolgirl. "Naw, not this time. I been thinkin' on it all morning." She still had yet to quite make eye contact.

Freddie shook his head once. "Well, as expected, it's really something."

As a *thank you,* a subtle exhalation escaped her— seemingly a laugh that died on conception. She squirmed bashfully, now outright tugging at her hair. She glanced around the parking lot seeking nothing in particular.

Her face brightened and her hands dropped. She finally met his eyes. "Want to see my collection?"

"Sure." *Collection?*

She turned and led him inside.

The building was a little taller than a single-story home, having been originally designed to accommodate industrial shelving accessible by forklifts. Whoever built out the low-budget habitat clearly had the intention of cramming in as many tenants as possible and had converted it to two stories. While indeed taller than a house, the building had insufficient space for two levels—at standard ceiling height.

A tight, closet-like space served as a makeshift foyer, so designed to provide private entrances for both stories. Against the facing wall stood a door to the lower level. Directly beside it, a narrow stairwell led to the dwelling above. He didn't think he'd be able to squeeze in, but he managed.

At the top of the stairs waited a landing of about six feet. On the wall to the right, the entrance to Julie's apartment. Some dumbass had installed a door with hinges on the right, making it necessary to pass the door and squeeze into the space beyond in order to enter. The landing was not wide enough for it to fully open, so scuffs marked the left wall where the edge of the door had collided with it over the years.

They crowded against the far wall as Julie twisted the knob.

"Sorry," she said as they edged inside.

In one step, Freddie seemed to enter a fantasy world light-years from the galaxy in which he resided.

While the ceiling was ridiculously low, the room was spacious. The walls, floor and ceiling were lined with economy-grade, unsanded plywood, installed in a hurry, not quite square. Caulked angled spaces were visible in almost every seam.

Every surface of the room had been brushed flat black. The lighting was dim, provided by low-wattage bulbs in ancient lamps featuring chiffon shades of lavender. They rested on coffee tables, all models from decades past, each having been painted with abstract shapes and designs.

He became aware of an incense aroma. It partially hid a subtle Goodwill pungence, like depleted mothballs and stale clothes long smoldering in the drawer of an abandoned wardrobe.

At first he was shocked to see that a banyan tree had grown through the floor in the far right corner. Its limbs clung to walls and ceiling like swollen vines. The branches were gnarly fingers, blindly seeking a way outside.

He realized it was paper mache. She'd meticulously crafted each of thousands of leaves from hair-thin wire and various shades of green silk. The smooth bark was not just brown—or gray or black. Like the surface of a real tree, it was a mosaic of hundreds of shades of all the above, complete with tufts of off-white lichen, accented by patches of dark green moss.

The illusion was convincing.

In the far left corner sat a furry white chair, the head and armrests of which were live sheep heads. At least they appeared to be living, although of course they sat perfectly still. The animals stared back at him through shiny glass or plastic orbs, the rims of the lids—and noses and lips—all glistening shades of pink and black that gave the impression of being moist.

He barely managed to contain a gasp as he turned farther left to the third corner of the room. A naked woman stood staring at him, holding twin babies on her right hip, which shot out dramatically.

Although completely unclothed, the woman stirred not the slightest hint of desire in him. In fact her image was almost repugnant, for she suffered from a severe case of scoliosis. Her spine curved impossibly to her right, providing the babies a ledge on which to sit.

Her left leg had apparently developed shorter—and the right longer—to compensate for the deformity. Even still, contortion of each limb was necessary, the left slightly bent and the right stretched to capacity.

Her face was a world unto itself. The eye sockets were disproportionately large and embedded in her skull too widely apart, almost to the sides rather than the front of her head. The nose was a wedge, as if designed for cleaving the air before her. Her laughing mouth was an abyss, also disproportionately large, and painted with the same moist colors as the sheep lips.

Of course the three were manikins, but again meticulously detailed to the point he expected the woman to come hobbling across the floor at him.

Her skin was imperfect—and thus realistic—bearing angry blemishes, moles, and even some razor burn on the upper thighs below the tuft where crippled legs met torso.

Her breasts were ironically perfect, a cruel reminder of the beauty that might have been. Small, perky and firm, each tart nipple had been painstakingly painted various shades of pink.

In fact, there were not three manikins but two. The babies she held, he realized, were Siamese twins, each connected diagonally from inside shoulder to shared hips.

But would that be one baby or two?

Like JZ, he—or they—were impossible to define as either singular or plural.

"That's Beebee," Julie said. "She was a real person. Lived back in Arkansas. Asked me to make her a manikin of herself for fittin' clothes. Once it was done, we decided it should be a art piece. After she died, I got carried away and done her face happy-like. She was sad in real life, so I wanted to make this Beebee *super* happy. Maybe she's sittin' up there with Jesus right now, smilin' like a Cheshire cat."

Super happy Beebee was indeed, although Batman's Joker could be said to have the same demeanor.

"The babies is Slash n Stitch," she said with that pathetic nervous laugh. "Beebee's favorite band was Guns n Roses. So one's named after Slash, their guitar player. Then Stitch is a joke, since they was born sewed together. She couldn't have babies in real life, so I made her two. And deformed like her. Kind of a, *This Is Who I am So Go To Hell World* statement about being a cripple, you know?" Again the nervous laugh that was one step from crying.

Freddie didn't "know," and was having trouble processing all this. He'd need a minute. Or two.

"Come on back and see my collection!"

Mid-wall on the right stood two doorways, the one farthest right the entrance to her bedroom. The other opened to the kitchen, in which her bike was parked.

The bedroom door had been sprayed with metallic paint, designed to resemble a submarine hatch. Complete with walnut-sized bolts around the edges and a round port window near the top, it appeared she'd used real hardware. Of course a sailor's face bearing grotesquely exaggerated features smiled through the faux portal. Waving insanely.

Freddie dodged banyan branches as he proceeded to the bedroom. It occurred to him that, due to the low ceiling height, the doorways must also be undersized.

In rooms with eight-foot ceilings, door openings were eighty-two inches tall. By necessity, these openings could be no more than six feet and change. *Where the hell had they found doors to fit?*

He didn't quite need to duck into Julie's bedroom, but did it anyway reflexively.

He gasped aloud this time, for lounging on the bed, cozy in long-sleeved pajamas, flaccid conical nightcap flowing from pate to breast, was Julie V. Ayers herself—or perhaps Zoe—reading a black-and-white checked Mother Goose book.

-Sneaky-

"Decker?" The wall-mounted air conditioner offered a steady hum. No lingering odors of cooked meals or recently worn clothes permeated the air.

"Zoe Decker!" No answer—as Bruce had expected.

Although the place felt like no one had been here in some time—in fact it felt deserted—he had to assume she'd return any moment.

At this point, his cover was blown. No repairman from any company would enter a residence uninvited. So he lifted the windbreaker, exposing the .45 at his back, and moved it to the front for quicker access.

The first thing he noticed was the end of a computer charger sitting on the nightstand. So where was the computer? Perhaps she'd taken it with her when she abandoned the place, if in fact she had. But then why hadn't she taken the charger? Maybe he'd discover the computer in a drawer or something when he conducted his search—but that felt wrong, too. Why wouldn't she leave it plugged in, ready for use? Or if she were going to hide the computer, wouldn't she have hidden the charger with it? No big deal, but something felt off about it.

He turned and went in search of anything else that might be of interest.

If Payne had been on the up and up, Decker could still have been his source—only she'd have been providing information destructive to the agency. Knowing the feisty woman, that scenario made more sense. He hoped that was the case because the last thing he wanted was to tangle with Zoe Decker.

After rummaging through drawers and a few other obvious places, being certain to leave things as he found them, he suddenly thought of their shared propensity for low tech.

So he opened the refrigerator. The hinges were on the left, and so once open, the sliding doors across the room and lush landscape beyond were visible over the top of the door. A ghost of himself stared back at him from those glass panels.

Bruce stood staring at the illusion, entranced—then shook it off and bent to the search.

Pickles, an almost empty half-gallon of milk, relish, mustard, a can of soda and a full jar of mayonnaise. Evidence of a monastic existence—and one with which he was familiar.

He unscrewed the jar of mayonnaise. Nothing but white goop.

He twisted the top of the soda can and it held strong. It was what it appeared to be.

He examined the milk jug. A week past the expiration date. Interesting . . .

After checking the remaining containers, he decided to take a look in the bathroom.

He started with the mirror cabinet. When sprayed briefly, a can of Degree demonstrated it was nothing but deodorant. A quick examination of several over-the-counter medicine bottles also proved fruitless.

He took a quick peek in the cabinets under the counter. Cleaning supplies, hygiene products, soaps and shampoos—all nothing but what they appeared.

He moved to the toilet, lifted the tank lid.

Just water and the ball valve.

He set the ceramic piece back in place—and stopped.

Wait a minute. While Decker may be prone to incorporate low tech, she wouldn't be obvious about it. She wouldn't use something just anyone could learn on YouTube or purchase on Amazon. No, she'd be slicker than that. Something piqued his memory of the last minute and a half.

He returned to the refrigerator. Holding the door open with his left hand, his right propped on the cool facing, his eyes fixed on the mayonnaise jar.

After a time, he picked it up. Hoisting the container in several quick successions, he felt a heft to it—about that of a full jar. But something seemed off. Holding the door open with his hip, he unscrewed the lid and studied the contents with more scrutiny.

Mayonnaise.

He dipped a small sample on his pinkie and, after sniffing it, risked a taste.

Still mayonnaise.

Just as he was about to replace the top, the lip of the jar caught his eye. It featured a brass lining along the rim. Strange, he'd never seen that before. Maybe it was just a new design, but he doubted it. He backed unconsciously away from the fridge, and the door fell closed. Grasping the shiny metal in his splayed fingers, he tugged at it. It felt snug, although he thought it may have budged a little. With more effort, it began to give. Finally, he pulled it free.

A cat food tin. Long since emptied, cleaned, and filled with mayonnaise, it was absent label and wrapped instead with several layers of electrical tape to keep it wedged in place.

He looked inside the jar. The interior had been sprayed flat white, a convincing illusion of creamy condiment when viewed through the clear plastic sides. Then the bottom had been filled an inch or two with plaster of Paris, which explained the heft. Finally, it had been lined with black craft foam to protect the paint job.

There on the bottom of the container sat a brushed-nickel zip drive.

Not family photos; he'd have bet his life on it.

"Why you sneaky little—"

Tires crunching gravel, someone eased into the driveway.

-Monster Under the Bed-

Startled, Bruce dropped everything—the jar, tin insert and lid. Despite skidding his feet back reflexively, a wad of mayonnaise shot onto the cuff of his pants. He sprang to the window. Quickly—but as subtly as possible—he pulled down a blind.

Another Broadcom van. With magnetic logos.

Clearly a violation of company policy.

He let the blind snap back into place.

He quickly scanned the floor for the zip drive.

Gone.

Fuck!

Stooping, he peered under the rolling cart.

Nothing.

Under the bed.

Dust bunnies.

He stood, perplexed.

His pulse quickened as he desperately searched farther out on the floor.

The van door closed outside.

Something suddenly occurred to him. He bent, snatched up the jar. There inside, seemingly taunting him, lay the zip drive. "Damn it." He dumped it into his palm.

The jar clattered to the floor. He quickly pocketed the zip drive, bolted to the glass door and drew the XD.

Somewhere in the distance, a flock of parrots cackled as they took wing.

He did not attempt to escape. Too late for that. Instead, he gently cracked the sliding door, became one with the right side of the frame. He took a firm, wall-supported shooter's stance. Pointing left toward the corner of the house.

The sites of the gun jittered in time with his pulse.

Nothing.

He leaned into the wall and tightened his grip on the weapon, closing his left eye, preparing to make the most of the too-distant shot.

Still nothing.

Shards of glass tinkled behind him. He glanced back to see the shades still twitching. A black cylinder the size of a Red Bull can clattered to the floor right in front of him, twirling on its side like a top. He knew exactly what it was, but stood transfixed.

The twirling slowed.

"Ah shit."

Bruce bolted to the refrigerator, snatched open the door, wheeled around it and squeezed himself as tightly as he could inside. His weight bent the shelves. The meager items clattered to the floor. A jar shattered. The container remained intact, held together by the label.

Still holding the pistol, he grasped the egg compartment lid with his right forefinger and yanked the door as tightly to himself as he could—even as he plugged his left ear, even as he lifted his feet, even as the blast tore through the room.

His teeth chattered with the concussion. His right ear rang painfully. He felt the impact of shrapnel against the fridge, and a few fragments managed to pierce through—but thankfully stuck in the door, a macabre metallic mosaic.

He knew what came next.

He sprang to his feet and rounded the door yet again to put it between himself and the window. Grasping the handle to keep it open. This time he couldn't lift his feet to protect his ankles. He hoped he'd get lucky.

Not a split second after he'd positioned himself, glass shattered more aggressively as an entire pane was cleared. Had he peered over the refrigerator door, he knew exactly what he'd have seen: The silenced tip of an automatic weapon peeking through the blinds, its muzzle a dead eye, subtle and small but a harbinger of death.

The muted spitting chatter was in stark contrast with the violence spewing forth. Rounds pocked-twanged-whined around the room, those making solid impact crashing noisily, all much louder than the mechanical chugging-tweeting of the suppressed machinegun. Dresser drawers splintered. Tufts of foam leaped from the bed. The door to which he desperately clung jarred and jostled. What remained of the sliding doors dissolved into safety glass pellets.

On it went, seemingly forever. A few rounds managed to penetrate the fridge door, their velocities stunted but no doubt still dangerous. Miraculously, none struck him.

It finally stopped.

He gave it three seconds . . . five to be safe . . . and stood.

Hushed voices from outside the window.

He considered for a split second the mystery door to the right of the bathroom.

No good. It could turn out to be a closet, which they'd certainly check—after peppering it with bullets. Even if it led farther into the house, they'd find him. He would win neither a game of cat-and-mouse nor a shootout with the team he knew was coming.

So in the next millisecond, Bruce decided to do what only an idiot would do—and thus what they'd least expect.

He bolted on hands and knees for the bed. Or what was left of it. Visibility was four feet tops. His lungs burned with acrid smoke. His right ear was ringing, throbbing. He thought he felt a trickle of blood oozing down his neck. Moving too fast *(Slow down!),* he slipped on the debris littering the coral tile, regained purchase—then shot under the bed. He maneuvered to his right side. Facing the entrance.

Just in time.

The cleanup crew arrived as expected. Two boots . . . four . . . then six. They hustled into room-clearing formation, the first moving right, the second left and the third straight ahead, halting at the foot of the bed. They spoke not a word, but Bruce knew there was an in-depth conversation of gestures going on between them.

They'd be wearing gasmasks and most likely body armor. The beams of their rifle-mounted flashlights stalked the room, agitated phantoms in the haze. Fingers would be resting on triggers, partially depressed. As forecasted, the third-man-in braced his feet. His machinegun sputtered, and the mystery door turned to splinters. The boots stepped forward and the bottom of the ruined door dragged open with a loud rasp. A closet, as Bruce had feared.

"Clear," the man whispered.

Heart pounding, Bruce wanted to fire, *needed* to start shooting—but forced himself to wait for the right moment as they scrambled around the room.

"Clear," whispered one of the others.

"Clear," whispered the last.

The team leader repositioned himself at the last uninspected doorway. Bruce knew he'd be chopping his left hand toward the bathroom area. They reconnoitered to breach. All crowded together.

A split second seemed to last an hour. He took a deep breath and slowly exhaled. If he missed even one shot, whoever remained standing would ravage the bed with a full magazine. He would not survive it.

Even now, he imagined signaling fists, shoulder taps and nods. Another second at best and they'd be through the door and out of range.

Hurry up while standing still.

He shot first one ankle, then two, then three, in quick succession but with careful aim, balancing the need for both speed and accuracy. Two grunts and a muted scream confirmed the shots had found their marks.

None were dead. Until they were, they'd be relentless in carrying out their mission. He repositioned his sites as the three men tumbled to the floor.

The .45 coughed once . . . pause to aim . . . twice. The first put a finger-sized hole through the eye of a gasmask.

The second ripped away the top of a skull, gore splattering on the baseboard behind it, gray matter spilling from the wound.

The third guy managed to roll to his right side, facing the bed, grimacing in pain. He gained tentative control of his weapon. Spraying lead as he went. The muzzle was high in proportion to the shooter—wide of the bed—aimed just short of the sliding glass door opening. To the spitting of suppressed reports, the feet of the dresser disintegrated.

Bruce fired, harmlessly punching the man's armor. The soldier pulled the weapon toward his body—closer to Bruce—and the growing snake of impacts slithered closer. Bruce fired again, this time striking the shooter's unprotected left shoulder. He screamed but refused to relent—and the fangs of the bullet-snake bit into the feet of the bed behind him.

Bruce thought, *Fuck it.*

He squeezed the trigger repeatedly, peppering the man with craters until he finally managed to take out the data processor. The body went limp, everything but the trigger finger. So the bullet teeth kept biting into the same spot, chewing the wall behind him and the foot of the bed in front of him to bits. Splinters stung Bruce's face like angry bees. He curled into fetal position.

Finally, the magazine ran dry.

So much for remembering to tape the hair back into place.

-Clown Suit-

At first, Freddie was electrified at discovering, after all, Zoe and Julie were indeed two different people, as he'd speculated in the beginning. He was fascinated having the two of them together in one place. Then it dawned on him—if there were two of them, why not three? Perhaps here were two of three artistic triplets, Zoe, currently missing, being the third and dominant of the group.

Then he leaned into his first step, and the Julie on the bed—and the bed itself—rippled, distorted . . . and he realized it was a self-portrait painted on both walls and floor. The concavity of the corner appeared instead convex, lending the illusion of three dimensions.

"I ain't *that* good a artist," the real Julie said from behind him. "I used a overhead projector with a photo of myself sittin' there like that, then traced and painted it. I took the picture at Macy's on one o' them fancy beds."

While stunning, the desired effect nonetheless materialized only from a precise position in the doorway. Moving even one step into the room shattered the illusion, and the painting proved to be distorted, stretched like a Salvador Dali piece. Watching it shift made him dizzy.

The Macy's bed in the painting was conjured from a princess dream—something he should have picked up on immediately. In contrast with her meager possessions, it boasted features inaccessible to this girl of modest means—golden bedposts, laced pillows, silk sheets and a billowing fluffy duvet. Her actual "bed" lay on the floor in another corner, a sheet of textured foam and threadbare blanket neatly rolled and belted, next to it a modest throw pillow presumably from an old couch.

Above the rendering on the wall was a real frame (at least he thought it was real; at this point he couldn't be certain) outlining two words, both upside down: *Stay Weird.*

Directly in front of him, a cartoon giraffe jutted its head through a window. Into the far right corner of the quarters had been added a small room, probably the bathroom.

Then to his immediate right was The Collection.

Crammed into six bookshelves that spanned from the bathroom wall to the one at which he stood, floor to ceiling, were the binding edges of hundreds of the same brand of journal notebook that Julie had shown him at Jongo's. He noticed that, starting from the lower right, they showed increasing signs of deterioration. Apparently, they were arranged in chronological order starting from the oldest in the upper left to the most recent in the lower right.

The sheer volume of work here was nothing short of breathtaking. Especially if she truly didn't bother writing down what she spontaneously composed on the spot.

"Julie," he muttered. "This is—" He shook his head. "—stunning."

"It's all the poems from my whole life. What's left of 'em, anyway. Victoria burned any she could get her hands on. Johnny showed me how to bury them in the back yard, inside old pickle jars so they wouldn't get ruint. The first hundred or so are all moldy and wrinkled. Some of the pencil wore off from rolling 'em up. I must've had a hundred jars buried out there by the time I left home."

At this point, there was little doubt Julie was the original split. She had clearly demonstrated the creativity and mental capacity to conjure up her protective Zoe—and trees and poems, sheep and giraffes, sculptures and paintings and then some.

She'd also, it seemed, revealed in her history the need to do so. While somewhat discouraging, this also compelled him to open his heart to the artist. She had considerably more depth than he'd given her credit for. And after all, as he'd surmised, weren't they indeed the same person anyway?

"So. Interested in going for a bike ride?"

She bobbed on her toes, her smile radiant. "Oh you bet I am!"

Freddie exited the apartment first then scooted around to wait in the stairwell. Julie deftly stood her bike on end in the holding space. She wrestled the door closed (she'd had practice at this), and then Freddie assisted her down to the parking lot. Before they left, he inflated her tires (he'd thought to bring the pump along). He noted they were badly weathered with little tread remaining. He decided he'd later offer her new ones as well as a general overhaul.

The promise of the roadside birds was fulfilled. Sunbeams like golden stilts seemed to rise from the street, cooled by an ocean breeze. The roads were deserted around the warehouse district Julie called her neighborhood, so they took up both lanes. She treated him to spontaneous poems about birds, abandoned cars, stray cats and discarded hats as they pedaled lazily along.

As she mused, Freddie considered how to broach the topic of her alter ego. Was Julie aware she suffered from Dissociative Identity Disorder? Had this kind of thing happened before? If so, when? And under what circumstances? There was much to glean here—if she was willing to talk about it.

Her reaction to the BT's incident suggested she was oblivious of the condition. They'd been able to have nothing more than a distracted conversation about it at the strip club. Then later, Jongo's had seemed the wrong time to delve into the topic as well. Here, alone in the quaint Bird Road art district, seemed the perfect time and place. He decided to just jump right in. "So Jules."

"Hmmm?"

They rolled past a dumpster full of scrapped manikins. Corpselike hands groped the air. A woman's head kept plastic secrets, stared blindly out at nothing.

"Remember how you wound up at my place the other night?"

"Aw man. That totally freaked me out!"

"Do you know what happened, Julie? How you got there?"

She sighed. "Well, I did wonder. I didn't wanna say nothing since you seemed kind of worked up about it. You know, at BT's? But now that you mention it, I guess I would like to know."

He noticed her front rim was warped; it wobbled on each rotation. It wasn't too bad. Had the bike depended on front hand brakes, it would have been a problem. As it was, with only coaster brakes, it wasn't a big deal. Still, he wanted to fix it for her. "From my perspective? I'm driving along, minding my own business, and you came darting across the road wearing nothing but a man's suit jacket and broken heels. You ran out in front of my van, and I hit you."

"Whaaaaat?" She seemed genuinely amazed, but her eyes never left the safety of the pavement.

"You somehow rolled out of it and landed on your feet. I unlocked the door, you hopped in and we took off."

A hand-painted sign announcing, *Café Cubano! Desayuno!* glided past, posted in front of a cheery yellow-concrete-block restaurant. Evidently, the shop was closed on Sundays, for neither patrons nor waitstaff circulated among the outdoor tables.

He said, "Do you remember that, Julie?"

When he focused on the girl, he found her shaking her head, eyebrows raised, still gazing at the pavement. "Naw, man. Like I said, I don't remember *nothin'.* I'z dancing to Rod Stewart, then all the sudden I woke up at your place."

By unspoken agreement, they made a right turn.

"Has that kind of thing ever happened to you before?"

She was already shaking her head. "Uh-uh. Never. I don't do drugs, neither. Smoke a little weed now and then, but nothing that'd make me forget where I was at. I thought maybe I'd smoked a doobie laced with something, you know? But I don't remember even seein' any weed that night, much less smoking any. I never buy it or sell it—just smoke some if one the girls has it to offer, that's all."

They passed an intersection. Freddie looked both ways, shivering at the memory of kids and cars. Julie seemed to just trust the way was clear and pedaled on.

As they crossed the street, she pulled ahead— "Race ya!" — and stood up on her pedals, pumping wildly. By the time Freddie realized what was happening, her skirt was already billowing in the draft.

He shook his head and grinned— "Oh no you don't!" — then took off after her.

Her laughter and squeals of delight simultaneously charmed and saddened him. Bittersweet, it reminded him of Stevie. He was heartened to see Julie enjoying herself and felt good about his decision to stick with her—regardless of who she happened to be at the moment.

He was a loyal man. Crazy as it may have been, in just a few short days, he'd thrown in his lot with this girl. And he'd stick by her until she asked him to leave.

"What's the matter back there, big boy? Gettin' tired?"

He was amazed at her speed. Indeed he was having a tough time catching up. He supposed dancing and riding a bicycle everywhere had fostered the development of strong legs and considerable stamina. He hoped he'd be able to get in better shape himself, riding with Julie.

With Julie.

Yes, they were indeed the same person, weren't they? He found himself as interested in the artist side of her as he was with that of the acrobat, and he considered that progress.

She screamed. Wobbled precariously, still flying like a bat out of hell. She lost control and tumbled skirt over handlebars into the side of a parked plumbing truck. The impact sounded horrendous.

"Julie!" He imagined broken bones and blood, Julie's blood, Stephanie's blood. He caught up, slammed on his brakes and jumped off the bike. "You okay?"

The woman untangled herself from the frame tube, stood up and stumbled away from the mess of bars and spokes. She peered around at the warehouses, the road, the sky . . . staggering in the middle of the street. Her eyes fell to her body. She stepped back, inspecting herself.

She looked up at Freddie. "A fucking *prairie dress?*"

CHAPTER THREE

CORROSIVE

-Hero-

Although it was probably over, Bruce fumbled in his windbreaker pocket for spare ammo. He kept his eyes glued to the back yard. Maneuvering was all but impossible in the cramped space under the bed.

He pressed the release button on the pistol, expecting the depleted magazine to slide out and clatter to the floor. Of course it didn't—because gravity couldn't assist in the process. He shook-twisted his wrist in an effort to dislodge it.

No good.

Holding the fresh magazine in the last three fingers of his left hand, he pinched the butt of the depleted one between thumb and forefinger. Trembling hands slick with sweat, he ended up dropping them both. Eyes still locked on the turf beyond the door, he blindly sifted through the dust bunnies and wood fragments—and finally snared a magazine.

The empty one.

Shit!

He tossed it aside and retrieved the fresh clip, remembering to blow off the dust and debris before slamming it into the magazine well—then thumbed the slide release.

Double-hand grip on the pistol, he pulled down on the back yard. His breath stuttered; his heart pounded.

Violent coughing spasms racked him. Smoke from the blast had filled the room. Worse, his own gunfire had further polluted the air trapped beneath the bed. He had to move. *Now.*

He shrimped his way out, both hands on the pistol, raking up dust, shredded foam and wood chips as he struggled. Lungs on fire, his tear-flooded eyes nevertheless maintained the vigil. Once vertical, he covered his mouth with the inside of his left elbow to dampen the coughing. The sights of the pistol led him at last into the yard.

He drew his first lungful of untainted air. Using his wind-breaker sleeve to wipe at his face, he rotated several times, peering over his sites at every potential hiding place in the faux jungle—of which there were many.

Finally he bent, hands on his knees, and hacked the gunk from his lungs.

The apartment was devastated. He almost chuckled when he imagined himself calling out, *"G' mornin'!"* with a hearty wave as the owners of the house pulled up to the shambles.

Standing upright, he crammed the pistol into his waist-band. He brushed himself off as he trudged toward the corner of the house. He followed the trail leading to the driveway, mulling over the ambush.

This failed hit all but confirmed everything he'd suspected. That made Zoe Decker an ally.

And it meant he'd in all likelihood killed Christie Payne's father needlessly. He had no compunctions about taking out anyone with even a distant connection to Muslim extremism. He would not, however, lift a finger to cover the agency—much less harm an innocent man.

In fact, his hostility toward his own government was not much less than what he felt toward the Jihadists. In the weeks following the kidnapping, his parents had scoured the Muslim slums of France in search of Amy. They'd been met with only contempt and derision.

Back in the states, they'd struggled for years—all in vain—to get their government moving on the investigation. He'd been a teenager when a representative from the state depart-ment had spoken with his parents.

His name was Gerard Terrance. At first glance, he seemed to be in his late twenties or early thirties. On closer inspection, however, young Bruce Vega suspected the illu-sion was achieved with Botox and clever grooming. He was probably closer to fifty, maybe as old as sixty. He wore a glistening silk suit that appeared to have cost more than the Vega home, and his fingernails were either coated with clear polish or had been recently buffed. His hair seemed sculpted rather than styled.

Like a cat, he lounged comfortably on the family couch. Capped teeth gleaming, legs crossed casually, his arms stretched across the tops of the backrest cushions like sunning pythons.

He was completely at ease, his voice mockingly subdued. "Lieutenant Vega. You've got to understand the sensitive nature of our position here. Our relationship with the Muslims is tentative at best. Trust me, everything that can *be done, is being done. But we can't just go barging into Islamic communities roughing up every Imam and cleric who resides within. These situations must be handled with kid gloves in order to keep the peace we've managed to achieve."*

His father was outraged. "Peace? You call what exists now peace? *There is no compromising with these people, Terrance! The only thing they understand is brute force. Why do you think that attack happened in the first place? Because France allowed that scum within its borders! If you don't respond with extreme prejudice to each and every act of terrorism, they're only emboldened to commit more of it."*

The politician smiled. "To the contrary, we've come to find violence only begets more violence. Sure, we want to prevent what incidents we can, but revenge does nothing to solve the problem. Hate *is a four letter word, Mr. Vega. Rather, tolerance is key.*

"Polling shows the majority of people agree with our position, which is why you'll find communities living in harmony with Islam in most parts of the world. Muslim neighborhoods are sprouting up everywhere, even right here in the good old U. S. of A."

"What the hell are you even talking about, Terrance? WE JUST WANT OUR DAUGHTER BACK!"

"Like I said, everything that can be done, has been done."
Now he was speaking in the past tense. "Look. I have a
daughter myself. I sympathize with your anguish. But trust
me, national security depends on discretion in these matters.
While using a heavier hand may increase the odds of finding
Ashley—"

"Amy, you asshole."

The man closed his eyes and jutted his chin, barely con-
taining his patience. "Yes of course. We could apply a heavi-
er hand in locating her, but if we were to stir up the wrong
hornets' nest in the process, we might find acts of terrorism
suddenly increasing. That would put the population as a
whole at greater risk. And so in saving one person, we may
in fact end up losing many more. Thus, looking at the big
picture, in a very real way, your daughter is a hero, Lieu-
tenant Vega."

Bruce spat at the foliage, snarling at the memory. His
mother had succumbed to cancer on Bruce's twenty-first
birthday. He suspected her real killer had been grief. And
grief was without a doubt the cause of his father's death, since
the man had sucked on the barrel of his service pistol two
years later.

He froze. Eased behind a patch of elephant ear.

The fourth member of the team sat checking his cell phone
in the cab of the van.

-What do you Want me to Do?-

"Hello, Zoe." As the artist often said, this was "totally
freaking him out, man." He'd called her Julie only seconds
ago. But gone was the easy drawl, replaced by the tart non-
regional dialect. Gone as well were any remnants of the timid
mouse, traded instead for the no-bullshit tiger. This removed

all doubt as to whether the two women were in fact one person.

He'd *seen* her change.

No amount of explanation on the Mayo clinic website could have prepared him for the impact of witnessing the transition firsthand.

So, how did one address the splits of someone suffering from Dissociative Identity Disorder? It seemed insane to play along, to use two different names—as well as different methods of interaction—for a single person. However, stubbornly referring to the feisty woman as "Julie" would surely result in *her* claiming *he* was crazy.

"What the hell's going on, Freddie?"

He chose directness. "Hey. *Slow down*. Nothing's going on with me, Zoe. But something is certainly going on with you. Just a moment ago, you were Julie. *Not Zoe.*"

"Julie." She scoffed, shook her head.

"*You* changed. *You* wrecked your bicycle. *You* jumped into *my* van. I am just here to help, as I have been since you ran out in front of me that night."

"I wrecked the bicycle," she yelled, "because, *I don't know* how *to ride a bicycle!*"

His heart sank at the thought of a little girl who never rode a bike. No handle-grip pompoms, no cute pink helmet. No parents patching skinned knees with cartoon Band-Aids then encouraging her as they pushed her along when the training wheels came off.

Except she *could* ride a bicycle. When she was Julie. "That's fine. I—"

"No, it's *not* fine. I busted my ass, Freddie!"

What he'd meant was, *I accept that*. But she had a way of turning his words around on him. He suspected she'd be as cunning in a tussle as she was in conversation. Infuriating as it was, he wondered why this spiciness drew him like the tide to the moon.

He held up his hands, looking at the pavement. She seemed to calm at the gesture.

Freddie had discovered an effective strategy for dealing with irate clients. When they got hysterical, a single question always seemed to bring them back to earth, convinced them to consider the situation objectively. "What do you want me to do?" He enunciated each word, so she'd *get it*.

She only stared at him. Her chest heaved a little less dramatically.

The strategy seemed to be working, seemed to make her understand she was being irrational—and that he was only trying to help. "What do you want me to do?" he repeated. "Because, I *helped* you, Zoe. You disappeared from *my* house, and I went to that shit-hole to make sure you were okay. You were there. Even when you'd told me you didn't do that."

"I *don't* do that. And I—"

He cut her off again with his calming hands. "I understand, and I believe you. But there's something strange going on here, and if you'll listen, I'll tell you where you live, where you've been the last several days, and what you were doing before you wrecked."

"Where I *was*," she said, more subdued now, "was having a bitch of a nightmare."

"Okay, I believe you. But from *my* perspective?" He laid his hands on his chest. "You were riding *that* bicycle—" He pointed to the wrecked Schwinn. "—as you have been for an hour now." He finished with the same question. "So, what do you want me to do?"

With a sigh, she finally relented and dropped her hands. She turned, stepped three paces and plopped to the curb. She laced her fingers in her hair. This one liked to be in charge, or at least feel she was in charge. So he waited.

Finally, with yet another sigh, she looked up at him. "Okay. First thing we do is get me out of this Sunday school dress."

Freddie grinned and opened his mouth to speak.

"Don't say it. Don't even *think* about it."

The pavement rolled by considerably more slowly when pushing the bikes rather than riding. Zoe shook her head. "God, I hope nobody sees me like this."

They passed a fenced junk-car lot. A beat-up convertible sat rusting several rows over, a mechanical metaphor for the woman walking beside him. "Would you prefer the coveralls?"

"Actually, I would." Her tone was lighter; she seemed to enjoy the banter.

Freddie chuckled. "So. Want to know what's been happening while you were . . . away? Want to know who you are and what you do?"

"Sure. Gimme the news, Mr. Fix-It." A *yes* would have sufficed. But no, she had to have him report to her in response to an order. He wondered why she was like that—and if she even realized she did it.

He smiled to himself. "The morning after you crashed at my place . . . no offense with the bike-wreck language—"

"None taken."

"—I woke up and made you breakfast, only to discover you'd disappeared." He continued with the whole story—the BT's calamity, the bicycle chain, Jongo's and the poetry. He finished by describing the bizarre artwork and bike ride. He decided to leave out the mini-cam and anything having to do with DID for now. Once or twice, she asked clarifying questions, but mostly she just listened carefully, occasionally shaking her head or scoffing with doubt.

"Wow. Now that is—" She shook her head again. "—unbelievable, frankly. I don't know who I am, but one thing's for sure. I'm no poet."

Freddie thought of an idea. He hoped she'd play along. "Hey. Why don't you try to make up a poem? Just see what happens."

"Okay," she said. "Give me paper and pencil and a year to think about it, and I'll give you something that sucks. I'm no poet, Freddie."

"Oh come on. Humor me."

She sighed. She did that a lot, he noticed. He guessed under these circumstances, he may develop the same habit.

She collected her thoughts as she pushed the bike steadily along. "Okay. Roses are red, violets are blue . . ." She paused, shook her head. "Sorry Freddie, that's the best I can do."

He burst out laughing. "That was clever! Not your best work, but at least it rhymed." Maybe Julie was somewhere back there in Zoe's subconscious, yearning to express herself. And maybe Zoe was in Julie's—but then why did he never see even a hint of toughness in the artist?

"Hey. It did, didn't it? Hell, maybe I am a poet. Today *Roses are Red,* tomorrow *The Raven.*"

She got back to business. "You're leaving something out, Freddie. Don't deny it. You said you know who I am, but you never mentioned that part."

He wondered if maybe she'd been a police interrogator in a past life. "Okay, go with me on this. I thought I realized what was happening that night at BT's. As it turns out, I was on to the something." He paused, took a deep breath, knowing she'd immediately shoot down the idea.

"Don't keep me waiting, nail banger."

"Hear me out now. I did some research on Dissociative Identity Disorder, aka DID, formerly known as Multiple Personality Disorder. You show all the signs and symptoms, and I've been hanging with you since you 'disappeared'—" He made an air quote with his free hand. "—that morning at my place. Only you've been Julie the poet all this time. Just a while ago, riding that bike, you transitioned, if that's the right term, into who you are now. Zoe the . . . uh . . . acrobat."

"Bullshit. No fucking way."

"I know. It's impossible, right? I wouldn't believe it either if I were in your shoes. But I'm telling you, I've seen it. And . . ." He was so stoked about this last part, he wanted to tantalize her with a dramatic pause.

"You're making me wait again, hammer head."

"I've got videos to prove it. I knew you'd be skeptical, and I don't blame you. But just wait 'til you watch them."

"Now that is indeed something I have to see." They rolled past the martial arts school.

"One more thing."

"Yeah?"

"We're here. Your place." He pointed to the warehouse.

-Innocent Flesh-

Don Gluth sat in the fake Broadcom van checking his text messages.

Money!

He'd received a "sext" from a sassy little piece he was working on. He drooled over the saucy image. "She's only *fifteen*," he muttered with mock concern, "for threee mooore years."

He chuckled then replied, *wow! hard to believe ur just 15! rock hard, lol. you look 23! hot hot hot!*

Young girls loved that shit. He was considering sending her something back, just that if he got caught sitting here with his dick in his hand when the team returned, he'd never hear the end of it.

And they wouldn't be long.

Girls also loved Gluth's dolphin smooth, steroid-enhanced physique. He glanced over at the naked woman sprawled on his right bicep. Multiple flexes made her tits jiggle and threatened to rip the seam of his olive-green t-shirt. Gluth kissed his left fingers and transferred it to the rock-hard muscle.

He'd drawn the short straw on this one. Stuck driving. All in all, he supposed, that was a good thing. This was a boring assignment. No one could have survived the initial blast, especially not with that hilarious hail-of-lead follow up. Chesney had emptied a whole damn magazine into the apartment. Gluth had laughed his ass off when he realized Chez was not going to let up 'til it ran dry. The man had turned to face the van when he was done and made Incredible Hulk arms. *"RRRRRR!"*

"Stop fucking around," the team leader scolded, and they'd double-timed it to the back in triangle formation.

They were just going through the motions. They'd do nothing more than snap a photo of the corpse and go home. No gunplay whatsoever.

He looked up at a burst of muted gunfire. After a beat, another burst—surely a full magazine.

He chuckled. Goddamn Chesney, the clown. He'd no doubt completely pulverized the body.

Gluth liked details involving a little action. He didn't even mind people shooting back. Preferred it, in fact. That just made it more exciting—and gave him an excuse to blow the fucker's brains out when he caught up to them. Another notch on his rifle.

He wondered what was taking so long.

He looked up from the flesh glowing on the screen, expecting to see the guys rounding the corner, gasmasks dangling from their hands. Team Leader chewing Chesney's ass.

His eyes turned to headlights and the phone clattered to the floorboard.

Staggering toward the van with his head lowered, hugging his belly, was one of the team. When the poor bastard looked up to navigate, Don was shocked to see a bloody bullet hole through one of the eyepieces.

"Holy *shit!*" He reached for the holster at his side—
remembered he wasn't wearing it—then leaned over and
snatched his Glock off the seat. He bolted out of the van. He
aimed over the man's slumped back, ready to shoot the first
non-friendly that fell into his sites. He couldn't help but note
the tanned musculature of his forearm behind the black steel.

He stuttered to a stop. "Come on! *Get up get up get up!*"
He leaned to offer a shoulder, never taking his eyes—or the
gun sites—from the corner of the house.

The guy stood.

The last thing Don Gluth saw before his lights went out
was that hole in the gasmask lens—and the wild eye behind
it—as the head on which it was mounted bashed into his face
like a giant hammer.

-Chartreuse-

"Oh, I definitely don't live here. If I did, I'd have slashed
my wrists by now."

"You do indeed. Where do you think the bicycle came
from?" They'd tried to wrestle it in the door, but eventually
gave up and stowed it in Old Mable instead. Evidently, as further evidenced by the bike wreck, skills developed by one split
were inaccessible to the others.

"So, where does she keep her clothes?"

Freddie was fascinated at the woman having referred to
herself in the third person. She thought of herself as two different people, as he had. In fact, however, Zoe in the girly
dress seemed about as right as Bruce Lee in a tutu.

"In her . . . in your bedroom, I'd presume. Oh and wait 'til
you see this." She followed him to the door and he held it
open, watching her reaction.

Zoe's gasp was audible. Then she relaxed as she proceeded inside, as he had.

"Son of a . . ." she stood staring at the mural of herself. "I gotta say, she may have crap taste in clothing, but she can sure as hell paint. And sculpt."

"You should hear her poetry." Freddie was amused to hear himself do it now. He was talking about Julie as if she were someone—and somewhere—else. *She was standing right in front of him!* Only she was trapped behind that mental barrier she'd built for herself inside that labyrinth of a mind. It boggled *his* mind.

There was a rolling closet rod crowded with dresses and blouses in the far left corner of the room beyond the foot of the faux bed. Beside it, closer to the door, sat a waist-high chest of drawers. Zoe proceeded directly to the clothes rack to assess her options.

Hangers squeaked noisily as she rifled through the garments. A few times, she commented. "Another Sunday school dress—this one's gotta be for Easter . . . "

More metallic scraping . . . "What's this, a fairy costume?"

The whole thing rocked precariously as she roughly flipped aside handfuls of clothes. "Oh and if she's invited to a quinceanera, this should work wonderfully."

Having come to accept Julie for who she was, Zoe's words seemed callous and offensive. He had assumed splits would naturally get along; he couldn't imagine them feeling disdain for one another. "Hey. She's an artist, okay? Give her a little slack."

"Yeah, I'm being a bitch, aren't I? Sorry. This is just . . . new to me. It's weird as hell."

"Ya think?" Freddie said. "But keep in mind, you're the same person."

"You've still yet to convince me of that, Mr. Honey-do."

"Hey, that's a good one. Maybe I should change my name to 'Honey-Do Handyman.'"

Zoe chuckled. "No, Freddie the Fixer is fine . . . alliteration unintended."

"Do you keep, like, a Rolodex of handyman epithets?"

"Okay, hanging clothes are out. Let's check the dresser. Keep your fingers crossed." She began opening drawers, rummaging briefly then slamming them shut.

Something caught her eye beside the dresser. She bent to a pile of clothes and snared some jeans and a chartreuse t-shirt. She held them up, scrutinizing. "Well, these will work, even though the shirt is pink. Better than a vacation bible school dress, but I hate wearing pink."

"It's chartreuse."

Zoe shot him a look. "Chartreuse is dark *pink.*"

Freddie just shook his head and smiled.

"And they're dirty." She took a whiff. "Not too bad, but still. The thought of wearing someone else's unwashed clothes is disgusting."

"Julie."

"Zoe, numb nails."

Freddie grinned despite himself. "Zoe. You two are the *same person.* Even if I humor you on being different people, you are without a doubt sharing the same body. So, do you ever wear your *own* clothes two days in a row?"

Zoe shook her head and sighed. "I suppose you're right and, like I said, they don't smell too bad." She raised her eyebrows at Freddie. "So . . ." After receiving no response, she nodded toward the door.

"Oh. Right." He backed out and shut the door behind him.

The lock engaged from the other side.

-Don't Say That-

"*Don't keep me waiting,*" she begged. "*Come on little sleeper. Don't pretend. I know you're there now.*"

Oh, he was there alright. But the thing was, he could never quite get his rocks off in a damn dream.

She slapped him. "Wake up, fucker!"

He raised a fist to hit her back— "*Wanna play rough, do you?*" *—only he couldn't.*

Because his hands were bound.

"*Open your eyes or I'll* shoot you now and be done with it."

Not a dream.

More like a waking nightmare, because this average looking guy from the briefing, with a haircut like the local weatherman—thrice dead from grenade, fusillade, and clean up crew—was right in his face.

"That's it," Bruce said. "Mornin', sunshine."

Don Gluth panicked. He was strapped to a chair, massive arms pulled cruelly behind him, sitting in the middle of a dimly lit cavernous space of some sort. It smelled like an old hardware store, like ancient lumber soaked with stale gasoline—and a hint of dead fish. The floors were wooden planks, oil-blackened and speckled with debris ground into the surface over decades.

Cloaked in shadows, aged wooden picnic tables lined the perimeter. They were cluttered with rusty tools and aging mechanical parts. Identifying them with any precision was impossible. Maybe old boat motors. In fact, he thought he could discern distant seagulls scolding the air and perhaps waves lapping at the sides of the building.

One of the tables had been dragged to within a few feet of him. On the table sat a battery powered lantern—the only source of light. It silhouetted the weatherman ominously. Also resting on the table were a gallon jug of clear liquid, a suit-case-sized chunk of concrete, a pair of pliers, a propane torch, a rusted hammer and a few other items.

He didn't like the look of them—he didn't like the look of them at all.

Underneath the table sat a filthy five-gallon bucket. It appeared to have once been orange. He couldn't help but imagine what it might contain.

"Who are you? What is this place?" Gluth knew who the man was. By *who are you,* he meant, *how the hell are you still breathing?*

His training had taught him to assess his surroundings for anything that might facilitate his escape or determine later where he'd been. This had been a piece of cake during simulation drills. But now Don's brain wasn't functioning as it should. The items on the table were forcing their way into his head. Tripping him up.

Bruce chuckled. "Now, why do people in your position always ask questions they know won't be answered? You're a company man. You should know better."

In fact, Don *did* know better. Just that, he'd never been in this situation before. Not exactly. He'd *done* to countless others what the weatherman was about to do, but he had never had it done *to* him.

Don Gluth liked action, but not this kind of action. Suddenly he didn't feel so tough. He took a few panicked breaths and tried to manufacture some courage.

The weatherman produced a photo from inside his sport coat. "You seen this girl, by chance?"

It was a kid. A little blonde-haired, faucet-nosed dismo. Why would he have ever seen the brat? "Fuck you!" He hawked up a loogie and spat. It fell short of its target. A little clung to his lower lip, now stretched down his chin like a snotty worm.

"Oh now, don't be rude—" Bruce slipped the photo back into his coat pocket. "—or I'll have to make this harder than it needs to be."

Into Don's mind floated the glowing image of the topless girl. Her tanned skin emphasized the nakedness of the creamy surfaces untouched by the sun. This beauty was in stark contrast to the ugliness of the tableau laid out on the table, and that somehow scared the shit out of him.

Would he ever get to caress those creamy curves? He tried to conjure up her naked body—her face, her hair, her voice—anything to drown out the thoughts of what was going to happen here. But while his imagination indeed supplied him with the images, they were marred with bubbling flesh, crushed knuckles, amputated earlobes. A shudder racked his spine. "Okay, fine. What do you want with me?"

"That's better." Bruce propped his foot on the chair and rested his elbows on his raised knee. "So. Donny. That is your name, right? That's what was in your cell phone."

"Yeah, sure. Donny. Or, Don."

"Okay! Ordon!" Bruce laughed. "I want to know why the hell you and your boys tried to tear me a new asshole back there. And did you come for me specifically? Or were you after someone else, and I just happened to be the one who was home?" He was careful not to use Decker's name, in order to prevent the prick from regurgitating information Bruce himself had revealed.

Gluth gyrated his head in frustration. The agency didn't have a lot of tolerance and understanding about spilling information. Even if you were under duress. The punishment would be stiff—as in graveyard stiff. "Hey man, that's classified. You know I can't . . ." He looked at the ceiling, his lap—then back at the weatherman. "I'm sorry. I can't say anything."

Bruce sighed. He nodded and stood. "About what I expected." He crossed his arms. "Tell me. Have you ever heard of Polyplacebic acid? Did you pay attention in science class, Ordon? Or were you busy texting underage girls back then, too?"

"Hey. She's eighteen, man."

"Let me see." Bruce referenced his memory. "I think it was, 'Wow. Hard to believe you are just 15. Rock hard, lol. You look 23. Hot hot hot.' That about right?"

"Oh man . . ."

"So. Polyplacebic acid?"

Ordon just stared at him.

"Well let me refresh your memory. PPA—that's how the boys in the lab refer to it, because it's a mouthful, right?—is about the most corrosive substance known to man. It will eat through steel, wood, concrete—and of course any type of flesh. Like say, a *cow.*" Bruce shrugged. "Or your leg. In fact, Ordon, about the only thing it won't dissolve is high-density polyethylene plastic, like that container sitting right over there on that table." Bruce pointed to the jug.

Don shuddered. But he tried to stay tough. "Bullshit. I've never heard of—"

"That's what I figured, Ordon. So I'm going to perform a little demonstration for you."

"No! I mean, you're not going to—"

"Oh now, don't go jumping to conclusions. I would never harm a fellow company man—" Bruce patted Don's face with mock affection. "—again." He strolled to the table. "Do you know what this dense material is, Ordon?" He touched the gray slab.

Don chose his words carefully. He didn't want to tweak the weatherman; the guy seemed a little . . . off. "Yeah sure. Concrete, right?" He shrugged. "Like, a piece of sidewalk? Or foundation or something?"

Bruce nodded. "Good! Maybe you were paying some attention in those classes after all. Now. Watch this." He wriggled his hands into a pair of thick black rubber gloves, then bounced his eyebrows before donning a pair of strap-on safety goggles. "Here we go . . ." He picked up the jug, carefully unscrewed the cap . . . then eased a thin stream onto the slab.

It began to sizzle. The hissing was subtle but ominous. Bruce kept pouring as it ate through the dirty chunk. The liquid, now laced with a white-swirled snotty substance, apparently ate through the table as well, for globs of the toxic goop plopped into the bucket. It sounded like a cow dropping a wet patty.

"Look at that, Ordon! It just keeps. On. *Going!*" Bruce laughed merrily. "Why, it could easily eat through, say, a rib eye steak—" He tilted his head, looked at the ceiling. "—then the plate it's sitting on, then the tabletop, then the linoleum, then the damn concrete foundation." Bruce lifted his hands in faux amazement, sloshing the contents of the jug. "Hell, it might have eaten its way to fucking *China* if it weren't for that polypropylene bucket! Right? Isn't that *cool,* Ordon?"

Gluth's chest heaved. Sweat had formed on his forehead.

Bruce carried the jug to the chair. He held it over Gluth's lap, tipped it until the liquid balanced on the rim. "Now. What were you guys doing at that house today? And heads up: I know a few things already—I just need you to fill in the gaps. So if you try to bullshit me, you're going to end up lying about something I already know and then—" He pointed at the container.

The liquid pulsed at the rim of the jug with each syllable the weatherman spoke. The stringent fumes burned Don's nose. He thought of his precious private parts, imagined them bubbling. "Alright al*right!* I'll tell you what you want to know. Just get away from me with that shit."

Bruce backed off and stabilized the container in both gloved hands.

Don thought carefully about the information he was about to reveal. This goggle-wearing goof would take it personally. "Don't get mad at me, okay? I was just following orders."

"Of course."

"Alright . . . we were there for you."

"Me? Why?"

"You were set up, okay? You took out that rat. The whistleblower. Payne. Alright? Then, and this is just what I heard, they wanted to take *you* out, like, to cover the trail. So no one ever knows what happened, right?"

Bruce's musings of disappearing hired hit men had evidently been accurate. And he'd referred to Payne as a whistleblower. Not a terrorist sympathizer.

"It didn't help when you kidnapped his kid."

"It wasn't kidnapping, Ordon. Her father was dead. Remember? The whistleblower?"

Gluth shook his head and continued. "And then Decker, she was passing Payne information about . . ."

"Go on."

"Oh man."

"Orrrdonnn . . . " He sloshed the jug.

"Okay al*right!*" He hadn't needed to mention Decker; it had just . . . slipped out. But that damned acid. "Decker was passing him information about the special project."

"What special project?"

Don thought about his career. The guns, the mystique, the thrill of the hunt.

Then he thought about losing his pecker. "Amber. Project Amber. That bitch was about to spill the beans on Amber, okay? Satisfied?"

"She's not a bitch, Ordon. Please don't use that word."

Don smirked and shook his head. "They're all bitches, man."

"Don't *say* that!" Bruce wasn't kidding. He recognized his emotions were taking over, and knew he needed to get them back in check. "Why me? For the setup?"

"Hey, I don't know. I've heard stuff. Like, you're all gungho to kill towel heads. Over your sister or some shit, I don't know. Like, and this is just what I heard now, you were losing it." He smiled sheepishly, wishing he'd left out that last part. The weatherman seemed to take it in stride. "So like, if anyone ever figured out you were the shooter, they could make it look like you did it because you thought the guy was in bed with terrorists."

Ironically, Bruce thought, that was precisely the case.

"They needed *somebody* to do it, and we're all expendable, right? So I guess you were just the *most* expendable." The weatherman wasn't responding. Not good. "Hey, like I said, their words, not mine."

Bruce nodded. "That's okay, Don." He supposed it made sense the agency knew about Amy—but slimy they'd never mentioned it.

It was humiliating, however, that they'd tumbled to his private vendetta. How could they have known? Was it that obvious? They'd done their homework; he had to give them that. They'd evidently been saving all this in case a situation arose in which they could use it.

Like now.

He couldn't seem to get back on track with the sarcastic shtick. "So tell me about Project Amber."

"I've heard things, but it's bullshit."

"I'll be the judge of that. Keep talking."

"Okay, they got this physicist, right? Working on some kind of E.S.P. shit. Then, and this is where it goes off the rails, okay? The Navy finds something. In like, this trench or something. In the ocean. Like, *miles* deep. An old carrier or something. Maybe an underwater cave, I don't know. But the point is, they found something *inside* it."

"What did they find?"

"Nobody knew at the time. But you know the DSA; they monitor everybody. So when the Navy brought this shit up and started testing it, we infiltrated their labs. Eventually stole it. Then burned the lab to make it look like everything was destroyed in the fire."

"And . . ."

"They say it does some weird shit to you."

Bruce approached with the jug.

"Hey wait a minute! I'm talking, okay?"

"What is the 'E.S.P. shit,' Don? And what does it do? Is that what Decker was passing information about to Payne?" Bruce tipped the container.

"I *swear,* man! The Navy found something, DSA has it, nobody knows what it is, and *I* don't know what it does. Maybe it helps with E.S.P. But *I don't know!*"

"Don . . ."

"You think I'd lie to you when you have that . . . that poly-whatever-it-is held over my crotch? I *told* you it was probably bullshit!"

This story was obviously a dead end, but perhaps it was indeed what the man had heard. Hell, maybe they'd even leaked it for this very reason—in case men like Gluth found themselves under interrogation.

That was one of the many challenges of running a rogue department. As with any crime syndicate, it was difficult if not impossible to acquire faithful and competent staff. If someone was willing to betray their country and the rule of law, why then would they suddenly develop a sense of dedication and loyalty to the agency?

After all, a backstabber is a backstabber.

There were two ways to achieve loyalty with such men: Money and fear. The problem was, if these hoods were offered more money or instilled with more fear by someone else, their faux honor would disappear like a virgin on prom night.

It did not escape Bruce that he himself worked for the same agency for reasons of his own.

The deep sea yarn and 'E.S.P. shit' was bogus—although Gluth was likely telling the truth as he understood it.

"I told you everything, man. So can I go now?"

"Sure, Donny. As soon as we're done here, I'll release you."

Don's shudders returned. "No you won't. Please, man . . ."

"Now now. Don't go soft on me, Ordon."

"Look. They're already after you. I can't do anything about that—and it's not my fault. But if you let me go, I can get you a head start, right? I'll tell them . . . I'll tell them you took off for Canada or something, you know? Then you could go south, like, to Mexico. That would at least be a head start, right? But if you kill me, you're on your own. Whadya say?"

Bruce shook his head once and grinned. "You know, Ordon, I believe you might really do as you say." And Bruce really did. But of course, he couldn't let him go.

"So we got a deal?"

"I'll think about it. You just answer a few more questions and I'll make this as painless as possible."

That didn't sound like a deal to Don Gluth. He tried the old Takeaway. "Okay, fuck you. Without me, you're dead. Like, *today* dead."

"One last thing. Where's Decker? Is she alive?" At this point, it seemed certain the woman had done nothing wrong. Nor had Payne—and about that, guilt had already begun its slow, never-ending acid drip on Bruce's heart.

But what was so important about this amber that the two of them would risk their lives to expose it? It was just ESP mumbo-jumbo. Or was there more to it? Right now, he desperately needed to speak with Decker. Knowing her whereabouts would make it easier to approach her with at least some degree of circumspection. If he had to hunt her down, there was a better than average chance she'd see him coming.

And take him out before he could let her know he was on her side.

Don smirked. "They've got her nailed down tight. Oh, she's alive. She'll live forever."

"What's that supposed to mean?"

"Let me go and I'll tell you." Don offered his best used-car salesman grin.

"I'm losing my patience, Ordon. You tell me everything, right now, or I'll pour this shit over your head and walk out of here while your skin crawls off. How about that?"

Gluth's eyes narrowed. "You'll find everything you need to know about that little bitch in drawer number seven."

"I told you, don't *say* that!" Bruce tried to keep his cool, but it was slipping away. Yes, they were just words, but he didn't buy into the whole sticks and stones thing. Words reflected principles. Words evolved into *action*. Perhaps, had words like these never been spoken, he and his sister could have grown up together. Maybe he wouldn't have had to spend the last fifteen years wondering whether she was dead—or alive but dead inside.

So, what was this drawer number seven? Did they have an entire file drawer dedicated to Decker? That seemed odd, since most records were kept digitally nowadays.

He was about to have Gluth clarify when the man spoke.

"Don't say what? *Bitch?*"

"I'm warning you . . ."

"They're *all* bitches, man."

"They're not bitches, Gluth! Stop calling them that. They're wives and daughters. Sisters. They're our *mothers,* for Christ's sake! Now, *where is Decker?*" Bruce's hands were shaking. He was holding the jug, but Gluth was leading the interrogation. He had to get hold of himself, get his emotions in check.

"Mothers?" Don scoffed. "How do you think they got that way, huh? How you think they got all bloated up with babies? 'Cause somebody got them *hot*. Yeah, they're daughters and wives alright—and mothers and sisters." He smirked. "Whatever. They melt like butter if you buy 'em flowers or someshit."

"Gluth . . ."

"Then they'll spread 'em back to their ears if you get 'em hot."

"Stop it!"

"Or, if that doesn't work, you hold 'em down, grope that crotch, mash their faces in the dirt—and they *all* get wet and *take it*. Bitches! Every one!"

Bruce took a step and turned the jug upside down over Don Gluth's head. The fluid came gurgling out, bathing the punk in liquid hell. When it was empty, he shook out the remaining droplets.

Gluth screamed.

Bruce tossed the empty container aside then turned to the table, deafened by the little imp's wailing. He removed his gloves and goggles and slapped them onto the table. He picked up the torch and twisted the knob, then whisked the sparker in the hissing stream of gas. With a subtle *poof,* the rippling air turned to flame.

Gluth's howls were subsiding. He grunted and coughed. Choking on the fumes. *"HA!"* He sputtered. "Your shit's bunk! It's not working like you said, like it did on the concrete. It's not doing *anything!"*

Bruce thought, *The pathetic fool is babbling delirium.*

Gluth spit again, shook his head and tried to blink his eyes clear. "You got another chance here, weatherman. Work with me. I could even set you up with my little hottie. Whatdya say?"

Weatherman? Bruce carried the torch to the chair. "It's not working like I said because it's Acetone, dumbass."

"Acetone?"

"Yeah. Like nail polish remover except with no perfume. Harmless to human flesh. Tastes like shit, but you could gargle with it."

"What? I thought you said poly—polyplu—"

"I made it up, shit-for-brains."

"But it ate through that slab!"

"It's Styrofoam."

"What?!"

"An old boat dock bumper. I didn't have any Pentothal handy, so I used your imagination. What little you have."

"Fucker."

"But what acetone *is,*" Bruce added, "is highly combustible. I probably need to tell you, that means flammable."

Gluth gawked at him.

"Highly . . . Flammable."

"Hey. No-no-no. We made a deal."

"We didn't make any deal, Gluth."

"Come on, man." He was whimpering now. "Have a little mercy here."

"Do you have mercy on the 'bitches,' Ordon?" Bruce's body shook as he imagined this man slobbering all over the fifteen-year-old, and the unspeakable atrocities that had in all likelihood been committed on Amy.

"Hey. That was just something I said. I was just trying to get under your skin, that's all."

"Well, you did." Bruce tossed the torch under the chair and backed quickly away. The *whoosh* of heat stole a gasp from him.

This time, Gluth's screams were genuine. The chair bumped and rattled on the floor with the man's thrashing. He shook his head violently, slinging burning liquid as far as ten feet out. Bruce retreated, devastated by the heat wave, eyes squinted almost shut.

The punk had indeed gotten under his skin, preventing him from learning more about this drawer number seven—although it likely meant nothing. Worse, however, Bruce had failed to acquire Decker's whereabouts. He had to give the man credit for that, at least.

Gluth's chair tipped over backwards. His feet pedaled for purchase.

The fire was blinding. Gluth's mouth was like a dragon's, spewing flames with every diminishing scream. Surely his eyeballs would melt soon, if they hadn't already.

Bruce headed for the door. He said under his breath, "Don't call them bitches."

-Twins-

Zoe had read the Mayo Clinic post Freddie had pulled up for her and seemed to absorb it like a sponge. Now she stood behind him, fists on her hips, skeptical. She watched impatiently as the Freddie on the screen eased cautiously through the door of BT's, then rolled her eyes when he began negotiating with the bouncer. She sighed dramatically as the strippers swarmed him. "Is this going to take long?"

"Just watch." Freddie's eyes stayed locked on the computer.

Then there was Julie. Unclear at this distance and angle for the moment, it was still enough to motivate Zoe to reach blindly behind her and pull up a chair. "Hoooly . . ." She sat, paying attention now.

Her jaw dropped as she watched herself, close enough to identify with clarity, pull Freddie by one lapel past the table where the jerk sat holding the camera *(fucking bums with tits)*. Julie's drawl was not clear on the recording, but Freddie was glad to see Zoe shake her head, amazed, the few times her alter ego's voice was audible.

Then she blushed as she watched herself dancing half naked on Freddie's lap. She continued watching, through the commotion of the punk's extraction from the club, all the way to the end when Freddie palmed the camera, shutting off the device.

"What the *hell?*"

"I told you! You're a stripper, see?"

"Like hell I am. *She's* the stripper."

Freddie pulled out his phone and, using a nearby tethering cord, quickly connected it to the computer. "Check this out."

"Am I at least wearing clothes in this one?"

"You're wearing what you're wearing now."

He waited for the file choice options box to appear.

Zoe said, "By the way, you better be glad I didn't see you going for a butt grab or something. Do anything like that while I'm . . . 'away' or whatever, you can bet your ass when I come back, I'll break a heel off in *your* foot, Fix-It Man."

"Zoe." Freddie shook his head. "She's practically a child." Again he was amazed at his falling back to referring to them as different people. "I get the feeling, even though she's a stripper, she's like, asexual. She's more into thinking up words that rhyme."

"You better hope so."

"Besides, I'm not interested."

"Hey!" Zoe laughed and punched his shoulder. Though she was clearly just teasing him, Freddie was encouraged. Maybe behind the banter was a hint of hope.

"Not interested in *her,*" Freddie clarified. He feigned concentration on the computer to mask his thinly veiled expression of interest—and the fact that the statement was not entirely true. He'd come to accept both splits as different manifestations of the same woman. Thus, while he was indeed more attracted to the Zoe version, he'd also come to appreciate Julie. After all, they were one and the same person.

It was rather like dealing with different moods in a spouse. If you truly loved someone, that meant you loved them regardless of their inevitably varying dispositions.

Whatever the case, her silence encouraged him. At least she hadn't cut him off at the knees again.

When the folder options box finally appeared, he selected *View Contents in Explorer* then opened the first file: Julie's recitation of *Cup of Coffee.*

Zoe leaned forward in her chair, rapt through each video, every poem. Freddie was impressed anew with the artist's singular talent.

It seemed Zoe had become a believer. "Julie V. Ayers, huh? Well, you were right. She's a hell of a poet."

"Okay, I have an idea. You've seen her now, up close and personal. So, why don't *you* send *her* a message? Let her know beyond doubt you exist. You see, you actually *are* Julie. After all, you have no memory of a past. Julie does. So you, Julie, created Zoe as a means of protecting you from bad experiences you had as a child.

"Nope." She shook her head adamantly.

"But—"

"I have memories too, Freddie. A history. I know I do. I just can't access them. But I'm certain it's there. Besides, according to the Mayo article, splits often fabricate their histories. Couldn't I, Zoe, have created Julie—and her past—as some sort of messed-up coping mechanism?"

Freddie reluctantly agreed.

"At the very least, it could be either of us. But I'm certain it's me."

She had a point. And regardless of who the real, original personality was, at least Zoe was up to speed with what was happening. "Point taken. Regardless, I think it would be a good idea to get the two of you . . . merged or whatever."

"What, you hoping maybe I'll start doing lap dances for you? Because that ain't gonna happen."

There she went again, turning his words around. Implying he meant something he didn't.

"She tries tricking me into doing that, she'll be writing poems about getting her ass kicked!"

"Now that I'd like to see. What, are you going punch yourself? You'd break your leg trying to kick your own ass."

Zoe chuffed and shook her head. "Yeah, right?"

"Look. I'm just saying. Right now, regardless of who's 're-al,' neither of you has awareness of—much less control over—the other. Even though you're in fact one person."

"I know the evidence seems conclusive, but I'm still convinced there's more to it than that."

Freddie was undeterred. "So if you 'merge,' I guess the word is, maybe the two of you will become one *mentally.* Then you get your life back, become aware of what you're doing twenty-four-seven. That would be nice, right?"

"Oh yeah. Real nice. I'll discover my hidden talent for poetry and sculpting Halloween manikins. And pole dancing. That would be *awesome!*"

Freddie tried playing to her personality. "So, you want to just leave her in charge half the time? Do you enjoy waking up naked at BT's? Or falling off a bicycle? Talk to her, Zoe. Make a connection."

She shook her head and blew out her breath. "Okay, fine. We doing this now?"

"No time like the present." Freddie opened the camera app on his phone. He pointed the device, staring at the woman through the tiny screen. "Roll 'em!"

Now this *was familiar.*

Quite the opposite of Julie, Zoe seemed intimidated by the camera. She overcompensated with bravado. "Uh ... Okay. Hi, Julie." Then aside, quietly: *"What the hell am I supposed to say, dude?"*

Freddie whispered, *"Anything. Just whatever's on your mind."*

Again with the sigh, then, "Alright, listen. *Stop stripping!* That shit's humiliating, man. Okay? Like it or not—and I don't—we're sharing my body."

"Zoe!"

"Fine. We're sharing *a* body. But, I don't fuck with you while you're away, so stop fucking with me, cool? Oh and, stop dressing like Mary Poppins. It's embarrassing. Get some t-shirts or something. And try to eat more. Every time I come around, I'm freakin' *starving*." She'd wolfed down a sandwich and a half bag of chips the moment she'd arrived at Freddie's.

"Can you say something nice?"

"Uh . . . yeah, okay. Your poetry is awesome. I mean it. And I'm sorry about Johnny. Life sucks sometimes, girl. But whining won't help. Chin up. Rely on yourself. At least you remember your past. Or uh . . . 'our' past? All I remember is my name. Zoe. Oh and uh . . . your artwork is impressive too. Just, no more freak sculptures, alright? That shit's creepy, dude." Then aside again, *"Is that good? I hate this, Freddie."*

"Just say goodbye. And be nice!"

"Okay uh . . . look. Regardless of who came first, I suppose we're kind of—" She shrugged. "—sisters, I guess. Like it or not. *Closer* than sisters. *Twins.*" She shook her head and chuffed. "You're me. I'm you. We're . . . *us,* I guess."

Since she was looking right at him through the camera app, Freddie couldn't help but imagine the *us* referred to Zoe and him.

"So, let's try and get along. Maybe we'll, like, find each other somehow. Take it easy. Zoe out." She finished with a salute, ending it by pointing a finger-gun at the camera and winking.

Freddie lowered the phone and made sure the video had saved. He looked back at Zoe. "Okay. We need to get you some clothes."

"That would be nice. But Freddie. I not only don't have my own clothes, I've got no car, no job, no home—not really—and no money. I'm not a mooch, Freddie. I'm not comfortable ow-ing anybody."

"You mean, you're not comfortable owing *me*?" He smiled and raised his eyebrows.

"Well, I did mean anybody, just that . . . I guess you're the only one I know right now." She looked perplexed. "So, what can I do, Freddie?"

"Listen. I want to help you, okay? We get you a wardrobe you're cool with, and we get this DID thing under control. Then we find you a job, get you set up. Like I said, we just—" He shrugged. "—get your life back."

"*We,* Freddie?"

Unexpected, his patience hit rock bottom. "Well what the hell are you going to do on your own, Zoe? You can't even depend on being *you* all the time! So how are you going to strike out on your own? Please tell me. Because, *I'd love to hear it!*"

She said nothing. Just stood steaming.

"Let's say you apply for a job as a cop—and God knows you'd be a good one—but during the interview, *you start improvising poetry!* What then, huh? Or let's say you somehow manage to finagle the job, then you're throwing some dirtbag against a squad car—which I have no doubt you could do—only suddenly you're Julie. Limp-wristed, head-in the-clouds Jules, who couldn't fight a fly with a bazooka. What'll you do then? How are you going to do *anything* that counts for shit, *when you can't even count on being you?*"

Zoe glared at him, hands fisted at her sides. She seemed to be doing her best to summon some anger, apparently her favorite mood. But despite her efforts, her fury was thwarted by hopelessness—and now, he realized, fear.

Tears welled in her eyes, but she held them at bay. She gritted her teeth and refused to look away.

He stepped forward, hands raised in surrender. "Okay, I'm sorry." More subdued now, he cautiously closed the distance—then gently touched her shoulders, tentatively . . . carefully . . .

It seemed she went to strike his arms aside, but it wasn't that. She gripped his sleeves fiercely and held him there. He wondered what that meant.

"All cards on the table?" Freddie locked on her eyes. "I need you as much as you need me. So it's an even trade."

"How could you possibly need—"

"Even trade," he insisted. He paused to let it sink in. "You move me, okay? I don't know what it is. Your sassy mouth, your fierce pride—but you've made an impression on me. Hell, changed me. I haven't allowed myself to truly know someone since . . ."

He stopped, and his eyes wandered, and his memory.

With some effort, he shoved the ghosts aside and continued. "Since I don't know when." He shrugged. "So there it is. You made the mistake of feeding this boot-footed puppy, and now he's followed you home. So you're stuck with him."

She just stared at him. She seemed confused.

"Hell, you're the best friend I've got. How pathetic is that? But I mean it. Anyone lays a hand on you, it'll be over my dead body." Of course she would point out that *she* could just as easily protect *him*. He beat her to the punch. "And I mean whether you're making wisecracks or writing poetry. Whether you're kicking bouncers' asses or painting murals. Whether you're rolling out of a hit-n-run or lumbering along on a bicycle. Who do you think has been watching over *Jula' V. Ayers* while you were God-only-knows-where? *Me,* Zoe. I am *here* for you. I can't explain it, but by God I want to *be* with you."

She slowly shook her head, and her eyes clouded.

"In any capacity; I can live with however this unfolds. I may not be rich, or particularly smart—although I am a first-rate handyman—"

She chuckled despite herself and her chin quivered.

"—but for whatever it's worth, you've got yourself an ally. A friend. You've got *me.*"

She opened her mouth, perhaps to debate, but no words came forth.

"It'd mean the world to me if you came to reflect my feelings, but I understand that may never happen. I'm not expecting love, money, sex—" She blushed at his bluntness. "—or anything else in return."

He lowered his voice and leaned forward. "My money, my time, my heart? All yours, Zoe. All you have to do is accept."

That piercing stare of hers—she seemed to be scanning for any sign of deceit, and that broke his heart. Looking from his left eye to his right, back and forth, eyebrows knitted, the jiggling threatening to spill the dreaded tears . . . she was flipping through the pages of his mind again—and this time he didn't care if she read it all.

"I need a moment," she said, and studiously summoned a blank expression as she stepped around him and hurried to the bathroom. The door closed and the vent fan started up.

Now it was Freddie's turn to sigh.

-Words Unspoken-

Bruce parked the van a few miles away in a shopping center parking lot then hiked back to the bus stop. He took only backstreets and alleys. Without a doubt, both vans had been equipped with transponders. He hadn't wasted time trying to locate the bugs because there was no way to be certain he'd found them all. They'd pick up his trail soon enough, but at least they wouldn't be able to jump right to it.

He had prepared for this contingency because an apostate agency could be expected to have no more loyalty to its henchmen than to its country's principles. After all, a backstabber is a backstabber.

He'd arranged bug-out bags throughout the country and a few overseas, all of which contained cash, a change of clothes, clean credit cards under aliases with accompanying identification, a pistol and a few fully loaded magazines.

All the guns and magazines were consistent—Springfield XD .45—because he didn't want to wind up holding a weapon incompatible with the ammo he had on hand.

Back in the day, it had been possible to employ train station and airport lockers for these purposes. But with the security measures instituted since 9-11, these options were no longer viable. So he used safe deposit boxes and storage units for the most part, paying for them as far in advance as was allowed. It was a pain keeping them current, especially since the payments needed to be untraceable. But it was well worth the effort.

He'd also sunken high-pressure containers under various waterways and buried simple plastic boxes in a few desolate wooded areas.

He'd picked up a bug-out bag and used some of the cash to purchase a laptop computer. He'd dared not open it under the bus shelter. Engrossed in the screen, he'd have been unable to see death coming before it was upon him.

Now he sat in the rear seat of a city bus, computer open on his lap. The diesel engine hum and occasional hiss of air-brakes comforted him. He inserted the zip drive and opened it in Explorer. His heart sank when he was presented with around twenty folders bearing names like *Family Photos, Michael BD Party, Our Files* and *Vegas Trip.* He was disappointed to see the stick contained nothing more than personal content, and perhaps not even that of Zoe Decker. Then it dawned on him that, again, she'd have gone the extra mile to make her information as difficult to find as possible.

She'd keep it simple, but she'd be thorough.

After all, mediators were not the only ones who could come across the drive. Her landlord's kids, a burglar, or any busybody could end up with it, especially if she got careless and left it open on her computer. Not likely, but it happens. How stupid would it have been to entitle the folders, "Project Amber Cover-up," "My Secret Files" or "Nuclear Launch Codes?"

Maybe . . .

He opened *Family Photos*. These proved to be nothing more than what the folder title described. Images of smiling kids at a fair, a silhouetted couple strolling hand in hand on a beach, a Galapagos turtle at a petting zoo.

He noted the superior quality of the photos. Either the photographer had professional experience—unlikely—or these were stock images, perhaps downloaded from the internet.

Also within *Family Photos* was a video file entitled *Denny's First Bike Ride*. He watched thirty seconds or so of a snaggletooth boy, helmet askew, wavering precariously on a little bicycle—sans training wheels probably for the first time. Bruce noticed the progress bar had barely moved—then that the duration window read 1:27:23. Cute as it might have been, he wasn't going sit here and watch an hour and a half of this kid falling over his bike.

He closed the video and moved on.

He opened *Our Files*. Here he found scans of phone and utility bills and a number of Word documents. There were letters, notes, memos, grocery lists and other random files. He doubted any of them were any more authentic than the ID currently occupying his wallet.

The contents of *Michael BD Party* were loyal to the title as well, presenting the same smiling boy—presumably Michael—donning a cone birthday hat, blowing out candles and opening gifts. Here he was wielding a plastic Star Wars lightsaber; there he was hugging a curly-haired puppy, fat red bow as a collar.

The boy was as glamorous as any movie star—as was every parent and child in attendance. Absent were the blemishes, bruises, braces, scraped knees, awkward eyeglasses and general dishevelment inevitable at any gathering of kids.

The home in which the party was held was completely free of clutter, crayon marks, or even a speck of dust. He doubted any child had ever set foot in that house—except on the day of the photo shoot.

Vegas Trip. Images of—gasp—a dazzling couple frolicking in the casinos of Nevada.

After several other dead ends, he closed the lid and stared out the window. They passed auto parts stores, bike shops and tax preparation firms. After a minute or so, they all began to look the same.

A traffic light brought the bus squeaking to a stop. They sat idling in front of a restaurant at which a young couple was entering the front door. The man was saying something funny—or that seemed to be the case since the young woman for whom he'd opened the door was giggling. Bruce smiled at the scene and chuffed, happy for them.

As the bus crept forward again, his smile faded. Bruce's twenties had come and gone, and now he'd entered his third decade. A devastating truth wrenched from him a subtle gasp. Wholesome experiences like this couple was sharing he'd unthinkingly sacrificed, filling his history instead with bitterness and death.

And for what? What had he accomplished? Nothing. Absolutely nothing. Amy was still gone, and he was a broken man. He'd wasted fifteen years kneeling at the altar of vengeance. In feeding that fiery god, he'd unwittingly fueled the flames of his own demise.

No more.

Although his life was in grave danger—more so than ever before—a burden had been lifted from his shoulders. Strangely, he was the happiest he'd ever been since the moment before the blast at the theatre.

The little girl with the Lalaloopsie doll had opened a door through which change was possible. He'd stepped through it. Bruce had come to realize there were things about which he could *do* something.

Amy's tragedy was not one of them.

Somehow, through Christie, he was able to let that go. He looked up at—or rather through—the ceiling of the creaking bus, past the graffiti peppered with crusted gum, into the heavens far above. He uttered *Thank you* to a God he'd never known—and with whom he'd never put forth even the slightest effort at making an acquaintance, much less building a rapport.

Maybe that would change too.

"Thank you," he whispered again.

He thought he'd feel at least a tinge of guilt or grief—not for deserting Amy, because he understood now he was doing no such thing—but for the relinquishing of his only link to her: The Insatiable Fire.

Instead, he felt a sense of almost jubilation, although tainted by a shade of remorse it had taken all these years— and a little girl with bed head—for him to get to this point. But he'd made it.

The agency would never stop looking for him. They'd be relentless in their search. Bruce had a card up his sleeve, one that may just cool their heels. At least for a while. Then perhaps with the passing of time, they'd lighten up. Especially when they realized he was gone for good and posed no threat to them.

Maybe.

He realized he'd be watching his back for the rest of his life, but that was okay. He just needed to lay down that card and make his play. When they hesitated, he'd bounce. With Christie.

Then it was over.

No more killing.

No more nightmares.

He had no idea what he'd do, exactly, but the myriad possibilities excited him. He could work in computers. Become a gunsmith. Paint houses. Hell, *go fishing!*

He also felt compelled to find Zoe Decker. He didn't know what, exactly, she'd gotten herself into, but he didn't care. Whatever it was, he was confident she was on the right side of it. He just needed to find a way to approach her without getting shot in the process.

Zoe Decker . . .

Had Bruce had his head screwed on straight way back when, he'd have pursued the woman. At the time, however, he'd been too immersed in anger to chase anything other than revenge.

Not that things had changed much.

Looking back at himself, he wondered how he'd been so stupid. Who knows what might have developed between them?

That is, if he'd even had a chance in hell.

First, Zoe was a looker. To say the least. She could have strutted into the barracks, any day, any time, pointed to any recruit and said, "You. Marriage. Now." —and the man would have stumbled out the door behind her, tail tucked between his legs pissing himself.

Though only slightly taller than average, her thick mane of curly blonde hair lent the illusion of increased height. Bruce chuckled to himself at the thought of her trying to straighten a curl to tape over the sliding glass door.

Her wet tresses would sometimes slip from her ponytail during training, and the effect of it clinging to her chiseled face was enough to dry the sweatshirts of every man on the range.

She was solid as a rock, strong as any man—yet she carried it well. She was ripped but by no means bulky.

Second, it didn't take three seconds on her radar to get the message, loud and clear: *Do. Not. Fuck with me.* Not that she was rude. She'd hand you change if you were short, or hold the door open for you. She'd offer you a hand from the mat after planting your ass on it. Even so, you always got the feeling she was utterly unapproachable, large and in charge, even in the presence of officers.

Still, fate had provided Bruce a shot.

The opportunity was presented when he'd come back early from a three day leave. Zoe was hammering away in the weight room, muscles pumped, glistening with sweat. Bruce had just happened to see her there as he passed. Beer bottle in hand, he'd stood leaning on the doorframe watching for half a minute, torn as to whether to strike up a conversation or just walk on by. He'd opted for the former.

"Aren't you tough enough already, Decker?" He pulled up a weight bench.

"Vega?" Zoe answered in greeting. She finished her bar curls without looking up—then set the weights down and plucked a towel from the rack. As she wiped her face, she shot a glance at the bottle. "Last I checked, alcohol's not allowed on the base." She offered a wink and a half grin.

"Yeeeah." He sighed dramatically. "I saw the sign, but I thought it said, *No Smoking.*"

She chuckled, draped the towel around her neck—and paused. Bruce got the impression she was deciding whether or not to lower her drawbridge for a moment. It was anyone's guess what she was guarding in there behind those castle walls, but it was something.

With a single nod, she plopped down across from him, astraddle the lat stool. "How you been, Bruce?"

He shook his head once and chuffed. *Feed the fire,* he was thinking. "How do you do it, Decker? You're like . . . a force of nature."

"And by that you mean . . . what? I'm a natural disaster?"

"No I'm serious. Here you are during a three day leave, in here busting your ass. I got a lot of respect for you and—" He shrugged. "—I just want to know how you do it. What's your motivation?"

She fidgeted, glanced around the room, gripping the ends of the towel. "Tsss. I'm no better than the next guy." She looked back at Bruce.

"Come on, Decker. Talk to me. No bullshit, now. Like, who were your parents? Seems to me you were raised by lions or something."

Zoe knitted her brow, those ice blue orbs burrowing into him, seemingly scanning for any sign of mockery. He could feel her there, poking around inside his head. It made him fidget.

Evidently finding no malice but only the sincerity with which he spoke, she relented. "I never met my parents."

Bruce's heart sank. She was not a friend per se, but his respect for the woman was considerable. He hated hearing this.

"I was raised in an orphanage. Or, orphanages plural. I was adopted a few times, but they always sent me back."

"What for?" Bruce took a pull from his Budweiser.

"Well for one, I was a hell-raiser." She stood again, returned to the curl bar. "Had a chip on my shoulder about my parents dumping me." She started pumping. "Got in a lot of fights, kicked in a lot of Drywall." She grimaced on the 5th rep. "I'd have sent me back, too."

"Hell, who could blame you? I bet a lot of those kids felt that way." He took another swig. "So, what's the other thing?"

Zoe set down the bar and moved to the seated row station. She settled in, set the tab in the stack, gripped the bar and braced herself. "Even when I was little, I realized I could never depend on anyone but myself." She yanked back and the weights glided up.

"Why's that? Surely there was someone in your life who gave a shit."

The weights clacked down and she pushed back again. "There were a few, I suppose, but I didn't *want* to depend on them. It was me, not them." She grimaced through another rep, apparently not just from the exertion.

"Oh man. Decker. That's sad, bro'."

"Just self-preservation. They all cut loose, Vega. They get distracted, find other interests . . . or the earth just opens up and swallows them whole." The weights clacked down to stay this time, and Zoe stood. "But they all cut loose."

Bruce couldn't help but imagine his sister voicing this very sentiment about her "hero" brother. He said nothing, both touched by her candor and troubled by her story.

Psychology had been one of his favorite subjects in school. During a lecture on child development, he'd learned that words unspoken had as much—and sometimes greater—impact than those voiced. Words like, *I love you kid, I'm so proud of you,* or *You are my special princess,* were precious, vital to normal development. Their absence left indelible voids in the soul.

Words have meaning. Convey emotions. Words shape people. Unlike mere thoughts, words fuel action. Intimate dialogue was where a person learned to trust and be trusted, to love and be loved. Without it, the spirit developed an impenetrable shell as a means of protection.

Self-preservation.

You grew to be detached and cold, guarded and distant. You ended up becoming . . . well, Zoe Decker.

But was there anything Bruce could say that would make a difference? Solutions had not been discussed during the course—or if they had, he couldn't remember. Besides, this sense of intimacy needed to be developed during the formative years. Ideally with parents.

He was only a friend. More like an acquaintance.

Still, he could change that, couldn't he? He could say *something,* could be at least that someone who gave a shit. It was by no means a fire, but certainly a tiny spark—or the potential for one. He was about to open his mouth when the door burst open.

"VEGA!" Damn Gunnery Sergeant Green. "Trash that contraband and give me fifty."

Zoe shot Bruce a wink. "Nice talking with you, Vega." Returning to the safety of her fortress, she reeled in the drawbridge and locked it tight. She saluted the sergeant *(Sir!)*, snared her towel and ducked out.

The clacking of the weights transformed into that of the bus door as it rattled and hissed open, releasing a kid with a skateboard to the freedom—and jungle—of the streets. Like they had on that moment so long ago, the doors slammed shut and the bus surged inexorably forward.

He'd never spoken alone with her since.

He supposed that attitude of cold self-preservation had served her well in this line of work. Without a doubt, it was what had driven her to become a martial arts expert in her life before the service. However, the isolation likely took its toll on her, like Bruce's aimless hate had eaten away at him. Maybe one day they could compare notes. Talk about it. Get it off their chests.

Perhaps while fishing.

He chuckled to himself, imagining Zoe storing lures in that mayonnaise jar, cat food tin long since discarded.

The mayonnaise jar . . .

Bruce snatched open the computer lid. He navigated to the video, *Denny's First Bike Ride.*

A kid on a bike.

He moved the slider all the way to the end.

Still the wobbling kid.

He slid the bar about a third of the way past the beginning.

Instead of a boy on a bike, Bruce found himself hovering, by way of the screen, a good 500 feet above the ocean. Radio chatter blared from the computer speakers, and he quickly turned it down. He looked up to see if he'd attracted attention. The only other riders were up front, asleep or faced forward, entranced by the drone of the road.

He returned to the screen.

Even viewed through this virtual window, Bruce's stomach flipped. The horizon swayed and dipped, then disappeared from view, replaced by the churning waves below. Apparently, the video had been shot through the open door of a helicopter. The handheld camera was unsteady, and Bruce's vertigo worsened to the point he had to look away to let it pass. When he peered back at the screen, he was circling a ring of frigate and cruiser ships, in the middle of which idled a Nimitz-class aircraft carrier the length of three football fields. It grew in size and clarified as the chopper descended.

Along the starboard side of the carrier, suspended on fat cables, a 100-foot cylindrical craft caught his attention. Crewmen swarmed it, apparently prepping for launch. Capsule-shaped, bright orange except for huge bubble viewing apertures fore and aft, it featured oversized twin props and some sort of robotic arms port and starboard, folded at the moment. Bruce had never seen one of this design, but he knew essentially what it was.

-Insta-Google-Tweet-Face-

She came walking nonchalantly out of the bathroom, fully composed as if nothing had happened. "Decker. My last name's Decker."

Freddie's face lit up. "*Decker?* You sure?"

Zoe shrugged. "Sure as I can be, considering."

"Considering?"

"That I don't remember anything else. It's just a big blur."

An idea occurred to him. Maybe she wouldn't *have* to remember—at least not unprompted.

He hurried to the computer, began opening a browser before he was even fully seated, then navigated to Gmail.

Zoe closed the gap and stood behind him. "Suddenly decide to clean out your inbox?"

"I have email, but I don't even remember the password. I'm not . . . social."

"I feel ya."

Freddie pecked at the keys, filling boxes and responding to prompts. "No surprise, ZoeDecker is taken. How about *ZoeDecker07@gmail.com?*"

"How about, *Who The Hells Going To Email Me Anyway @gmail.com?*"

"We'll go with 07. Doesn't matter—it's just for access to FaceBook."

"FaceBook?" She stiffened. "Uuuh . . . I don't know, Freddie. "

He kept working until he'd cleared the final digital hurtles. The new account splashed across the screen. Satisfied, he navigated to FaceBook.

"Stop."

He turned in the chair to face her. "What's wrong?"

Her expression clouded and she shook her head. "I just . . ." But she couldn't finish.

Why was she so nervous? How could opening a FaceBook account be in any way dangerous? Even kids did it all the time. "Hey. It's okay." He tried to calm her with his eyes, but she still looked skeptical. "Look. I hate this Insta-Google-Tweet-Face stuff too. But if we open an account, enter as much information as you can remember, post a few photos . . . who knows? Maybe we'll get lucky and someone will recognize you."

"That's what worries me."

"No reason to worry. Considering we may be able to verify your past—or that you even have one—it's worth the risk." Freddie turned to the computer again and proceeded on FaceBook. "Besides, I think we could handle a stalker, no problem."

Zoe took a deep breath and blew it out through pursed lips. She watched over his shoulder as he proceeded.

Within a few minutes, FaceBook.com/ZoeDecker was introduced to the World Wide Web. They shot a few quick photos—Zoe smirking, Freddie insisting she smile. He was sure to feature her face with clarity.

Interests: *Martial Arts* was an obvious choice. *Acrobatics* was not an option, so they went with *Gymnastics*. For good measure, they included *Fitness*.

After some discussion and more than a little debate, they finally added *Firearms*. Zoe couldn't recall any specifics on learning to shoot, but she assured him she was adept at it.

They used Freddie's contact information. They'd get her a cell phone and update that later.

Freddie logged out, closed the browser, then leaned back in his chair. "Now we cross our fingers."

Zoe shook her head once and sighed. "Okay. Let's go shopping."

-Lottery-

Freddie negotiated the back streets as Zoe took in the lay of the land around his neighborhood. Although she struck up a conversation, he was certain her eyes missed nothing. "So you were married."

At first he was shocked she knew that about him—then remembered he still had family collages displayed around the house. "I was." He nodded. "Fifteen years."

"Divorce?" She didn't seem to mind jumping right in.

"No. She passed. Ten years ago. Stephanie."

"Sorry. It's none of my business."

"No need to apologize. Glad you're interested."

Zoe stared out the passenger window as Freddie wound through the neighborhood. After a minute or so, she finally looked over. "What happened, Freddie?" Her tone was subdued and sympathetic—a first. Much as he'd have liked to meet her halfway, Freddie hadn't spoken of this since Stevie had left. In fact, he'd made a concerted effort to avoid the subject—which meant avoiding relationships any closer than clients. It was only now he realized—or perhaps acknowledged—that in so doing, he'd been avoiding life itself. He also realized he didn't mind talking about it with Zoe.

He spoke before he lost his nerve. "We won a sort of lottery."

"The lottery?" She creased her brow with a half smile as if waiting for the punch line.

"Some people win the state lottery. Or a box top contest. Or they're just born into the lucky sperm club. One chance in millions. What happened to us was one in *billions.*"

She waited in silence.

"Sinkholes are fairly common occurrences, although few are big enough to be serious. People dying in them is rare." They proceeded a few blocks, slowed for a line of ducks. "In February 2007, a sinkhole in Guatemala dropped some thirty stories into the earth. Almost instantly. Over a thousand had to be rescued, and five died."

Zoe shuddered and shook her head.

"Two years later, right here in Miami, a historic sinkhole event occurred. It's funny. When I read about it now, it's undeniably accurate. Yet, it's not *real* somehow.

They paused at a stop sign then proceeded.

Freddie took a breath, braced himself. "The hole itself wasn't so big—nowhere near the size of Guatemala's—but it gave way under a parking garage. We were near the top of it."

Freddie paused, examining how he felt after saying those words. "I should have been able to save her. In retrospect, it would have been easy."

"Hindsight's twenty-twenty."

Freddie hadn't even heard her. "One in billions," he said, slowly shaking his head at the irony of it. *"Billions."* He laughed, but he didn't smile.

He reviewed the day for her, the breaking of the piggy bank, Stevie counting his money . . . the trip to the mall, checking out with the bike . . . "They were both in the car. I told them to get out." Freddie was navigating on autopilot, eyes on that sunny day so long ago. "Stephanie either didn't hear me or couldn't get her seatbelt unbuckled in time. Something. But she got stuck."

"I'm sorry, Freddie. You don't have to do this."

He relived it, all of it, finally relinquishing the burden, or some of it, as he hadn't since the day it happened.

"Get out of the car!"

Stevie opened his door and stuck his head out. "What?"

The floor dropped. At least five feet. One moment the concrete was there, the next it simply *wasn't.* Freddie found himself floating in space—everything but his stomach, which had plummeted with the floor. Every vehicle—every car, every truck, every discarded paper cup—floated with him.

His eyes saw, but his mind couldn't process it. For a split second, he was in Apollo 13, astronauts and orange juice floating like plankton in the capsule, viewers at home riveted to their TVs.

The floor came up to greet him. Slammed him back to earth. Freddie's knees buckled. His palms burned and bled, cheese grated on the broom-finished concrete. He hadn't even realized he'd fallen. He watched helplessly as the Cayenne ejected his son like a circus cannon.

Rumble now deafening, the very earth rent asunder five floors below. Car alarms blared, lights flashing, a mechanical symphony. Freddie's heart jumped the starting gun in a race with panic.

Gargantuan tablets of concrete cracked, the fracturing of which registered in his sternum. Guy wires as thick as a man's wrist stretched to capacity. Humming like the strings of a mammoth death-metal guitar.

Dazed, he sat sprawled on his ass. Bloody hands splayed behind him. A fault in the floor raced from beneath the Cayenne, right under Freddie's crotch, spitting angry crumbs as it sped along.

Stephanie . . .

"STEPHANIE GET OUT OF THE—"

Above the Cayenne, one end of a cement girder like the trunk of a sequoia broke free. Solid chunks of jagged shrapnel blew out from the rupture. The girder hung there, suspended precariously by one end.

The weight of cured concrete was about 150 pounds per cubic foot. Judging by the girder's length—about twenty feet—and girth—about two by three feet—the girder must have tipped the scale at no less than nine tons.

"Stephanie—" Quietly, to himself.

The beam broke free, a mammoth guillotine. It smashed the Cayenne like an eggshell. Right at the windshield.

"Mommy!"

Mommy? Stevie said *Mom*. And *Dad*. He hadn't used *Mommy* since he was six years old. So strange he should notice something like that at a time like this.

The floor shook with the impact. Freddie scrambled up, weaved over the trampoline concrete.

At the car. He teetered with another wave. He braced himself—right hand on the roof of the vehicle, left on the fallen girder—and peered inside.

Stephanie. Covered in gummy safety glass pellets.

Every window shattered.

Eyes open.

Dashboard crushed.

Eyes moving. Dazed but alive.

Pinned.

Reaching for him.

Pinned!

Face dotted with blood, but alive.

PINNED!

"Freddie. My legs."

Stevie suddenly at his side. "What's happening, Daddy?"

Freddie and his wife locked wrists in a mountain climber's grip. He tugged with all his might. Stephanie grunted in pain. Freddie braced his right boot on the ruined Cayenne, using both hands now, and pulled harder still.

"Stop . . . Freddie *stop!*"

He released her. Examined her predicament. The dash was Jaws himself. Biting into her thighs. She'd have a nasty bruise the shape of a steering wheel across both legs. Freddie fought off images of crushed bone, of wheelchairs and colostomy bags.

"I'm stuck."

Alarms still blaring, lights a dizzying strobe.

"I'm *stuck.*"

But the rumbling had eased.

"Oh God, Freddie *I'm stuck!*"

The girder . . . Have to somehow lift the Goddamned girder.

"Daddy?" From right beside him.

"Help me out, little buddy." The kid's assistance would be of little or no use. But it would give him something to do.

Freddie fumbled for purchase along the bottom of the beam, lifted with all his might. A fierce pride swelled in his heart as his son growled with effort, bony knees bent, bird muscles rippling, heaving alongside his father.

The girder held fast.

Freddie stood back. *(Daddy?)* Think. *(Daddy?!)*

Think!

A lever of some sort.

Stephanie groaning.

He scanned the ruined garage.

What are you doing, Daddy?

There! A work truck a few spaces down and across the aisle from them. Laden with disassembled scaffolding.

"Get me one of those poles!"

"What for?"

"Stevie!"

The boy bolted. Another tremor crescendoed and fell. Freddie studiously ignored it. Lime dust bit at his sinuses.

Stephanie, through gasps: "What are you doing?"

Freddie didn't answer. He located an ice-chest-sized chunk of rubble. Adrenaline surging, he heaved it like a sack of sugar. Laid it toward the low end of the girder.

"Here!" Stevie. Already back with the scaffolding. Good boy. *Good boy!*

Freddie wedged the pole under the beam, laid it across the impromptu fulcrum. "When I lift, you help your mother." He glanced at Stephanie. "Ready?"

She nodded, panting through pursed lips. Freddie was catapulted back to the day Stevie was born. *(Push!)*

He bore down on the makeshift lever. His son grimaced with effort, Stephanie grunting, straining in vain to birth her legs from the wreckage womb.

The stubborn beam stayed put.

Freddie ignored the alarms. Shut his eyes to the blinking lights. Rejected the pain in his bloody hands. He dropped all his weight, summoned every ounce of strength . . .

And the girder moved. Only a budge, but it *moved.*

"It's working!" Stevie or Stephanie? Doesn't matter. Go. *Go!* He strained harder still.

"Hey!" They were laughing joyously. "It's—"

The scaffolding bent. Creased right at the fulcrum. The end in his hand plummeted. Freddie crumbled, busted his elbow. He snarled in pain.

The rumble returned. The worst yet. Somewhere deep in the garage, a fuel tank ruptured, exploded. Nauseous black smoke billowed up, swirling around the guardrail like a gangrenous ghost. It flooded their level, heated the air, poisoned their lungs. Visibility obscured, eyes burning . . .

Think. *Think!* How to lift an impossibly heavy object. Lever? *(Fail)* Inclined plane? *(Not applicable)* House Jack?

Car jack!

From somewhere below, the crackle of a fire, the acrid stink of burning tires.

The fissure beneath the Cayenne sprouted branches. An arm of the web skittered under Freddie's feet. He could feel the concrete separating.

Block it out.

Bolt to the cargo door.

Locked. Electronics dead. Keys jammed under the crumpled dash.

Freddie sprinted for the scaffolding truck. Peered into the cab. *(Daddy?)* Tried the door. Locked. Chambered his elbow.

With one devastating blow, the glass disintegrated. *(Freddie!)* Opened the door. Popped the seat. *(Hurry!)*

Freddie rose with the car jack.

At the far end of the level, a section of garage floor slowly tilted like an adjustable bed. Tilted *out.* Freddie stopped in his tracks. The car parked there eased slowly forward, smashed through the guardrail, disappeared over the edge. Gone forever. Just . . . gone.

Three seconds later, a distant wrenching of metal and smashing glass split the air. He thought he heard flames erupt.

Freddie bolted for the Cayenne. He didn't remember setting up the jack, only found himself pumping insanely.

"Daddy help me."

He kept pumping.

"Freddie!"

Kept pumping . . .

"Daddy!" Right at his side.

"What!?"

"She's free!"

The crumpled Great White dash had relaxed its bite enough to allow Steph to part her legs slightly, free of the steering wheel.

"You did it baby!" Tears cut jagged paths through the dust on her face.

Freddie grasped her arms.

Stephanie wriggled her hips, flexed her legs. Inching her way out. "I swear I'll never complain about your Jerry-rigging again." She laughed nervously as she struggled. "Not ever again, baby."

As Freddie tugged, metallic teeth in plastic jaws bit at Stephanie's legs.

She screamed.

Freddie relented.

The rumble was building again.

"It's-okay-it's-okay! Just pull. *PULL!*"

The floor dropped another several feet. No, not the whole floor. Just the section supporting the Cayenne.

They were afloat aboard a jagged ice flow—now sinking—in a sea of dissolving concrete. The growing crack revealed a Honda Civic burning several floors below.

Freddie's stomach flipped. *Where are the other floors?*

The beam and jack remained undisturbed, opening more space between the girder and the SUV. Freddie renewed his efforts, ignoring Stephanie's cursing and shouts of pain. *(I can see the crown . . . There's the head . . . One—more—big— PUSH!)*

"Freddie!"

The aggregate-packed ice flow broke free of the raging concrete current. The car plummeted; Stephanie's hand slipped away. The Cayenne—atop the stone glacier—floated through space . . . shrinking . . . falling . . . seemingly forever . . .

Freddie teetered on the edge of the abyss. Watching in shock. Steph's torso hung out the window, hair and blouse billowing, face a mask of horror. Shrieking. Eye's locked on Freddie's.

The car smashed to a stop. Choked off Stephanie's scream. Insanely, over the impact, a single merry tinkle of the bicycle bell.

The entire hood section had either crumpled or was buried to the front doors. Steph's body lay limp in the detritus. Fathoms below.

"Steph?" His voice cracked.

There was no answer.

A person could survive this. Okay, not likely, but there was hope. He clung desperately to hope.

The tailgate popped open as if by a ghostly hand. The bicycle lay there, perfectly intact, glimmering through the dust and smoke like a beacon. A *sign*. They'd laugh about this later.

She'd be okay.

The car exploded.

Two seconds later, the heat wave knocked Freddie back from the edge, rudely onto his ass. He sat there, stunned. Realized he was in shock. Almost laughed.

Time passed. Minutes? Seconds? He woke to more rumbles. Creaking. Groaning. Smoke. Heat.

"Daaad!" Strangely muted. Echoing as if from a celestial post.

"DAAAAD!"

"Stevie?" Where *was* he? *"Ste*vie*!"*

"Down here!"

Freddie scrambled on hands and knees back to the gaping hole. His stomach flipped. The flaming coffin car was nestled at the bottom of a gargantuan satanic sculpture of wreckage and destruction.

Grief.

Tossed cars were floating bodies after a shipwreck, slabs of concrete like displaced islands, all streaked with blood and oil . . . Pipes and boulders, stone and steel . . .

There beneath him, seemingly miles away, clinging desperately to a strand of rebar over the fiery abyss, dangled his son. His precious son. Stevie.

Freddie leaned over, extended his hand. Couldn't reach. He plopped onto his belly. Still couldn't reach. Scooted dangerously over the edge . . . as far as he dared . . . stretched . . . groping desperately . . .

Got him!

The heat was unbearable. He didn't notice at the time. Later, he'd be treated for burns.

Freddie found himself staring at a parking sign at the mall: *Remember your spot! D27.* It was as if the parking structure from the past had been at one moment a shambles, the next renewed. He didn't even recall driving up the ramp, and wondered how he hadn't crashed. He looked over at Zoe, and his heart melted.

"You had him?"

"I had him."

"So what happened? Where is he?"

Freddie's eyes faded. His lips moved but nothing came out. He traveled to a past he was no longer sure existed. "Stevie blamed me."

"What do you mean?"

"It was on me to save her. I failed." He nodded once, owning his guilt. Period. End of story. Case closed. "Stevie couldn't take it." He took a breath and let it out. "So he left." He slowly shook his head. "If only I'd . . . If only . . ."

Hand in hand, seemingly galaxies away, a mother and young daughter strolled past behind them. The girl's lively chatter echoed through the structure, muted by the walls of the van.

Freddie descended to earth. Found himself clinging to Zoe's gaze. He was lost, as he had been for a decade. Her eyes were a beacon in the mist, showing him the way back home.

"Freddie?"

"Yeah?"

Eyebrows knitted, she was doing it again. Waltzing right into his head. "I see you."

Entranced, he could not look away.

"I *know* you, Freddie." She chuffed. "More than makes any kind of sense."

He just nodded.

"Not everything, not even a lot yet, but this much is clear to me."

"Yeah?" He liked the word *yet*.

"If *you* couldn't save her?" She shook her head once. "Then no one could."

Freddie's chin quivered. He took a deep breath and blew it out. "Thanks for saying it, Zoe."

She nodded once as a *You're welcome*. "Now—"

"Yeah?"

"Let's *do it!*" She punched his shoulder with a wink.

Freddie shook his head and conjured a smile.

-Sushi-

They were upstairs at Sunset Place, a billion-dollar, two-story, open-air shopping destination. It featured diverse dining options and every kind of store imaginable: Fashion shops, casual clothing, pet stores, toy places, even an AMC theater with sixteen screens.

Due to the popularity of the mall, rental rates for shop space were through the roof. If you found something you liked, it was best to buy it immediately. The next day the store in which you found it could well be gone—replaced overnight by something utterly different, as if by industrious elves.

A stone-lined stream circulated throughout, so natural in appearance it seemed as if the structure had been built around it. Waterfalls fussed with fountains, an endless buoyant babbling.

Freddie was waiting outside a dressing room at Old Navy, bombarded by a techno groove blasting from the overhead speakers. Everyone seemed fine with it. It made Freddie nervous. Occasionally, raised voices wafted in from outside. Probably kids horsing around on the sidewalk.

He wondered when Muzak had changed from Roberta Flack to these acid-rush, mechanically-generated beat-riffs. He guessed he'd been absent for the transition.

"This'll do," Zoe said, appearing at his side. She was wearing beige belted cargo pants, cinched to her ankles. She'd tucked in her new olive-green t-shirt. A pair of black tactical boots completed the ensemble. Made of leather and nylon, they appeared both flexible and durable. She looked sharp.

And to Freddie, beautiful.

He could conjure not an ounce of interest in the sick kitten type. He supposed that was due to his own placid nature. Despite his size, within his chest beat the heart of a lamb.

Nature abhors a vacuum; strives always to even the scales. So perhaps it was only to the heart of a lion that he could be drawn, in order for balance to be achieved.

They checked out then stepped through the exit. A shopping bag hung from each of their left hands. Freddie's bag between them. As subtly as possible, he switched his bag to his right, leaving his left hand available.

Zoe's hands remained at her side.

Sparrows flitted about, ever vigilant for spilled popcorn or other treats. Mothers pushed strollers, and children played chase around the pavilion. Helium balloons were everywhere.

They'd been at it a few hours, and it was about dinner time. "Feel like Don Shula's?" Freddie suggested.

"How about Japanese take out? You eat sushi?"

Freddie chuckled. "Look at me. I'll eat anything."

"Cool with you if we take it back to your place and eat while we play checkers or something?"

"Sounds like a plan."

Sushi sacks and shopping bags bulging in their arms, their footsteps echoed through the parking garage.

"That sushi chef was awesome." Zoe stared at the pavement ahead. "You see the way he chatted us up as if we were the first people he'd seen in weeks? All the while slicing that fish like a surgeon?" She shook her head and grinned. "I love Japanese culture. The honor, respect, discipline—That's how it used to be anyway."

Had they passed a brass band belting out a Rumba, Freddie doubted she'd have even noticed. He was touched to see her finally let her guard down a little with him.

"It's a shame," she said. "For the last few decades, the influence of the west has been flooding in there. Instead of hakamas, they got jeans now. Instead of sushi joints, there's a McDonald's on every corner. Gone are all but a few dojos, replaced by gangs. Just like the good old U.S. of A." She shook her head and winced.

The wonderful mélange emanating from the takeout was slightly tainted by a hint of exhaust fumes. Old Mable sat in a space ahead and to the left, the driver's side visible to them.

Freddie slowed—then came to a halt.

Zoe forged ahead, still engrossed in her dialogue. Realizing her companion was no longer at her side, she stopped mid-sentence as she glanced up and turned to see what was delaying him. "What?" She shrugged with a half smile.

Leaning against the van door, arms crossed casually over his bulk, was a man about the size of a compact car. Dazzling rings flashed in brilliant contrast with the black leather jacket sleeves over which they rested. Stretched to the limit, the seams screamed for relief. Freddie's mind replayed the last thing he'd heard him say as he entered the strip bar:

Welcome to BT's enjoy y'self.

-The Others-

The scene switched, and Bruce found himself peering out the viewing port of what was apparently the orange craft from the deck of the carrier. He'd never seen—much less been in—a submarine with exterior windows.

Words barely discernable over the ambient noise of the engines, he could nevertheless tell the voices aboard ship struggled to contain their excitement. The camera panned around the research team, each member waving and smiling.

Without a doubt civilians, a few wore ponytails and unruly beards. Several appeared beady-eyed through thick eyeglasses. Some wore t-shirts bearing science symbols and jokes, only one of which was legible: *Science: It's like magic, but real.* All were tucked into what appeared to be spacesuits; the upper portions trailed behind them.

The camera returned to the viewing ports, this time aimed at the leviathan hulls on the surface. Each churning prop was the size of an SUV. Silhouetted by the diffused sunlight from above, the inverted waves crashing against the iron mountains were disorienting. Bruce wanted to look away to ease his vertigo, but he sat transfixed.

As the sub descended, the camera lowered to eye level. He gasped at the monolithic dull-gray tube suspended mid-ocean no more than fifty yards Starboard: an Ohio class nuclear submarine. Although he was familiar with the vessel, its presence seemed alien in this space.

Aircraft carriers were never deployed alone, but rather as the key member of a Strike Group. These floating cities of steel were escorted by a contingent of other warships and supply vessels, all of which he'd seen on the surface. The only member of the group as yet unaccounted for was the giant before him.

The team was necessary in order for an operation to be carried out. The armament of the Nimitz class carrier was made up of short-range defensive weapons useful only as a last line of defense.

As are all surface ships, the carrier is particularly vulnerable to attack from below. A Nimitz class was insanely expensive and hard to replace—a strategically valuable asset. Therefore, logically, the ship had a significant target value as well.

As a result of this value and vulnerability, the strike group always included at least one submarine. The other vessels provided additional defensive capabilities such as long-range Tomahawk missiles or the Aegis Combat System.

A typical Strike Group may include, in addition to an aircraft carrier, frigates, guided missile cruisers and guided missile destroyers, one or two attack submarines—and ammunition, oiler, and supply ships of Military Sealift Command to provide logistical support.

The precise structure and number of each type ship could vary between groups depending on the objective of the deployment.

While the sub on which Bruce was "riding" was civilian, its function scientific, this was most certainly a military operation, the importance of which could not be overstated. The operating expense for a strike group was around seven million dollars—*per day*. Even considering the government's propensity for waste, that kind of money would not be spent unless the mission was of a critical nature.

What the hell were they doing down here?

Deep in the darkness now, the chatter aboard the explorer diminished and took on a more subdued, even apprehensive tone. Fish and creatures like swimming Volkswagens glided lazily through the halogen beams cleaving the darkness. Some nosed the thick glass, lifeless eyes staring blindly. Sensing nothing edible, they turned slithering into the depths.

Although he viewed the scene from the safety of a computer screen, Bruce shuddered.

Down they went, inexorably down, like Jesus descending to His three-day sentence in hell. With each passing fathom, the marine life took on new strangeness—then disappeared altogether as if instinct warned them of what lay below. Absent this instinct, or ignoring it, man always seemed to blunder ahead where no creature dared go. What atrocities in man's history could have been avoided had we heeded nature's warnings?

A few minutes later, miles below any hint of sunlight, something began to materialize in the ambient glow of the spotlights. Something on the seabed—something foreign and *wrong*—a dead thing, seething at light, thriving in darkness. Like a siren song, it seemingly called out—quietly, sweetly—then more insistently as the crushing depths swallowed them.

At first made up only of murky shadows, the structure slowly resolved. Points of strange towers and thick antennae rose toward the sub, looming. Each shape was distorted by decades—perhaps centuries—of coral on the surfaces, infected fingers of a long dead giant groping desperately for oxygen and light.

As the sub descended, the fingers seemed to close in on it. There was no way to even guess at the structure's size; it faded into murkiness in all directions. It most certainly dwarfed any craft floating above—or any of which Bruce was even aware. However, the overall geometric slope of its base and strange excrescences thereon left little doubt this was put here by something other than nature.

The sub slowed its descent and trudged forward. More protrusions, serving God knows what purpose, appeared in the port windows then vanished as they passed, only to be replaced by others, all different but equally strange.

They were approaching a light. It silhouetted the spears, lending them a ghostly aspect. Each cast haunting shadows that bled into the darkness. As the light neared, Bruce realized this was a man-made luminance. They'd apparently burrowed some sort of station into this . . . city? Is that what it was? The ancient infrastructure of some aquatic civilization long past? But a civilization of whom? Or what?

Or had it come from somewhere else?

The idea of alien weaponry and even superior intelligence didn't much bother him. Sure, we may endure a pounding. But sooner or later, mankind would figure a way to defeat any enemy of which it could conceive.

But what about life beyond our comprehension, to which we were utterly oblivious? Like a character is to the author who created him? It was a big universe out there. Eventually, our paths would cross with The Others.

They'd write us out of existence with no more mercy than a writer shows for the distraught mother who decides to hang her children in *Act III*—then herself; beet-faced and gagging, she twitches there, staring at her babies, wondering what had come over her, why on earth she'd thrown it all away.

Sweat formed on Bruce's upper lip.

There were two airlocks on the station: one for docking, the other sealed to the structure. The latter suggested this drowned behemoth was hollow and secreted something within.

The sub slowed almost to an idle . . . then finally bumped against the docking station. Bruce's stomach dipped with the camera. The pilot began tethering procedures with someone on the other end of the radio. The camera shook as the vessel slid first port . . . then starboard . . . reversed, changed pitch, crept forward, ever so gradually . . . then bumped the docking station and stuck. More radio chatter, apparently coordinated with the soft mechanical whirring, clicking, and metallic banging from deeper in the sub.

The engines slowed to a stop.

The shot panned to the pilot. He sat between two technicians. As the crew shut down their consoles and removed their headphones, the pilot stood, turned to face the camera and said solemnly, "It's time."

-Rattle Click Snap-

"You're leaning on my ride." She relieved herself of all cargo but the takeout, eyes locked with the bouncer's.

"Zoe," Freddie cautioned. He began easing toward her.

Tank just looked on, deadpan. He made no move to take his weight off the driver's door.

Zoe turned to Freddie, but never far enough that the van was out of her peripheral. "What. We supposed to just stand here twiddling our thumbs until 'Roid-Rage finishes his nap?"

Tank: "You know the rules, Star. No boyfriends. Why you wanna go causin' problems?"

Freddie appeared behind Zoe. "Hey, look. We don't want any problems. We just—"

"You done *got* problems. You best shut the fuck up before you make 'em worse."

She turned back to Tank. "The name's Zoe, *asshole*. And if you're the problem, I'm the solution. So why don't you take a step back before I solve your fat ass?"

"Now, *that's* funny!" From behind them.

Freddie snapped his head toward the voice. The accomplice was about half the size of his partner at the van—but his Dahmer smile was surgeon's smile, a mirthless smile under jackal eyes.

Then to Freddie's dismay, a third tough unfolded from an electric-blue classic Plymouth behind the smaller man, even as a blade rattled open in the hand of the latter. The smiler unconsciously toyed with the weapon—a butterfly knife, Freddie thought it was called. Open-shut-open *(rattle click snap)*; he seemed not even to realize he was doing it.

"Zoe?"

"Yeah, I see them." Her eyes remained locked on Tank.

(Rattle click snap)

Big Man from the Plymouth: *"Pokey!"*

"What? I ain't doing nothing."

"Just . . . be cool, alright?"

"I'm cool!" *(Rattle click snap)*

Big Man turned his attention to Zoe. "Hey, Jules. How you doing?" His soothing tone spoke more than his words, conveyed a genuine desire to de-escalate the situation. He wore a thin tie neatly clipped to a bleached-white shirt under a black suit jacket, from which he produced that bed-sheet-sized hanky and wiped non-existent sweat from his brow. "You just be cool now. You know we gotta take you to see Paxyl, but I make sure everything turn out okay."

"Paxyl?" Zoe scoffed. "What's that, a Lego character?"

(Rattle click snap)

Tank's eyes flicked to Big Man's. Big Man stared back at him. The smiler—evidently "Pokey"—seemed only amused and continued fidgeting the blade. Freddie looked from one of them to the other.

Big Man, clearly the friendliest of the group, shook his head and raised his eyebrows. "Now, Jules, we gonna pretend we didn't hear that, alright? Just . . . get on in the car now."

Freddie's veins flooded with battery acid.

Zoe was cool as ice cubes. She seemed aware of everyone present, and their positions: Tank at the van, Freddie directly behind her, Pokey five steps beyond that, Big Man behind the open door of the Plymouth, one foot still inside—even a passel of noisy teenagers making their way into the garage. She'd probably taken a headcount of the kids. Hell, Freddie was certain of it.

Tank said mockingly, "Yeah, *Zoe,* get your ass in the car. *Now.*"

(Rattle click snap)

She'd decided Tank was the leader, so she ignored everyone but him.

Freddie's father had once given him a lecture on confronting a gang of bullies. The same lecture, he supposed, every kid heard sooner or later: *Determine who the leader is and hit him just as hard as you can. When the others see him go down, they'll cut and run.* Freddie couldn't help but add, *probably.* It was the *probably* that worried him, if this woman was about to do what he thought she was about to do.

She started toward Tank.

"Zoe!"

Tank shoved himself away from the van and turned to face her. He seemed to stiffen as if something rabid approached him. Freddie supposed that was actually kind of the case.

Somewhere on a lower level, the chirp of a car lock, the carefree laughter of kids on their way to a movie or toy shopping. *Only one floor down,* he thought, *life goes on.*

Zoe screamed, like Geronimo as he launched his final flight. Freddie thought for an instant she was going to ram the guy. Crazy.

A split second before she did just that, Tank's hands rose.

The takeout bag dropped to the floor. Zoe spun and knelt. Facing away from her opponent. She hammered the butt of her fist just above his knee. Tank bent and howled in pain. Zoe *exploded* up and slammed the back of her head into his face.

Only then did Freddie realize a chopstick bristled from Tank's thigh. Skewed sideways, it had apparently grazed the femur. Just above the knee. Or maybe it had broken on impact; he couldn't tell.

As Tank staggered backwards, Zoe bent for the takeout. Why would she choose now to recover their dinner? As Tank steadied himself, Zoe snatched something from the bag.

Ah. Miso soup.

Hot Miso soup.

Tank blinked himself back to awareness, nose gushing—and Zoe was there.

She kicked at his crotch. His hands dropped reflexively. Although the block was successful, it was Tank's undoing. Zoe could have cared less whether her kick landed.

She just needed his hands down.

With another rebel yell, she clapped her hands into his ears as if crashing cymbals during the grand finale of a Beethoven symphony.

In her right hand, the steaming bowl.

Tank screamed. He turned away, his shovel-sized hands trembling before him.

Freddie sensed more than saw Pokey slipping by. Into his head flashed the surgeon smile, the predator eyes.

He'd seen ungodly cuts on worksites. Flesh laid open like a Christmas turkey. He pictured gushing blood, severed tendons. Hideous scars.

He was a fixer, not a fighter. Pokey was comfortable with violence. Seemed thrilled by it. So if Freddie let this turn into a sparring match, he was finished.

His body tensed. His heart seized up.

He spun counterclockwise just as hard as he could. Right arm outstretched. Lined up with Pokey's throat.

The firewood diameter clothesline snapped Pokey's head back like a Pez dispenser. The bouncer's feet kept running on autopilot toward the scuffle. The pavement smacked the back of his head and craned his neck with a sickening thud. His alligator shoes dead-stopped to the concrete.

Freddie gawked at the limp body. His breath came in ragged gasps. He rested his hands on his knees and tried to dim the lightshow building behind his eyes.

Zoe: *"Damn* it! That was *hot!"* As if all was well, she examined her hand as she strolled back toward Freddie.

Tank rose behind her and shook his head, slinging blood-swirled Miso onto the van. His left eye was an angry lump.

Freddie gasped.

Tank roared, thumbed open the jacket with his left hand.

Like a machine on overdrive, Zoe turned on her heel and marched determinedly back toward the monster. Not running but with measured haste. She stepped on the takeout bag, not even seeming to notice. Freddie imagined the destroyed flesh within.

Tank drew the Glock. Late by a millisecond. As the 9 reached Zoe's face, her left hand blocked it away. Monkey-pawed the slide. Fingers and thumb over the pistol and away from her. Tank's gun in her left hand, his lapel in her right, she vaulted up and head-butted his already-battered face.

Even as she landed, she wrenched the pistol inward. Twisted it clockwise. Pinkie now toward Tank.

His trigger finger bent backwards at an impossible angle.

She snatched the Glock out of his hand as he tipped like a falling sequoia. Freddie's gaze fixed on the knuckle skin gathered at the end of Tank's pointer, wire-stripped by the trigger guard.

Tank smashed to the pavement. Zoe pounced. Straddled him.

She jammed the gun in his face—and squeezed the trigger without so much as a flinch.

Click.

"What?" She examined the pistol. "You don't even keep one in the *chamber?*" She snatched the slide. "When you're coming for *me?*" She returned the muzzle to his face. "Here's how this works, asshole." She squeezed the trigger, unblinkingly, to within an ounce of transforming this mishap into a complete disaster, beyond which there could be no return . . .

"ZOE!"

Freddie's voice echoed around the parking garage. The gun hovered at Tank's nose. Unfired, still cool to the touch.

Silence, save for the rumble of cars navigating the ramps below, a muted horn in the distance.

Each of the teenagers held a cell phone before them. Frozen, goggle-eyed, they watched the show from their screens.

"Ah, hell, Freddie." Zoe's eyes stayed locked on the bouncer. "We're just havin' a little fun here." She raised the weapon and released the magazine. It slid out and bounced off the man's chest, rattled to the floor. Eyes squeezed shut, head lolling on the concrete, Tank didn't even seem to notice.

She racked the gun, sent the brass spiraling. As the bullet thumped the van, she thumbed a lever, freed the slide, stripped the barrel, loosed the spring . . .

She tossed the whole mess over her shoulder. In the stillness, the clinking of metal on concrete was deafening. She smacked Tank's face in mock affection, then stood.

Freddie remembered the kids and whipped his head around. "Guys. What are you doing?"

The teens just stared. Phones lowered.

Freddie held a shrug in a *what-the-hell* gesture. *"Beat it, man!"*

They hightailed it.

Freddie fished his own cell from his pocket. "I'm calling the cops." He dialed 9-1—   .

"I wouldn't do that." Big Man. He'd eased up behind them.

Freddie flinched and turned, poised to fight. Big Man froze with his hands raised. One held the handkerchief like a white flag, having apparently just completed another wipe-down.

Seeing him in daylight, Freddie was shocked at his size. A good bit heavier than even he himself, the man was intimidating. But his kempt dress and calm demeanor belied any threat.

When Freddie relaxed, Big Man cautiously moved forward. "Paxyl, he smart." The handkerchief disappeared into his suit jacket. "There was a murder."

Zoe appeared at Freddie's side. "So?"

Everything was cool for the moment, and Freddie prayed it would stay that way. Pokey stirred and groaned through sealed eyelids.

"Freddie, your DNA at the scene."

Freddie and Zoe shared a glance then looked back to Big Man.

"How can that be?" Freddie asked.

Zoe's eyes were on the bouncer, but she spoke to Freddie. "Your shower drain. Or your comb, or your pillow."

For a moment it didn't compute. Then it did.

"That's right," Big Man said. "It don't take much. Just a few hairs in her hand like she tried to fight you off."

Freddie's head was spinning.

"Long as there's no match for the DNA, you be alright. But if they ever decide to take a sample from you—like if somebody make a call?"

Freddie knew how it would go. Police were overloaded. Dramatically so. There were piles of rap sheets, mountains of case files. Few would ever see the light of day, much less be solved. They had to sleep with that. He imagined few of them slept well.

"Yeah, well," Zoe said. "That's a two-way street. I could start singing a song about prostitution and trafficking, get them sniffing around BT's. Then they might start seeing that evidence for the bullshit it is. Whatdya think?"

If the police managed to actually *close* a case? With something solid like DNA evidence? To secure a charge that actually stuck? That would go down like a spoonful of vanilla ice cream.

Big Man said, "You could do that, Jules—or Zoe if that's what you callin' yourself now."

"It is."

Whatever appeal Freddie could assemble from prison would fall on deaf ears. They'd have their trophy and would not willingly give it up. Within a year, they'd no longer even remember his name.

"But wouldn't it be easier just to go back to how things was? You got a job, I got a job, Paxyl happy, everybody happy."

Freddie saw that Zoe was addressing this with cold calculation. He felt lucky to have her by his side, and thankful she was *on* his side.

"Weeell, see now, that's the thing." She shook her head once. "I'm *not* happy. Not at BT's." As if she even remembered the place.

Big Man took a long hard look at her. "You changed, Jules. What happened to you?"

"I got wise. Shouldn't you do the same?"

"Yeah, well—" He shrugged.

"Yeah well *what?* Just get out."

"It ain't that easy, Jules. Where am I gonna go? What am I gonna do, huh?"

Big Man seemed comfortable confiding in the woman. Freddie supposed it was to the mild-mannered poet that he bared his soul, like perhaps they shared some history. Or maybe the new, bolder split had earned his trust; Freddie couldn't tell.

"I don't like some the things Paxyl does, but he take good care of me. He take good care of you again too, if you let him."

Freddie finally piped in. "You mean after her *punishment?*"

"Like I said. I don't like some the things—"

"How about this, big man." Zoe had tumbled to his handle without realizing it. "I don't fuck with you guys, you don't fuck with me. Cool?"

"Fine by me, but you know Paxyl don't—"

"I'll take that as a yes." Then to Freddie, "Come on. Let's order pizza."

Big Man stood watching as she gathered the Old Navy bags and carried them to the van. Freddie was waiting with the rear cargo door open. She threw in the packages.

Freddie slammed the door, then turned to Big Man. "Uh. Sorry about this. Take care." Now *that* sounded stupid. He wished he'd said something else, or nothing at all.

Big Man remained motionless as they backed out, and still didn't budge as Freddie threw it in drive and crept past.

As they pulled away, Freddie checked his rearview. Big Man strained his suit pants as he bent to Pokey, wiping the back of his neck with the hanky as he knelt.

CHAPTER FOUR

STRANGE

-Tenzi-

"It's called Tenzi. You roll your dice, hoping for as many of the number you chose as possible," Freddie said. "You collect and set aside the ones that land on that number, then roll the ones you have left. You repeat this until your dice are all set aside. Meanwhile, I'm doing the same with mine. Whoever finishes first wins."

They sat facing each other on the living room floor, a pizza box containing only crusts to the side.

"You choose your number before you start?"

Shaded lamps set their faces aglow but left every corner shrouded in darkness. "Actually, no. You roll all ten dice the first time, look them over, and choose whatever you have most of. Then that's your number."

Between them, twenty dotted cubes cast red and green shadows on the tile. It was about 9:30 p.m.

"Don't we need a ref?" Zoe's eyes narrowed. "If I'm concentrating on *my* dice, how do I know you're being honest?"

In the distance, a low rumble heralded a storm to come, stirring the racial memories of anyone under a roof. Every house was a warm cave, every primal inhabitant fearful of the pending lightning as they huddled in their dry redoubts.

"Honor system. You'll just have to trust me."

"And *you'll* just have to trust *me.*" She conjured her best Arnold Schwarzenegger. "Biiiig mistake."

The impersonation was far more charming to him than it should have been. "Okay, ready?"

"Ready."

Rattles muted in their cupped hands, they stared each other down like gunslingers.

"*Go!*"

The cubes clattered to the floor.

"Fives! Seven left!" Zoe deftly gathered the fives, slid them aside and scooped up the rest.

"Threes!" Freddie followed the same steps.

"Five left!"

(Slide-scoop-rattle)

"Six left!"

"Three left!"

"Ha-haaa, *two* left!"

They both scooped and dropped in quick succession until Freddie shouted "DONE!"

"Oh you *so* cheated!"

"What? You think my dice are loaded? Think I use them to stalk the alleys at night cheating homeless guys out of their day's take?"

"Yeah well. How about we switch then? You're green and I'll take the red."

With another, more insistent volley, the battlefield in the distance advanced.

Freddie asked, "So, were you scared at all back there? With those guys at the mall?"

Zoe slid the red to her, the green to Freddie. "Sure I was."

Freddie collected his new color. "Didn't seem like it. It seemed like you almost . . . enjoyed it."

She chuckled, fidgeted. "I don't enjoy violence. I'm just—" She shrugged. "—good at it."

"How do you know that?"

"Wasn't it obvious?" She said it in a hushed tone, as if she were ashamed of her ability to fight, regretful she'd had to do what she did.

"You were going to kill that guy, Zoe."

She locked eyes with Freddie. "He was going to kill us. At the very least, had they gotten me in that car, I had some serious pain coming."

"What makes you say that?"

She propped on one arm. "Pokey and Tank? They're damaged goods. Gone to the dark side, never coming back. Big Man? He's okay. He's just . . . stuck. Or thinks he is."

"How can you know all that?"

"I don't know how. I just . . . know." She sighed. "Look, I didn't like it, Freddie. I just . . . I just relinquished control and the training took over."

Freddie raised his eyebrows. "Training? Got some memories rattling around back there?"

She stared at the dice, sliding them absently with her finger. "Kind of . . . not really. It's just . . . once I realized we were in trouble, 'it' just took over."

"It?" Freddie fidgeted his own dice, focused on the woman.

She shrugged. "It's like . . . a switch threw in my head and I went into attack mode. I guess I see there's a reason for it, some explanation lodged in my head somewhere—but the images are foggy, the voices all muted."

Freddie chose silence. Maybe a breakthrough was imminent.

"Under threat, attack what's attacking you. With all other options exhausted, the most aggressive gets to live. He who hesitates dies." She knitted her eyebrows and stared at the dice.

"That's some heavy shit. Sounds like military training."

She peered slyly up at him. "Sounds to me like you're delaying." She scooped up her dice, threw them to the floor. "Sixes! Seven left!"

"You jumped the gun. Fives. *Six* left!"

"Four left!"

"Four left!"

"One left!"

Freddie scooped and rolled, scooped and rolled . . .

"Done!"

"Waaaait wait-wait-wait, Brucette Lee. That was a little *too* fast."

They both laughed. Whoever she was, whatever her past, it was clear she carried a burden. She was in desperate need of downtime, and he was happy to be sharing some with her. Maybe this was good therapy for DID.

Maybe not.

Regardless, this was nice.

"Too fast for *you*," she challenged.

"Tell you what. Let's do it like this." He leaned back, straightened his right leg and wrestled his cell from his pocket. It took a moment . . .

"Having some trouble there, board head?"

Diffused by the curtains, the first flashes of light gilded the windows, accompanied by spatters on the roof—residual shrapnel from liquid mortars in the distance.

Freddie finally retrieved the phone, tapped the screen and slid his thumb a few times. He set it face up with the stopwatch app open. "How about we take turns timing it?"

"Fine. You're still going to lose, mister. I got the hang of this now." She slid the phone around, oriented to her. "You first. Ready?"

Freddie scooped up his dice and started rattling.

"Go!"

He made his throw. "Fours!"

"I'm watching, numb nails."

"And distracting me. Six left." Freddie rolled and scooped in vain, growled in frustration. "Four left."

Three more failed rolls, then "Three left."

(Rattle-roll-scoop, Rattle-roll-scoop)

"Done!"

Zoe consulted the stopwatch. "Eighteen seconds. Pretty pathetic, Handy Heinie. No offense."

"Offense definitely taken. Your turn." He took the phone and cleared the readout. "Ready?"

Zoe collected her dice. "I was born ready, baby."

"Go!"

The cubes hit the tile. "Sixes again. Seven left."

"Now who's stating the obvious?"

She rolled again. "Three left!"

"Okay, that was just lucky."

One final roll, then, "Done!"

Six seconds flat. He sat stunned, entranced by the steadily increasing rataplan from above. He'd played a lot of Tenzi in his past life, but never had he seen a round like this. "Whoa. Now that was just . . . freaky."

"Not freaky. Skills, hammer head. Your turn."

Freddie did not relinquish the phone. "No, you go again."

She did *gimme* fingers. "Give me the phone."

"No seriously. I've got to see that again." He smiled slyly. "If you can do it again, that is."

Zoe shrugged. "Okay, no problem. But it ain't gonna change anything, *loser.*" She said it with a half grin, collecting the dice as Freddie prepped the stopwatch.

They locked eyes. Freddie could have sat there like that all night.

"Something wrong, Mr. Timer?"

He shook himself out of it. *"Go!"*

The dice fell. "Threes! Five left!"

Freddie gawked.

"Done!" she cried, then whooped with delight.

The light flashing in the windows silhouetted blue trickles sliding like tears down the glass, followed seconds later by a volley of angry cannon balls rolling nearer.

Freddie shook his head.

Zoe just laughed, delighted at her luck. After a beat, Freddie chuffed and shook his head. "Okay seriously. How'd you do that?"

"Just talent. Wanna see it again?"

Rumbles rattled the walls, and the intermittent splats on the roof segued to a chatter.

Freddie said, "Ready?"

"Hang on, let me get in the zone . . ." She rattled the cubes in her cupped palms, eyes closed in mock concentration. "Okay, ready."

"Go!"

The dice bounced to the floor. This time, each spun like a top with an energy uncharacteristic of the game pieces. Thunder like a cannon startled Freddie, but he sat transfixed. For several seconds, no cube stopped. Possible but . . . unusual. Then three turned up fives. Then another, then two more. Zoe scooped up the remaining four, dropped them immediately. Three dead-stopped on fives as if they'd landed on glue strips. The final dice spun for a second, then toppled once, twice . . . too slowly to be explained by gravity . . . then landed on five.

A shiver crept up Freddie's spine.

"You gonna press stop?"

They both stared at the dice.

"Okay," said Freddie. "Maybe it *is* the dice. Try the green ones again." He was grasping at straws. The dice in the Tenzi set were normal. It was not the dice.

Still . . .

They exchanged cubes.

Blue light flooded the room then vanished, shortly followed by a crash as thunder split the night.

This time, more somber, Freddie said, "Ready?"

Zoe held the dice clamped in her fist. "I don't know, Freddie."

"It's freaky, but they're just dice. Concentrate like you did before."

"I wasn't really concentrating. Just kidding around."

"Well, concentrate anyway." He waited while she took a breath and closed her eyes—then opened them. "Okay, ready."

"Go."

She rolled the dice. They spun out of control, twirling like cubed green flamenco dancers. She locked in on them, focused, eyebrows knitted. Two skittered to a stop. "Snake eyes," she said.

The remaining eight kept spinning like gyroscopes; it seemed they'd go on forever.

Zoe focused harder still.

Two more ones. Then three more . . . then two . . .

"Whoa." Freddie set the phone aside.

The last dice slowed, balanced on a corner . . . landed five up . . . then tipped slowly over to one.

Zoe looked up. "Yeah, that's definitely freaky."

Freddie realized he could hear the wall clock ticking, even over the noise of the storm—something he hadn't noticed until now. "What's your lucky number?" The chatter above transformed into skeins of rain.

"Add up the dots on any two facing sides of a dice. That's my lucky number."

Freddie picked one up, examined each side. "Well I'll be damned."

With a blinding flash and startling blast from the heavens, the house shook and the lights went out.

-Strange Love-

Freddie had stashed headlamps throughout the house for easy access in the event of a power failure, a common occurrence in Florida. They'd felt like coal miners, shafts of light dancing in the dark before them. Neither had spoken of the dice.

Zoe exited the bathroom in a fluffy turban and oversized robe.

"Sure you don't want me to take you home?" Freddie had set out candles, put away the game and straightened the kitchen while she showered. He was leaned back on the counter drying his hands on a checkered dish towel.

"Thanks, but Julie's place feels less like home than yours."

He passed on reminding her that Julie's place was, in fact, her place. He tossed the towel on the counter.

She thought a moment, then said, "Hey, Freddie?" She padded over to him, hands cozy in the roomy pockets of the robe.

His heart stuttered at her freshly scrubbed fragrance, at the glow of her face in the candlelight. She stood on bare toes and kissed his cheek. "Thank you."

"For what?" He realized he was ever so slightly dizzy.

She punched him lightly on the tummy. "For everything, bonehead. Your time, my clothes, lunch, dinner, a place to lay my head and . . ."

"And?"

She shrugged. "Just for your kindness. I don't know why you give a shit—"

"It's your karate moves."

"—but you do. I see that now."

The rain had died to a drizzle, accented by occasional sleepy grumbles of thunder.

She took his hands and squeezed them. "Thank you."

The heat of her touch made him blush. "You're welcome, Zoe."

She nodded once, her gratitude expressed, and turned for the electronics room. Her bare feet made not the slightest sound on the cool tile. Over the threshold, she glanced back, said goodnight and closed the door.

Freddie noticed, with a silent jubilance, she did not lock it behind her.

Later, during his nightly ritual with the ceiling fan, he mulled it all over. While his familiarity with the woman had grown, so had the mystery of her. Each opening of one door seemed only to reveal three others, behind each of which worlds of wonder awaited. Who *was* she?

While it was quite conceivable that Julie had conjured the tougher Zoe as a protector, wouldn't there necessarily be limitations to this scenario? Sure, Julie could make the other split "tough," but Zoe was more than just tough. She was *trained.* You couldn't just make up the ability to maneuver like she had at the mall. You couldn't manufacture from thin air the skill to wrench a gun out of someone's hand, or spin and strike with such precision. Or for that matter, the ability to roll out of a fall as she had when the van hit her. That pointed to Zoe being the "real" identity, as she'd argued.

But if that were the case, why was it Zoe who suffered from amnesia? About the only thing Julie couldn't remember was the time spans in which Zoe had been in control. This lucid recall of a history seemed to point toward Julie being the core identity.

The Mayo Clinic article had mentioned amnesia, but he'd assumed this referred to the idea of one split being unaware of what the other was doing, the lost time perhaps only an *illusion* of amnesia. But Zoe seemed to have forgotten experiences *that Julie never could have had.* Like military training. Maybe this was all part of the whole condition, he just didn't know.

And how about the bicycle? Surely, like the ability to walk, one split would inherit this kind of coordination from the other—or at least "borrow" it in cases of self-preservation. He'd read that other opposing characteristics like handedness and even the need for eyeglasses existed in the splits of DID victims, but still. It didn't seem to make sense.

What really threw a wrench in the works was this: If Julie had created Zoe as a protector, where had Zoe been when this Paxyl was cracking her skull with his ring? Yes, perhaps protection was not the only motivation for creating an alter ego— and so Zoe may well indeed have created Julie for purposes

Freddie would never understand. But whoever was the core identity, *where had Zoe been when she was needed?*

Freddie sighed, entranced by the drizzle and distant rolling thunder. What the hell did he know, anyway? Maybe he could convince them—her—to see a psychologist. He laughed aloud at that idea, enough so that he covered his mouth with his hand. What a circus that would be. The doctor overwhelmed, Julie improvising poetry and Zoe kicking the shit out of the poor bastard if he made the mistake of referring to her condition as a "disability."

As he calmed himself, the hypnotic tapping on the roof lulled him . . . began to echo. The drops of liquid cured solid . . . tiny grains of aggregate shrapnel . . .

"Hold on, Stevie!"

The boy seemed to shift positions, stiffly, the strobe effect of myriad flashing car lights. In the dream, they were the only source of illumination: Red (dark), amber (gloom), blinding white (blackness)—all from impossible angles.

Deformed shadows of Stevie flashed and vanished from walls, crushed cars, rubble, ceiling. The deafening blasts of car alarms—horns, sirens, screaming whistles—hammered his ears, reverberated in his skull.

"Don't drop me, Daddy!"

Circling behind him on the garage floor, a demon biker gang. Heavy wheels of the Harleys passed dangerously close to his legs. The roar of engines was like the tub-voiced cackle of a demented giant. Over the rumble, the pallid riders chanted in unison. "Dead. Dead. Dead."

Something moving. Down below. Something birthing from the Cayenne. Stephanie? Stephanie!

Not Stephanie.

("Don't let me go!")

Something bigger. Something slamming through the seats. Something enormous . . . thrusting the seatbacks, to-

ward them . . . almost free. A gray snout (SLAM!), then teeth, gnawing whatever crossed its maw (SLAM!). An entire seat ripped to shreds, the bicycle mangled like a bread tie.

It burst from the car, streaked with blood, skeins of snotty afterbirth drooping from its gills. Jaws of molded plastic, teeth of glass and twisted steel, fish flesh and car parts—a great white shark.

Suddenly the chasm was water-filled. Crystal clear. The mammoth cyborg shimmered with every sinewy movement. He watched helplessly as it slithered and spun, cutting a path, streaming crimson trails through pristine liquid, up . . . up . . . jaws yawning to capacity. Coming right at them. Right at Stevie.

"No! NO!"

Dead eyes rolling over white, the shark clamped down on his son's legs.

Stevie screamed.

Freddie found himself back at home. He sat at the table, one leg crossed casually over the other. Stevie was on the couch. Freddie just . . . knew this. Because he couldn't see his son. The darkness had substance, clung to him like wet clothes. "Want to ride our bikes to the park today, little buddy?" His voice trembled.

"You dropped her, Dad." Stevie. But something was wrong. His words were garbled. Wet.

"So heavy . . ." He closed his eyes, blind now in the darkness.

The couch springs complained.

Freddie's eyelids burst open. His pulse quickened. Something dripping. From Stevie. "It's time for me to go, Dad."

"No!" Freddie shook his head, kept shaking it. "No, please . . ."

"Let me go." Something sliding now . . . somewhere in the gloom . . . toward Freddie . . .

"I . . . I *can't let you go. I could never—*"

"*Wake up, Dad. I can't stay here.*" *A light squeak—perhaps a tennis shoe dragging along the tile.*

"*But you're my own flesh and blood, son. I—*"

"*Wake up. You have to let me go.*"

(Slide . . . squeak. Slide . . . squeak)

An imaginary strap cinched his chest. "*Please, Stevie. Don't—*"

"*Let. Me. Go.*" *Through a mouthful of worms.*

"*I can't.*" *Tremors racked his body.* "*Don't you see?*" *His dry tongue flicked over drier lips.* "*We are one person. In two bodies.*" *His chin quivered.* "*You and me.*"

"*Wake up.*"

A cold finger touched his face . . . Stink of burnt tires, burnt flesh.

"*You're all I have left.*"

Sliding down his neck.

"*Let me go.*"

Now a hand against his chest—

"*I can't. I . . .*"

—shoving him, challenging him.

"*Wake up.*" *Insistently.* "*Wake up.*" *Shaking him.*

"Wake up."

He couldn't tell who had spoken the words, but Zoe was there, watching over him, chasing away the demons. His pulse subsided and his breath slowed. The smell of smoke dissipated; the alarms fell silent. The Harleys faded—the shark, the zombie . . . fading . . . fading . . .

The horror vanished, locked within the labyrinth of his subconscious, beyond recall.

Pleasant chills swam throughout his body, emanating from where her warm palm met his bare chest. His ears rang and his head swam, but not from the nightmare.

She was absent the towel turban and oversized robe.

His pulse pounded in his neck; his vision blurred. Though she stood naked before him—now slipping in beside him— though her redolence intoxicated him, though her warmth all but burned his skin—he was simply unable to fathom this, could not wrap his head around it, refused to believe it was happening.

An almost painful yet not unpleasant shudder ran up his spine.

She somehow slid beneath him, never taking her eyes from his. As if by a spell cast by some benign giggling sorceress, their minds seemed to synchronize—and then with a subtle gasp and widening of her eyes, their bodies.

The gasp.

Her eyes.

The deafening silence.

It was more than he could take.

Exhilarated, confused, he started to speak.

"Shhhhhh . . ." She placed a finger across his lips.

It had been so long; he suddenly remembered the magic of it, remembered how this was a spiritual thing. How could he have forgotten?

And the two shall become one flesh.

Mark 10:8. It was right there, plain as day for all to see— yet encoded, hidden in plain sight. So easy to read the verse and miss the meaning, the passage would remain nothing but senseless words for the celibate—and for those who engaged in the physical act without benefit of love.

She pulled desperately at him, not just with hands but with her eyes. When he tried to take in the rest of her, she gently took his face in her hands and pulled it back to hers, hungry for his gaze.

Kissing. She couldn't get enough of his lips . . . or his eyes . . . and yes, he discovered, she was right, wasn't she? The eyes were the windows to the soul, and *that's* what they were sharing.

And the two became one.

How did she always seem to just . . . *know?* She plowed through life like a freight train, always a step ahead, always in charge, doggedly determined to defend what's right, what's good, what's true.

She'd die to defend her honor.

With an "anybody's," who would have cared what she shared? It could belong to anyone, free to all. But Zoe was *nobody's*. Nobody's fool, nobody's victim, nobody's lover, nobody's anything.

Until now.

Her eyes missed nothing. They gathered the world around her, gathered *everything*—and now, by God, they were capturing him . . . pulling him deeper into her, her magical mind . . . He was drowning in it, but he didn't care . . . Warmer . . . Maybe he'd finally get to see her in here, the real Zoe, finally solve the mystery of her—through her eyes . . .

Rhythmic gentle breathing as one, then more insistent . . . he lost himself in those gleaming pools.

He didn't know how long it had been—he hoped long enough—but he lay atop her, panting, fireworks blasting behind his eyelids. After a time, he descended, the fire quenched.

He began to worry she couldn't breathe and rose on his elbows.

"I'z hopin' you wasn't gonna smother me, cowboy."

Freddie's breath caught in his throat.

She gently took his face in her hands, then kissed his lips.

An avalanche came crashing down on him. He hadn't realized such a mix of emotions was possible. Befuddlement. Elation. Embarrassment. Love.

Confusion.

All tainted by the slightest hint of fear.

She ran her fingers through his hair, then giggled as she ruffled it.

Into Freddie's mind flashed a scene from a movie he'd once seen. When his wife had confronted him, the slimeball husband had lied, *I'd been drinking, and I thought she was you.* Even through the other, more complex emotions, he panicked when a laugh nearly escaped him.

"I ain't a virgin no more, I guess." Julie's smile seemed to glow in the dim light. "I knew I'd know when it was time, and this was it, sure'z rain."

So now was added a touch of guilt.

And speaking of guilt, what would Zoe think? Would she feel betrayed? Deceived? Had he ruined everything?

"I got a poem for ever' occasion. But this time, Freddie Schaeffer, you got me stumped."

He started to panic—then relaxed. After all, they were in fact one and the same person, weren't they? Like different moods in a woman with normal psychology, there was nothing wrong with loving both demeanors.

He finally spoke. "Maybe you'll think of one for the mirror in the morning."

The storm had passed, and now only occasional drips fell from the eves, luring them toward the land of Nod.

"MMMmmm . . ." It was half laugh, half drunken ecstasy. Her eyes fell slowly closed. "Maybe so." She took a breath, let it out. "'Til then, hold me?"

-Black Abyss-

"I am Lieutenant Daniel Hames. This operation is under military jurisdiction. Failure to comply with the protocol in your briefings can and will result in imprisonment. You will take nothing, move nothing, touch nothing or even so much as look at anything without my direct consent."

The resolution was clearer, evidently due to a camera upgrade. They were in the airlock. The speaker stood before a portal reminiscent of a submarine hatch. The tubular walls barricading them from the depths consisted of a transparent rigid material, through which the outer hull was visible through the murky water.

The semi-clear walls deformed the strange excrescences. They seemed to twist and turn stealthily, but that was just the effect of currents and distortion.

There was no reply, only murmurs among the civilians.

Hames continued. "We are here not only to monitor your work, but to protect you. The purpose of this entity's presence is as yet undetermined, and could be hostile."

There were snickers and scoffs amongst the scientists.

"Something funny, Dr. Ingles?"

The camera panned to one of the brains, presumably Dr. Ingles. He wore an unruly beard under unkempt hair. Adjusting his thick glasses, he said, "Uh. Yeah. *Entity?*" His facial hair concealed his entire mouth. "Are you implying there's actually something *alive* in there?" He seemed to be channeling a disembodied voice. "I mean, come on. It has to have been here for centuries. Nothing could possibly have survived—"

"Up to now, we haven't seen them—"

Ingles shrugged as if Hames were making his point.

"—but that doesn't mean they aren't there."

"What does that even—"

"Once inside," Hames interrupted, "nobody removes a helmet, or in any way breaches the containment suits. The air has been determined safe to breathe, but only by preliminary testing. Moreover, we want to keep contamination of its environment to a minimum." He paused, eyeing each of them. "I am in command of this mission. Nobody lifts a finger without my say-so. Clear?"

The camera panned around the airlock. The civilians shook their heads and smirked. Someone muttered, "Whatever."

Bruce had been on assignments involving civilians. They just didn't understand the concept of threat risk, had no frame of reference, no experience of violence with which to temper their confidence. They were impetuous. Naïve. This operation had all the telltale signs of an impending cluster-fuck. He wondered if Hames realized this.

"This is Sergeant Cole, Sergeant Wilkins first class, Corporal Conner and Corporal Evans. If there are no more questions, mount your headgear."

The helmets—mics and earpieces within—locked in place with the containment suits. Headlamps were mounted on each. Visibility was provided by a face-width cylindrical window. The suits were bulky, clumsy—peripheral vision only possible by turning the entire body. Bruce felt claustrophobic just watching them.

The military personnel were armed with suppressed submachine guns, the trigger guards enlarged to accommodate gloves. Their suits were equipped with backpacks, radios and Velcro-sealed compartments that could have contained anything.

Hames punched a code into a wall-mounted keypad. The portal hissed open.

Bruce's expectation of a narrow entrance hall was not realized. Rather, they stepped into a spacious cavern, the walls of which were lined with miniaturized versions of the gnarly antennae bristling from the outer hull. Unlike most all manmade structures, this enclosure was in no way cubical. It more resembled the domed interior of a cave.

The slashing beams of the headlamps were disorienting, and his vertigo returned. Strangely, the beams seemed to produce no ambient light, illuminated nothing except that upon which they fell directly. It was as if the environment somehow consumed and instantly digested the light.

"This way." Hames led them toward a tunnel to which metal-grate catwalks had been added.

The camera panned down. Bruce's stomach flipped when he realized there was no floor, per se. The cavern they were traversing was in fact roughly spherical, a mammoth inverted sea urchin. Absent gravity, one orientation would have served as well as another. The tunnel ahead was of the same design. Only on the catwalks could they navigate the jutting excrescences.

Bruce's vertigo turned to nausea. He looked away, blinked repeatedly and took slow, deep breaths. Someone on the video asked, "What's this?"

Bruce looked back to the screen. They'd proceeded a ways into the tunnel.

Hames: "That's what we brought you guys for. What do you make of it?" The voices through the headset mics sounded tinny and artificial.

"It's a doorway of some sort but . . . not like any I've ever seen."

"Tell us something we don't know. Like how to open it."

One of the scientists, *Albertson* scrawled on white duct tape across the front of his helmet, felt along the border of a mini-bus sized indentation in the knobby wall. "I don't know. It doesn't seem to be designed for manual operation. Perhaps there's some sort of keypad. Or . . ." He removed a glove.

"Goddamn it!" Hames' shout distorted the headsets.

"Just relax." He fondled each protrusion in succession with his bare hand.

"That just looks . . . wrong, man."

Hames: "Put a lid on it, Conner."

Albertson stopped on one of the projections. Bruce gasped when the indentation seemed to . . . fade. Ever so slightly. Or maybe it was just the lighting.

"Help me out here, Dr. Ingles."

"Yeah yeah. I see it." Ingles removed one of his gloves as well. Hames sighed under his breath.

Both researchers bared both hands. Together, they gripped four protrusions. The gateway faded . . . then disappeared.

Someone, maybe Conner, muttered, "Whaaat thaaa fuuuck . . ."

Bruce thought about the anatomy of whomever—or whatever—this gateway was designed for. Then he stopped thinking about it.

The scientists started inside.

Hames shoved one of them aside. "You guys better get your shit straight, *right now,* or you're going to find yourselves working as fluffers for a porn shop in *Leavenworth!*" Then to his subordinates: "Conner. Evans. On me. Wilkins and Cole, you're with the research team."

The soldiers breached the doorway. Weapons up. They stumbled and stuttered, awkward in their suits as they navigated the impassable terrain.

The camera followed them from across the threshold. Residual light revealed nothing, for there was none. Strange shapes flashed and vanished in the slashing beams.

After a few moments, the lamps converged on a coffin-sized capsule like a crushed couch—infected with elephantitis, snarling with spikes and prongs. Bruce could discern no legs supporting it, nor did it rest on a ledge. It seemed to simply float, although it was utterly still as if frozen in place.

One of the beams pulled away and flashed into the lens. "Clear."

Conner puzzled over the casket, rifle strapped behind him. "What the hell *is* it?"

They were careful where they stepped, for this compartment had not been modified for human locomotion. The "floor" just as easily could have been a ceiling in an upturned subterranean room. A miniature version of the cavern through which they'd entered, about the size of a large living room, nasty barbs were everywhere.

"Let me see." Albertson. Ingles navigated his way over and Conner stepped aside. Without speaking, the scientists tried the same technique with which they'd opened the portal.

The capsule faded . . . then vanished altogether. Glowing dimly in its place, evidently still contained by some invisible outer shell, an amber colored, semi-liquid mass. Perhaps it was an illusion caused by lighting and angle, but something seemed to stir inside it, like x-ray footage of a butterfly chrysalis.

After a beat, Ingles gasped. Albertson cried out in alarm. They stumbled backwards, tripping over themselves and the treacherous spears.

Conner crept forward. At the amber mass, he yanked off his helmet and cast it aside—haunted eyes, face slick with sweat.

Hames: "Everyone just calm down." No one seemed to hear him.

Conner: "Just because you cannot see them, doesn't mean they aren't there."

"Back off, Conner."

"Just because you *think* you see it, doesn't mean it *is*." He drew his knife.

"Conner?"

The kid bent to the amber, savage grunts, the sick sound of the blade like a shovel penetrating wet cement.

Everything went to hell.

(Last stop.)

Everyone shouting. Hames barking commands, unheeded.

Wilkins moved forward to assist. He froze, crossed himself, retreated. Fumbled with his helmet. Bumped the camera as he passed.

His retches accented the mêlée.

Conner rose, smiled around the room, arms wide like a crazed evangelist. "Just because it's right before us, doesn't mean it's really there!"

The thing in the amber gained clarity as the camera crept forward. Bruce could almost make it out . . .

A shot of the floor slid up the screen, then of an upside-down Wilkins vomiting into the ceiling.

Conner was the calmest among them: "Just because you see it, doesn't mean it's real."

The camera plummeted, a laser show of flashing human forms. It came to rest directed up at the amber. Conner was an alien profit, looming over the mass.

(End o' the line.)

"Tsk tsk tsk." He shook his head, chuckling— "Would look at my sloppy work?" —and racked the machinegun. "I'll just finish the job."

"CONNER!"

The chugging/tweeting of suppressed gunfire punctuated the retching and screams. Everyone dove for cover. Chunks of putrid gelatin flew everywhere.

Something slopped onto the lens, writhed away. The remaining footage was blurred with smears: amber swirled in scarlet. He'd have to examine the frames individually later, but Bruce thought it may have been a human hand.

Birds suddenly singing. A dog yapped, whined for attention. Denny on his bicycle, parents cheering, an All-American family on a beautiful day.

Bruce's eyes remained saucers.

"End of the line."

He jumped in place, barely managed to snag the laptop as it fell.

He stared up into the face of his assassin.

Such a personal thing, murder. More intimate even than sex when you really thought about it. Your killer escorts you—and most times it was just the two of you—through the most private, monumental event any creature would ever experience, save for his birth: Reunion with his maker.

Or the black abyss.

How could he have been so stupid?

"Didn't you hear me? Last stop. I'm headed back to the station."

Bruce blinked, flummoxed.

Not an assassin.

The bus driver.

-The Color Green-

He'd been dozing on and off, the aromas of bacon and coffee ever so gradually coaxing him from his dreams. He'd realized a few nods ago that Julie was already up, and he missed her warmth.

She elbowed through the door bearing a tray, cuddly in the oversized robe, her freshly brushed hair draped over the collar. "Mornin', sleepy head." She looked happier than he'd ever seen her.

She set the tray aside and propped a couple of pillows on the headboard, then patted them: *Sit right here.*

Freddie wrestled himself into position and rubbed his eyes. "You're up early."

"Wanted to serve you breakfast in bed." She set the tray before him.

Plate loaded with bacon and eggs and wedges of toast, all arranged in a smiley face, the tray was garnished with morning glory petals he recognized as having come from his back yard. Condensation lined a chilled glass of orange juice, and a cup of coffee sat steaming beside the plate.

"Thanks, Jules. This was really sweet."

She snuggled in beside him and hugged his left arm. A comfortable silence fell between them, broken only by Freddie's occasional grunts of approval as he wolfed down the feast.

Julie said, "After you're done, we gotta drive over and pick me up some clothes."

Freddie grunted through a mouthful of eggs. After nodding them down, he said, "We already got you some. Yesterday at the mall. I'll help you find them."

"I did find 'em. I appreciate it, but I can't wear green. Makes me sick."

Freddie took a sip of coffee, trying to decipher what that meant. "You mean, you don't like green?"

"Nah, it ain't that. I like it much as any other color. It's just, *wearin'* green makes me sick. Another curse o' the ole black cat, I guess."

Her nervous laugh was missing—and the apprehensive disposition from whence it came.

In retrospect, he realized she'd made direct eye contact upon entering the room. A mirrored sliding closet door faced the bed, and she met his eyes comfortably there as well.

Now. This black cat business.

He set down his fork and turned to face her. She looked up at him, directly into his eyes. Freddie's heart melted. "Hey. Did last night mean anything to you?" She didn't answer. Just gazed into his eyes. "Huh?" he prodded.

"Last night meant the world to me, Freddie Schaeffer. And I hope it meant somethin' to you, too."

"It did," he said. "It meant everything." Freddie brushed a strand of hair back from her face. "But listen. I'm allergic to cats, okay? At least the bad luck variety. So, that old thing has to go."

She let out a sigh and smiled, then rested her head on his shoulder.

"Seriously, Julie. You have me now. We have *Us*. Would you be willing to let that feline go? In exchange for this worn out old handyman?"

She thought about it, looked back up at him, from one of his eyes to the other, reminiscent of her bolder alter ego. She nodded once, creased her brow and said, "By golly, I *am* willing." Then, more playfully, waving her left fist, "Call 911! Get animal control on the line! See ya later, cat!" She laughed, a healthy, happy laugh.

Freddie nodded, satisfied. "So. Why not green?"

She snuggled in again and met his eyes in the mirror. "Well, see, it's my complexion. Green clashes with my skin. Makes me look sick. And so when people see me wearin' green, they start *treatin'* me like I'm sick. And then next thing you know, the way they're treatin' me, starts makin' me *feel* sick. Then I *git* sick."

In the middle of a sip of orange juice, a sudden chuckle burst forth from Freddie. Once escaped, there was no holding it back—and it morphed into full-fledged laughter. Orange juice squirted from his nose. Julie squealed with delight, laughing herself, and ran out to retrieve a towel. She returned as Freddie calmed himself, and started dabbing at the mess. He considered mentioning how Zoe had worn green all day yesterday with no problems whatsoever, but decided to let it go. Take this one step at a time.

As she stood and set the towel aside, Freddie said, "Okay, fine. We'll go get you some non-green clothes. But hopefully, you'll want to bring them back over here?"

She turned to him. "Oh, Freddie . . . You bet I'll want to."

"Good." He set the tray aside. "So let me get dressed and we'll go."

The oversized robe dropped to the floor. "Okay but . . . make love to me again first?"

-Blood Red-

Julie had been willing to compromise and wear Zoe's clothes from yesterday, including the green shirt, at least for the trip to her place. Strangely, they seemed to fit more loosely on the artist. Freddie donned his usual day-off attire, cargo shorts and a tank top, crocs on his feet. They were headed out the door when Freddie remembered something. "Oh. You've got to see this first."

"What is it?"

Freddie hustled to the computer and tethered his cell. "Just watch. It's for you." He navigated to the DCIM folder and opened Zoe's video to Julie.

Zoe appeared on the screen, less composed than Julie at the moment. *(What the hell am I supposed to say, dude?)*

Julie's jaw fell open. After the first few lines from the Spitfire, she said, *"Whaaat?"* Then, surprisingly, she giggled and hugged herself when Zoe lectured her in no uncertain terms about wearing prairie dresses and the self-demeaning nature of stripping. When the video ended, Julie tilted her head, stared at the ceiling.

Then she launched into verse:

Hey Little Blood Red,
Sing us a song,
Lively and strong,
Steal the show.
Brilliant bravado battlement boasting . . .
But I know your heart.

Hey Little Blood Red,
Chase it away,
Ghost of yourself.
Dash your skeleton,
Delicate delegate,
Against my pain,
Widow windowed.
Yes, I know your heart.

Hey Little Blood Red,
Dare I care?
To wonder where?
Is that *you* there?

No, Little Blood Red!
Crimson heap, Scarlet on scarlet,
Furrowed breast from
Dagger claw,
Earth and feline fed . . .
I know, Little Blood Red,
They are your heart,
Helpless and blind,
Cuddled and warm, nestled,
Nuzzlin' Mama's wing.
One day you'll sing,
'Cause Daddy done the martyr thing . . .
Will *you* know his heart?

Hey Little Blood Red,
Fly away home,
Where blissful you'll roam, for
You got the last laugh,
And I know your heart.

By God she still had it, Freddie was pleased to see. Despite last night's writer's block. "I think it's your best yet," he said. "And I think your alter ego would be impressed."

"Oh, she ain't me. No sir. She's somebody totally different—although we do share one heart."

Strange, Zoe had insisted the same thing. *This is not me.* So, this now from both of them, even in the face of video evidence. Perhaps splits insisted on their autonomy.

Still, the verses showed signs of progress. Clearly it was about Julie and her protector. He nudged her toward that revelation. "But the poem. What does it mean? What's it about?"

"A daddy cardinal and the family he's sworn to protect, of course."

"Yeah but, Zoe is the cardinal? You're the family? She's protecting you, right?"

Julie laughed and closed the gap between them. She put her arms around Freddie's waist and lay her head on his chest. "No, silly. She's both. The family, *and* the daddy bird. I know her heart, 'cause we share the same one.

"See, she's got something in her past needs protecting. That's the little bird family. And Zoe's willing to die defending it. The cardinal, he defends with distraction. His color and his boldness. Me, I turn to ink and paper. With her, it's bravado." She raised her head and looked up at him. "All that tough talk? That's just her lookin' out for the scared little girl inside her."

Freddie slowly nodded. She was right, of course. Now that she'd pointed it out, it seemed obvious, and he wondered how he'd missed it. He wondered what Julie knew about *him*. What monsters of his mind did she see with clarity, spooks that to he himself were invisible?

"See? I know her heart." She looked back at the computer as if she expected Zoe to be standing there. "And even though we never met, I love her like a sister."

Jules was on fire during the drive to the warehouse, spitting out verses and clever quips about anything noteworthy. "Blue Bicycle Banishing Boy Boredom." "Fat Cat, Chase a Rat, Where's he at? SPLAT!" When they passed an old man sitting on his porch in a rocker, watching the birds peck away at their breadcrumb breakfast, she whipped out a verse of thirty seconds or so, the title of which Freddie imagined to be, *Thinker in a Chair. (Old man sittin' over there, Are you a thinker, in a chair?)*

They pulled into the parking lot of the warehouse, Freddie laughing at a poem she'd just concocted, Julie in a wordsmithing frenzy. He found a space, navigated Old Mable between the faded lines and threw it in park.

Unbuckling his seat belt, he froze.

The male end of the restraint hovered over the buckle. Julie's voice trailed off in the middle of a verse about an abandoned car seat.

The door to the apartment stood open.

Had he and Zoe left it that way?

No. He remembered with clarity locking up behind himself.

So maybe Julie had been the victim of a common thief.

Possible, he supposed, but . . .

Freddie glanced around the parking lot for the classic Plymouth. It was not here.

Not here *now*.

He released the seat belt and fished his cell from his pants pocket. He got as far as 9-1 . . . then stopped, finger suspended over the keypad.

(There was a murder last night.)

He cleared the dial pad then stuffed the phone back in his pocket. "Wait here."

"But my stuff's in there. I need to—"

"Don't worry, we'll get it. Just . . . wait." Freddie rummaged blindly behind the seat, never taking his eyes from the gaping doorway. He produced an L-shaped tire tool and hefted it a few times. Satisfied it would do the trick, he opened his door.

"Freddie?"

"It's okay, just wait here."

"Freddie." More insistent this time.

"What?!" he said, more forcefully than he'd intended. He finally looked at her.

"Be careful."

Freddie held her gaze for a beat—then leaned back inside. Julie, understanding, met him halfway.

A brief kiss, then he closed the door and headed for the apartment.

-Book Burning-

With every step toward the warehouse, it seemed to move farther away. Freddie carefully scanned the lot as he stalked forward, ever vigilant for the haunted Plymouth. Sweat formed between his palm and the tire tool—though the latter remained cool to the touch. He struggled to avoid tiring out his hand before he even reached the Building.

He found himself at the door. With one last scan of the lot, and with more caution than was probably necessary, he eased through the door, stepped into the foyer . . . and waited. He didn't know whether he should call out or opt for stealth.

He mounted the rickety stairs, makeshift weapon held ready. Each step would have been supported at the ends, so he hugged the wall in order to produce the least amount of noise. Not that it did much good.

He cursed silently at each faint squeak.

About halfway up, he crinkled his nose at the stringency of recently charred plastic and burned insulation.

After an eternity, he reached the backwards-mounted door, which also proved to be slightly ajar. Again he was in a quandary. Sneak in stealthily or burst through and ambush them? Neither option seemed prudent. In fact, he supposed it was stupid even coming up here. But what choice did he have? And were they even still here?

The last question seemed to be answered when a faint squeak eked out from inside the apartment. Chills tickled his spine and he resisted the reflexive urge to bolt back down the stairs. Frozen, he raised the tire tool.

Freddie was torn. Perhaps he should just get the hell out of here and call the police, and to hell with the consequences. In fact, couldn't Big Man have been lying about the murder and planted evidence? Was Freddie willing to take that chance? He hadn't thought to check the paper or watch the news to confirm the claim. But, he reasoned, why would they have gone to that much trouble and risk? If they were capable of murder, why not just kill him and be done with it?

He supposed it was impossible to follow the logic of evil men, to think like a violent criminal. If he could, wouldn't that make *him* a violent criminal?

Truth or dare? Go or stay? Fight or flee? Why wasn't anything ever easy?

The creaking returned. He tightened his grip on the tire tool.

The sound wafted out yet again. He realized it seemed stationary—as if someone were shifting his weight over a loose floor joist. But the span between each whine was too great to have been caused by impatient fidgeting, and too short to have been someone changing positions after having stood too long in one spot.

EEeeek . . . EEeeek . . .

"Ah fuck it." Freddie took a step past the door then snatched it open and burst inside.

Hanging from an exposed rafter, Slash and Stitch shattered on the floor beneath her, swung Beebee, neck constricted in a noose. She'd been burned beyond recognition. Plastic flesh singed to scar tissue. Glob of a wig now fused to her skull, her melted face brought bile to his throat. Nailed to her left breast was a napkin bearing a gold leaf BT's seal. Scribbled in block letters, the note read:

COME SEE ME YOU SICK BITCH.

He took in the rest of the room. The Banyan leaves had all been ravaged, the intricate detail of the bark charred to a crisp.

Puddles of water spotted the floor, most of it having soaked into the plywood. Every sheet was warped at the corners.

The windows were open, apparently with the intent of letting the place air out. The draft explained the gently rocking synthetic corpse.

They had carefully planned this for maximum effect. One bouncer had immolated the home, the other following close behind with water to make sure the blaze didn't get out of control. Besides attracting the attention of the authorities, burning the entire building would have had less emotional impact on Julie. They wanted this to be personal and needed her to see it.

Freddie would spare her that indignity.

A gasp startled him and he turned to the door, tire tool raised.

Julie stood just inside the threshold, aghast.

Freddie wanted to say, *I thought you were going to wait in the van,* or, *I'm so sorry,* or *something*—but found himself mute.

Julie's breath quickened, as if she were building toward some hideous orgasm of shock.

Her panicked eyes met Freddie's—but didn't see him. He opened his mouth to speak but could think of nothing to say.

She bolted for the bedroom.

"Julie!"

She breached the doorway. "Oh, no . . . Oh, no no *nooo!*" Her muted wailing from within those hidden quarters tore at his heart. Guilt bit at him. He should have been at her side.

He dropped the tire tool and hurried over.

There in place of her collection sat a fifty-gallon steel drum, the type around which the homeless could be seen warming their hands in winter. Within it, about two feet deep, a black rancid sludge of soaked ashes speckled with flecks of gray and white.

"They took it from me." She was trembling. "Burnt it." Her face was blank, eyes dead. "They burnt up my whole life."

The shelves had been ripped from the wall, necessary in order to leave, crudely rendered in black spray paint, the giant face of a cat.

Under it had been scrawled:

BAD LUCK.

Julie's words turned to gibberish, then to unabashed wailing like a child whose mother had abandoned her at daycare.

Freddie didn't know what to do. He felt big and stupid, a dumb clumsy Shrek, suddenly claustrophobic in this enclosed space.

He went to her. "Julie . . . " He placed a tentative hand on her shoulder.

"Don't *touch* me!" She shrank from him, hunched like a cornered animal, arms crossed defensively. "Don't you *touch* me anymore!"

Badly stung, Freddie was nevertheless convinced she spoke not to him but to a ghost once buried in her past, safely interred within the verses. That corpse is what she saw now, risen from the dead, the paper grave laid open.

He offered only his sympathetic gaze, for it's all he had left to give.

Julie, keening, chest heaving, peered back at someone who was not Freddie . . . then realized where she was and with whom she was speaking.

She fell into his arms. "I'm sorry!" She didn't embrace him, but clutched her arms tightly to herself as if she were freezing.

Freddie held her. "Shhhh . . . It's okay."

"I'm so sorry," she repeated, words torn by ragged sobs.

"I'm sorry, Julie. I am so, so sorry."

She let it out, wept openly into his chest. He just held her, staring at the ceiling, sickened by thoughts of breaking bones, busting heads—yet powerless to stop them. He gnashed his teeth. Lips in a snarl. He closed his eyes and took a deep breath. Did his best to remember this was about Julie, not the bouncers.

For now.

Her head was turned toward the wall, spellbound by the hateful image staring back at her.

The feline face had been sprayed in haste by an unprac- ticed hand. But perhaps some malevolent spirit had guided the work, because the message of mental oppression came bleeding through.

The eyes were grotesquely oversized. Giant, flat-black holes, each seemed to bustle with legions of lamenting souls who'd suffered the misfortune of falling within its vortex.

The mouth stretched ear to ear, a jagged grinning gash. They'd held the can too close, perhaps intentionally; bloody black paint drips ran down its chin and face.

She was shuddering. He turned her face up to his with his massive hands. "Hey . . . hey hey hey. No black cat. Just stupid scrawling from some dumb jerks who are in *desperate* need of an ass-kicking."

She chuckled once despite herself, but the tears kept flowing.

"So listen." He didn't know what he was about to say, just prayed for the right words. Her sobs slowed, but again he said, "Listen," because he needed her to *hear* him.

She engaged, her face streaked with tears.

"Those guys?" He shrugged. "Yeah, they took your poems. Your precious word sculptures."

Her eyes squeezed shut and her chin began to quiver.

"But listen . . ." he eased himself back nearly to arm's length. She opened her eyes.

"They took them, yes. But . . ."

She stared at him, perplexed.

"What they *didn't* get?" He gently tapped her forehead. "Was the machine that makes 'em." He let that sink in. "Those poems? Julie, they were great. And they expressed something important to you. It's a real tragedy they're gone, but here's the thing."

Her face begged for his words to mean something.

"They were sad, Julie. Tortured. And yes, they needed to be. But you know what?"

"What?" Sunlight seemed to be breaking through the clouds in her eyes.

"We're together now. *Us.* No more black cat. Even the poems you made up on the way over here, they were bright.

Funny. *Jubilant*. Maybe all that sad stuff—maybe it was time to let it go anyway. Those assholes? Hey. Maybe without realizing it, they actually did you a favor."

Julie gazed at his chest, absently fingering his buttons.

"Yeah," he said. "A favor. If you have the brains—and the guts—to look at it that way. I do. We've started something cool here, haven't we? And I don't know about you, but I think it's going to be something precious and fine. Starting today, you're going to write *hundreds* of poems."

"Thousands," she said, wiping at her tears.

Freddie's heart soared. "Our new life is going to be *exciting*. Full of art and poetry. Pizza and pancakes. Bike rides and bounce houses. And these *new* poems? They're going to document our life together, going to paint a picture of all that happiness for the world to see."

He pulled her to him. "You and me."

After a beat, she added, "And Zoe too."

Freddie shook his head at the ceiling and couldn't resist a chuckle. "Yeah, and Zoe too."

-The Voice-

What was with that hotel smell? From the finest Ritz Carlton to the cheapest Motel 6, they all seemed to have it. Bruce had once surmised it was cigarette smoke residue, but the odor remained, long after smoking had been banned in hotels.

He powered on the prepaid cell. When the screen blinked to life, he entered eleven numbers then held the phone to his ear. After the prompt, he entered seventeen more.

The line begin ringing.

Perhaps they all used the same detergents. But what were the odds of that? They certainly wouldn't coordinate their cleaning product purchases. And even if they did, surely at least one inn would throw caution to the wind and boldly risk trying a new soap with its own unique scent.

"Creed."

"I know everything, chief."

"Excuse me?"

Maybe it was the guests. People each seemed to have their own subtly unique scent. And due to diet, colognes, and perhaps home environments, one could even speculate as to ethnicity based on fragrance.

"In the event of my death, it all comes out."

"What are you talking about?"

"High crimes and misdemeanors, Colonel. All the kidnapping, theft, bribes, murder . . ." Bruce paused for effect. "It would be the scandal of the century."

The response was only line noise over which he could discern Creed's troubled breathing. Then, "Bullshit."

Perhaps it was a cumulative effect. That had to be it. Cleaners produced in bulk, Suave and Geri Curl, Old Spice and patchouli, Arrid and Right Guard—Sweat residue infused with curry powder, casserole, chitterlings, chilly pepper and of course alcohol—perhaps all these odors combined over weeks and months and years to create that unique hotel mélange.

"Your password."

"What are you talking about?"

Bruce sighed. "I know your password, Colonel. I've had it for years."

The fetor of myriad body fluids must also be added to the mix, but he tried not to think about that.

"There's no way—"

"JesusIsLordFive6SevenSky. First letters capitalized. Five and seven spelled out."

More line static. If they'd been scrambling to trace the call, Creed had stopped them.

"You know what we do here, and why we do it. I've only done my duty. For the country."

"You know that and I know that, chief. But I don't think John Q. Public would be quite so understanding. Or the news media."

Again there was no reply. Bruce could almost hear the handset fracturing on the other end of the line. He imagined white knuckles, gritted teeth. "Hey. I get it. I understand why you came after me. But if you do it again, you're finished."

This time the reply was only a sharp exhalation.

"Relax, chief. Here's the good news. I'm out. I'll be coming for Christie, and you'll facilitate that process. Then you'll put us out of your mind and go about your business saving the country."

"You know I can't—"

"But if you decide to follow me, you're either fucked or dead or both." Bruce clicked the off button and removed the battery. The phone would never be used again.

He'd cast off the bedspread (they were rarely laundered) and now lay on the cool top sheet in his sock feet, legs crossed, eyes closed, fingers laced behind his head. The TV was playing, but he was not watching it. Nor was he listening, not really; it only served as background noise—a distraction from thoughts of Christie, Project Amber, Zoe Decker, Phantoms under the sea—and the hysterical death throes of Don Gluth. He desperately needed sleep, but with a sigh resigned himself to the fact it wasn't going to happen.

His eyes eased open and found a water stain on the ceiling. It reminded him of a spreading pool of blood.

Maybe if he organized his thoughts, he'd be better able to tuck them away for a time so he could drift off.

First, the botched interrogation confirmed the agency had indeed set him up. He'd contained the threat for the time being, but he'd use caution in his upcoming moves.

Second, Gluth's story corroborated the existence of Project Amber. Bruce still didn't know what it was or what it meant— only that it had something to do with telekinesis (Gluth had referred to it as "some E.S.P. shit") and this "amber," supposedly from the bottom of the sea.

Was that what he'd seen on the video? CGI was capable of creating convincing representations of impossible things— from aliens to avatars. And actors won much-deserved Oscars for their portrayals of every emotion imaginable. He applauded all that, but Bruce's experience with real violence had ruined cinema for him.

Special effects and acting were downright amazing these days. In fact, they were *too* good. Real violence—real life itself—was messier. Unrehearsed, unpolished, untimed and imperfect. He doubted anyone would ever be able to precisely duplicate the genuine article.

There was something about the rawness of life, and especially violence, that was lost the very moment you laid a plan, something about the rhythm and subtlety of real dialogue that dissipated the moment you wrote a script. Even with improvised lines, the actors were still aware they were acting. And so with the slightest scrutiny, the illusion was broken even as it was created.

He was convinced the video was real, or at least real to the people in it.

A TV chef was preparing a dish alongside a soap opera star of decades past. A sampled morsel was of course proclaimed superb. The audience, or a canned laugh track, roared with laughter at a sassy comment from the washed-up actress.

Who in the hell watched this crap? He imagined a reeking, 500-pound hermit sitting in gloom, slick with sweat. That or a geriatric prune too incapacitated to search for the remote.

Or a burned out spy in desperate need of distraction.

More important was what Bruce had *failed* to discover. Decker's whereabouts.

According to Gluth, the agency had her. This may or may not be true, but it felt right.

A jubilant big band theme came crashing over the final fading words of the TV chef, spiced with cackles from the has-been. The plastic audience clapped like seals. After a few seconds, the cacophony was interrupted by something more dramatic. Tympanic thunder, cymbal swells, and trumpets as if from a mountaintop heralded the coming of drama, dilemma, disaster and scandal. Like the damn world was coming to an end.

Maybe it was.

As the action theme faded, it was replaced by the solemn words of the all-knowing, all-caring, and perpetually concerned Raven Stryker.

As if one phony name wasn't enough, he'd come to be known in media circles as "The Voice." Though camera angle and scale were carefully arranged to conceal it, the smug prick was obviously short. Nothing wrong with that; Bruce had had his ass handed to him plenty of times by men who could stand under his arm.

But some guys just couldn't get over it.

Stryker sported a hairstyle carefully sculpted to accumulate every millimeter of height possible—but without revealing what it really was: a pile of hair. It didn't make him look tall; it just looked like a possum had died on his head.

He puffed out his chest, the result of which offered little in the way of counterfeiting size—but caused his voice to sound pinched.

He held his chin ever so slightly raised. He'd evidently worked tirelessly to achieve an angle at which no one would notice the altered posture—but was sufficient to give the subtle impression of talking down to his audience.   Apparently, he'd convinced himself he had everyone in TV land believing he was a giant—of both media and stature.

No one was fooled.

A trim salt and pepper beard framed Stryker's perpetually tart lips. Bruce imagined it was intended to give the impression of virility.

Power.

Manliness.

Raven Stryker was something alright, but it wasn't a man.

Bruce had no more respect for TV journalism than print. What modern news boiled down to was entertainment—if you could call it even that. These assholes reported only items sure to arouse suspicion.

Worry.

Dread.

Like print news, *how* they conveyed information—as well as what they left out—had as much if not greater impact than what they reported.

But it wasn't entirely the fault of the media. People seemed to be addicted to the narcotic of emotional stimulation.

Anger.

Hate.

Even fear would do.

So the media fed them exactly what they asked for, provided their nightly fix.

Giving up on sleep, he finally sat up as Stryker husked out the highlights of the evening. Bruce vigorously rubbed his face in his hands then snared a glass of water sitting on the nightstand. He drank greedily. As he returned the container, wiping his mouth with his sleeve, he shot a nasty glance at the anchor as the smug prick launched into the first story.

"Sergeant-Major Abdelaziz Hashim al-Atassi, of the Fort Smith Arkansas air force base, opened fire today in the base cafeteria, killing five and wounding seven. According to witnesses, al-Atassi shouted 'God is Great' in Arabic as he went on his shooting spree. Investigators are still working to piece together a motive for the rampage, but officials say they will not rest until—"

Bruce hefted himself from the bed and approached the TV, barely resisting the temptation to toss the damn thing out the window. "Motive my ass." God forbid they consider *(gasp)* terrorism. No, it had to be filed under "safer" labels. Like workplace violence. Disgruntled employ. Tragic childhood.

And why "God is Great in Arabic?" Why not report what he *actually said:* "Allahu Akbar?" Allahu meant "God is," but as Bruce had learned long ago, Akbar did not mean "great," but *"greater."* As in greater than whomever *your* God happens to be.

He searched for the off button, bubbling toward the boiling point.

Not on the front. Of course it wasn't. Why put the buttons on the front where you could find them? Not on the sides either. Nor on the top; not even on the back.

"According to investigators here in the Voice Chamber, al-Atassi's social media posts paint a picture of a tortured man from a troubled past, with a history of—"

Bruce threw up his hands—then remembered only remotes were used to control TVs nowadays. So you could lose it, rendering the device useless.

And buy another one.

He glanced around the room. There. Bracketed to the nightstand.

"Damn it," he muttered, and shuffled back.

He reached for the remote . . .

His finger hovered over the power button, but he made no move to press it.

Social media posts . . .

Now why hadn't he thought of that? If the agency had Decker, an internet search for her would be pointless. But maybe they didn't. If she were still out there somewhere, perhaps she'd use the web to track down or communicate with another journalist.

Covert interaction was relatively secure with just a public email account. Each collaborator need only log in and draft a message. But never click send. The other collaborator(s) would read the draft and add a reply. As long as nothing was ever sent, it was all but impossible to trace.

The agency wouldn't even know where to start looking. Of course, Bruce wouldn't either, but it was worth a shot. Because once you started typing and clicking, your odds of leaving a trail increased exponentially. She'd be careful, wouldn't blaze a lighted highway—but all Bruce needed was breadcrumbs.

Maybe he'd get lucky.

He pressed the off button. Sweet silence.

He snatched the duffel bag from the other bed and plucked out his laptop. He opened Google Chrome and sighed. You had to start somewhere, so he searched "Zoe Decker," knowing he'd find nothing on the first try.

Wrong.

-Drop-in Guest-

There had been nothing to salvage. Not one stitch of clothing—no paintbrush, no toothbrush, no furniture, no food. Not even silverware had survived—actually Dollar Store plasticware—all melted into globs, petrified plastic dinosaur dung. Julie was officially homeless, utterly dependent on Freddie. At least for the duration.

Her landlord accepted only cash, week to week. No lease had been signed. He'd find the apartment abandoned, have his crew give it a once over—and a new itinerate musician or fly-by-night business would be snuggled into their brand new home-sweet-home within days.

The place was a rat hole, but it had been *her* place. Her artwork had been everything. Despite Freddie's consolation, Julie had been subdued as she'd watched her home fade away in the rearview mirror.

Shopping for clothes somewhat lifted her spirits—although he had to constantly steer her away from lacy tops, teen-jeans adorned with rainbows and butterflies, and of course dresses as if from Snow White's enchanted wardrobe.

Julie was cooperative, even asked a few times, "Do you think she might like this?" Freddie hated himself every time he said no. He relented when she just couldn't live without a pair of white bunny slippers, complete with marble black eyes, pink plastic noses and filament whiskers. He was reminded of the sheep chair. Maybe she was too.

The dying day seemed to slip through her fingers. The waning sunlight spilled down her hair, gilding it in shades of gold as she sat swaying with the road, staring out her window.

They passed a man walking down Freddie's street in the same direction. He held a clipboard in the crook of one arm. Of average height, dressed in average looking jeans topped by an average sport coat over a polo shirt—none of any remarkable colors—Freddie noticed the guy only because he was so *un*noticeable.

A glance in the rearview suggested he was anywhere from twenty-five to forty-five, and thus of average age. His face proved to be a match for his outfit: an everyday mug framed by a weatherman haircut. Under "typical guy" in the dictionary, you'd find this guy's picture.

In fact, Freddie had forgotten about him by the time he steered Old Mable into his driveway.

They carried the bags inside. Freddie set his on the table then headed for the kitchen. He grabbed two cups from the dish strainer. "Water?"

Julie was relieving herself of her own cargo at the table. "Sure, thanks," she said. Then, "Hey! Come on in," just as a light knocking arose from the front porch. They hadn't shut the door yet.

Now who could that be? He wasn't at all concerned, just stumped. Freddie had lots of satisfied customers, but none he could call friends without fidgeting a little.

When he rounded the corner, he recognized the guest. The average guy, the walker, complete with sport coat and clipboard.

"Hi. Bill Vargas." He extended his hand with a disarming smile.

"Freddie Schaeffer." He shook the man's hand, still clueless. For an average guy, Vargas had a firm grip. "And this is Julie," he added, indicating the girl as she came to Freddie's side.

"Hey there!"

Freddie was touched by her sudden buoyancy. Only with him did she reveal her genuine mood.

Addressing their curiosity, Vargas said, "I live a few doors down from the Zaydons. Joe Zaydon?"

Freddie nodded recognition.

"I'm sorry to impose on you—" He handed Freddie a flyer. "—but this won't take but a minute or two."

Freddie scanned the flyer as Vargas spoke: *Neighborhood Watch*.

A few minutes later, they were sitting at the table, waters all around, the couple answering a list of pro forma questions: First and last names. Contact information. How long have you lived in the neighborhood? Pets? Where do you work? Freddie answered most of the questions as Vargas scribbled away on the clipboard, nodding. Julie, for the most part, just sat by looking pretty.

They finished the interview and were all headed for the door with the usual *good to meet you*s and *we must get together sometime*s, when Julie made the strangest of comments. "Ever have trouble sleeping? I mean, with all the noise?"

Freddie looked at her, baffled. Her southern accent was suddenly strained. In fact, he realized, it was totally fabricated—although Zoe did a decent job of faking it. He wondered if Vargas noticed. *What is she doing?*

"Noise?" Vargas shook his head. His smile remained plastered in place—but faded, ever so slightly. Freddie himself was completely stumped. *Noise?*

"You know, Joe's new Harley. Scares the shit out of us every time he drives by." She shook her head and chuckled. "Wakes us up when he drives by at night."

Vargas nodded dramatically, his memory ostensibly jogged. "Oh yeah," he said. *"That* thing." Now he shook his head, sharing her sentiment. "Good thing I have impact glass." He shrugged. "Heck, a bomb could go off next to my window and I'd sleep right through it." He nodded, raised his eyebrows and turned to the door with his clipboard.

"Hell, the *color* of that thing is as loud as the muffler!" Zoe renewed her chuckle.

"Obnoxious, right?" Vargas said over his shoulder. "Thanks for your time, guys." He reached for the knob.

Zoe cut in front of him. "Please. Allow me." She held the knob but didn't turn it. After a beat, she looked back at Bill Vargas.

"Oh. Of course. Sorry." He stepped back respectfully and waited, clipboard resting at his belt buckle in both hands.

Zoe just stood there, eyes locked on Average Bill. She was reading him. Freddie did not envy the guy.

Vargas sniffed and wiped at his nose. When he realized he was under scrutiny, he looked first at Freddie, then at Zoe.

"What?" When no one answered, he repeated, *"What?"* with a strained smile.

"I made it up." The drawl was gone.

"Excuse me?"

"The motorcycle. It's not loud. In sound *or* color. In fact, if it's any color at all, I guess it would be clear."

"What?" Vargas shook his head.

"Joe is terrified of motorcycles. He'd never own one."

Vargas tried a smile, immediately checked it. "Well, I thought you meant—"

"Cut the shit. Who are you?"

Freddie decided it was time to step in. "Whoa whoa whoa. Let's just back up a minute. I think surely there must be some kind of—"

Zoe held up a hand to cut him off, never taking her eyes from Vargas. "I feel like maybe I know you from somewhere. 'Bill' is close. But it's not Vargas, is it? Who are you, *Bill?* What do you want from us?" Into the silence, she added, "The truth."

Vargas raised the clipboard in his left hand as if waving a white flag. Recalling it later, Freddie realized the man's right had simultaneously crept toward his hip.

"Whatever you're reaching for?" Zoe said, cold as ice. "I hope it's a sandwich. Because if you pull it out, you're going to eat it."

Freddie's skin was suddenly hosting ant races.

Vargas smiled, slowly raised both hands. "Amazing. Absolutely stunning."

Now it was Freddie's turn to ask, *"What?"*

Never taking his eyes from the woman, Bruce Vega—alias Bill Vargas—said to Freddie, "That's not Zoe Decker." He shook his head once. "But if I'd been blindfolded, she sure as hell could've fooled me."

-|nterview-

Whoever this Julie Ayers was—and he doubted that even *was* her name—Bruce had to admit she was good. He'd immediately recognized the motorcycle thing for what it was. Either Zaydon really owned a motorcycle or he didn't. Bruce's response would tag him as neighbor or imposter. Fifty-fifty shot.

She'd chosen something unlikely to show up on a quick DMV search conducted ahead of time: A *new* motorcycle. Intentional or dumb luck?

He trusted his bullshit detector better than any polygraph. He'd bought the story, paid the full tab and left a fat tip. Damn it, she'd sold it like free beer at a frat party.

He had no resentment about being outclassed. In fact, the woman had won his respect, even charmed him. That would make killing her and the Handyman a sad thing. If it came to that.

Now they were back at the table, this time all cards on it.

Bruce said, "First let me say, I'm sorry I had to deceive you."

"Tried to deceive us, tough guy," the woman corrected.

Despite the chilling similarities in personality—hell, the outright *match*—the woman obviously wasn't Decker. Even if she'd resorted to plastic surgery—and he could think of no reason for such a radical move—decreasing height by six inches was impossible. Without cutting off your feet. But if he closed his eyes, he could *see* Zoe Decker, sitting right in front of him, quick wit blasting away through both barrels of that sassy-ass mouth.

Such an uncanny impersonation would be impossible—even, Bruce surmised, with extensive study of the spy. And why would they go to such lengths anyway? What good was impersonating an operative if you looked nothing like her?

"Right," Bruce conceded. "So here it is, as much as I'm at liberty to say. More than I should say, really."

Ayers looked at Schaeffer. "He's going to tell us some truth now."

"Some?" said the Shrek.

"Only as much as he has to."

Bruce smiled inwardly. That was Decker alright. Except it wasn't. "I represent a government agency investigating the disappearance of—"

"Which agency?" she interrupted.

"A major one."

"Homeland security? Sanitation department? *Which agency?*"

Bruce resisted a chuckle.

"Hey," Schaeffer said calmly. He reached out and covered Ayer's hand with his. When she glanced at him, he gave it a gentle squeeze and tipped his head toward Bruce. "Let's just hear him out."

She pulled away and crossed her arms. After a beat, she gestured at him with one hand: *Go ahead.*

"I'm investigating the disappearance of Zoe Decker. Naturally, when we ran across your FaceBook account, we had to check it out." Decker was drilling into him, just like always. *She's not Decker, damn it!* "So we just need to know why you created that account in her name instead of your own."

"It *is* my own."

"You introduced yourself as Julie. Julie Ayers, you said. On the questionnaire."

The woman and Schaeffer shared a glance. Schaeffer raised his eyebrows, a private question.

The woman answered with a quick shrug.

Bruce looked from one of them to the other. "Well?"

Schaeffer took the reigns. "DID."

"Did?"

"Dissociative Identity Disorder."

Oh, here we go. He maintained a poker face and heard the man out.

"She's two people," Schaeffer explained. "Well, two personalities. Splits, they're called. Sometimes she's Julie Ayers, who you met. Other times, like now, she's Zoe Decker. Julie is a poet and artist. Zoe is . . . well, we haven't quite figured that out yet."

"Why not?"

The couple shared another glance. Ayers shrugged again.

Back to Bruce, Schaeffer said, "The main problem with the Zoe split is, she's got amnesia."

Isn't that convenient. "Tell me about her. Everything you can remember." He tried to sound curious rather than interrogative.

After another shared glance, and another shrug from the woman, Schaeffer continued. "Thus far, all she remembers with any certainty is her name. But we think maybe she has some sort of martial arts or military training."

"Do you?" Bruce asked the woman.

Ayers only shrugged again. She seemed furious, arms crossed, listening to the men talk about her as if she weren't here.

Schaeffer continued. "Wherever she learned it, she most certainly has—" He thought about it. "—'skills,' I guess you'd say."

Bruce remembered the fight in the parking lot he'd watched on YouTube. Evidently posted by some teenager who'd captured the scene on his phone, it had been entitled, *Zoe is her name, and she kicks ass!* In fact, only when coupled with the video had the FaceBook post piqued his interest enough to pursue.

He decided to go out on a limb. He removed from his inside coat pocket a three by five manila envelope. From it, he extracted sixteen portrait photographs of different women and laid them out in a grid on the table. "Any of these ring a bell?"

She leaned forward and scanned the photos. Almost immediately, she gasped. "Oh shit." She pointed to the third row, second photograph. Still looking at it, she said, "That's me." Then to Schaeffer, "That's *me.*" She shook her head and her face contorted.

"It's okay," Schaeffer consoled. "I mean, this is good, right?"

"I don't know." She stared back at the photo.

"Whatever this is, we'll get through it." He took her hand and added, "Together."

If she was faking it, she was doing a hell of a job. Of course, Bruce had already determined she was good. But the woman seemed genuinely chastened. Shocked. That type reaction was difficult to fabricate.

More curious was why she would admit recognizing the photograph—much less make the ludicrous claim it was her— if indeed these two were up to something. He'd come for answers but was ending up with only more questions.

As if by the flipping of a switch, she . . . changed. Her face relaxed. Her shoulders seemed to slump, almost imperceptibly. She looked up at him and offered a hint of a smile.

"Wait a minute," Bruce said. "You're saying that's *you?*"

"Huh?" She seemed confused.

"This one." He leaned forward and tapped the face she'd indicated. "You said, *That's me.* What did you mean by that?"

"I'm sorry. I lost time again." She said it with an awkward kind of laugh, a touch too dramatic as she were one step from crying. Blatantly obvious, the drawl was back.

"The photograph?" Bruce prompted.

She looked at the faces again, the image at which Bruce held his finger. "Oh I *wish* that was me! She's pretty."

Bruce blinked twice. "You said that *was* you. Just now. Why would you say that?"

"No, that ain't me. I never seen her in my life."

Bruce threw up his hands, let them fall to his lap. He looked to Schaeffer for guidance.

"That's how it happens. There's no rhyme or reason, nothing that triggers the change. Not that we can determine."

Yeah I'll bet. Bruce shook his head and plucked the grid of faces from the table. "Fair enough." He stuffed them neatly into the envelope, which disappeared into his coat.

Schaeffer said, "Mind if we hang on to that photo?"

"Sorry, no can do."

"Can we at least make a copy?"

Bruce shook his head slowly, pursed his lips. "I took a risk even showing it to you." He stood.

Freddie followed suit. Ayers rose as well, less distressed than the men, sipping her water as she stood.

"But we've already seen it. What harm could it possibly—"

"Sorry. Now if you'll excuse me . . ."

Julie had padded around behind them on her way to the door. "Well, it's been nice havin' you."

Bruce followed her, Freddie close behind.

Almost to the door, Bruce turned to the handyman. "Mr. Schaeffer?" he said with a nod, in way of a goodbye. The men shook hands.

When Bruce turned, the woman was there. "I hope you— *AH!*" She ran right into him, cup first, splashing water all over his damn coat. "Oh my!" She blushed, began brushing at the spill with her left hand ("Now look what I done."), cup in her right ("I am *so sorry!"),* checking under his lapel, tugging at his collar . . .

Then she dropped the cup, ejecting the remaining water onto his shoes and pants.

"Oooh!" This time she could only laugh. Bruce didn't blame her; she'd really just totally klutzed it. She bent to one pant leg, wiping at it with the tail of her shirt.

"It's okay, don't worry." Bruce was thinking, *What a clusterfuck.* He stepped back away from the puddle, out of reach of the woman's fretting.

"I'll go get a towel." She disappeared around the corner, fussing and laughing at herself.

Schaeffer said, "I'm so sorry. Will you be back? Next time maybe in a bathing suit?"

Despite himself, Bruce laughed. Connecting with people was unwise in this business, but he couldn't help liking these guys. "I'll report my findings and see what they say. Chances are, you'll be hearing from me."

Julie appeared with a towel. Before she could attack him with it, Bruce said thanks and took it from her. Most of the water had already soaked in, but he managed to dab up a little. He handed the towel back and Julie bent to wipe the floor.

Meanwhile, Schaeffer had opened the door.

Bruce finally took his leave amidst a flurry of apologies and well-wishes.

-Tail-

As Bruce drove away, he barely registered the electric-blue classic Plymouth a block or so behind him. He wouldn't have noticed at all had the doors not been rattling off the damn thing, to the subsonic thump and hum of gansta rap. Why did they do that? Probably the same reason a peacock broke its back with nine pounds of superfluous feathers during mating season.

Street thugs didn't phase him. They wouldn't start any shit unless you gave them shit. And if they did, there was little out of which he couldn't talk his way—or kill his way if they made him. They meant nothing more to him than the inconvenience of calling for a cleanup crew.

From the backseat of the Plymouth, a voice as if from a gremlin said, "Stay back."

Tank reached to turn down the music.

"Don't touch it."

"I can't hear nothing!" Tank glanced at Pokey in the passenger's seat for some support. Pokey only scowled at the windshield, his cheeks scrunched over the rim of his neck brace.

"The beat our cover." The gremlin's abrasive voice was somehow audible over the music, even without raising it.

"Cover?" Tank glanced in the rearview. All he could see was two glowing eyes and a perfect set of gleaming white teeth. "The whole neighborhood know we here!"

The perfect teeth cackled and sat back. "That's right. Now who in their right mind gonna tail somebody with their music blastin'?"

The hoodlum beside the gremlin, in dreadlocks and shades, nodded and smiled at his boss.

Tank said, "Who you think he is?"

"Bodyguard, cop, don't matter."

"Why we followin' him?"

The teeth in the rearview just grinned.

When they reached the hotel, the gremlin leaned over the seat. "Drive on past." About a block later, he said, "Make a U. Cut the tunes."

Tank obeyed.

The gremlin had him park across the street from the hotel, just as the bodyguard entered his room.

"There he go," said Pokey. He reached for the door handle.

"No," said the gremlin, stopping him. "He know somethin'."

"Know somethin'?" asked Dreads.

"Like Karate or somethin'."

"Karate?" Tank said. "Who the fuck care about some damn *Karate?"*

The gremlin shook his head and laughed. "Not Karate. *Like* Karate. Dude know how to handle his self. Always watchin' but don't *look* like he watchin'. Packin' for sure."

"What we gonna do then, *watch* him to death?"

They all got a kick out of that, even the gremlin. He said, "We give him a little bit. He'll come on out later, feel more comfortable. Relaxed. Let his guard down a little."

"How you know?" Pokey asked.

"Just watch," said the Gremlin. "Here's what we do."

-Sleepers-

Twenty minutes later, Bruce was locking himself in his room. He'd been mulling it over the entire trip back to the hotel. *Who the hell* were *those people?*

He threw the clipboard on the bed.

Why would the woman claim to be someone she clearly wasn't? What were they up to, if anything? Had to be something. Had to be.

The possibility of their being sleepers for the Russians—or anyone else for that matter—had occurred to him.

He removed the hip holster and set the whole rig on the dresser.

Thing is, he knew a sleeper when he saw one, if he spent any time at all with them. Yes, they were pros at assimilating. But they themselves always knew what they were. There was a transience about them, especially when it came to their living space. There were either too many family photos—or not enough. The dwellings were almost always tidy and well-maintained, absent the clutter of most American households. It was as if, subconsciously, they were living out of boxes, ready to move on a moments notice. Because it wasn't truly their home, not really. It wasn't even their country.

He started to remove his sport coat . . . then stopped. He shrugged it back on and patted himself down. Outer pockets, breast pocket . . . then finally the inner pockets, through the outside of the coat. He blushed, closed his eyes, shook his head. He stuck his right hand in the left inner pocket, then his left hand in the right. Amy's photo was there as always, but nothing more.

He rummaged through his pants pockets just to be thorough.

It wasn't here. No envelope of women's faces. No *Decker's* face.

She'd done it again.

-Girl's gotta Make a Living-

As soon as the door fell shut, Julie scampered to the kitchen. Freddie locked up and followed. Julie came running back, halting him, hands behind her.

"Close your eyes." She was beaming like a birthday girl.

Freddie cocked his head—then closed his eyes.

After a pause, she said, "Okay. Open!"

Dirty little grin on her face, she held out an envelope. *The* envelope. Freddie slowly took it, thinking, *Surely not.* Eyes on the girl, he opened it and fished out the photos. After a pause, he shuffled through to Zoe's face.

His gaze returned to Julie. "How did you—"

"Girl's gotta make a livin' somehow between jobs." She shrugged then bobbed on her toes.

"Why you sneaky little . . ." To her squeals of delight, Freddie lifted Julie and spun her around in a bear hug.

CHAPTER FIVE

DANGEROUS

-Somnambulism-

*B*ionic bouncers tossed cars from their paths like card-board boxes. Freddie, Julie's hand in his, muddled through all that remained of her life—waist deep in acrid gray sludge. Julie became Zoe, and Zoe turned on the bouncers. "Sea level," she said calmly—as if that made any sense. "Desalt."

"What are you saying?!"

"Drawer number seven."

Freddie bolted upright. He reached for Julie but found only cold sheets in the darkness.

Someone was in the room.

Standing at the foot of the bed, a human form—hazy but more substantive than a mere shadow.

"I'm learning," she said. "They're teaching me."

It was Julie. Or Zoe.

Or perhaps he was still dreaming, the voice no more real than the sliver of ice sliding down his spine. At that moment, he saw this strange psychology not as novel, not as a singularly interesting puzzle—but as a tangible thing, sinister, something from which he should have fled long ago.

"She's jumping the carousel." Deeper, like she was impersonating a man. "Worse than before."

His hands trembled. A sense of dread spiked his stark fear. After all, what did he really know about Dissociative Identity Disorder? How stable—or unstable—was a victim of the condition? Did it involve a malady of a physical nature? A pinhole in the brain, perhaps? A tiny puncture in one of a billion cranial capillaries, releasing a minutia of blood—or spinal or cerebral fluid or what-the-hell-ever circulated in there—into a place it didn't belong? Was it slowly flooding the part of her brain that took in the world, causing it to perceive reality as a nightmare fantasy? Was the pressure spiking? About to blow?

Suddenly his armchair research seemed pathetically naïve. How could he have kidded himself like this? He should have gotten her to a doctor. "Zoe?" His voice quivered.

Slowly, he slid to the edge of the bed, then stood. He approached her, carefully . . . cautiously.

She seemed to be touching her temple with her right hand, as if massaging a headache. But the angle of her arm was off. As he neared and she resolved in the gloom, he realized why.

In her hand, muzzle pressed firmly to her skull, was the fully loaded Smith and Wesson 357 magnum revolver he kept in his nightstand. He cursed himself for failing to forecast a scenario such as this. After all, there was someone with a mental disorder living in the house. He should have secured the firearm.

Too late.

The gun was cocked. In this condition, the lightest of touches—even the cold breath of a ghostly breeze upon the trigger—would loose the hammer. Even now, he could hear the deafening thunder. Through the gloom, in his mind's eye, he was nauseated by the macabre maroon mosaic sliding down the mirrored closet door.

"Zoe?" Instinct told him that's who was present now, not the poet.

"Sea level. Desalt. Drawer number seven."

Her eyes were open. They looked cataracted. Dead. It was just the effect of distilled moonlight bleeding through the curtains. Her eyes were perfectly fine. That's what he told himself.

"Sea level. Desalt. Drawer number seven." She spoke it deadpan, with not a hint of anguish.

Somnambulism.

She's sleepwalking!

She was wandering, eyes wide open, through a world of dark fantasy, or perhaps living old memories. Unmoored from reality, she could perceive Freddie himself as an angel, a monster—or anything at all. His spine tingled when he realized that, with but a flick of her wrist, the pistol could be turned on him.

And fired in a heartbeat.

To hell with it, he thought. *In for a penny, in for a pound.* He would by God figure this out or he would die trying. "Zoe, honey, give me the gun." He reached his right hand for the weapon, his left for her wrist, lest she decide to swing the gun toward him. She was fast; he knew that. But perhaps her dream state would delay her ever so slightly, maybe at least give him a ghost of a chance.

"I'm not ready yet."

Freddie thought the statement referred to his suggestion of surrendering the 357.

Then she continued. "I'm learning though." She stared at something in the darkness. Unmoving. "Testing is teaching."

Silence. A cat howled outside then bolted into the night.

"When I'm ready, I'm going to kill you all."

Freddie's chills loosed anew. He realized he and Julie had fallen asleep naked. Bodies laid bare, and their minds. Utterly vulnerable.

"Give me the gun," he said again, closing the gap between his quivering hand and the cold steel.

"Within my grasp," she whispered, "is the power of a *god*."

It seemed obvious she was talking about the pistol. Yet somehow he knew this wasn't the case. Again she'd changed her voice dramatically; it seemed she was impersonating a man. Even the dialect was different.

Could this be the manifestation of a third split? He hoped not. It was hard enough living with two women in one body. He didn't think he'd be able to cope with adding a man to the mix.

"Sea level."

He moved closer . . .

"Desalt!"

He flinched—then kept creeping forward.

"Drawer number seven."

He finally made it to the pistol and grasped it by the cylinder, his thumb between the grip and trigger guard.

"It won't let me die."

With a quiet *snick* and startling pinch, the hammer fell on the web of his thumb.

-Ice Machine-

Bruce had considered jetting back over to the Schaeffer's to confront them, even had his hand on the knob.

He'd decided against it. Of course Julie Ayers would deny having picked his pocket. But even if she admitted it—and returned the envelope complete with an apology, wet kiss and a heart-shaped box of chocolates—he could never be certain they hadn't copied the photo. Or posted it all over the damn internet. No, in the end, he just had to chalk up another one for the woman.

A half smile stole over his face. Henceforth, he'd keep a closer eye on the little shit.

Now he laid sprawled on the bed, still fully dressed. He thought about his exit strategy, with or without Decker. He'd made his play with Creed, but that didn't mean it would be smooth sailing.

In this business, you didn't just quit. Apply for a new job. Clap your old x-boss on the back when you saw him on the street years later. No, in this business, your x-boss *shot* you in the back when he saw you on the street years later. After all, Bruce knew where all the bodies were buried.

He thought he could pull it off. He had plenty of money and knew how to vanish. He had Creed by the short hairs, and it seemed as though the Colonel had gotten the message. By no means a guarantee of impunity, it was at least decent insurance.

He'd move out to the country, somewhere off the grid. Raise Christie as his own. Get another shot at some semblance of a life. Make up for lost time with his sister. And if they did manage to catch up with them?

Well, he wouldn't allow either of them to be taken alive.

A sudden craving for a Coke overcame him. He rose, plucked his holster off the dresser and withdrew the pistol. He screwed on the suppressor. It wasn't likely he'd need the weapon, but you just never knew.

He stuck the gun in his belt and shrugged on his sport coat. He grabbed the ice bucket, made sure he had his swipe card and cash on him, then headed out the door.

The sidewalk was sheltered by the walkway of the floor above, lit by screw-in fluorescents mounted at each door. Bugs, of which there were many, twittered around the lights.

The only sound was the subtle hum of membranous wings, and carapaces bashing the bulbs. A translucent gecko slinked silently amongst them, snapping up moths. With one eye like a tiny anthracite marble, it maintained a vigil on Bruce as if he might make a sudden lunge for its wriggly dinner.

Bruce stiffened at the crescendo of approaching wheels on squeaky bearings. He walked on, relaxed but vigilant.

A housekeeper—black male, mid to late twenties, below average height—turned the corner toward him. Pushing a cleaning cart.

Bruce immediately knew something wasn't right. First, it was a guy. Sexist stereotype or not, these positions were usually filled by women. Usually.

And wasn't it a little late for housekeeping? Maybe not. Maybe the staff was working overtime prepping rooms for tomorrow morning.

The guy wore a hotel smock complete with embroidered logo. But his hair was out of control, bunched up in blunt spiky dreads. Surely the hotel would have made him tone it down. Of course, who knew these days? Criticizing someone's hairstyle might be considered "insensitive."

The housekeeper wore a vapid grin, as if something was funny, but only to him. Then he began whistling. When they passed on the walkway, Bruce raised his chin in greeting, met his eyes directly, letting him know he'd been spotted and scrutinized.

"Wha's up?" The guy had a voice like an overgrown gremlin.

The squeak faded, and the carefree whistling, and Bruce made it to the vending area without having to shoot anyone.

He filled the bucket with ice, watching his six while noise from the machine might mask a stealthy approach.

The walkway remained deserted.

He inserted six quarters in the Coke machine *(Jesus! A buck and a half!),* stewing on what, exactly, to do with Schaeffer and the woman.

The Coke clunked into the delivery compartment. He fished it out, mashed it down into the ice and headed back out onto the walkway.

She was not Zoe Decker. But the likeness in mannerisms and speech was simply uncanny. This was perplexing, almost a little disturbing when coupled with the fact that she claimed to *be* Decker.

Sometimes.

He shook his head, puzzling it over.

It would be worth one more interview just to see what else he might be able to glean. Besides, it was sure to be at least interesting.

He turned the corner . . .

And froze.

The cleaning cart. Parked sideways. Obstructing his path. Staring at him over the top, the unlikely housekeeper. Still grinning ear to ear. Bruce now saw the expression for what it was. Not vapid, not blissful, but deranged. His skin prickled.

"Was' up?"

He dropped the bucket, thumbed open the sport coat and went for his piece. Finger already on the trigger, he raised the gun in a flash.

A fist like a sledgehammer came down from behind him. Right on his forearm. Hand instantly numb. The pistol discharged harmlessly into the sod. The clatter of steel on concrete was louder than the report.

Before Bruce could turn, a hand like a fat steak covered his mouth. Crushed his face. Pinned him head to torso. Bruce's arms instinctively shot up and back, seeking eyes, lips, nostrils—anything he could rip or gouge in defense. His hands found only a chest like a side of beef.

Something slammed against his kidneys. His eyes grew to dinner plates, locked on the freak behind the cleaning cart. The man behind him hit his kidneys again—then repeatedly.

Bruce found himself floating on a cloud of euphoria. His thoughts were cast back decades, to a memory long forgotten. He'd fallen off the monkey bars at the park. He'd have cried, but his lungs wouldn't work. He panicked, unable to breath.

Amy appeared over him. She tugged at his sleeve. "Don't worry, Bruce! I'll save you!"

His struggles waned. His will leaked away like blood from a stuck pig. The strikes, he realized, had not been so much *against* his kidneys, as *into* them.

The euphoric cloud curdled as skeins of pain bolted like lightning, around his waist, up his spine, through his solar-plexus and into his brain.

The world begin to spin. His arms dropped. His knees buckled. The Goliath released him and he collapsed like a crumbling conquered castle.

He somehow managed to roll onto his back.

Bruce knew enough about anatomy to know he was finished.

In Hollywood, when stealthy murder was portrayed, spies slit the throats of their victims. This was only so the violence could be viewed in concert with the chiseled faces of the stars. In fact, with all the gurgling and spewing, this was much too noisy. Not to mention messy. And while indeed fatal, the victim could live, and in some cases put up a considerable fight, for many seconds or even minutes.

The most effective way to quickly and quietly neutralize a target was to destroy the kidneys. The victim went into immediate shock, as Bruce had. They'd still have plenty of time to ponder their demise, but they'd do it silently, peacefully.

As Bruce was.

Man, what would they think back at the agency? Bruce Vega, taken out by a couple of common street fucks.

The gremlin appeared above him. "Ain't never heard one of these." He was examining Bruce's pistol. "That shit *quiet.*"

Bruce's trembling hand slipped beneath his coat. The gremlin, grinning, turned the Springfield on him.

"Now—" Bruce did his best to conjure a smile. "—don't go jumping to conclusions." He choked, fought off the nausea, and slowly drew out his hand. In it, the photo. "You guys—" A coughing spasm ejected blood onto his face. He spit, sucked in a breath. "You guys . . . by chance . . . seen this girl?" He held up the photo. His hand shook much too violently for anything in it to be examined.

The freak lowered the gun and turned to the walking house. After a beat, he broke into laughter. Then looked back down at Bruce. "Maaan, you *trippin'!*"

Bruce laughed along with them—until another coughing spasm sobered him.

Shadows like ghosts stalked the sidewalk, cast by Kamikazes bashing the bulbs, drunk on the light. The gecko stole another bite.

"Ready?" Solemn. Almost kind. But grinning, always grinning. The freak pointed the Springfield down at Bruce.

Funny, this was the first time Bruce had ever seen it from this perspective. It looked downright intimidating. Badass.

He turned the photo to himself. He saw it as he never had before. She spoke to him, as never she had before.

He smiled back at her. "I'll find you."

And he would.

The freak shot Bruce in the face.

-Stand at the Door-

Freddie nearly jumped out of his skin. His entire body shuddered at the thought that only a split second—and a delicate flap of flesh—had lain between the subtle click and tragedy.

She willingly relinquished the Smith. Her arm fell to her side.

Without taking his eyes from her, he popped the cylinder and shook out the heavy gleaming rounds. He reached over and dropped the bullets on the dresser. The hushed clatter was deafening in the silence. Then he squatted, still watching her, and set the neutralized weapon at the foot of the bed.

He stood once more before her. She radiated heat like a furnace.

"No offense." He just blurted it out without thinking.

She cocked her head as if listening for something. "None taken."

Slowly, cautiously, he embraced her. Despite himself, he realized, a stir of arousal crept through him. Maybe it had something to do with his relief that the crisis was contained. Maybe it was her warmth—and of course their nakedness. Regardless, it was involuntary. The more he resisted it the more insistent it became.

That damned male instinct. It seemed God had cursed his gender with it, he supposed in order to ensure there would be a next generation. And perhaps the female instinct for intimacy to be intertwined with order and security ensured the next generation would actually survive.

"Freddie Schaeffer." His words were muffled, lips pressed to her hair. Her scent was intoxicating.

"Zoe Decker. Pleased to—" She gasped and stiffened, fully alert now. She snapped her head left—then right—taking in her surroundings.

She returned his embrace, perhaps unconsciously. Her heart raced against his tummy like a frightened bird. Though he tried to block it from his mind, the heat of her breasts sent a shiver through him. He held her there, doing his best to resist the steady crescendo of desire.

Her pulse slowed. She looked up at him. "Why is it every time I come around, *you're* here?" Affectionately, not as an accusation.

He wondered if she was aware of what had grown between them. At this point, he wondered how she could *not* feel it. There wasn't a chance in hell she'd believe it had risen involuntarily. He was embarrassed, and this somehow further fueled his arousal.

"And of course I just happen to be naked." She stood on bare toes and kissed him, this time not chastely at all.

Her feet left the floor—and he found himself encoiled as if by a python. Then, still locked in a kiss, she somehow guided him inside her. It was Freddie's turn to gasp.

As in all things, Zoe took charge. She pleasured herself with him—biting his shoulder, *using* him—but that was okay with Freddie. When she finished, a sheen of sweat now slick on her back, one delicate foot took to the floor and she deftly pivoted and pulled him to the bed, now under him. *Your turn,* she seemed to be saying.

But she wasn't finished. Crimson trails tracing his back, she used him again, which only inflamed his desire further.

On and on, she flipped around, knelt and twisted, spun and stood, now at the mirror, now the dresser, then back to the bed, all a blur, his vision swimming, subconscious thoughts previously hidden to him like horses battering the walls of their stables, now running wild and free, out of control.

When she finally allowed his release, it seemed to have happened years ago in a time long forgotten.

The blades of the ceiling fan cut the air above him, drying his sweat, the stallions sated, ambling back to the stable like old nags.

He felt like he'd just been through a UFC match. Full contact, no holds barred. Biting and clawing not only permitted but encouraged. It seemed to have been a dream, but the burning scores on his shoulders and back assured him it had been real.

Pleasure and pain.

Bittersweet.

Life itself.

Julie had claimed the women shared one heart. He wondered whether she—or Zoe—would be as tolerant about sharing *this*. Guilt bit at him, as if he'd cheated on them both. But what the hell was he supposed to do?

And how utterly different they'd been! Stunning, really. Julie, seemingly terrified of his gaze by day, had wordlessly begged him not to look away. Zoe, whose eyes sucked you in like a collapsed star, *demanding* direct contact—had met his eyes not once, not one single time, as if she were ashamed of or intimidated by the intimacy.

"Don't get the wrong idea," she said. "This doesn't mean we're picking out curtains together or something." But her head lay on his shoulder, body warm against his, her fingers toying absently with the hair on his chest.

"Ah. I prefer shades anyway."

She chuffed, amused.

Freddie considered asking about the sleepwalking incident. They'd learn more if they spoke while it was fresh. But then again, that would ruin the moment. No, he'd take it up with her in the morning.

Through the dim light, she said, "Tell me about Stevie."

Though he tried to hide it, Freddie tensed. He was moved by her inquiry; the unveiled sympathy was unlike her. Of course, she'd expressed it as a demand rather than a question *(Would you feel comfortable talking about Stevie?),* but still. Concern for another human being—allowing one's self to care—was an emotional risk. Especially for Zoe. How had Julie put it?

All that tough talk? That's just her looking out for the scared little girl inside her.

Zoe had taken a risk, so Freddie would too—as much as he was able. He thought about Stevie, all the things that had happened, all the things that hadn't, and sighed. "He blames me. For his mother."

"Did you talk to him about it?"

"A few times." He creased his brow. He was sure they'd discussed it, but couldn't recall any specific conversation.

He didn't want to talk about this. It scared him somehow. Terrified him. If it hadn't been Zoe, he'd have told her to go pound sand.

"Surely you could make him understand, point out you did all you could."

The blades kept turning, each revolution ticking off another second since he'd spoken with his son.

Tick tock. Tick tock.

"I could never convince Stevie because I don't believe it myself."

"That is so much bullshit." She said it softly, snuggling up to him as she spoke.

Freddie said nothing. His pulse was quickening.

"Where is he now?"

His growing sense of dread baffled him. "Out in California. Working as a barista, singing in a heavy metal band. I've heard their stuff on YouTube. They're good, but the lyrics are obscene. Harsh as all hell. Angry." He knew this was the case, but he could not have quoted a single harsh lyric.

"Ya think?" Zoe kissed his shoulder. "When's the last time you spoke with him?"

Freddie had begun to tremble. He simply could not talk about it. Not this.

He forged ahead anyway. "Maybe five years ago?" It wasn't five years. In truth, he had no idea how long it had been. Five sounded about right; five would work.

Zoe rose on her elbow, staring down at him in the darkness. "Five *years?*"

Freddie pretended the question was rhetorical, but Zoe's gaze burned the side of his face. He glanced at her, then back up at the ceiling fan. "Something like that."

She lay back down.

After a time, she said, "Call him, Freddie." Her words were quiet, the night's effort catching up to her.

Freddie stared at the murky blades above, cutting the air like anguish cut at his heart. "There's nothing I could say." Eyes wide open, he was frozen. Still as a corpse. "He won't let me in."

He thought she'd nodded off. He lay there in dark solitude, and the blades just kept on cutting.

She whispered, "Then just stand at the door."

-Watchers-

A few minutes later, as Freddie and Zoe lay dead to the world, the lights of the classic blue Plymouth blinked to life three doors down and across the street at an abandoned lot.

Tank said, "We ghosted the bodyguard, so how come we not takin' out the Shrek?"

The gremlin smiled. "Respect. He got big-ups. You don't kill that. Not 'til you let him try a little."

Tank didn't understand, but he didn't argue.

With no music playing, the car pulled away.

-Nail-

There was nothing like the smell of freshly brewed coffee in the morning.

Freddie sat up and stretched, heaved himself off the bed and slipped on some boxers and a t-shirt.

He padded to the bathroom. As he stood relieving himself, one hand braced on the wall above the toilet, he wondered who he'd find in the kitchen this morning. He figured if it were Jules, she'd have been working on breakfast.

No merry tinkling of cookware rang out from the kitchen, nor could he discern the aromas of bacon, eggs, biscuits—or anything for that matter. Just coffee.

He loosed a big yawn, trying not to let it screw up his aim.

Zoe then. That was good, because they had much to discuss. Not sex, of course. He'd long since realized that, while men enjoyed a review of highlights the morning after—if not a full-blown play-by-play—women seemed to prefer pretending it never happened. At most, they may allow a *Mornin', sexy* or something like that.

At most.

Best bet was to just keep your mouth shut—and hope it wouldn't be too long before the next time.

He flushed the toilet and did a closer inspection of his mug. No good. He cranked the spigot and splashed water over his face and through his hair.

No, what he wanted to talk about was sleepwalking.

She'd said some strange things—outright disturbing things. Maybe it was a just a nightmare, but even so. Some small detail of the event, seemingly insignificant at the time, may result in the recall of even just a moment from her past. He'd take that.

Because perhaps that moment would represent a pinhole in the dike that barricaded her memory. With a little prodding, perhaps the perforation would become a fissure, the fissure a crack, and the crack an all-out disintegration of the dam, the breaching of which would allow the spilling forth of all the memories of her life.

Enlivened by the hope of a breakthrough, he dried his face on a hand towel, after which he consulted the mirror one final time.

Close enough.

"Good morning," he called, flipping out the bathroom light as he rounded the corner. He was careful to avoid using either of her names. He passed through the kitchen on the way to the living room, glancing at the countertops, confirming the absence of pots, pans, spatulas or spoons—or any breakfast bouquet. Just as he entered the larger quarters, he realized what he did smell.

Spicy cologne.

Sprawled on the couch, legs crossed casually, sipping coffee from Freddie's favorite mug, sat Pokey the bouncer in a neck brace. In his lap lay a battery operated nailgun. Freddie recognized it as the exact model he himself used. He kept it in the van. In fact, he realized, they were one and the same tool.

A flood of emotions swept through him. He felt bested. Violated. Outmaneuvered. *Infuriated* . . . then suddenly terrified as it dawned on him the woman was nowhere to be seen.

"Mornin' Sunshine!" said the bouncer.

Something slammed the base of Freddie's skull.

Flash of light.

Buzzing.

Ringing.

Dancing spots.

Freddie found himself on his hands and knees, watching a tear-blurred line of his drool puddle on the floor. Had it been but a minute? Seconds? Or had he been laying here for an hour, only now recovering enough to make it to his knees?

Muted voices:

"Why you gotta . . . *something* . . . 'bout killed his ass, dumb fuck!"

"Paxyl say . . . *something* . . . if he . . . *something* . . . "

Freddie shook his head, lazily—and realized he was crawling.

Interesting. He wasn't *trying* to crawl; his hands and knees seemed to have just made the decision on their own.

The voices continued, unintelligible.

Delirium.

Watching the grout lines pass as he proceeded, seemingly for miles, his progress was stunted when his head bumped into something.

Huh?

He looked up, wobbling with the effort.

Oh.

End table.

With a monumental effort, he lifted his left hand and slapped it palm down, fingers splayed for stability, onto the tabletop. He hefted himself to his knees and shook his head more forcefully.

Mistake.

The room faded and resolved, rocking like a ship in stormy waters.

His stomach rolled.

Choke it down.

Breathe. That's it . . .

Pokey: "Hey." Closer, from directly behind him. "Shrek."

Freddie turned his head, slowly lest another wave of nausea seize him. He faltered, almost fell, then caught himself. He pressed his left hand even tighter to the table, his right hovering for balance.

The bouncer moved to the side of the table so Freddie wouldn't have to crane his neck so far. "*Hey!*" he repeated. "You with us, big boy?"

"*What?*" Freddie mumbled, as if he'd just heard something incredible.

The bouncer leaned down to him, shouting this time. "Do-you-understand-the-words-that's-comin'-out-my-mouth?" He enunciated clearly as if Freddie were hard of hearing—which he kind of was at the moment.

Freddie just gaped, but his head was clearing—a little.

"Gotta a message for you! From Paxyl!" Pokey pressed the nailgun to the back of Freddie's hand.

Freddie gawked at the tool—then back up at Pokey. *"What?!"*

With a deafening report, Pokey nailed Freddie's hand to the table.

-Pain-

Searing.

Biting.

Pain, Freddie realized, was a living thing—a pervasive, insistent, *animal* thing—on him, *in* him, demanding his immediate, undivided attention.

He sucked a breath, long and deep. Even that subtle movement shot bolts of lightning from the breach in his hand, across his wrist, up his arm, through his shoulder, around his skull and into his brain—where it proceeded to burn a pinhole in his delicate gray matter. He was shockingly aware of every nerve around the injury, each screaming louder than the next, all fighting for priority placement on the lava lightning.

He released the pent-up breath in a scream, but it came out only as a muted snarl.

Shuffling.

Garbled voices.

Freddie released another breath he hadn't realized he'd taken.

His vision blurred.

A hammer clattered to the end table, inches from his violated flesh. He flinched, rocketing new signals of trauma along the scorched path to his head.

"G' luck," said Pokey. "Stay away from Star. Last warning."

The words registered, but Freddie could muster not one ounce of concern for them, his attention—the entire essence of his being—focused on the nail.

Time stood still.

Keening . . . his.

Somewhere in this waking nightmare, Pokey's voice cut through the dreamscape. *"Something something . . .* 'cause the den ain't got no power."

The Den.

Freddie knew this was important, but he had trouble figuring out why, exactly. Nor did he particularly care.

Tick tock. Tick tock.

Hands frozen in place.

(Icy cold, white-hot . . .)

The front door slammed.

An eternity passed.

Ragged breathing . . .

The Plymouth started in the driveway, ran for a moment (they were in no hurry), then gravel crunched as it slowly backed out. He thought he heard it pull away.

Alone.

(Pain)

Just Freddie and the nail.

(Lightning)

And the hammer—oh Jesus, the hammer. He started to panic—caught himself.

(Breathe . . .)

In for two, out for two.

Again . . . That's it . . .

(PAIN!)

He risked a glance at his hand. As expected, a length of shaft gleamed above his flesh. Freddie knew it was precisely one-quarter inch. That's how he'd last set the gun, and that— thank God—is how it had functioned. Had he set it to countersink . . .

The wound.

Surprisingly, the whole tableau was rather anti-climactic. Matter of fact. Just a hand—*his* hand—still splayed on the coffee table, the only odd thing being that quarter inch of steel exposed above the flesh. Like some macabre jewelry, it glittered between the metacarpals of his pointer and middle fingers—his peace sign.

Pierced peace.

The bones appeared to be untouched and intact, the smooth shaft having penetrated only flesh—a Godsend. Had either bone been clipped, much less penetrated, he'd have needed medical attention sooner rather than later. They'd have questioned him as to how this had happened. They'd have viewed with suspicion any lie of which Freddie could think at the moment. They may have summoned the police.

(There was a murder last night.)

Besides, he had places he needed to be.

He thought he could avoid the emergency room. Probably. Hopefully.

There was little blood and no bruising. Yet.

Just pain.

Okay, so here he was. Panic wouldn't help. He'd been injured on the job before, although certainly not this badly. Still, it was only an injury.

Just a nail.

(And pain.)

Zoe!

They'd taken her.

No. Not Zoe.

Had it been Zoe, he'd have discovered two corpses on the living room floor, bound in lamp cord and duct tape, the woman curled on the couch, casually sipping her morning brew.

(Mornin' Sunshine.)

Julie then. They had to have taken her while she was Julie. Had they been watching? Lounging on the couch, waiting? Had they taken her the moment she entered the kitchen? Or in the yard while she was out picking morning glories? The poor sweet thing wouldn't have lifted a finger to stop them. Was she afraid? Did she just blindly trust that Freddie would come for her? He thought of the poem she'd improvised seemingly an eternity ago.

(My boy, who's come to rescue me.)

He would come for her alright. And he'd by God come for the bouncers. And this time, he'd—

PAIN!

Stop it.

That was for later.

What did he need to do—*right now?*

Now was now. Now was the nail—the nail—the gleaming fucking nail, the matter of fact, eternally patient, diamond hard, white-hot, searing Goddamn nail.

He grimaced as he hefted the hammer with his right hand. A bead of sweat trickled down his brow and found its way into his eye. He raised his hand to wipe it away, of course bonking his head with the hammer in the process.

Dancing spots.

He tried the obvious first, which was fixing the claw of the hammer under the nail head. The electric touch of metal-on-metal was like a high voltage shock to the exposed nerve of a rotten tooth.

Ignoring the pain—and the spittle flying from between his clenched teeth—he fixed the claw in place, tested several angles.

No good.

The counter-pressure necessary to pull the nail free would inflict severe damage on the rest of his hand. He was going to need it fully functional—

(for later)

—or at least in some semblance of working order.

He tried positioning the hammer under the table. He realized he'd need to situate himself so that he could see the target at which he intended to swing.

He didn't do it. There was insufficient space to chamber the tool.

Okay, so back up a step. What was the problem here? What was the heart of the matter; what was the *real* problem? And what was the simplest solution?

(Pain)

Conventional wisdom dictated this was an injury, a situation, an *emergency*—and that he focus solely on his hand.

But what was it *really?*

Just a nail.

So how would he proceed if his hand were not involved?

He'd extract the nail, of course.

And what was the most effective way to do that?

Why, he'd simply flip the table upside down, throw a brace under each end and hammer the nail back out the way it had gone in.

If his hand were not involved.

He secured a firm, one kneed stance, set the hammer on the arm of the couch and took a few rapid breaths.

"Come on, Fixer. You can do this." He placed his right hand under the table, directly opposite his skewered left, the sharp tip of the nail in the crux of his right peace sign. Before he could think too much about it, he hefted the table. It was tricky, the weight at first born by his right hand, then by his left as he flipped it upside down. Sandwiching the top between his hands held it fairly securely—but hurt like hell.

A muted grunt escaped him, followed by air rasping—in-out-in-out—rapidly between his teeth.

He stood.

He grayed out—paused a moment to ensure he'd maintain consciousness. God only knew what horrific damage he'd do if he passed out, leaving the table to career about uncontrolled. He shuddered at the thought.

Okay, all good.

He cat-stepped toward the kitchen. Left bicep screaming.

Wire cutters were necessary for the procedure he planned, and he kept a pair—along with a few other simple tools—in the rolling kitchen-cart.

Halfway there.

Balance . . . careful . . .

(Pain)

Of course they wouldn't be there. Of course they'd be out in the workshop, requiring him to navigate the yard while balancing this topsy-turvy turkey platter from hell. A thousand trip-and-fall scenarios played through his mind, all of which ended with the guts of his hand dangling from the nail head.

He found himself at the cart.

Please be there . . .

Now what?

The tabletop was sandwiched between his hands, minimizing sway and jiggle. If he removed his right, would he discover his impaled left was slightly off center? Would the table lurch left? Or right? Or away from him? Would he wind up juggling the damn thing, inevitably dropping it?

A bolt of lightning shot up his left arm.

(Breathe . . .)

He slowly *(Carefully!)* leaned the legs of the table against the wall, then pressed his body to the edge, pinning it there. Awkward, but it held.

Keeping his eye on the table, watching for even the slightest movement, he cautiously lifted his right hand.

So far so good.

He shot a glance at the front of the cart to locate the drawer pull then immediately refocused on the table. Without looking, he slowly pulled open the drawer and felt blindly inside.

Tape measure. Box end wrench. Scissors. Wire cutters.

Wire cutters!

He grasped the tool firmly (God knows he didn't want to stoop to retrieve it), placed it gently on the upturned table, re-sandwiched his hands and headed back into the living room.

Two chairs, both of which he needed to re-position, sat under the dining table, near the couch and within easy reach of the hammer. This time, in order to perform the necessary furniture arrangement, he was forced to balance the table single-handedly like a pizza tray.

A *heavy-ass* pizza tray.

Nailed to his hand.

His left bicep quivered.

Slowly, carefully, right hand working blindly, ready to abandon mission and support his left if need be, he arranged the chairs facing one another, leaving about a six-inch space between.

Using his right hand for support again, he knelt and allowed the chairs to assume the weight of the upturned end table, his injured hand in the six-inch space beneath. His bicep throbbed with relief. He fought to resist a charley horse.

(Breathe . . .)

Now the hammer.

After setting the wire cutters on the kitchen table, he carefully took the hammer from the arm of the sofa. Grasping the handle firmly, he gently set the head of the tool on the sharp tip of the nail, calibrating the strike he needed to make.

He could do this.

(If his hand were not involved.)

He'd done it a thousand times.

(Pain!)

He slowly pantomimed the strike . . . once . . . twice . . . then raised the hammer to his shoulder, death grip on the handle . . . grimaced . . .

Chickened out.

(Just a nail.)

"Come on, buddy. Julie's waiting."

Then he thought of something. What should he do with his left hand when the nail burst through? Keep it pressed to the table? That would leave no space between his hand and the table, no metal to grasp with the wire cutters when it came time for that phase of the procedure. Moreover, the nail would blast through the wound, dragging God only knew what kind of germs from the wood into his hand.

But if he pulled away as he struck, he risked yanking his hand *too* hard—right over the nail head—and pulling a tangle of veins and tendon from his palm in the process.

So. Push against the table and let the nail shoot through. That seemed the least risky—albeit the most painful.

He balanced the head of the hammer on the sharp tip once more.

He tested the strike one final time.

He pressed his left palm to the upturned tabletop . . . ignoring the warm slickness . . . clenched his jaws tight . . . eyes wide open . . .

He raised the hammer high . . . hesitated . . .

"Fuck it." He slammed it down, *hard*.

An eternity later, a ringing in his ears dragged him back to consciousness.

His eyes were squeezed shut.

The ringing faded and revealed a light rattling: the head of the hammer resting lightly on the table bottom, transmitting via the handle vibrations from his trembling right hand.

His eyes closed even tighter.

He knew what had happened. He was sure of it. He'd only grazed the nail, the shaft of which was now bent ninety degrees, embedded in the wood, locking it firmly in place. He'd have to pry it upright and try again.

Don't pass out . . . Breathe . . .

He opened his eyes.

The nail was gone.

For a moment he was confounded—then realized . . .

He'd slammed it home, all the way through. One shot. The now blunt tip was barely visible in the tiny wood hole.

Good handyman. *GOOOOOD* handyman!

He tossed the hammer aside, forgotten. It sounded like it cracked some tile upon landing. He didn't care.

He hefted the table one last time, flipped it upright, and set it on the floor. It was easy; he was getting used to this.

He grabbed the wire cutters from the dining table and, before he could think too much about it, pulled his pierced hand slowly upward, the puncture wound sliding along the shaft of the nail. His fingers writhed like beheaded snakes.

Quickly now, before he passed out . . . under his hand, grasp the shaft of the nail with the wire cutters . . . sides of the blades pressed to the table . . .

He pried upward. The muted whine of metal on wood was like fingernails on a chalkboard.

(Head swimming.)

Do it again. *Now!*

Another bite with the cutters . . . Another sickening whine . . .

His hand pulled free at last.

Freddie fell back on the floor. Gasping. Tears trickled into his ears, although he didn't think he was crying.

When the glowing ant races behind his eyelids finally dimmed, he hefted himself from the cold tile and headed for the bathroom, left hand cradled in his right.

He snatched open the mirror medicine-cabinet door *(Stranger Danger)* and searched for the Hydrogen Peroxide.

There.

Behind a forest of other products.

He swiped them aside, most landing in the sink. A small bottle shattered on the floor. Using his teeth, he tore open the top of the Peroxide, poured it into his cupped left palm, soaking the nail, his skin, and half the damn bathroom.

After a minute or so of bubbling, he turned his injured hand palm down.

One last task.

With a haunting Bigfoot bellow, he grasped the head of the nail and yanked with all his might.

The nail pulled free.

(*PAIN!*)

He bellowed again and shot the spike clattering into the bathtub. His vision blurred with the effort.

He ran a trickle of warm water into his cupped hand. He made a loose fist under the stream—then opened it . . . repeated the process . . . A little stiff, but not as bad as he'd have expected.

The red swirls turned to pink—then finally to clear—and he closed the faucet. He disinfected one last time, found an old doxycycline prescription bottle on the floor and popped two tablets. He snatched the ibuprofen from the sink basin, opened it and shook out three.

Better make it four . . .

Sucking water from the tap, he washed them all down.

After a generous slathering of Neosporin, he wrapped the hand in gauze, noting again the curious minimal bleeding. He didn't know whether that was good or bad. He thought bleeding was supposed to aid in the removal of contaminants but . . . he was no doctor.

Fuck it.

Almost there.

He stormed into the bedroom, trauma turning to anger, anger to rage. His hands shook. He jerked yesterday's clothes from the hook on the back of his door and found himself standing in them with no memory of having dressed.

He snatched the .357 from the foot of the bed, gathered the cartridges from the dresser, slid them into the cylinder and snapped it shut. From the nightstand, he snared a box of spare ammo and crammed it into his cargo pocket.

He was moving now, in the groove.

He stuffed the revolver in the back of his waistband and headed for the hallway, absently flicking off the bedroom light as he proceeded.

All the agitation stung his injuries anew. Good. The pain would feed his rage, which he needed right now.

Without slowing, he snared his keys off the hook by the refrigerator, headed for the door, almost stumbled over a seat cushion—then burst outside.

He slammed the door behind him. It failed to catch, bounced off the frame and crept back open.

He didn't care.

In the saddle now, Old Mable rumbling to life . . .

Tires spitting gravel, pinging the sides of the van as he backed out—then burning rubber as he sped away . . .

Going . . . going . . . gone.

-Polite Host-

Years ago, Freddie had built a bathroom addition for a beat cop—the father of one of the boys on Stevie's soccer team—Sergeant Manny Inquanzo. Manny was a jolly character, packed a few extra pounds, was quick with a joke and an ardent fan of the team. Freddie would never have pegged him as a cop, not in a million years. He'd have been less surprised to discover the guy was a junior high basketball coach. Or a Chuck E. Cheese character.

There were times when his exuberant sideline shouts and whistles bordered on embarrassing, but somehow with Manny, the cheering came off as good-natured rather than fanatic.

Freddie squealed around a corner, right on red. His heart leaped into his throat as a car barreling from his left, horn blaring, nearly plowed into him.

It didn't take much to launch Manny into war stories of his escapades on the street. He'd once busted a prostitute, the girlfriend of the assistant to a lieutenant of Pablo Escobar. According to Manny, his collar facilitated other arrests up the food chain which eventually led to taking down the kingpin. Of course, Manny had never so much as laid eyes on Escobar himself.

Freddie's spine tingled as he sped past an SUV in a no-passing zone just before the street narrowed to a one-way lane. Old Mable, God bless her, handled the maneuver like a Ferrari. The driver of the SUV, evidently engrossed in thumbing a novel on her cell phone, never even saw the van.

During a lunch break while building out the addition, Manny had once shared a story involving the old Fox's Sherron Inn. "Real shame. Second oldest liquor license in Miami," he always managed to work in.

Originally constructed as an eight-room hotel in the forties, it had undergone ownership change and major renovation in the sixties. The ground floor had been converted to a quaint dining room, kitchen, and bar—the four rooms on the second floor to apartments. It had been a cult favorite in Miami since.

That is, until the owner passed and left the place to his sons—who turned it into a rave bar. Decades of loyal clientele were alienated, replaced my millennials with a taste for ecstasy rather than alcohol. Fights broke out. Drug raids ensued. Profits plummeted. Tempers flared, harsh words exchanged.

Freddie laid on the horn when a '69 Rambler, wisp of blue hair peeking over the driver's seat, braked to a stop at a roundabout. If Old Mable didn't kiss the car's bumper as they blew past, she sure missed a good opportunity.

The van bounced over the curb, jarring Freddie's spine. Tools exploded into the cargo area and shrubs raked the undercarriage.

Fox's had closed nearly five years ago, a sad day for every-one in the area. Since that time, ownership of the property had been in hot dispute, tied up in probate court. The build-ing remained boarded to this day.

Boarded, however, was not synonymous with vacant. Inev-itably, some crack head pried off a sheet of plywood and crawled in to crash for the night. "There's nothing more re-sourceful than a junkie," Manny often said. It didn't take long before drug dealers, prostitutes, and the occasional bold lov-ers were slinking in and out of there like it was Grand Central Station.

Soon, Fox's was back in business—if you had a loose inter-pretation of the term *business*. Available for sale and ex-change were all varieties of contraband and vice, the flavor selection and price dependent on the night, availability of products or services, and who'd claimed the crack house—or crack hotel as it were—as their turf.

Freddie had no recollection of even the vaguest details of Manny's case, but he did remember one thing. Apparently because of the name *Fox's,* and the ten-foot red fox logo that had somehow managed to survive the scrawls of graffiti art-ists, people on the street called it the Fox's Den.

Aka, The Den.

That's what the bouncer had said. *The Den*. So it had to be Fox's.

Freddie cursed and struck the wheel with his left palm *(PAIN!)* when he got caught at a traffic light. Achingly, Fox's was but a block ahead. He debated stopping right there in the middle of traffic and hoofing it the rest of the way. No, he de-cided; he may end up needing to make a hasty exit. Besides, he couldn't be certain he'd even find them there.

He thought of something else. Maybe it was time to bring in the cops. Yes, just call it in and let the chips fall where they may. Perhaps he could reach out to Manny personally, see what he had to say about it. At this point, he'd pretty much decided the murder and planted evidence was a fabrication anyway, concocted either by Big Man or this Paxyl. Probably the latter. Big Man struck Freddie as guileless, despite the employer he'd chosen.

Or maybe the employer had chosen *him*.

He leaned over and dug in his right pocket for the cell phone.

Empty.

Oh shit.

He tried the cargo pocket.

Just his knife.

He threw the van in park so he could focus on the search, then leaned the other way, checked his left hip and cargo pockets.

Only the box of cartridges.

He arched his back to check the rear pockets, but he knew it was pointless. He'd left in a hurry and forgotten to grab his damn phone. The device was an essential part of his daily "carry kit," and he felt naked without it. Had this been any other day, he'd have turned back for it, regardless of the time it took.

Not today.

A horn complained behind him. Freddie looked up to discover the light had changed. He pressed the accelerator—realized it was in park—threw it in gear and surged forward. He weaved from lane to lane, earning the derision of every driver he passed. To hell with them.

He screeched right onto the side street before Fox's, then swerved left onto the back road that led to the alley entrance—now the main entrance. He skidded to a halt and threw it in park. He ripped open the door, not bothering to close it behind him or even shut off the engine. He bounded out. Headed for The Den.

A dumpster with a missing wheel sat askew to the left of the entrance. The door whined open and two black men stepped out—not A.M.E. evangelists, he'd have bet his life on it.

Thank God, Freddie thought. He could think of no other situation in which he'd be glad to be confronting a couple of street thugs. He steamed toward the doorway, utterly undeterred by the hoodlums.

Manny had bored Freddie stiff with all sorts of street advice and tactical strategies. Since it was Manny, Freddie had offered his ear politely, although he had no interest in such things. Now he was glad he'd listened.

One of Manny's tactics was the concept of "Being a Polite Host." When you have company, the strategy theorized, it's polite to provide everyone a little something, then return as quickly as possible to present more substantial offerings on a second trip. That way you kept everyone occupied, left no one empty-handed.

In the same way, when facing multiple opponents, it was prudent to address each of them briefly—as in with a single shot—then return for a second round where necessary to finish them off.

Freddie would be a polite host now.

The first man out the door was tall, almost Freddie's height, and wore dreadlocks and shades—this despite the fact he'd been inside, probably with no lights. The second was an average-sized fellow in slick looking pants—silk maybe?—printed all the way up the legs with multi-footed, snarling dragons. Because of the pants, Freddie didn't even notice his shirt. "Dreads" was on Freddie's right, "Dragon Pants" on his left by the dumpster.

Dreads spoke out, expecting to intimidate Freddie to a halt: "Whassup, white bo . . ."

Freddie never even slowed down. He grasped a fistful of braids in each hand as if a passionate kiss were intended. Instead of a lip smack, he head-butted him just as hard as he could. The bouncer's nose exploded. The shades fractured. A spritz of scarlet sprayed over both faces. Freddie's neck injury shot lightning bolts down his spine.

Before the second man had time to react, Freddie grasped his collars, slammed him into Dreads. Then back against the dumpster.

He turned right to Dreads with a left hook. The nail wound sang soprano.

He spun once more to Dragon Pants with a right cross.

Dreads was falling into him, well on his way to La-la land. Freddie met the fall with an uppercut elbow. The man's head snapped back and he went down, stayed down.

Dragon Pants was shaking his head, eyes rolling. One last devastating headbutt and the two men lay in a heap at the doorstep.

Freddie, crazed and panting, realized a trickle of blood flowed from a gash on his forehead. He wiped it away, stepped over the bouncers and across the threshold.

-Dread-

Dim turned to black as the door fell shut behind him. He took a moment to calm his nerves. As his eyes adjusted to the gloom, dust-speckled beams of sunlight revealed themselves, laser-planes and pin-spots burning through cracks in the boarded windows. A rat scurried through a blade of light.

Stifled by the walls, passing traffic whispered ancient tales from the pages of his past.

Freddie had been here with Stephanie on occasion, long ago in another life. It no longer seemed like *his* life. Crippling nostalgia washed over him as memories flooded in. Planning a date, nailing down a babysitter, dressing up, laughing with his wife on the drive over . . .

They always sat at the same table. Freddie ordered "his usual" (all the waitstaff knew it) while Stephanie liked to try something new each time. He glanced to where their table should have been, half expecting to see Stephanie sitting there waiting for him.

Of course the table was long since gone.

And Stephanie.

His life.

But before him glimmered an unwalked path, down which worlds of wonder awaited, among the treasures love, perhaps even peace.

A new life.

And he was here to get it.

Muted voices bled through the ceiling. Freddie looked up when a rafter quietly complained. Although he knew the main dining area well, he'd never been upstairs to the old guestrooms. So of course they were upstairs where he was unfamiliar with the layout.

He drew the Smith from his waistband and navigated his way through the debris to the stairwell. This time, he hoped he'd find more than a melted manikin at the top.

Again he hugged the wall where each step rested on its support, and again the stairs whined anyway. "Ah to hell with it."

He took them two at a time, stealth forgotten.

He launched into the upstairs hallway. The second door to the right stood open. A glow emanated from within, apparently from sunlight through more substantial breaches in the window boards.

Five quick steps brought him to the threshold. He burst inside, assumed a shooter's stance, pistol raised in a two-hand grip. He instantly registered the size of the room, about twenty by twenty, roughly that of an elementary school classroom. Rusted sconces hung askew from opposite walls, the globes long since shattered.

He counted six bouncers along the perimeter, including Tank and the mild-mannered Big Man. Pokey was there, still in a neck brace.

In addition to the six stood another man positioned in the middle of the room.

The dancer's stance of the seventh character gave the impression he was pausing on stage, having been interrupted during a performance. Although smaller than most of the others, he seemed somehow larger than he appeared. Freddie wondered if the illusion would hold up in a photograph.

He wore black jeans and a white silk shirt accented by a maroon scarf, the ends of which disappeared into his collars.

His hair was a freak show. Divided into a three-inch grid across his scalp, each square of the mane was gathered into a burly dread bristling straight out about two inches off his head—railroad spikes nailed to his skull.

None of the men had drawn weapons, but clearly visible in several waistbands were black contoured handles, probably Glock 9's. Manny had advised him this was the weapon of choice for gangbangers.

Freddie adjusted his stance, pointing first at one bouncer, then snapping back to another, doing his best to cover them all. The men seemed amused. Not frightened in the least. Some leaned against walls, others stood with their arms crossed casually. None so much as even shifted positions.

The freak in the middle took charge. "Well, look. At. *You!*" With a welcoming smile, he bent backwards at the waist for punctuation, arms flung wide. Cast about like a ragdoll in his right hand, the nailgun. Freddie's palm burned anew.

"Ya look like *shit,* man!" A voice like grinding gears. "Face all bloody . . ." A gremlin's voice. "Hand all fucked up . . ." He pointed at Freddie's bandage.

As if suddenly sympathetic, his smile faded and his arms dropped. Worry lines etched his face. He shook his head slowly. "You just don't stop, do you?" Softly, sincerely, as if he genuinely admired Freddie.

The floor was littered with debris. Soup and tuna cans, lids hanging by a shred of metal, crumpled fast food bags, depleted Sterno tins, a shriveled condom in one corner, broken bottles and dirty needles—among other detritus.

The dancer glanced around the room at his crew. "Gentlemen? Take note. This is the kind of dedication and perseverance I seek in my foot soldiers."

Up to now, he'd spoken with the expected gangbanger dialect. This last statement could have been from a professor, politician, or CEO—not a trace of hood evident in his voice. The bouncers offered no response, evidently accustomed to these performances.

Now he incorporated a British accent when he declared, "In commendation of bravery and persistence above and beyond the call of duty, you, sir, shall be granted free passage from the premises." He paused, beaming, seemingly expecting applause.

Despite himself, the instinct to flee indeed overcame Freddie—but of course he didn't move.

The dancer chuckled politely. "I just playin', man." Like dying sunlight when a cloud passes overhead, his countenance darkened. He sighed dramatically. Took a step sideways.

Behind him, in a dilapidated old upholstered chair, pretty and passive as ever, sat Julie. Innocent, meek, sweet, sweet Julie. Her slender arms rested casually along the upholstered armrests, legs uncrossed—a completely neutral, and thus unnatural position.

Her eyes locked on Freddie's. He thought maybe she was trembling.

She said, "Freddie, this is Paxyl."

-Gangrene-

(Freddie, this is Paxyl)

Freddie had figured as much—although he'd pictured the pimp as a towering, muscle-bound, base-timbered man of few words. A bitter bastard.

Paxyl was none of those things.

He was a shrimp! And suffered from diarrhea of the mouth, seemed to spout off whatever came to mind.

(Paxyl, he's funny.)

Energized, crazed perpetual grin—anything but bitter—he seemed to be enjoying life. And, Freddie surmised, the taking of it.

(Not like funny ha-ha, funny like scary funny.)

His vacant stare spoke to the insanity behind his eyes.

(Crazy funny.)

Freddie said, "I just want Julie. Nobody has to get hurt."

Paxyl raised his eyebrows, paused for a beat—then burst out laughing. "Wait-wait-wait. Say it again." Through his guffaws, he gestured *keep rolling* with his finger. "Go on, go on, say it again!"

Freddie didn't humor him.

The freak composed himself, cleared his throat. "What we've got here is . . . a *fayl-ya* to communicate."

Freddie recognized the line. The impersonation was spot on, complete with the cackling drawl.

Paxyl closed the two-step gap between himself and Julie, placed the nailgun to her temple . . . and waited.

Grinning.

Freddie made no move to surrender.

"Oh my God. Are you gonna make me *count?*" And here was the baritone voice of Negan, the *Walking Dead* villain who bashed people's skulls in with a barbed-wire-wrapped baseball bat, smiling all the while.

Freddie's mind offered myriad responses, all of which he deemed worthless. He might as well be talking to a moving picture on a silk screen. How did you reason with or appeal to someone who didn't exist? To a *character*?

"Okay, Freddie. You win. I—am—*counting!*"

He knew what came next.

"Three!"

He tightened his grip on the Smith.

"Two!"

He cocked the hammer, knowing it was useless, knowing he'd never squeeze the trigger—and knowing they all knew it.

Paxyl shoved the nailgun into Julie's skull hard enough to tilt her head sideways. "This is *it!*"

Freddie sighed. "Okay, okay." He de-cocked the revolver and squatted. "I'm setting it down." He placed it on the floor, left hand raised in surrender, then stood. "It's cool."

"It is anything *but* cool, Freddie." The gremlin was back. Apparently, this was Paxyl playing himself. Freddie decided he preferred the characters.

(Don't nobody mess with Paxyl.)

A scraping sound at his feet. He glanced down as Pokey took the 357. When the neck-braced bouncer looked back at Paxyl, the pimp was holding out a pair of pliers-sized, curved-bladed pruning shears.

Freddie's pruning shears.

Pokey approached the freak. Reached for the tool.

Paxyl withdrew it. "Naw, man." He directed the shears to his left. *"Big Man!"*

The sharp-dressed giant paused in the middle of wiping his forehead. "Huh?" He stood frozen, hanky suspended mid-swipe.

"Don't go soft on me now."

Big Man cut his eyes to Julie, then back to Paxyl. "I won't." He made his way to the tattered chair and accepted the tool. He hefted it several times, considering the grisly task before him—then looked down at the girl. His face contorted with anguish. "Jules . . ."

"Make it neat now. I don't want no gangrene or nothin'. Horny mother fuckers won't notice a pinky missing, but they ain't gonna fuck no *arm* stump."

This couldn't be happening. Not to them. Not to a handyman nobody and his mentally impaired girlfriend. Not to the peaceful couple who rode bikes, made love and minded their own business.

But it *was* happening.

Hope lost.

Unless . . .

Freddie looked to the girl. "Zoe . . ."

A look of sympathy fell across her face.

Big Man bent to her left hand, lifted it gently, and placed his handkerchief beneath it. "I be gentle as I can. Be over in a jiffy." He touched her shoulder, a vow.

Paxyl chuckled. "Ain't that sweet." He shifted his eyes to Pokey and nodded toward Big Man. Pokey stepped forward, jammed Freddie's gun at the giant and cocked the hammer.

"You're Zoe, don't you see?" Freddie pleaded. "Just be *Zoe.*"

Yes, somehow, someway, she'd amaze them all, storm around the room like a cyclone, fists and feet flying. She would claw her way out of this. She would *will* their salvation, and it would come to pass.

If she were Zoe.

"Oh, Sweetie. I told you. I ain't her."

"God*damn* it Julie! You *are!* You're Julie, *and* you're Zoe! If you would just . . ." But just *what,* exactly? Did she have the ability to transform at will? Or was the switch locked away in the same corner of her brain that sent commands to her heart? Or scripted her dreams?

"What the *hell* you talking about?" Paxyl glanced around at his henchmen, then back at Freddie. "That ain't no *Zoe*. That's *Star!*" Then to Julie, "And you 'bout to get scratched, girl." He nudged Big Man. When the giant looked up, Paxyl handed him a thick rubber band and bottle of alcohol.

Big Man paused—then, understanding, accepted the items. He poured the disinfectant over the shears, then bent to Julie's hand. He soaked it as well, then wound the band several times behind the outermost knuckle of her left pinkie. Stringent fumes overlaid the stench of the detritus.

Paxyl said, "Don't let me down."

"I *won't!*" Big Man lifted his hand to his forehead, then realized the hanky wasn't in it. He used his jacket sleeve instead.

Pokey adjusted his grip on the pistol.

Freddie was unable to contain a choked sob. "Zoe . . ." Only Julie stared back.

Big Man positioned the shears. "Now don't look. I take care o' you like always." He took a deep breath . . . let it out. He glanced back at Paxyl, big face pleading.

Paxyl just grinned and raised his eyebrows.

Big Man looked to Freddie, a silent apology.

Freddie saw nothing but the girl. *"Please."* Her image blurred, then resolved as a tear spilled down his face. She gazed back at him, only at him, reassuring him, loving him.

The snip sounded like a bomb in the silence.

-Taxidermy-

Snip

Freddie's eyes never left Julie's. In his periphery, an ejaculation of scarlet, in stark contrast with the bleach white of Big Man's handkerchief.

She did not scream or even weep.

Only gasped.

He was catapulted back to that enchanted evening, to the moment she'd offered her virginity and he'd accepted, to the second they'd passed the point of no return, the very *instant* they'd consummated their love.

She'd gasped.

That belonged to *them,* damn it! Only the two of them, Julie and Freddie, and now these cruel bastards had taken not only her finger but that sacred moment. Strangely, he felt more violated at their knowing her gasp than when they'd known her body—along with the eyes of every swinging dick at BT's Gentlemen's club. Freddie realized this was irrational, but it was real to him.

Big Man picked up the severed finger. He looked about, confused, finally dropped it in his jacket pocket. He bent once more to Julie and wrapped the oozing stump in his handkerchief. His hands were surprisingly dexterous and gentle.

Freddie was trembling. Julie's eyes never left his, her expression blank, face tear-streaked. Maybe she'd gone into shock.

"Uh-*uh.*" Paxyl did *gimme* fingers. "I do me some *taxidermy,* Goddamn it. Make me a necklace out that shit. Remind Star about that black cat every time she see it."

Big Man retrieved the gray lump and handed it over.

It disappeared into Paxyl's hip pocket. "You lookin' a little pale for a black man!" He smiled heartily. "Don't pass out on me now."

Staring at a point somewhere between his eyes and the floor— "I won't." —Big Man shuffled back to his station.

Pokey lowered the gun and did the same.

Paxyl situated himself behind the upholstered chair. Looked down at Julie. Slowly shaking his head, dread spikes bristling, he began stroking her hair. "Tsk tsk tsk . . . Girl, bad luck sit on your head like a big ole, fat black cat. One day while you sleepin', he gonna suck the life right out of you." He peered up at Freddie, teeth gleaming . . . and winked.

Winked at him!

Julie just stared straight ahead, no longer at Freddie but through him.

Paxyl's eyes fell back to her. "You ready to let bygones be bygones?"

There was no answer.

Paxyl kept stroking. "After all I done for you? Put a roof over your head? Show you the way? *Protect* you?"

Nothing.

"I need to hear you say it, girl." His grin was radiant. "I need you to tell me, 'Paxyl, I appreciate all you done, I'm sorry for being a bitch, and I'm ready to come on back home.'"

Julie just stared into space. Her lips moved subtly as if mouthing a hushed poem.

Paxyl's smile began to fade. "You lay down for this ugly motha fucker, but you won't lay down for *me?* For y'*self?* That hurts, girl." The pimp tried to maintain his cool, but it seemed to be slipping. "Maybe you just needed to see what it feel like first." He tried to revive the smile, but it faltered. "Now you know, so you can—"

"I ain't no whore."

Paxyl's face hardened, a storm brewing. The left corner of his upper lip quivered. Freddie thought the man might explode, perhaps kill everyone in the room.

Instead, the cyclone slowly passed and the smile (was it forced?) pushed through the clouds once more.

He chuckled. Switched hands with the nailgun. He fondled one hand with the other as he circled to the front of the chair to face Julie.

Freddie realized what the fondling meant.

Paxyl raised his right hand, twisting his body into the chamber. He brought it around like a baseball bat. The ring cracked the left side of her skull.

Julie's head snapped/spun sideways, slinging her hair wildly. The chair—Julie with it—tipped over, tumbled to the floor, scattering disintegrated food bags and rusty tin cans. The men on that side of the room shuffled their feet, dodging the trash.

Freddie caught a glimpse of another rat—or maybe the same rat—scuttling along the baseboard behind the bouncers. Inconvenienced by the ruckus, the animal was utterly unconcerned with the drama unfolding above, headed off to some other hideaway to resume its regularly scheduled rodent tasks.

Paxyl shook out his hand then spun his ring back around. He leaned over and set the chair upright. "Tank. Put a gun on top that bitch head."

Julie sat up and slinked away. Cowering from the monster.

"If she say anything or Freddie move the wrong way, fuck it." He shrugged. "Blow her brains down into her titties."

"'Bout time." Tank fumbled out his pistol left-handed, his right pointer bound in gauze. He limped over to stand his post. Freddie remembered the chopstick.

Paxyl patted the back of the hot seat. "Sit y' ass in that chair."

Freddie found himself sitting, facing the side of the room toward Julie. Tank's Glock looked like a cannon against her delicate head.

Teeth gleaming, Paxyl pressed the nailgun to Freddie's forehead . . . then flicked it to the wooden trim along the back of the chair and fired it. The concussion tore an instant ringing from his ear.

"God *Damn* take a look at that!" Paxyl was now a redneck. He leaned in to inspect the nail. He grasped it by the head and pulled—then wiggled vigorously. It didn't budge.

"That shit ain't goin' *nowhere!*" He peeked around the chair. "Pokey? You all right." The gangster tang returned. "I appreciate you pickin' up these *show grips!*"

Show grips? Weren't stagehands called grips? Was this part of the whole theater shtick? Freddie didn't get it . . . then he did.

Sure-Grips.

As in construction fastener.

Freddie had last loaded the nailgun with smooth-shanked nails—thank God—which was why he'd been so easily able to extract one from his hand. If you could call what he'd done easy.

But now they'd loaded the tool with Sure-Grips. Each nail was coated in a green waxy dry-glue, the shaft banded with hundreds of razor-sharp, backwards-leaning micro-rings, so designed to prevent retraction caused by time and vibration.

Once in place, removing one would require destruction of that into which it had been fired.

Paxyl held up the tool for inspection then posed as if reporting the news. "In February 2014, Richard Talley was found dead in the garage of his Aurora home, the result of six finishing nails fired from a nailgun into his chest and skull." This was Raven Stryker, an anchorman known as *The Voice*. "There have been other nailgun suicides, all of which stir my inquisitive imagination." Mid-sentence, he segued to a perfect British accent. An English professor, perhaps.

"Mr. Schaeffer *(Mis-*tah Shaeffah), regale us with your hypothesis of what went through Talley's mind just as the first shaft of steel penetrated his gray matter. Besides, of course, the nail." Paxyl chuckled.

Freddie opened his mouth, not to answer but to plead for their lives.

"Never mind! Indeed we shall discover for ourselves."

The bouncers looked on, lazy-eyed—except for Big Man, who just seemed vacant. One of them shifted positions.

Freddie's eyes drifted to Julie.

"I will stimulate—or disrupt, as it were—a particular region of the brain. After insertion, Mr. Schaeffer will report to us the effects of the procedure."

She shook her head, blinking. The bloody bandage caught her eye. She examined it, seemingly confused. Neither Paxyl nor the bouncers seemed to notice.

"You will reveal whether you're able to move body parts on your right side. Or your left." He glanced at the ceiling. "Did your *vision* become impaired? Can you speak?" He paused for effect. "Or interpret . . . speech?"

Julie slowly unwound the handkerchief. He wanted to tell her to leave it alone, that if she exposed the wound it might get infected. Of all things, why had he thought of that?

Freddie's eyes squeezed shut as the nailgun kissed the left side of his skull, toward the back. "This is the parietal lobe," the professor lectured. "Our first point of insertion."

Freddie opened his right eye, still grimaced for the blow. Julie's hands were shaking. Bandage freed, she gaped at the horror beneath.

"That step completed, I will stimulate or disrupt, in sequence, the frontal lobe, (memory), temporal lobe, (speech and emotions)—"

Wide-eyed, staring straight ahead, she began slowly stroking the floor in wide arcs. Freddie was reminded of an old carpet commercial in which a scantily clad model sat caressing her new ivory shag.

"—the occipital lobe, (vision), and the cerebellum, which of course handles fine motor control—"

Dizzy with panic, drunk on fear, he wondered whether what he was seeing was even real.

"—after each of which, Mr. Schaeffer shall submit his findings—" He fixed on Freddie. "—until we've tested the organ to failure."

Eyes locked with Paxyl's, vision swimming, Freddie monitored Julie only peripherally. Her fingers sensed an old tin can in which he imagined the gooey remnants of God-knows-what, squirming with maggots. Her fingers crawled over it like a starfish devouring a clam. Slowly, absently, she brought it to her lap and began twisting at the lid.

Had Paxyl finally driven her mad? Was she delusional enough to consume the contents? Why was Julie fidgeting with the filthy fucking can?

"Time for the first insertion," Paxyl said. "Ready?"

Because, Freddie realized, she was not Julie.

-Demons-

(Ready?)

Paxyl pressed the nailgun firmly against Freddie's skull. Right at the parietal lobe. The pimp stared into his eyes, amused at Freddie's panic—or perhaps ready to observe the effects of the "insertion."

Tank now rapt with the promise of violence, he failed to notice when Zoe tore the can lid free then padded her hand with the handkerchief. She grasped the makeshift blade firmly in her fist.

Paxyl slowly depressed the trigger, eyes burrowed into Freddie's. Observing.

Zoe spun like a break dancer. With a sickening slash, the lid sliced Paxy's Achilles' tendon.

The nailgun exploded.

Pain flowered in Freddie's skull.

She kept spinning, now upside down, her tripod base now hands and face. Tank's gun between her calves. She flipped it from his grip and sent it spiraling across the room like a bird shot dead midflight—all in but an instant—then kept spinning, axis shifting again, now to her back, now her feet.

Tank's carotid artery spewed like a ruptured fire hose. Zoe's hand had been a blur as it passed his throat, but the serrated lid must have made contact. Just enough.

Tank didn't seem to grasp the fact he was bleeding. *Gushing*. His expression turned inquisitive; he reached up to see what was wrong. The crimson geyser sprayed his fingers. He collapsed to his knees.

"Get that mutha fucker!"

Gunfire.

From all directions.

Deafening.

Paxyl was laughing hysterically. Somewhere behind Freddie. He wanted to rise and fight—or dive for cover. He dared not, lest he inflict irreparable damage to his nail-punctured brain.

Besides, Zoe seemed to be doing all right on her own.

She ran straight into a hail of lead, toward the bouncer in the left rear corner of the room.

What was she doing?

Dodging bullets as she flew.

Was that even possible?

(BOOM!) Juke left.

Freddie did a quick analysis of his ability to process information.

(BOOM!) Juke right.

Could what he was seeing be real?

Zoe took flight—

Could he still speak?

—having leaped toward a boarded window to her left.

Or interpret speech?

("Shit. How this muh-fucker work. There we go.")

A trail of nails followed her progress, her path forever memorialized in steel shanks. Freddie turned to see Paxyl firing the nailgun, hobbling on one foot. Laughing insanely.

How was that possible? The gun required pressure at the muzzle in order to function. Then he realized the pimp's left fingers held the pressure safeties as if parting labia.

Zoe soared, seemingly chambered for a kick.

It seemed her intent was to break through the opening and risk a fall to the street. But surely she wouldn't leave him in a lurch.

Was he thinking clearly?

Her left foot landed on the wooden planks. Boards complained and dust erupted like mini volcanoes.

Perceiving the world around him as he should?

She vaulted from the boards, pivoted mid-flight and slammed her left shin into the bouncer's head. His gun exploded one final time and he flipped—a full 360—and plummeted to the floor. Zoe landed. Spun. Ducked a nail. Snared the gun and popped a round into the man's skull before his body even settled.

She rotated once more and fired at Paxyl. The pimp cackled and ducked behind Freddie.

She pivoted again, found Tank on his knees. Throat gushing through groping fingers. "I *told* you how this works, asshole."

She shot him through the forehead.

Zoe leaped again in response to nails flying at her shins.

("Yeah bitch! Take that! And that!")

Paxyl was firing the vaginal space-pistol from beneath the chair—and still howling with laughter. Freddie realized the pimp had become the Joker from *The Dark Knight*. He wondered what the freak's Google Play account must look like.

Zoe landed spraddle-legged. Nails whizzed through the triangle. She fired two rounds beneath the chair, between Freddie's feet. Paxyl yelled, *"SHIT!"* and the nails ceased. Then she spun and took out two more bouncers, quick pops, one two, both head shots. The tinkling brass sounded like lightning, the bodies thunder as they hit the floor.

Pokey stepped forward.

Zoe pivoted, squeezed the trigger—realized the slide was locked back.

She slowly lowered the weapon. It clattered to the floor.

Pokey raised Freddie's 357.

CLICK

He cycled through five more empty chambers, shoving the gun forward on each pull of the trigger.

He tossed the Smith aside.

Zoe crouched like a tiger.

Pokey reached behind his neck and, with a tearing of Velcro, ripped off the brace. He pitched it to the floor, leaned his head left *(crack),* then right *(crack)*—and the knife fluttered out. *(Rattle click snap.)*

Zoe dodged.

The blade sliced the air again as Zoe scooted deftly back. Pokey shot the steel forward. Zoe parried with her left hand and jabbed with her right. Freddie felt the smack of knuckles on meat in his own teeth.

Paxyl from behind the chair: *"Get* her!"

Pokey retreated and wiped at his lip. He checked his fingers for blood—found it there.

Zoe raised her eyebrows: *How'd you like* that?

Pokey flipped the blade and lunged forward in a *Psycho* attack.

("Stab *that bitch!"*)

She sidestepped and roundhoused his solar plexus as he passed.

The bouncer grunted and held his gut—but held his ground. Knife bristling.

Zoe faked, Pokey slashed. She faked again and this time he caught her wrist, yanked her forward and tried to decapitate her. He failed, but a thin trail of blood now etched her cheek.

("Got*choo, mother fucker!"*)

This time Pokey raised *his* eyebrows. Zoe wiped her face and acknowledged the point with a nod.

The pair circled. Zoe feigning, Pokey slashing.

As he watched, Freddie reached for his head. Hand shaking, skin icy hot, he fingered blindly . . . gently . . . bracing himself for the bristling steel . . .

There.

The nail was only buttonhooked through his scalp. He prayed the bone beneath was un-scored.

Pokey thrust forward. Zoe caught his wrist in her right hand and pulled it past her as she rotated clockwise, her back now to him. She whipped her left arm over his bicep, under his elbow, then monkey pawed her own right forearm with her left palm, right hand still grasping his upturned wrist.

Pokey was caught in a nasty triangle.

She flexed with all her might. Grimacing. Trying to hyperextend the stubborn limb. Pokey grunted with his effort at resistance. Veins bulged on the belly of his arm, knife in a death grip. He landed a few ineffective punches to Zoe's head with his left fist. She ignored the blows and strained harder still.

It seemed to be a stalemate . . . then Zoe's left elbow shot back into Pokey's face and returned instantly to the triangle she'd left unattended. The strike had a dazing effect, but not enough. So she did it again. Then a third time.

Pokey, nose gushing, faltered.

With a resounding *POP,* the arm bent backwards. The knife clattered to the floor.

Pokey screamed.

Zoe elbowed again, this time following through, snaring the bouncer in an upside-down headlock as he fell backwards. She held him there a moment . . . Pokey's screams muted under her armpit . . . She thrust forward, raised her hips, and Pokey's head bent impossibly backwards with a sickening crunch.

Zoe dropped the corpse to the floor.

Freddie felt pressure on top of his skull.

"Hooly *SHIT!*" Paxyl. "You are *bad—ASS!*" He showed not the least concern that his crew was dead.

All but one.

"You see that, Big Man? She like, hai-*ya! BAY*-yam! Kick one nigga, shoot another . . ."

Zoe stalked toward the chair, eyes directed above Freddie, apparently locked with Paxyl's.

The nailgun pressed even harder. Digging into Freddie's scalp. Inches from the buttonhooked nail.

"Uh-uh-*uh,*" the pimp warned.

Zoe froze, chest heaving, teeth gritted behind snarling lips.

Paxyl revived the British professor. "The hemispheres of the brain communicate with one another through a thick band of 200 million some odd nerve fibers called the corpus callosum. Interruption of said communication results in . . . shall we say . . . *interesting* phenomena?" The gangbanger dialect returned. "Ain't that right, Big Man?"

Big Man.

Somehow, he'd remained invisible through the mêlée. Dazed throughout the entire bloody battle, he'd been perhaps oblivious of the threat to his own life. Freddie hadn't even noticed him.

"Get her, Big Man!"

"I won't."

"What?" He paused, then, "What you say to me, motha fucker?"

"I *won't."* The pressure on Freddie's head relented. The nailgun crashed to the floor.

"I *won't!"* Big Man lifted the pimp by scruff and ass, slammed him to the ground.

Paxyl started his insanity cackle and kicked at Big Man's shins.

The giant wasn't even fazed. He plopped onto Paxyl's chest.

In a whiny tone, Paxyl said, "Stop it, Steven. You're *hurting* me!"

"I won't!" Big Man's fist came crashing down.

"Didn't hurt!"

"I *won't!"* Another crushing blow; blood spattered across the filthy floor.

"Now *that* shit hurt."

"I WON'T!" Big Man rose and hefted the pimp above his head.

"Come on now, *help me out,* Freddie!" Paxyl howled with laughter.

Freddie bolted from the chair.

"I *WON'T!"* Big Man smashed the pimp across the chair back.

Paxyl only laughed.

Big Man lifted him again.

"Aaaa-ha-ha! *PUT-ME-DOWN!* "

"I WON'T!"

The body plummeted.

"I insist you stop this insanity—*immediately!"*

With every crushing blow *(I WON'T!)*, Paxyl joked and jeered *(I can see my house from up here)*, each time in a different voice *(I WON'T!)*. It was as if demons were fleeing the body *(Un-HAND me, sir!)*, realizing they'd soon require alternate refuge *(I WON'T!)*.

Freddie wondered how many monsters occupied the freak's labyrinth mind.

"*I'm meeeltiiing!!*"

Freddie wondered how much more the pimp could endure.

"I WON'T!"

The insane babble ceased.

"I WON'T!" *(SLAM!)*

"I WON'T!" *(CRUNCH!)*

Big Man bellowed at the top of his lungs; his voice cracked with the effort. "I . . . . *WON'T!*"

He tossed the body all the way across the room. It struck a wall and slid to the floor in a heap.

Big Man, eyes wild, seeking nothing in an imagined eternity, sucked in mighty waves of air and ejected them through gritted teeth. His chest heaved; his fists clenched. Again and again . . . ragged breathing . . . then slower as his rage dissipated.

He opened his hands and shook them out, seemed to descend like a falling leaf back to reality.

Freddie looked on, stunned.

Zoe watched the bouncer, cautious.

Big Man took one final breath then slowly let it out. His shoulders relaxed.

Zoe broke the silence. "We cool, Big Man?"

He looked back at her. "Dexter. Dexter Grant." Despite the dim light, it seemed somehow brighter. "I'm real sorry, Julie. Or . . . Zoe." His big voice rumbled softly. "For everything."

"So, what happened? Why did—"

"I got wise. Like you." He peered at Paxyl's corpse and seemed to tense. "He had this . . . mad kind of juju. He could just . . . He made everybody . . ." His breath kicked up a notch. "I shoulda seen it. I shouldn't have let him . . ."

"Hey. Dexter."

Big Man looked back at her, seemingly lost.

"You saw it, you acted. That's all that counts."

He shook his head. "But I should have—"

"No. It was always going to be this way."

Dexter wiped his hand down his face and took a calming breath.

Freddie said, "Thank you, Dexter."

Big Man nodded, then moved toward the rightmost side of the room. "I need to sit a spell." He turned, leaned against the wall and slid down with a long sigh.

While Dexter was gathering his wits, Freddie retrieved the Smith.

Zoe scanned the floor. Fixed on Paxyl's mangled corpse. She walked over and rolled him to his back with her right hand, the left cradled at her tummy. She rummaged through his pockets then stood with her grisly prize.

She looked from one man to the other as she slipped the finger into her shirt pocket. "Hey." She shrugged. "You never know."

Big Man's eyes narrowed. With a sly grin, he said, "I think it's good we finally gave him the finger."

Zoe pursed her lips, but a snort escaped through her nose.

Dexter also tried to resist, chest bouncing . . .

"Next time," Zoe said, "let's give him *yours*."

A single chuckle escaped Dexter . . . and another from Zoe . . . then all three burst into guffaws.

Zoe bent double and slapped her knee with her left hand—gasped and started dancing in place. *"FUUUUCK!"*

They all laughed even harder.

This should not have been funny. Freddie feared they all stood precariously balanced on the precipice of insanity—but he couldn't stop.

Finally, the gales began to subside, punctuated with chuckles and sighs.

Dexter took a deep breath. "Oooo-*eee!*" He thrust his chin at Freddie. "How's y' head?"

"He really nailed me."

"Stop it," Zoe said before they all lost it again. Then to Big Man, "Coming with us to the ER?"

Dexter's brow furled. "Why would you—"

On cue, Freddie stepped over and offered his hand.

Dexter looked up at him, considering . . . then finally nodded. "Alright then." He slapped his palm into Freddie's and stood.

The men locked eyes. Their clasped hands became a handshake.

Freddie smiled. Big Man chuffed and nodded.

Zoe passed them on the way to the door. "Hey. When you two are done with your bromance, can we maybe haul ass to the hospital?"

Dexter said, "She always like this now?"

"Only when she's Zoe."

"I ain't even gonna *pretend* to know what that means."

Zoe said, "Talk about it in the van. Let's bounce."

-Big Man's-

It took awhile, but they fell into a comfortable routine, free from worry, moving about where they pleased with no need to watch over their shoulders. For a while, their lives seemed almost normal.

BT's Gentlemen's Club shut down. The building was demolished. From the rubble rose a new venture, *Best Lighting*. They sold no fixtures. Rather, they offered every bulb imaginable. What they didn't have in stock, they could order.

Every employ at Best Lighting went about their workday fully clothed. There were no fistfights. No bar, no bouncers, no rancid cloud of cigarette smoke—no destitute souls walking a razor's edge between survival and woe.

Still, they could not bring themselves to go anywhere near the property, avoiding even so much as a glance in that direction when they drove past. They bought their bulbs at Walmart.

For the first several months, Dexter Grant worked with Freddie. At six-six and a good 300 pounds, the nickname "Big Man" stuck to Dexter like gum on his shoe—despite his best efforts to wipe or peel or scrape it away. Unprompted, even strangers would tumble to it eventually. For a while he did his best to avoid answering to the moniker, but the effort was futile. Some things were just meant to be.

A sobriquet also evolved for the two men as a team. They came to be affectionately referred to as "Miami Vice," an allusion to the bi-racial stars of the 80's crime drama series.

One day while framing out an addition, Big Man let slip his dream of becoming a bartender. Somehow this seemed a natural fit, and Freddie wondered why it had never occurred to any of them before. Apparently, the vision had been germinating in Dexter's mind for some time. He'd just been too shy to talk about it. Once voiced with his trusted friend, the dream proved plausible and he opened up about it.

"Not just a bartender," Big Man explained as he unbuckled his tool belt. "I want to *own* the place."

"I thought you'd have had enough of the tavern life."

"BT's wasn't no tavern. It was a cesspool." Dexter draped his tool belt over a sawhorse and ambled toward a broom leaning in the corner. The floors creaked with his weight.

Freddie nodded as he wound up a cord. "Okay, so how does one go about making his tavern . . . a wholesome place?"

Dexter paused, grinning ear to ear, bristles of the broom resting against the floor. "I like that word. Wholesome." He thought about it, nodded his enormous head, then kept sweeping.

"Know what?" The broom paused again. "I'll run me a family tavern."

"A *family* tavern? Could there even be such a thing?"

"Sure could." Big Man started sweeping again. "During the day, we offer kid's menus, ice cream, coloring pages, that kind of stuff. At night, we take care o' Mom and Dad. Give 'em some alone time away from the kids."

Freddie nodded and raised his eyebrows, considering the possibility as he tossed another bound cord into the bin.

"Won't tolerate no fights," Dexter continued. "No smokin', no cursin', no nonsense." He left a pile of sawdust and headed for a mess in another corner. After a minute or two, as they cleaned up together, he said, "I get me a *juke*box!"

"Now there's an idea."

"Put me some Motown in there. Elvis, Frank Sinatra—maybe some hits from the 70's and 80's, too. Rock-n-roll. But none of that heavy metal or gangsta rap they got nowadays."

"You'd sure earn some quarters from me."

On they dreamed together, that day and the next, and every day after. Big Man would cook. He'd work the bar. He went on for five minutes one afternoon about buffing the gleaming lacquered oak with a rag.

He'd know all his customers by name.

Freddie encouraged his friend, and the vision grew. One day they decided it was time to stop dreaming and start doing.

As it turned out, Fox's had finally come on the market. They jumped on it, offered more than the asking price, and won the bidding war. Freddie co-signed for the loan, offering his dormant insurance account as collateral. It was just sitting there anyway.

After a month of waiting on pins and needles for appraisals and title checks, they finally found themselves at the bank signing papers. The day after, they were standing in the dim shell of Fox's, keys in hand.

After two months of grueling renovations, Big Man hung out an *Open* sign. Freddie and Jules were his first customers. They selected *Proud Mary* as the first song ever played during business hours.

In respect of history, Dexter kept the original name of the place. Julie renovated the red foxes on each side of the building. Even so, everyone called it "Big Man's." Some things were just meant to be.

Although Julie was as prolific as ever when it came to improvising poetry, she had a strange aversion to learning to type—perhaps due to her pinkie tip, which ER doctors were unable to reattach.

But neither did she bother writing anything down. Apparently, her previous obsession with chronicling her work had been about journaling her life of struggle. Those who forget history are doomed to repeat it. But this new history she'd have repeated a thousand times, would have lived it for eternity.

Freddie never pushed her about it, but sometimes worried there would come a day he'd regret his lack of encouragement.

Staying busy for the poet was not a problem. She painted and sculpted, sold her work at fairs and festivals. It wasn't long before a Julie V. Ayers piece was something people sought out. She made murals of the living room walls— Styrofoam-stamped jungle leaves of lavender and thick red vines winding through a background of baby blue. Neither Dexter nor Freddie understood it, really—but both agreed it livened up the place.

Zoe, on the other hand, had trouble finding meaningful work. While adept in martial arts (though they could never quite nail down any particular style), hiring herself out as an instructor was all but impossible. While Zoe's impersonation of Julie at an art festival was passable, there was simply no way Julie could fake teaching a self-defense class. Zoe tried making her some tutorial videos, but Julie proved to be utterly incompetent. Fighting was just not in her DNA.

Zoe taught Freddie on occasion; they even got a bag to hang from the towering banyan out back. While Freddie's interest wasn't much greater than Julie's, he was surprised to discover he could bend the bag in half with a kick after only brief instruction on the technique. She taught him the gun-snatching trick, but he never practiced.

When Zoe and Big Man tried horsing around one night, barbeque grill smoking on the back patio, he stooped and snatched her up by the ankle, chuckling as if from a 50-gallon drum. Swinging like a jewelry pendulum, staring at Big Man's belt buckle, Zoe had squirmed and struck out in vain, laughing all the while. "Put me down, fucker! I'll kick your ass!"

The splits continued to appear randomly. None of them could determine any trigger for the switch. The duration of Zoe's presence was utterly unpredictable—ranging anywhere from a few minutes to a full day. There were times she didn't show for close to a week.

Freddie remained averse to socializing. He shared his life only with his circle of friends, his family. Dexter and Julie. And Zoe. More like a pathetic triangle, really. He was a regular at Big Man's, even had his own barstool. But any seeds of friendship inadvertently sown at the bar were neglected, instantly forgotten beyond the door with the red fox, dead before any sprout ever broke the soil.

He racked up hours puzzling over the photo. Zoe herself was disturbed by the image, and after a time refused to look at or even discuss it. Who the hell had that Vargas character been anyway? Why had he come here, and why had he never returned? The whole thing nagged at Freddie like a sore in his mouth that never healed because he just couldn't stop tonguing it.

He'd done some research on facial recognition software with the intent of somehow searching the face online. He'd discovered the technology just wasn't there, at least not for average consumers over the public web.

As always, the Stevie paradox plagued him. He wanted to reach out, longed to reconnect with his son. Yet he couldn't find it in himself to just pick up the phone and dial the number. God knows he tried sometimes, even made it to pulling out his phone and opening the contacts app. His efforts were rewarded with only confusion and panic—accompanied by fever sweats and a splitting headache.

Work remained an effective inoculation against the scourge, most times.

One night, Zoe awoke alone in bed. She slipped on a robe and went in search of her man. She'd intended to check the bathroom first, but a soft glow emanating from the living room revealed his location. As she navigated the dark hallway, the soft chatter of keyboard strokes identified the source of light.

She tiptoed up behind him, curious. He was working in Microsoft Word. Not intending to snoop, she nevertheless couldn't help but notice random snippets of content: " . . . so proud of you . . . if only I could . . . think you'd really like her . . . miss you so much . . ."

Freddie turned to Zoe with a start—then immediately back to the computer. He fumbled with the mouse, closed the program.

Just before the page disappeared, she caught a glimpse of a small caption in the footer of the document: *Page 587.*

Freddie sat in the glow of the desktop, unsure what to do.

From behind him, Zoe bent and crossed her arms over his chest. "Sorry. Didn't mean to startle you." She kissed the back of his neck. She propped her chin on his shoulder, staring at the screen with him. Freddie reached up and caressed her arm.

She said, "What are you working on, night owl?"

Freddie slowly shook his head.

"I'm sorry. It's none of my business. I just thought—"

"It's a letter."

"A letter?" She was thinking, *587 pages.*

"To Stevie. A kind of journal of our lives together. It's the only way I've found to . . . connect."

Zoe sighed. "Oh, Freddie. Baby. Why won't you just—"

Freddie pushed back from the desk and rose, careful not to topple the woman. Zoe's arms slid from their embrace. He stood staring at the screen for a beat, then turned to her. "I can't."

"But if you just—"

"I *can't,*" he said, more emphatically. "I know I . . ." He shook his head, looked at the ceiling, then back at Zoe. "I'm sorry." His gaze wandered downward—to a pencil on the desk, to Zoe's feet. His brow furled as if straining to remember something. He searched the floor—but not the floor—for something floating in the space just above it. After a beat, he drew a deep breath. His eyes found Zoe's again. He gently touched her face—then padded to the hallway. Rounding the corner without looking back, he said, "I just can't."

Though clearly she cared, Julie was less instructive on the matter. The few times the subject flitted into their conversation like a lost butterfly, she would simply listen, wait, and let it go. On one occasion, she shook her head, eyes full of sorrow, and gently touched Freddie's chest. "I know your heart," she said, "and I feel your anguish." She kissed his cheek, then turned and walked away, leaving him to his solitude.

About the only problem of any significance was Zoe's somnambulism. She never ventured outside in her sleep, thank God, but Freddie worried about her nonetheless. He'd locked up the firearms, but on occasion he discovered her in strange places, engaged in sometimes alarming exploits.

Once, he found her fully submerged in the bathtub, nightgown floating like a dead jellyfish. Her eyes stared up at nothing through the water. His heart leaped into his throat when he thought she'd drowned, but she'd been fine.

On another occasion, huddled in the shadows of the kitchen, she stood mesmerized in a cloud of steam, a boiling pot before her. He vowed to find a way to disconnect the stove before bed, but never did.

His skin nearly crawled off one night when he woke to discover her bedside, staring into the shadows—absently slicing at her thigh with a butcher knife. Most of the cuts were superficial, though one required stitches.

Freddie installed a motion detector above the mirrored closet door, integrated with a soft beeping alarm on the headboard shelves. This worked well for containment of the incidences but did nothing to prevent them.

The nightmares varied in frequency but most always included disturbing, one-sided dialogue. She whispered myriad messages, sometimes troubling, always cryptic. Often recurring in her aimless babbling were the words she'd uttered that first night in the electronics room, what Freddie came to call her Dream Phrase: Sea level. Desalt. Drawer number seven.

Sea level. Desalt. Drawer number seven.

The phrase vexed him, chilled him. What did it mean, if anything? Why would she keep coming back to that? He conducted many a Google inquiry—for Zoe Decker, of course—but also for conditions involving somnambulism. He searched in vain for psychological meaning behind mention of the ocean, sea level, salt water, desalinization, numbered drawers . . . His hope was that he'd find something—anything—some research or even vague theory on those words, perhaps discovered previously in the study of dreams. Nothing ever came of his efforts.

The event that brought it all to a head, that led to so much destruction and death, was precipitated by the mildest of nightmare incidences. Freddie was awakened not by the hushed beeping of the motion detector but by Zoe herself.

She was tossing and turning on sheets soaked with sweat. "Sea level. Desalt. Drawer number seven."

He gently shook her from her torment. She sighed, rolled over without opening her eyes, and slept.

Freddie checked the bedside clock: 11:00 p.m. He laced his fingers behind his head and stared at the motionless ceiling fan. Things were better now. Life was good. So why the continued nightmares? For that matter, why was there no change in the DID in general? It seemed as though either issue should be associated with stress, symptoms of a traumatic life. But no improvement. Nothing had changed.

Sea level. Desalt. Drawer number seven.

What could that possibly mean? Uttered once, probably nothing. But for months on end? Surely it had to mean *something*.

They'd procrastinated seeking professional help in hopes that time and peace would prove effective remedies. Maybe it was time they took that step.

Julie would be cooperative if not receptive to the idea. He thought he could talk Zoe into it as well. But if that didn't work? What then? It occurred to him that perhaps the reason they'd put it off was the simple fact it was their last recourse.

If, after extended psychological therapy, the doctor threw up his hands in defeat—there would be nothing left to try.

Sea level. Desalt. Drawer number seven.

Freddie glanced at the clock again: 12:15 a.m. He was shocked so much time had passed. Maybe he'd dozed without realizing it, but he didn't think so. He quietly rose and slipped into some pants and a t-shirt.

Fox's, better known as Big Man's, 12:30 a.m.: The tavern door creaked open, then closed itself with a squeak of springs. Billy Idol was yelling something about the midnight hour on the jukebox. He cried *more, more, more.*

The lounge was sparsely populated, but the patio was busier. College kids gathered at the picnic tables out there, custom built complete with canvas umbrellas by Miami Vice, Inc.

Dexter was polishing the already spotless bar. He seemed to be using drops of sweat from his forehead as cleaning solution. A barstool complained with Freddie's weight.

"Freddie da Fixer!" Dexter's big face broadened.

"Big Man?" Freddie said in way of a greeting.

Dexter's smile vanished. "What you doin' here so late?" He traded the bar towel for his hanky and polished his face as he had the lacquered oak. "Everything okay?"

"Ah, yeah. All good."

Big Man was already running an Amber Bock from the tap. He watched Freddie as he did it, eyes patient for a more honest answer.

Freddie gave it to him. "It happened again. Nothing major. I just couldn't take it tonight is all." He slapped a twenty on the counter as Dexter slid the frosty mug before him.

"You know your money's no good here."

"It's not for you. It's for your kids."

Dexter crossed his arms on the bar and grinned slyly. "What kids?"

Freddie shook his head once and raised his eyebrows. "Guess it'd be hard to make kids by yourself."

Big Man chuckled.

"So, put it toward a date. Maybe you could get one—if you paid her enough."

Big man's laughter practically rattled the bottles glowing behind him on the glass liquor shelves. When he settled down, he said, "Wanna talk about it?"

"Eh . . ." Freddie sipped foam off his brew. He licked his lips then turned up the glass. He had a deep thirst.

"Look," Dexter said. "I know it gets hard sometimes. Does with any couple. But you hang with her. Things'll get better."

"What if they don't?" Freddie set his beer on the bar and wiped his lips with his shirt sleeve.

"Manners," Dexter teased, and a stack of bar napkins appeared beside the mug. "You love her?" He stood back and crossed his massive arms.

"You know I do."

"There you go then."

"It's just that—"

"Just that nothin'. You love her, you stick by her. Thick and thin. Simple as that."

Freddie sighed. "Hell I know that," he confessed, and took another sip.

Big Man was polishing the bar again. "I know you do. I'z just reminding you."

They moved on to lighter subjects—the tavern business, the handyman business, life's truths and politicians' lies. They passed the time comfortably, and Freddie was amazed at how much better he felt as he polished off a second round.

He pleaded exhaustion, shared a fist bump with Big Man and heaved himself off the barstool. As his friend turned to retrieve a whiskey from the shelf, Freddie snatched the twenty from the bar and stuffed it in the tip jar.

"I seen that," Big Man called over his shoulder.

"Get a date." Freddie pushed out the door with the red fox, to Dexter's hearty laughter.

Outside, he looked first one way up the street then back down the other. The night breeze teased at his hair, coaxing from him a pleasant chill. His eyes fixed on a huddle of college kids gathered around a table. Curiously comforted by their youthful exuberance, he stood watching them.

There seemed to be a leader of the group, reading from what was apparently a tabloid. Maybe the National Enquirer. One moment, the night would be silent but for the reader's muted voice. The next, peals of laughter would ripple the stillness.

Freddie chuckled as he headed for the van. He detoured toward the table, inconspicuously, for perhaps a hint at what tickled them so. A girl with a glint of a nose ring flicked her hair back and caught Freddie's eye. She offered a half smile and a wink then returned to the story.

Proximity brought the reader's words into hearing range.

"UFO ... *(something)*... Navy ... *(something)* ... conspiracy ..." The group roared with laughter.

Freddie drew closer still.

"The extraterrestrial craft—" (a few chuckled) "—was claimed by the Navy to have disappeared without a trace." *(Oh riiight right.)* "However, our anonymous sources speculate that something from aboard the ship is being secreted in the 'Salt Mine,' the legendary subterranean network of research labs at the notorious Department of Scientific Alternatives."

Freddie walked on, smiling to himself, still well within earshot.

"The DSA, sometimes referred to as D-SAlt—" *(D-SAlt. Fuckers!)* "—is infamous for its corruption. Suspected of interdepartmental espionage, unauthorized military operations and illegal interrogation, D-SAlt seems immune to accountability."

One of the girls, maybe the winker, said, "Tell us something we don't know."

"When will we wake up? When will Congress tighten the reins on . . ."

Freddie had stopped walking. He stood very still. He stared into the parking lot but saw nothing. A nighthawk swooped by, not ten feet overhead. Subconsciously, he registered a light crunch as the bird snared a bite of dinner midflight then vanished into the blackness.

He turned and headed for the table. More subdued now, the kids had all taken seats, the article concluded. Some still shook their heads and chuckled. A few had lit cigarettes. Coals burned in the night with each puff, faces momentarily aglow in the strange orange luminance.

"Say, you guys done with this?" Freddie indicated the tabloid.

"What, this? Sure." The girl with the nose ring. She handed him the paper then took a drag from her cigarette, squinting one eye at him through the smoke.

"Thanks."

CHAPTER SIX

WHO'S WHO
&
WHAT'S WHAT

-Bunker-

Colonel Taggart Creed pored over the Amber file. While by far the most extraordinary substance D-SAlt had ever possessed, amber was proving to be of little or no practical use. Their black swan was producing impressive results—but only intermittently. Every time they stood at the brink of success, the geeks downstairs drooling all over their clipboards, she'd just . . . shut down. "Jumping the carousel," Constantine called it. What the hell did that even mean? And why couldn't they simply *do* something about it?

They balked at any mention of money. He tried to explain that he just needed something—anything—he could take to Washington. It didn't matter what, just something to keep the spigot open. Didn't they get it? In order to continue this line of research, they needed funding. Otherwise, all their lofty beard pulling would come to a screeching halt. The boys in Congress didn't respond well to potential. They needed something into which they could sink their teeth.

"You have visitors, sir."

Creed shifted his focus to the intercom. He pressed the transmit button. "Visitors?"

"At the checkpoint."

He could recall no appointments scheduled for today. He minimized the Amber file and pulled up his notifications. "I don't see them on today's roster."

"No sir. They just showed up. The guard told them to make an appointment, but they insist it's urgent."

"You know my policy, Gloria."

"They mentioned a Bill Vargas?" He was about to tell her to send them away. Then she added, "And something about a drawer? Drawer number seven?"

Creed stared at the wall and his brow furled. "Where are they?"

"The checkpoint, sir." Gloria was ever patient.

Creed pulled up the security camera display and clicked *Chkpnt*. A man and woman with tote bags slung over their shoulders shuffled nervously at the boom barrier. The man was a considerable specimen, his size evident despite the neutralizing effects of the video image.

He didn't know them—but *they* knew something about Project Amber. How the hell could that be? And how much, exactly, did they know? Perhaps they were conspiracy chasers and did not understand what they had. Maybe they read about it somewhere.

He made a mental note to make a sweep of all publications, especially tabloids. He hoped he wouldn't discover another security breach.

It did not escape him that the initials of "Bill Vargas" matched those of Bruce Vega. He couldn't recall any Vargas identity as one of Vega's agency-issued aliases, but that didn't mean much. He may have concocted the name on the spot if he hadn't needed documentation.

These two didn't appear to be a threat—just your average everyday-Joes. But then of course, any decent spook would cultivate that appearance.

"Have one of the sentries drive them over. Tell him to keep a tight rein, but be cordial."

"Yes sir."

Perhaps they were delivering a message from Vega, possibly without they themselves even being aware of it. That made sense. Vega had been a ghost the past several months. Maybe he was finally making contact. God knew Creed was anxious to settle things with him—and to get the kid the hell out of here.

And what if they *were* spooks? Maybe someone had tortured information out of Vega. That made sense as well. First, given enough time and the right drugs and interrogation tactics, anyone could be broken. Without exception.

Then there was the fact Vega was disgruntled. To say the least. Not only was his loyalty in question, it was nonexistent. He'd have made a deal in a heartbeat, no interrogation necessary.

The intercom crackled. "On their way, sir."

Gloria, as it had turned out, was quite the child psychologist. Although she avoided actually spending time with Christie, she seemed to have a knack for understanding the kid's needs.

She'd sold them on customizing an apartment for the girl. The regular deadbolt, thumb latch on the inside, had been replaced with a double-cylinder lockset keyed on both sides.

They'd hidden cameras in every room to monitor the kid's moods and behavior. They'd supplied her with toys, coloring books, Barbie dolls, painting supplies, stuffed animals—and drawers and shelves and footlockers in which to store it all.

She had her own TV, which was connected to NetFlix and other services. She could watch any cartoon or children's movie ever created.

Still, the kid wasn't right. She missed her father. They'd pacified her for the time being with the fantasy yarn that he was on a secret mission and would soon return. That wouldn't hold forever. Creed had a feeling there would be consequences for playing an innocent child for a fool. Sooner or later, she'd demand to see her father. And then . . . retribution.

Recognizing Christie's need for human interaction beyond the little she got from custodians and meal delivery, Gloria had suggested an academic regimen. While in no way a substitute for parents, it would at least provide a little company and keep her mind occupied until Vega showed up.

Of course sending her to school was out of the question, so they'd arranged professional tutoring. Christie had reading and grammar—at which she excelled—on Tuesdays and Thursdays. A guy in a wheelchair taught math and science on

Wednesdays. Mondays and Fridays, a coach took her upstairs for fitness which included swimming in the company pool.

It was getting downright ridiculous. Too many eyes. People would talk; security breaches were all but inevitable. If Christie's presence here ever made it to the wrong set of ears . . .

"They're here, sir."

Creed unsnapped his holster and made sure he was cocked and locked. "Bring them on in."

Creed yearned for Vega's return—and his hasty departure. He'd once seen a Porta-Potty pumper truck on the side of which was emblazoned, *You love to see us coming, you love to see us go!* He chuckled to himself, but he didn't smile.

Preceded by a light knock, his office door opened. "Here we are," said Gloria to the couple.

The hulk thanked her and squeezed through the doorway.

"Wow." Creed rose to greet his guests, hand extended. "Your mama must have had a go of it carrying all of you around!"

With a broad smile, the hulk shook his hand. "I was smaller then." Both men chuckled.

"Colonel Taggart Creed."

"Freddie Schaeffer. This is Julie Ayers."

Creed nodded politely at the woman. "Pleasure."

When they'd all taken a seat, Creed said, "How may I be of assistance?"

The couple shared a glance then joined hands over the arms of the chairs. The hulk took the wheel. "Until now, I hadn't really thought of how complicated this whole thing would be to explain. And how crazy it will sound."

"Try me." Creed smiled with his whole face.

"Well, it started about a year back, when I met Julie here." He looked to the girl for support. She nodded and squeezed his hand. Back to Creed, he said, "She suffers from Dissociative Identity Disorder. Here with us now is Julie Ayers, poet extraordinaire." The girl blushed and hung her head. "Other times, she's Zoe Decker, evidently a martial arts expert. Whoever she happens to be at the moment, she's always sweet."

Creed kept smiling, but his heart was a renegade stallion. He made a steeple of his fingers and nodded, rocking his desk chair gently. He felt like he was clinging to the safety bar of a runaway roller coaster.

"Zoe has amnesia, so we can't figure out what the deal is with her. It would seem that Julie fabricated the personality, except that Zoe has skills that would have required extensive training—which Julie never had. That we know of. Both insist they're unique people."

Percy's voice sounded in Creed's head. *What else might it be doing?*

"And Zoe has these strange nightmares. She says things."

"What kinds of things?"

"Creepy stuff. Most of it's random, but there are some recurrences."

"Like?" Creed felt the first drop of perspiration trickle down his rib cage.

"Well, 'desalt' for example. That's what led us here."

"How so?"

"This guy Bill Vargas dropped in one night, out of the blue, inquiring about a Facebook post we made in Zoe's name. We'd done it to try and connect with old friends or acquaintances, anyone who may know her. Vargas said he worked for a major government agency. Showed us this photo." Schaeffer leaned over to reach into his pants pocket.

Creed's hand eased toward his gun, but never made it. Indeed the man fished out only a photo, which he handed over.

"Obviously," Schaeffer explained, "it's not her face." He tipped his head toward the girl. "Yet she insists it's hers. Her *real* face, she says. When she's Zoe. Julie didn't recognize it."

There on the smooth surface of the photo paper was none other than Zoe Decker herself, smiling back at him, mocking him with those gentian-blue eyes. Creed willed his hand to remain steady, sent up a silent prayer for tranquility.

"Then later, I ran across an article that mentioned you guys, the DSA. It said, *also known as D-SAlt*. Naturally, since Vargas had said he worked with a major department, I made the connection." He shrugged. "Maybe she wasn't babbling about ocean water after all. Given Vargas's interest, I figured there was a good chance she'd been referring to this department. D-SAlt."

Creed placed the photo gently on his desk, struggling to maintain his composure. What the hell was Vega up to? Why had he done this? Who were these people? "You mentioned something else. At the checkpoint." He carefully avoided saying it in case perhaps he—or the sentry or Gloria—had misinterpreted the words.

"Yeah. Drawer number seven. We have no idea what that means."

Shit. Impossibly, they knew. It was apparent they didn't know *what* they knew, but they knew.

"So here we are. We just want to settle this, learn all we can about Zoe Decker and why there's so much confusion as to who she is, exactly."

Creed sat back and pressed his palms together as if he were about to launch into prayer. He tapped his lips with his steeple fingers. After a beat, he took a deep breath. "You've come to the right place."

Schaeffer sighed with relief. "So, do you know Zoe Decker? Is this her?" He indicated the girl at his side. "Or is that her in the picture?"

Creed thought carefully about how to play this. He couldn't let them go, of course, but he needed to handle the situation with kid gloves. God only knew who he was dealing with here. He'd need to get Constantine's input. Hell, Percy's too. He needed to figure this out, needed a chance to *think*. "I'll need some time, but I think maybe I can help you."

"You do?" The Ayers girl. It was the first time she'd spoken.

"Indeed I do." Creed smiled at her. "Where are you staying tonight?" He crossed his mental fingers, praying for the answer he expected.

The couple shared a glance, then Schaeffer looked back at him. "Actually, we haven't planned that far ahead. We Ubered over straight from the airport."

"Well, how about if the federal government puts you up for the night? Our treat."

Again with the shared glance, then Schaeffer said, "You have a hotel in the area?"

Creed proceeded carefully. "Even better. We have ample accommodations right here in the bunker. All the accouterments of a five-star hotel. Top rate kitchen, swimming pool, fitness area . . . " He shrugged. "Not to mention the best security on the planet. The one caveat is, you'd have a little roommate."

"Little?"

Creed chuckled. Rounding his desk, he said, "Come with me."

-Accommodations-

After navigating miles of winding roads through unending scrubland, they'd finally arrived at Mt. Chastain, home of the DSA. The Uber driver had been stopped at a checkpoint about 200 yards from the compound. The guard had advised them that access was by appointment only and was unmoved by mention of the name Bill Vargas.

They'd asked him to run it by his superiors. The sentry had initially refused. When they'd pointed out the creek in which he'd find himself, and that he'd be up it without benefit of a paddle should the name turn out to mean something, he'd finally relented.

As the sentry had spoken to someone on the phone, Freddie had motioned for him. When he'd gotten the sentry's attention, he'd mentioned the dream phrase.

"Hold on." Then to Freddie, phone against his chest, *"What?"*

"Drawer number seven." He didn't bother including the rest of it. In fact, maybe he shouldn't have mentioned it at all. To his own ear, he sounded like a kook. It had just occurred to him, so he'd said it.

Later, it dawned on him he may well have just shoved his pointers knuckle-deep into a Chinese finger trap. After all, these guys' reputation wasn't exactly stellar. He'd reassured himself there were always plenty of conspiracy nuts suspicious of any government agency. But this was still the United States, wasn't it? Where the government was of, by, and for the people?

That's what he told himself.

Nevertheless, he'd taken careful note of his surroundings.

Football-field-sized parking lots bordered the checkpoint. In one lot was tethered a military helicopter. The windshield, a giant dead eye, lent the craft an insectile aspect—a behemoth sleeping hornet.

Jutting from the chopper's sides were what appeared to be wings. Too small to serve any aerodynamic purpose, each was nevertheless substantial enough to support an intimidating array of missiles.

The road to the mountain was bordered by a twelve-foot chain link fence through the top of which wound a tunnel of nasty-looking razor wire. Signs every twenty feet depicted a stickman, each eye an X, being zapped by a lightning bolt, all in blood red on a background of white. No language barrier would obscure the signs' message.

The sentry had parked at the end of the road, right at the base of the mountain. Jutting from each side of the entrance was several feet of a massive, solid steel pocket door. A good two feet thick, he surmised they were blast doors, and looked like they could withstand quite a pounding. Electronically operated, they were conveyed on rollers by enormous chains—like motorcycle chains but easily three times the width.

Once inside, they boarded an electric vehicle. That made sense. After all, they were entering a cave, a sealed environment.

A one-man guard station reminiscent of a toll booth monitored the gateway from inside—uninhabited at the moment. The glass appeared thick. Probably bulletproof. On the wall to the right of the booth was mounted a folded fire hose, an ax and a crowbar. Below them sat a large metal Jobox filled with perhaps respirators and other firefighting gear. That set up made sense, too. After all, a fire inside a cave would suck up every cubic inch of oxygen within minutes.

As the EV whispered down the dimly lit tunnel, two more sets of blast doors revealed themselves, complete with firefighting equipment and guard booths. One marked the halfway point—about three hundred yards in. The other preceded the end of the tunnel and entrance to the facility.

The sentry had escorted them on foot through a man-sized door on which was emblazoned the capital letter *A*—the topmost level of the termite mound. Topmost, but still hundreds of feet below ground level. After a few turns, they arrived at an elevator.

Due to the lightest tickle of unease, Freddie carefully noted the path they'd taken, lest a hasty unescorted retreat became necessary. Unlikely, but you just never knew. Inside the elevator, they were presented two choices: A and B. The sentry pressed B, after which they slowly sunk like a doomed ship to the level below. A few more turns and they were at Creed's office for the interview.

Now they stood at the door of what would apparently serve as their accommodations. Creed had explained on the walk over that their roommate, a five-year-old girl named Christie, had lost her father in the line of duty. He made sure they understood the girl had not yet been informed of her loss. She would only be here another week or so until her grandmother arrived from Europe.

There was no mother in the picture. According to Creed. Freddie wondered why it would take so long for the grandmother to book a flight, especially considering the circumstances. He wondered, with all their resources, why the DSA hadn't flown one of the ladies to the other.

Creed knocked politely, waited a beat, then opened the door. "Hello hello!"

On the sofa, now glancing back at them, sat about the cutest little girl Freddie had ever seen.

She bounded from the couch. "Hi! I'm Chwistie!" Her glided *R*s were as endearing as her glee. His heart ached at the fact her bliss would soon come to a devastating end.

"Why, hello yourself, little lady!" Julie knelt to the girl, the men forgotten. "Whatcha watchin' over there?"

"Just a cartoon movie about bugs. I've seen it before. They talk."

Julie led the girl by the hand back to the couch. As they departed, Julie's voice faded. "Talkin' bugs? Why, it just so happens I got a poem about talking bugs . . ."

Creed explained the layout to Freddie. "Bedroom's back there." He pointed to the hallway beyond the kitchen. "Kitchen, obviously," he added, jutting his chin directly to the left. "And of course the living room. If you need anything, phone's right there." He indicated a wall-mounted telephone over the counter. "One on your nightstand, too. Just pick up and it'll start ringing. Someone will answer and bring you whatever you need.

"Pool, little sandwich shop, even a wet bar all up on A-level." His face tightened and he hitched up his pants. "Now, security's pretty tight around here, so don't go wandering the halls. If you need something or want to go upstairs, just let us know and we'll send an escort."

Freddie wondered why this would be. Surely security was focused on prevention of intruders *entering* the complex. Like at an airport, it seemed those cleared for access should be allowed to move about freely. But they were the experts. He wrote it off as typical military redundancy and let it go.

"Well, I'll leave you to it. Just let us know; we'll see that you get whatever you need."

The men shook hands. Freddie offered a final thanks as Creed departed.

As the girls giggled (they were playing a hand-clapping game now), Freddie dug out his cell and clicked Dexter Grant's icon. He put the phone to his ear.

Nothing.

He waited . . . still nothing.

He pulled the phone away to inspect the display.

No signal.

Yes, he was surrounded by a billion tons of earth and stone. And yes, he was calling from a high-security military installation. Even so, that tickle of unease he'd been feeling since his arrival grew almost to a nagging itch.

-Whispers-

Creed: "Could this have anything at all to do with Amber?"

Arms crossed, Doctor Aldus Constantine sat across the conference table from Lyle Percy. Twin fluorescent fixtures gleamed in the thick lenses of Constantine's eyeglasses. Only Colonel Creed stood, pacing as he spoke.

"Of course it does," Percy said. "We'd be fools not to assume it has *everything* to do with Amber. As I've said before—"

"Speaking of fools," Constantine interrupted, "we all know what *ass*uming does. There is no evidence whatsoever that amber—"

"It is *self*-evident, doctor! What further evidence do you—"
(Gentlemen?)

"Self-evident? Lyle. If you understood—"

"I have a title, just like you. It's *Doctor* Percy. I'd appreciate it if you showed just a modicum of—"

"Oh good Lord. If you knew anything at all about the scientific process—"

(Gentlemen!)

"What I understand," Percy shouted in his pathetic prepubescent tone, "is that you are *drunk* with power. Otherwise, you'd admit that . . . that *shit* down there—" He stabbed his finger at the floor. "—should be *incinerated!* Not later tonight, not tomorrow, but—"

"Shut up!" Creed slammed a bloated manual on the tabletop.

The scientists jumped in their seats.

Creed glared at each egghead, then stood upright and tossed the manual aside. He closed his eyes, drew a deep breath, then cracked his neck. He sent up a silent prayer: *God, save us from ourselves, Amen.*

He opened his eyes. "One at a time, gentlemen. Either of you interrupts again, I'll see to it you spend the remainder of your careers studying cow farts at the EPA." He looked from one of them to the other, then nodded. "Now. Doctor Constantine."

"Amber represents not only the solution to our problems, but the dawn of a new awakening. A paradigm shift for our civilization and for mankind in general. God could have placed this material in the hands of anyone He chose. But He placed it with *us*. As stewards of this blessing, it is our duty to use it for good, to learn all we possibly can from it."

"And Decker?"

"Yet another blessing. Black swans are one in a million. While surely others exist, the odds of finding one are so small as to be statically nonexistent."

Creed nodded.

"While the odds of a finding a black swan are minuscule, the odds of amber landing here, on this planet—and us acquiring it—well, look up at the stars and ponder that for yourself. But the odds of ending up with both? Together? Right when we needed them? That, sir, is simply impossible." He paused for effect, stole a quick glance at Percy, then locked eyes with the colonel again. "A miracle."

The physicist playing to his Christianity was not lost on Creed, and he strove to contain his resentment. The man before him was certainly not a believer, and quite likely an outright Atheist. Creed had never asked. He didn't like knowing the fate of people's souls, especially when they were all but certain to wind up burning in hell.

He looked at Percy. "And you?"

"I agree amber is a miracle." He glanced at Constantine, back at Creed. "But a miracle from *whom?* And serving what purpose?" He licked his lips. "A meteor annihilating the planet could be considered a miracle. The sun burning out would certainly qualify as miraculous." He was practically trembling. "Sir, have you taken a long hard look at them? Or what's left of them in some cases? Mired in that . . ." He pointed to the floor, shook his finger, unable to finish. "Have you even *seen* them, sir?"

Creed was notified of the project's every step but was unable to give the photos more than an indirect glance. The text of the reports alone mortified him. Even now, just talking about it, his stomach churned.

Percy continued. "But that's not the primary point here. Consider what we know about amber. Its origins. The disturbing phenomena it induces." He paused to let it soak in. "Then ask yourself, if it's doing those things, what *else* might it be doing? Things of which we are unaware?"

Creed thought, *Here we go.*

"The seeds of cancer could well be germinating, right now as we speak, deep in our brains. And that would be a best-case scenario." He took a deep breath, blew it out, then made his closing statement. "Considering the plight of those . . . those *things?*" He shook his head. "I myself would welcome brain cancer."

They all fell silent. Constantine was seething, but he dared not speak.

Creed sighed. He hadn't been seeking a sales pitch for or against Project Amber. He should have known that was all he'd get from these two. He was disappointed but not surprised. After all, they were scientists, not problem solvers.

The primary issues still remained unaddressed: Who was the couple down the hall, what did they know, and how did they know it? All he'd accomplished was cultivating further disgust with this whole damned project.

He nodded. "I want you to watch a video. In silence. Tell me what you think *afterwards.* Anyone says a word before it's over, so help me God . . ."

He turned to a rolling cart on top of which sat a flat-screen TV. He plucked a remote from beside the screen. After one more glare at the nerds, he clicked play.

They'd put the kid to bed maybe an hour before. Now the hulk and the poet sat talking in hushed tones at the dinette table. Once in a while, one of them smiled or chuckled.

Creed increased the volume a touch.

Schaeffer nodded toward the bedrooms. "You're good with her."

"I cain't have babies." The girl just blurted it out, her tone grave, out of character with their placid conversation. Wisely, the hulk remained silent, although he seemed moved—or perhaps didn't know what to say.

The girl continued. "It was a . . . accident. When I'z about Christie's age." She looked away, first toward the living room, then to her lap.

Creed hated himself for eavesdropping on these intimacies. He wondered how much longer he could withstand the pressures of this job. Of course, he was well aware of the severance package.

Schaeffer asked, "Was it Victoria?"

The girl did not respond. She remained frozen in place—one hand, like a corpse's hand, resting peacefully on the table.

Schaeffer reached over and took it in his. "I'm so sorry, Jules."

"But I love kids." She placed her other hand on Schaeffer's. "Maybe that's why, see. Cause I can't have any of my own. I always hoped maybe someday I could adopt one." She shook a strand of hair from her face. "But it never did seem like more 'n a crazy dream." She sat staring at Schaeffer, then added, "'Til now."

Creed fidgeted. He willed the video to come to an end, urged his mind to erase the private moments he'd stolen from this couple. Seconds passed.

"I'm sorry." Ayers shook her head. "I shouldn't have—"
She gasped. She . . . *changed*.

"Here it is," said Creed, grateful to be moving forward.

On the screen, the woman stood. All business now. She surveyed the room. She looked like a panther, ready to bolt into the night—or to maul him to death.

He didn't know Ayers, but he thought he knew the woman she was impersonating. Creed looked over to make sure the lab team was paying attention.

"Where are we?" It was Ayers's voice, yet . . . *not* her voice.

Schaeffer also stood. "It's okay. We just—"

"Where *are* we, Freddie?"

"In Colorado. Like we planned." He went to her side and tried to embrace her.

She was having none of it. "Tell me everything that's happened. Everyone you've met here."

Seemingly reluctantly, the man launched into their whole story. The flight, the Uber ride, checkpoint, security fences . . . the guard booths, blast doors . . . "Creed told us that—"

"Who?"

"Colonel Creed. He said we'd—"

"First name."

"What?"

"His *name,* Freddie."

Creed paused the video. "What's going on here? Any theories?"

Percy shrugged. Constantine creased his brow, shook his head and said, "Not at the moment, but . . . interesting."

Creed sighed and clicked play.

Back on the video, the hulk answered. "Taggart. Colonel Taggart Creed."

"Oh shit."

"What?"

"I *know* him."

"But you—"

"Goddamn it, I *know* him!" She planted her palms on her temples. "Why can't I *remember?*" Her hands dropped. "Anyone else?"

The man shrugged. "Just Christie."

"Christie?"

"Our five-year-old roommate."

"A *kid?*"

"Yeah," he said. "A kid. She's asleep back there." He nodded toward the bedrooms. "We should keep our voices down."

"Why the kid? What'd they say about her?"

Schaeffer glanced toward the bedrooms again, then back at the woman. "They said her father was killed in action or something. Said she's staying here a week or two until her grandmother comes to pick her up."

The woman glared at Freddie. "A *week or two?*" She shook her head and scoffed. "Did that not seem a little odd to you?"

"Well, as a matter of fact, I—"

"I'd say it's bullshit, except it would be an insult to bulls."

Damn it, Creed thought, now *that* story was shot to hell.

The woman continued. "We've got to get out of here. I don't know how I know it, but I know it."

"But we—"

"Freddie!"

"Hey. Keep your voice—"

"We are in *danger,* Freddie. The kid too. I can't . . . *think,* damn it, but that guy? Vargas? His name wasn't Vargas. His name is . . ." She stuck her fist to her forehead, staring at the floor. "It's *right there!*" After a beat, she looked back up at Schaeffer. "And this Creed. I need to see him. I think if I did, I might remember—" She studied the ceiling, shook her head. "—*something.*"

"But you *have* seen him. Just today we—"

"That was Julie. *I* need to see him, Freddie." She began pacing . . . then stopped. She glanced around the room. She hurried into the living room, bent to the TV. She turned to a nearby painting, left it, picked up a lamp, studied the bottom, set it back in place. Then, to Creed's alarm, she stared directly into the camera, *right at them.* As she approached, her face swelled and distorted like a reflection in a funhouse mirror.

Despite the fact he watched only a video image, Creed took a step back.

The woman stopped. Her gaze dropped, ever so slightly. Then her face shrank, proportions returning to normal as she backed away. "Oh, Freddie . . ." She retreated to her boyfriend and fell into his arms.

"Now watch."

The couple was standing sideways to the hidden camera, Schaeffer on the left, Ayers on the right.

She buried her face in his chest. "I'm sorry." Her shoulders bounced gently as if she were sobbing.

Schaeffer stared at the ceiling, evidently frustrated.

"Watch . . ."

She turned her face up as if to kiss him. The hulk bent to meet her. Their lips brushed—

"Here!"

—but never connected. Instead, her face disappeared behind Schaeffer's head. At first his expression showed only pity. Then, and this was difficult to discern with the grainy resolution, but it seemed his brow furled, like his face darkened.

Creed stopped the video and looked to Percy.

"What?"

He shifted his focus to Constantine.

The physicist shrugged, also oblivious.

Creed sighed and shook his head. "She was *telling* him something."

-Watchers-

Freddie laid awake, staring at the ceiling, nostalgic for his old friend the ceiling fan.

Julie really had been something with that kid. He supposed that made sense; Julie was, after all, a kid herself at heart. He wondered about the "accident" she'd mentioned, wondered about her tragic past. Maybe one day they'd fly to Arkansas.

In fact, exploring Julie's past might shed more light on her malady than this place. He'd been digging into Zoe's elusive history but curiously had never thought to examine Julie's. Why had he never Googled "Johnny Ayers," for example? Or "Victoria Ayers?" Or "Julie Ayers" for that matter? Perhaps he'd find some martial arts training or gymnastics experience in her past after all. It seemed unlikely, but why not at least exhaust the possibility?

But he was here now, to tap what he could from this well. Why had Creed been so evasive? If he knew something about Zoe, why hadn't he just said so? Or said no, for that matter?

Why had they been so eager to let them stay here? They'd been accommodating, yes—but perhaps too accommodating?

Yes, this place had secrets to reveal—yet Freddie found himself shrinking from them. What had seemed on his travels a sparkling gift in brilliant wrapping now seemed more like the door to a crypt, with only death and rot awaiting his discovery.

This was in large part due to what Zoe had whispered as she'd pretended to cry. Frustratingly, she'd departed almost as soon as she'd appeared. Her warning, although unsubstantiated, had set his nagging unease in motion again. Although his concerns hadn't sunken to the level of worry, much less the basement of fear, she'd certainly put them on the down escalator. He tried to take it with a grain of salt, told himself she was overreacting. Paranoid. That's what he told himself.

She'd said, *"They're watching us."*

-The Man who Wasn't There-

There was a crooked man,
who walked a crooked mile.
He found a crooked sixpence,
against a crooked stile.
He bought a crooked cat,
which caught a crooked mouse,
And they all lived together
in a crooked little house.

Christie giggled with delight. "More!"

Freddie foraged in the kitchen for some breakfast. The girls' chatter from the living room seemed almost hypnotic. Had it not been for the smoke detector he was studiously ignoring, this may have been a scene from some bizarre version of a Norman Rockwell painting: *Dysfunctional Dissociative Family of Orphaned Child.*

He opened the refrigerator and found it well stocked. He brought out a gallon of milk, a carton of eggs, a pound of bacon and a bag of fresh roasted coffee.

"Oh, you're gonna like this one. Try to see him—if you can."

Julie launched once more into verse:

Yesterday upon the stair,
I met a man who wasn't there.
He wasn't there again today.
(She added a theatric frown and slapped her forehead.)
Oh my—I wish he'd go away!

The girl burst into laughter. "Again! Again!"

Freddie fell into a groove, frying up bacon, brewing coffee and scrambling eggs. As always, work comforted him. Entranced by the sizzle of the pan, he considered their options.

He could play dumb and pretend nothing had happened yesterday with Zoe. They could plead time constraints or other plans, then take their leave; simply tell Creed to call them if and when he decided he could tell them anything.

And what if they won't let us leave?

Instead of a second recitation, Julie spun a new verse:

When I came home last night at three,
The man was waiting there for me.
But when I looked around the hall,
I couldn't see him there at all!

"You're silly." Christie giggled. "How could he be there (they-uh) and *not* there?"

He could also confront Creed directly. However, until he determined something untoward was happening here, this seemed unwise. What if everything was exactly as it appeared? Just a high-security military complex exercising normal precautions? He'd look like a paranoid fool, which he supposed he probably was. It may also plant the seeds of discord and create more problems than it solved. No, he'd save that option for last.

Then I was falling *down* the stair,
And met a *bump* that wasn't there.
It might have put me on a shelf,
Except— (Julie gasped.) —I wasn't there *myself!*

Over the girl's delighted laughter, Freddie called out, "Breakfast is ready!"

They bounded over and joined him at the table. Christie scooted her chair right up next to Julie's, crowding her. Julie, beaming, stole a glance at Freddie and winked.

Freddie took his seat as Julie served first the girl then herself.

"You guys seemed to be enjoying yourselves." He crunched a bite of bacon.

"She's my BFF," Christie said, hugging Julie's arm.

"BFF?"

"Best Friends *Forever!*"

Freddie set down his coffee mug. "So, BFF, are you ever going to start writing this stuff down again? That sounded real good in there." The tinkle of silverware on ceramic plates was soothing.

"Oh, that wasn't me. That was Mother Goose. And William Hughes Mearns. Antigonish. Johnny taught it to me when I'z little."

"Who's Johnny?" Christie hadn't touched a bite of her breakfast.

"He was kinda like my daddy."

"He sounds fun. My daddy's fun too. He makes words. On paper and on the line. He's coming to get me soon." A strip of bacon poised before her, she whispered, "He's on a special *mission!*"

Julie and Freddie shared a glance. Freddie raised his eyebrows then bent to his plate.

"Hey," Julie said to Christie, "how 'bout if me and you go up to the pool a little later?"

"YAY!"

"Okay, eat up that breakfast then."

Enjoying a meal together, enlivened by the kid's chatter, they talked about the day's plans. Freddie would connect with Creed and, with or without any new information, bring their visit to a close. Julie and Christie would trek to the pool. The only potential issue was if Zoe showed up. She knew about Christie, but still—as she'd said herself, kids were a labyrinth to her. There was no danger for Christie; it just might be disturbing to see her "BFF" suddenly change into . . . something else.

Freddie dropped his napkin on his plate, rose and carried his dishes to the sink.

Behind him, Christie said, "I want *dessert!*"

Freddie glanced back at her. "Dessert? Like what kind of dessert?" *Dessert with breakfast?*

"Ciminum rolls!"

He'd seen nothing that even remotely resembled rolls, anywhere in the kitchen. He could call about it, but as always, his tendency was to keep to himself. He didn't like owing people, nor did he like people owing him. Especially when the debts were due in social currency. And after all, accommodating or not, these people were at work.

Freddie was going to deny the request.

Julie's girlish grin and sparkling eyes convinced him otherwise. Why not? Hadn't Creed said they had about everything upstairs?

He picked up the phone to call room service—or whatever the hell it was. As Creed had instructed, he waited for the line to start ringing on the other end.

Nothing.

No ringing, no dial tone.

The line was not entirely dead. Just within hearing range, an ominous hum transported his mind, by way of his ear, fathoms beneath the foaming surface of a storm-swept sea. He creased his brow. "Hello?" After a pause, he repeated, *"Hello?"* While no voice responded, he got the disquieting feeling someone was there. Listening.

(They're watching us.)

He replaced the handset.

Freddie stood thinking, hand still gripping the phone in the cradle.

Julie said, "Freddie?"

He shook his head. "To hell with this," he grumbled, and strode to the door. He twisted the knob and pulled.

The door held firm.

He instinctively reached for the thumb turn of the deadbolt, only to discover there was none.

Brow furled, he twisted the knob again, pushed and pulled, shook the door roughly. *"Damn* it!" he said under his breath, doing his best not to upset the girls.

Twinset locks, keyed on both sides, were sometimes installed on doors featuring windowed panes. This prevented an intruder from breaking the glass and reaching through from outside to turn the interior latch. With this arrangement, a key should have been hanging just inside the door, close enough to access in an emergency—but not so close a burglar could reach it.

This door had no glass panes. And there was no danger of burglars.

His eyes traced the door trim. No key.

Okay, don't hit the panic button. They just forgot to give us a key is all.

He hurried to the kitchen, opened several drawers in succession. Only silverware and cooking utensils.

Why had they installed a twinset lock in the first place?

Well, Christie was usually in here alone. They wouldn't want her wandering out unattended.

And why is she in here alone? Come to think of it, why would they trust two strangers with her?

"How 'bout the bedroom phone," Julie suggested.

Freddie nodded and headed back. Once there, he snatched up the handset. Pressed it to his ear. He prayed for a ringtone, dial tone, anything.

Only silence—and the disturbing hum from the bottomless depths. Imagined silhouettes, shapes and shadows, taunted him in that murkiness. They whispered to him. He didn't want to hear their admonitions, refused to listen. He heard them anyway.

We're in trouble.

The front door opened.

Freddie dropped the phone, not bothering to place it in the cradle.

"Why hello there!" Julie from the kitchen, muffled by the intervening walls.

Spine tingling, Freddie turned to the bedroom door, listening.

She was answered by a man's voice, words indiscernible.

-Desperation-

"That door was *locked*." Freddie jabbed his finger at the double-keyed lockset.

The doctor looked perplexed. "Was it?" He glanced at the door. "Are you sure? It wasn't locked when I came in." He'd introduced himself as Doctor Aldus Constantine, head of research and development. He was draped in a lab coat, a metal briefcase dangling from one hand.

"It was *locked*."

"Maybe you pushed when you should have pulled?"

"Don't patronize me."

Constantine shrugged. "Well, I'll put in an order for maintenance to give it a once-over, but—"

"Don't bother." Then to Julie, never taking his eyes from the doctor, "Get your stuff, Jules. We're leaving."

"Please," said Constantine. As Julie rose, he raised his tone. "Please. Wait."

Julie stopped, looked to Freddie for guidance.

To the doctor, Freddie said, *"What?"*

Constantine turned to Christie. "My dear, have you something to keep you occupied? Elsewhere in the apartment? A doll, perhaps?" Uninvited, he took a seat next to the girl. She shrank from him.

Freddie thought, *What a jackass.*

Christie looked to her new BFF. Julie reassured her. "It's okay, sweetie. Go on back and play for a bit. I'll be along soon."

Reluctantly, the girl padded back to her bedroom.

When they were alone, Constantine said, "I'm afraid your departure will have to be delayed somewhat."

"Unless I woke up in Russia this morning," Freddie challenged, "we're free to leave any time we damn well please."

"Yes but you see, there are matters you yourselves brought to light here. Matters of . . . national security."

"National security." Freddie scoffed under his breath. "How about if I yank your ass out of that chair and beat the shit out of you? How would *that* be for national security?"

"You could certainly do that—" The prick brandished a smug smile. "—but such precipitous actions would serve only to further delay your release."

Freddie considered the guard booths, the blast doors, the sentries. Indeed they wouldn't be leaving unless they were *allowed* to leave.

Admittedly, this whole Julie/Zoe puzzle was troubling. And this was a major department engaged in God-only-knew what, charged with monumental responsibilities. Perhaps there were indeed issues of which he was unaware, issues of importance to the department, to the nation—issues that only Julie, or Zoe, could clarify.

He fixated on the word *delay*. They'd be released; it was only a matter of when. Maybe if they just cooperated and gave this airbag what he wanted, they'd soon be free to go.

Never before had Freddie missed Miami like he did right now. "Okay, what do you want from us?"

"We simply need Ms. Ayers to shed some light on a few matters of concern to us. That's all."

"What is drawer number seven?"

"Excuse me?"

The scientist seemed flustered, so Freddie persisted. "You heard me. Where's the file and what's in it? And what does it have to do with the sea level?"

Constantine adjusted his glasses. "What we do downstairs, sir, is *classified.*" He jutted his chin at Freddie. *"Highly* . . . classified." The men glared at one another. "So now, if you don't mind?" He tipped his head toward Julie.

Freddie scoffed. He leaned against the wall, arms and legs crossed.

Constantine nodded. "Ms. Ayers?" He motioned to the chair next to him.

When she was seated, Constantine opened his briefcase on the table. He withdrew a tangle of devices, all tethered to the equipment in the case by various types of cords. One ended in a plastic clip. "Place your hand on the table."

Freddie said, "What's that?"

"Only a polygraph," Constantine assured him. "Nothing to be concerned about."

When Julie glanced over at him, Freddie nodded.

Constantine secured the clip to her index finger. He attached a Velcro band to her wrist—probably to monitor pulse. He repeated similar procedures with several other devices. After they were all in place, she looked like a cyborg, the machine part of her within the case.

Finally, he produced a gallon-sized baggie from which he fished a handful of Styrofoam peanuts. He sprinkled them on the table. After flipping a series of switches on the machine, he began the questionnaire.

"What is your name?"

"Julie V. Ayers."

Constantine studied the readout, nodded approval. "When were you born?"

"August 8th, 1990."

"How long have you been here, at D-SAlt?"

"Since yesterday."

"How long have you been *here,* at the DSA?"

Julie knitted her brow. "Since yesterday?"

He made an adjustment on the machine. "When was your last carousel?"

"What?"

"When was your last carousel?"

"I don't know what you mean by that."

"When was your last carousel?" he repeated, more machine than the contents of the case.

Julie said nothing. She'd given her answer.

Constantine batted his eyes and lifted his nose at her. "How old are you?"

"It ain't polite, askin' a lady her age."

"How old are you?"

"I told you when I'z born."

"How old are you?"

She sighed. "Thirty."

"As a child, what was your favorite pet?"

"I wasn't allowed no pets."

"As a child, what was your favorite pet?"

"I told you. I never had no pets." The girl was getting frustrated. Freddie didn't blame her.

"Where are you right now?"

Julie glanced at Freddie, then turned back to the scientist. "Why, I'm sittin' right here."

"Where are you, *right now?*"

"At the DSA?"

"What is your name?"

"I told you that."

"What is your name?"

"Julie V. Ayers."

"How long have you gone by Julie V. Ayers?"

"Since I'z born, I guess."

Constantine paused, frowning at the machine. "Zoe Decker."

Julie didn't respond.

"Zoe Decker."

Freddie cut in. "What's this all about?"

The scientist ignored him. "Zoe Decker."

They all fell silent, Julie tense, the machine clicking, mysterious readouts reflected in the doctor's glasses.

"What is your weapon of choice?"

"The pen is mightier than the sword."

"What is your name?"

Julie's chin began to quiver.

"What is your name?"

The first tears pooled in her eyes. "Julie," she said quietly.

Another pause . . . "Move the peanuts." It sounded less like a request than an order.

Julie crinkled her brow, stole a glance at Freddie, then lifted her hand to comply with the request.

"No no," said Constantine. "You don't need your hands, Zoe."

"I ain't Zoe," Julie insisted. Her voice trembled.

"Zoe Decker."

"Aw man . . ."

"Move the peanuts."

Julie bent to the Styrofoam pieces and blew. The peanuts scattered to the floor.

"Ah," Constantine said. "Clever."

"I need a little break?"

"Black swan."

"Huh?"

"Zoe Decker."

Julie's voice broke as she said, "I already told you. I ain't—"

"Zoe Decker."

Constantine was engrossed in the machine. Sniffling, Julie lifted her hand to his face. He gasped when she touched him, tried to draw away. Tears streaming now, she leaned forward, following him, maintaining contact. "You don't have to do it like this."

"What ever do you—"

"I can make you happy. If you let me."

Freddie stood glued to the wall. His mouth fell open.

The scientist bolted to his feet. The chair toppled behind him.

Julie, anticipating the move, was already rising. "Please." She drew closer. "I'll be good." She began stroking the lapels of his lab coat. Freddie was reminded of the intoxicating feeling of her hands that first night at BT's.

Constantine retreated, backed into the wall. "Don't . . ." He raised his hands in surrender. He seemed reluctant to touch her somehow.

Julie stayed with him. The finger clip pulled away and fell to the floor. Several other devices disconnected. The armband, more firmly secured, dragged the briefcase to the floor. Unfazed by the commotion, she continued seductively. "I used to be a dancer, you know." Her fingers wormed their way beneath the lab coat. She was suddenly caressing his chest. "I don't do that no more." Her fingers blindly, perhaps inadvertently, brushed his nipple. As the man gasped, her hands roamed to his sides, then snaked all the way behind him. She drew her body against his. "But I could again—" She lifted her face to his. "—for you."

"Please . . ." Constantine's chin quivered, head turned away, eyes clenched shut. His arms were plastered palms out to the wall above him. Julie's hands were fevered ivy, encircling him, clinging, exploring him. She kissed his neck.

Freddie broke his paralysis and pushed off the wall. "What the hell, Julie!"

"For you." She seemed oblivious of Freddie as he lunged forward.

"For you . . ." Only a whisper now.

Freddie grasped her shoulders and attempted to peel her away. She held on stubbornly, now pressing her hips into Constantine's.

"For you . . ."

"Julie!" He worked his hands around her, secured the girl in a bear hug.

"No!" she shouted. Freddie hefted her and finally tore her away.

"No no *no!*" Eyes locked on the doctor, she reached desperately for him.

Constantine stood trembling. He looked about the room, face greasy with sweat. Fog was creeping in from the perimeter of each eyeglass lens. He glanced at the floor, the table, the walls.

What was he, humiliated? Ashamed?

By God, he's afraid of her.

Eyes on the doctor, Freddie released the girl. She hid her face in her hands. Still sobbing.

The door burst open. A guard. "What the hell is this?" He was armed but had not drawn his weapon. Constantine, having determined a path of escape, bolted for the door. The sound of his hurried footsteps indicated the speed at which he retreated down the hall.

"You sick bitch," grunted the guard as he collected the gear. He slowly backed away. He took his leave and closed the door behind him. This time, all pretenses dropped, he slammed the deadbolt home from outside.

One hand to her lips, Julie scurried toward the bedroom, almost at a run.

-When the Time is Right-

Christie was at the door to her room as Freddie passed. "Is Miss Jewels okay?"

"She's fine, honey. Just a little upset is all."

"Did that man hurt Miss Jewels?"

Freddie knelt and brushed the hair back from her face. "Hey. Nobody's going to lay a finger on anybody around here. Not on Miss Jules, and not on you either. They'd have to come through old Mr. Freddie first."

She didn't seem convinced.

"Listen, Christie. I'm going to go talk to her, see if I can make her feel better." He thought of an idea. "Miss Jules loves flowers, you know."

"She does?"

"Sure does. So why don't you draw her some? Color 'em up real pretty with your brightest crayons. Then when we're done talking, you can show them to her. That'd *really* cheer her up."

The girl nodded, still unsmiling—and turned obediently to her coloring table.

Julie was a lump under the bedspread. She'd pulled the covers over her head, apparently humiliated. Freddie eased up beside the bed. "Jules?"

She did not reply.

He sighed and peeled back the covers. As she had done, he submerged himself beneath the blankets. He spooned her, held her tight. "Want to talk about it?"

She flipped around to face him, then felt blindly for his hand, perhaps to hold it. But it wasn't that. She was giving him something.

A ring of keys.

A laugh nearly escaped him, but he contained it.

"We can use 'em whenever you think the time is right," she whispered. "But we might better do it soon, 'fore he figures out what happened."

"You're like, scary good at that, Jules." He felt her squirm with excitement at his approval, imagined her mischievous grin, her eyes sparkling in the dark. "Christie's a little upset that *you're* upset. You sold it pretty well, you know. Hell, I thought you'd lost it, too."

"Aw man. Christie . . ."

"Yeah. Why don't you go talk to her? I'm going to think on this a bit."

She just laid there with him, holding his hand beneath the covers. "I love you, Freddie."

"Love you too." He tweaked her nose and added, "You little thief."

Julie giggled, threw back the covers and headed to see Christie.

-Sea Level-

Even as Julie departed, Freddie stashed the keys away in his pocket. He was careful to keep them squeezed in a bundle lest a betraying jingle reveal his secret.

He was clueless as to the audio sensitivity of hidden cameras—if in fact there even were any. Zoe was convinced of it, and he trusted her instincts. Even so, would they be so brash as to monitor the bedrooms? He didn't think so, but he'd assume the worst.

He threw the covers aside and rose to the edge of the bed.

The room was dark, but that didn't mean anything. Night vision came standard on security systems available even at Best Buy. In fact, he wondered what they might be seeing now, things to which he himself was blind.

He got up and turned on the light. He chuckled when Christie's giggles bubbled in from her room.

Something about the interview nagged at him. Of course, the entire thing had been disconcerting. That only served to obscure the revelation, or possible revelation, that he intended to re-examine now.

He padded back to the bed and plucked a Newsweek off the nightstand. He laid down, crossed his sock feet, propped his head on two pillows and opened the magazine. He had no intentions of reading a single word.

The AC kicked on, and the hushed breath of forced air from the vents was relaxing.

Of interest to him was Constantine's response to Freddie's own inquisition before Julie's interview had begun. Freddie had asked about drawer number seven, and what it had to do with the sea level. He remembered Constantine's guarded response.

What we do downstairs, sir, is classified.

He imagined just about everything they did here was classified, so that hadn't bothered him. Rather, it was another word that interested him, one he believed Constantine had perhaps let slip without thinking. It had seemed insignificant at the time but now seemed to be of great importance. Or maybe it meant nothing, had been only an honest mistake. There was just no way to be certain.

He flipped a page in the magazine and shifted his gaze to the left side of the spread. He hoped he appeared convincing.

Downstairs.

That was the word that bothered him.

According to the elevator buttons, there were only two levels in the complex.

A and B.

A was the upper level, on which they'd entered. They were currently on level B, the lowest.

Yet Constantine, right here on level B, had said *downstairs*. Maybe the man had been disoriented, had imagined himself for the moment to be on level A. Or maybe he'd simply misspoken.

Maybe not.

What really made it an issue was Creed's little orientation speech.

Pool, little sandwich shop, even a wet bar—all up on A-level.

Not "level A," as Freddie would have called it, but the evidently more military *A-level*.

If indeed an undisclosed "downstairs" existed, he could safely assume that would be level C.

Or, as they expressed it here, C-level.

He thought he now knew where to find the elusive file cabinet. The puzzle would perhaps be solved when he discovered what, exactly, was secreted within.

The lights blinked out.

-Storm Brewing-

Up until now, the DID transformations had struck Freddie as nothing more than interesting. Unusual but harmless. And of course oftentimes frustrating. Now, the change seemingly triggered by the power outage, it for the first time disturbed him.

"Freddie?" Zoe from Christie's bedroom.

"In here." He tossed the magazine on the nightstand and stood. He realized how hypnotic the hushed breath of the AC had been. Without it, the tension concealed within him was laid bare.

The apartment was not completely blanketed in blackness. An odd illumination, bright but pinpointed, was provided by plastic battery boxes with two small flood lamps mounted on top, one in each room of the apartment. Ominous shadows stalked him everywhere.

"What happened to the lights?" Though she strove to disguise it, Christie's voice was laced with concern.

"It's alright, kid," Zoe said as he entered the girl's room. Then to Freddie, "What's going on? We still here?"

"Yeah. But I managed to lift some keys."

"How did you—"

"No time. If we're doing this, I think it needs to be now."

"That math works for me."

Freddie snagged his boots from inside their bedroom door then they hastily made for the living room, Christie hot on their tails. He practically skidded to a stop in his sock feet then quickly sat in a kitchen chair and slipped on his boots.

With the dexterity of a crotchetier, he had them laced and tied in seconds.

He stood, turned, and gingerly pressed his ear to the door.

From outside, distant shouts. Somewhere deep in the complex, a door banged shut. He strained to ascertain voices—or footsteps or doors or any sound at all—from nearby. Nothing. The voices retreated farther still . . . then faded to silence. He withdrew from the door and glanced at Zoe.

"Now or never," she said.

Freddie fished the keys from his pocket, wondering if they were still watching from the smoke detector. Were the cameras equipped with backup power? Surely not—surely they were not that important.

He lifted the key ring to a beam of light, trying to determine a likely match for the deadbolt.

Even if they were, things seemed to be in disarray out there. Maybe—hopefully—whoever monitored the camera feed was up running around like the people he'd heard down the hall. No definitive answers were available to him. While by no means a sure bet, now seemed like their best chance.

He located a Schlage. The only possible match. The other keys were of unfamiliar designs, none of which stood even a remote chance of fitting.

"Where are we going?" Christie.

Shit. The girl.

Zoe said, "We're getting the hell out of here, kid."

"Zoe." Freddie glanced at Christie, then back to the woman.

"Sorry." Then to the girl, "We're leaving. That's where we're going."

Freddie had inserted the key in the lock—but did not turn it. He left the whole ring dangling from the deadbolt and turned to Zoe. "We can't leave just yet."

"Why not?"

"I think I know where to find this drawer number seven. Not positive, but pretty sure. We're here, it's here, and I'm convinced it's important to us. To you."

Zoe's breath quickened. Her eyes wandered, seemingly in search of her troubled thoughts. She looked back at Freddie. "You're right, it's important somehow. But we better make it fast."

"What about Christie?"

Zoe looked down at the girl. Christie peered back and forth between the grown-ups.

Zoe knelt to her, gripped her shoulders. "Are you brave?"

"Miss Jewels. Why are you talking funny?"

Zoe closed her eyes and dropped her head. After a beat, she looked back up. "You like secret missions?" She was doing her best Julie impersonation.

The girl didn't seem convinced, but at least she was listening. "What kind of mission?"

"The secret kind. Me and Mr. Freddie, we really need to look for something. You, you need to stay here."

"Why?"

"To guard the fort."

"Guard the fort?"

"Yes. And your dollies."

"But I'll be scared."

Zoe sighed. "I asked if you were brave, kid."

"I'm brave," she insisted. "But it's *dark!*"

"Brave doesn't mean 'not scared,' baby sister. Brave means you do what you have to do, even though you *are* scared. When something tries to scare me? I *attack* it!" She balled her fist to emphasize the point. "Usually, you'll find it's more afraid of you than you are of it. If it's not, you *make* it afraid of you."

Christie knitted her brow.

"Look kid. This is important. I need you to do this. I need you to be *brave.*"

"Will you be back soon?"

"Yes," Zoe assured her. *"Real* soon." She stole a glance at Freddie then looked back to the girl. "Stay in your room. Keep busy. Color, play with your dollies. That way you won't even have to think about it. If it gets to be too much, just hide under your covers. Who's your favorite dolly?"

"Betsy."

"Hide under the blankets with Betsy."

"But—"

"But nothing, kid. Stay busy, or hide under the blankets with Betsy. We'll be back. Real soon."

Christie looked up at Freddie. He forced a smile and nodded agreement.

Christie seemed to consider the proposal. "Well . . ."

Indeed kids were a labyrinth to Zoe, but strangely, she seemed to have a knack for connecting— "Well what? You brave or chicken?" —in a tough-bitch big sister kind of way.

"I'm brave," Christie decided, offering her best little tough-girl face.

"Yeah, I thought you were." Zoe gave her a wink. "Now *go."* She pointed back to the bedrooms.

The kid scampered away. Zoe stood up and said, "Let's do it."

Freddie turned to the door and twisted the key. He let out a pent up breath when it turned without resistance. He gently pulled open the door, peered outside. The hallway was empty. He looked back at Zoe and shrugged. She shrugged back, and they slipped out.

As he carefully pulled the door to, Zoe whispered, "Lock it."

"What for? We'll be—"

"Christie might wander out. And if they check, they'll expect to find it locked."

Freddie nodded agreement and locked the door.

At a stealthy jog, they headed back the direction from which they'd come on the way here, toward Creed's office. Freddie had made note of an elevator just around the corner.

They slowed as they reached the turn. Freddie slid his back against the wall the final few feet, then tipped his head around the bend. All clear. He looked back at Zoe and shrugged again. She shrugged back again, and they rounded the corner. Moving fast now.

The elevator was just ahead. As they neared, something occurred to him. How could they take the elevator if the power was out? He silently cursed himself for that oversight as they arrived at the steel doors.

Zoe said, "Uh oh."

Echoing somewhere from deep within the complex, hurried footsteps. Hurrying to where? Then Freddie's heart tripped at an echo of voices.

He rifled through their options.

They could pry the doors open, then wait inside the car until the power returned. However, the doors may wind up stuck open—and there was a strong chance the car was not waiting behind them. Abandoning the gaping elevator shaft would leave evidence something was amiss. And if the car was there, they'd be exposed as they waited.

The echoes from the bowels of the complex drew nearer. Freddie's upper lip began to sweat.

They could try to find another door—to an office, a conference room, *something*—but sooner or later, the occupant of said quarters would return. Even if the room in which they hid remained empty, foot traffic would resume as they waited. Their window of opportunity would have passed.

This time they both jumped when the slam of a door seemed to come from right beside them.

They could also bolt back to the apartment and regroup. Freddie was about to voice that option when the power returned. As eerie as the meager lighting had been, the stark brilliance of the overhead fluorescents was worse. He felt like a mouse in the shadow of an owl, exposed by an inexplicable sudden sunrise.

Julie gasped. "Christie!"

Shit. He loved both versions of the girl, but damn it, Zoe was certainly the preferable split in this situation. Again it occurred to him the transition happened in direct correlation with the power status change.

"She's back in the room," Freddie said quietly. "We're looking for . . ." He shook his head. "It would take too long—"

"Just tell me what to do."

The elevator chimed. Too late to run, nowhere to hide. Freddie resigned himself to their imminent capture.

The doors slid apart.

The car was empty.

He grabbed Julie's wrist and yanked her inside.

She examined the buttons, raised a finger to test one.

"No!" Freddie warned. "Wait."

As he'd remembered, A and B were the only options. However, to the right of the panel was mounted a small screen with *Creston* etched along the top of the frame. A bit larger than an average hand, it may have been a palm scanner.

Of their own volition, the doors began sliding inward. Julie stepped toward them.

Freddie gently placed a staying hand on her shoulder. "Let it close."

The panels met, locked.

For a moment, they stood glancing nervously around the car. Then it jumped, subtly . . . and started down.

At first, Freddie was jubilant they'd lucked into a way to beat the security system and reach the elusive C-level. The next instant, it dawned on him the only reason the car would be moving.

Julie said, "Uh oh."

Despite himself, Freddie had to chuckle at the splits' twin responses. "What do we do?" he asked, mostly to himself. There was nothing they *could* do. They were simply busted.

"Quick! Stand over there!" Julie peeled off her shirt.

Understanding, Freddie squeezed into the corner, next to the Creston palm scanner, if that's what it was, and waited.

Julie tossed the shirt in the corner opposite Freddie, then shot him a wink and a nervous smile as she struggled out of her bra. She tossed it over with the shirt.

She unsnapped her jeans, slid them down a little, peeled off a sneaker and kicked it away. As a last thought, she tousled her hair. She slid down the wall, hands protecting her breasts.

-Field of Dreams-

Lyle Percy monitored the floor indicator above the elevator door. "Come on, come on . . ."

He'd had enough. His warnings about Project Amber fell on deaf ears. They treated him like a lab assistant, despite the fact his qualifications equaled, and perhaps exceeded, those of "Doctor" Aldus Constantine. Percy had a doctorate, too. Three of them! But they referred to him only as *Percy.* Sometimes even just *Lyle,* as if he were a boy. Never *Doctor Percy.* He hated the fact he lacked the guts to toss it right back at them. *Sure,* Aldus. *Whatever you say,* Taggart.

What was taking so long? He jacked the call button repeatedly.

Normally, a power outage would be nothing to lose your head over. He wasn't afraid of the dark; although like anyone, it did creep him out a little. Especially when he was working down here alone. With the amber.

The outage had probably been due to a thunderstorm topside. Storms always seemed to do it. Other times, the system just malfunctioned. In a normal medical building or laboratory, it would have been but a trivial matter. He wouldn't even have noticed. But in this place? It simply should *never* happen. He was well aware of the decontamination protocol. It would "decontaminate" everything for *miles!*

What if one day the system decided it needed to call the process due to power failure? Or a faulty filtration reading? Or just out of the blue, for reasons no one would ever get the chance to determine?

They'd all be locked in. Decontaminated. Over a computer glitch.

Ding!

Finally.

The doors slid open. He was just leaning into his first step—but halted midstride.

"Help me . . ."

Lyle Percy's entire thought process jammed. Crouched on the floor, leaning against the back of the car, trembling like a cornered animal, huddled a half-naked girl. It was her, the one from the video. From B-level. That's where she was *supposed* to be. What had happened to her? Why was she out? *How* was she out?

"Please? Help me?"

She'd lost her top. Her jeans hung askew, the creamy flesh below her tan line exposed. One shoe missing, bare toes curled. Vulnerable. The whole look was somehow . . . sexy. Despite himself, he caught his eyes caressing her silken private places. He shook his head and forced his gaze to her face. Maybe she'd been raped? Wouldn't surprise him with all these thugs roaming the halls like Roman centurions.

Reaching desperately for him, shaking, her left hand ventured from its post at her breasts, leaving a nipple exposed between her right fingers. Her bare foot slipped forward then pulled back. "Please . . ."

Stop it! Why had he noticed the nipple? Because he'd been looking, that's why. He squeezed his eyes shut. "Sorry."

"It's okay. Just, please. I need you."

He finally managed to break his paralysis. Demanding that his eyes obey the laws of chivalry, he stepped forward. Her other hand fell away as she leaned for him, exposing *everything*.

His eyes broke the law.

Ah to heck with it. He was powerless anyway, simply unable to stop himself from drinking it in. So he gulped it, lapped it up, every last drop. But at least he was helping her. Who knew? Maybe this would lead to something some day. Maybe. You just never could tell.

He bent to take her outstretched hand.

Just before entering a warm, wet, dream-filled sleep, where he frolicked naked in a field of daisies, hand-in-hand with the girl, he registered in his periphery a fist about the size of a Christmas turkey missiling toward his head. It slammed into his jaw. Right under the left ear. Just before his lights went out, he thought maybe he heard something shatter in there.

-Files-

As Freddie shook pain from his wrist, Julie examined the little man sprawled on the elevator floor. He was out cold, but his eyes remained open. "Poor thang," she said. "I think you might o' broke his jaw, babe. Look at this." She reached down and gently brushed the doctor's eyelids shut.

"Forget him. I've about had it with these people."

Julie was already slipping on her bra.

Freddie stepped over the limp body then turned and grabbed the man's ankles. He dragged him roughly, the man's hands trailing above his head, lab coat gathered at his armpits. He left the exposed trunk across the metal threshold to prevent the elevator doors from closing. "Come on." He released the ankles. The heels of the penny loafers plopped to the floor.

Freddie steamed down the hall, hands fisted, his shadow leaping ahead then falling behind under each brilliant florescent. Julie jogged to keep up as she shrugged into her t-shirt.

They passed several doors as they proceeded. *Archives, Supplies, Electron Studio, Processing,* and *A1A3 Viral strains* emblazoned with a red biohazard emblem. He opened a door labeled *Data Storage,* only to find a room crowded with racks of what appeared to be hard drives. Dissonant hums of varying frequencies offended. Freezing air blasted from the vents, yet the room was sweltering. Busy mechanical clicking was like the stealthy skittering of insects, alien, menacing.

No file drawers. He closed the door and continued down the hall.

He passed *Main Laboratory*—then came to an abrupt halt. Julie nearly collided with him. He was seeking files, ideally in a tall cabinet with drawers conveniently marked one through seven. But the lab would most certainly be used on a regular basis, so maybe they kept important files within easy reach, right inside with them. It was worth a shot.

He pushed through the door.

The room was roughly thirty by thirty, the wall opposite the entrance made up entirely of dark glass. The sudden movement of his reflection startled him, then disturbed him as his face materialized. He saw fear in those haunted eyes, which was no surprise. What he hadn't expected to find was a capacity for violence.

He hurried into the lab. The lingering odor of formaldehyde—or alcohol or floor cleaner—was subtle but nauseating. A workspace island seemed to float in the middle of the room, a ring of waist-high Formica countertop. The middle of the ring was crowded with padded stools. He counted eight flat-screen monitors, one for each stool.

Various devices awaited use between the screens. There were microscopes, centrifuges, beakers and scanners. A rack of test tubes, some of which contained brightly colored liquids. Two printers. Several stainless-steel boxes fronted by windowed doors somewhat resembled tiny microwaves. Lots of other strange equipment at which attempts of identification were futile.

He stopped at the first computer, stooped over and shook the mouse. A three-dimensional cube blinked onto the screen, segmented on all three planes by a grid of blue lines. In the middle of the box floated a naked human figure. Certain points of the cubed grid were marked by bold dots, connected each to another by red lines. Every line intersected the body, triangulating on various organs within the torso.

When he moved the mouse, he discovered the pointer was attached to one end of a new red line, the opposite end to a point on the grid. No amount of clicking or shaking would free the pointer from the scarlet thread. It jumped about the screen, shrinking and stretching like a filament of spider web stuck to his finger. The escape key proved useless as well. While curious, this was a dead end.

"Look at this." Julie from a corner of the room. Freddie glanced up to discover the girl holding hands with a skeleton. An instant of horror seized him—then he realized the skeleton was a model suspended by its skull from a steel cable on a white metal stand. It appeared imperfect, somewhat discolored—and thus real. He hoped that wasn't the case, but he didn't dwell on it. "Sweetie. We're looking for drawer number seven. Zoe's drawer."

"Sorry." She dropped the bony hand. The skeleton rattled and swayed as the fleshless arm fell back into place.

Freddie glanced under the counters.

File drawers.

He began yanking them open and slamming them shut in quick succession: Printer cartridges. Spare test tubes. Electronic meters. Petri dishes. He gasped when one drawer revealed glistening internal organs—then relaxed when he realized they were odorless. Silicone, most likely. Some were embossed with letters and numbers in white ink. Others were pierced by long needles of various colors. He slammed the synthetic guts back into their tiny sarcophagus and looked up toward the wall, the one with the door through which they'd entered.

Lined with four-drawer file cabinets.

Freddie maneuvered himself out from the island and to the first cabinet. He eased along, examining the labels: A-C. D-H. All the way to Z. Chemical Profiles. Viral Strains. Dates. Division directives.

No numbers.

"Freddie?"

He opened a random drawer and rifled through the folders: Various forms, incomprehensible medical data, unintelligible grids of numbers.

"Freddie."

A sheath of photographs caught his eye. He snatched it out and opened it: A Naval ship, the photo shot from high above, maybe from a satellite or hovering helicopter. A moist sea creature on a stainless steel tray. A rodent of some sort, partially dissected, furry face twisted in rage.

A monkey like a pincushion.

A human cadaver.

Freddie's heart was a panicked herd, hooves on asphalt.

"Freddie!"

"What?!" He turned to the girl.

"Sorry," she said. "I think I found it."

Her face was awash with concern. Why would a file drawer elicit feelings of foreboding? He walked to the dark glass, which he now realized was a floor-to-ceiling viewing window.

The edges of her palms were still pressed to it, the fog of her breath just vanishing from the surface. He placed the edges of his own palms to the glass, still staring at Julie. Finally, he looked into the dark tunnel that was his own cupped hands.

He found himself searching a gloomy research theater about the size of a basketball gymnasium. Stainless steel tables were spaced every twenty feet or so, each populated by random objects: Piles of coins, a kite, a remote control model car . . . balls of various sizes and colors, plastic blocks, a line of dominoes . . .

On one table, a pile of Styrofoam peanuts like the ones Julie had been instructed to move. Without use of her hands.

The room was a labyrinth of curious instruments and complex devices, some on tables, others on rolling carts.

Opposite the window through which he peered, the back wall was lined with two rows of gauges, dials, button and switches—one at eye level, the other along the floor. Cords exited at one point and entered through receptacles at another.

His breath stopped, in concert with his heart. Between the console rows, side by side, were crowded several stainless-steel panels, about thirty-six-inches square. Each was labeled with a foot-high gold-foil digit. One through ten.

He fixed on number seven.

These were much too large to be the fronts of file drawers. Dread crept over him when he realized what they had to be.

-Drawer #7-

Had Freddie proceeded only one door farther, he'd have found it the first time—although the label, *Theater,* offered not the slightest clue that the object of his search awaited discovery inside.

They'd been unable to locate a light switch, so it was in the gloom that they examined the thick steel panels. Sealed tightly to the wall, no handles offered a means of manual operation. The tight seams left insufficient space for even a slip of paper, much less a prying finger. Although there were countless switches and buttons on the console, Freddie dared not test any lest he set off some process that triggered an alarm.

He reached for his jackknife, then remembered he hadn't brought it along. He'd have had to check it during their flight, and they'd decided to travel light with only carry-on luggage.

"See if we can find a tool. Maybe a screwdriver and hammer or something."

"Sure . . ." Julie answered absently, studying the mysterious dials and gauges.

"Come on, babe. We don't have much time." He hurried to the first table, which contained only lightweight items: The Styrofoam peanuts, several Post-it Note pads, paper airplanes (why the hell would a bunch of eggheads be making paper airplanes?), a stack of towels. Freddie passed it over.

The next table held bins of other random objects serving God only knew what purpose. Dolls, Matchbox cars and other toys—a cheap pair of plastic walkie-talkies, several cell phones, a set of wind chimes—nothing with which he could pry at the panels.

Among the items on the third table was a handheld recorder. It didn't seem to fit, like perhaps it had been left behind inadvertently. Time leaked as if from a sieve. He could spare not a single second—*needed* to ignore it—but his curiosity defeated him. He snatched up the device and pressed play.

A tinny voice—that of a man in his early twenties, Freddie thought—spoke unintelligible babble. He sounded distressed. *"Ow deeta may . . ."*

It was followed immediately by another speaker, clear and composed. "Listen to me."

"Ow deeta quay is a me he . . ."

"Please, listen to me . . ."

He realized the second voice was that of a translator decoding the desperate pleas of the first.

"Vie qui locum ookay . . ." The words transformed into sobs.

"Woe unto all who enter here . . ."

"Serva may. Pla chera dee oova may . . ."

"Help me, please help me . . ."

"Es tina ternoom . . ."

"It's forever in here . . ."

Then the translator's tone changed, as if he were addressing a third party. "Where ever did you find this recording?"

The troubled young man, evidently via recording, continued babbling in the background.

A third voice responded. "What is it? Italian? Latin?" Freddie recognized it as that of Doctor Aldus Constantine, the jackass who'd interrogated Julie.

The translator: "Latin. I can't be certain, but based on his accent and the clothing you showed me, my best guess is that it's from the era of the Roman Empire. That dialect has been dead for centuries. Please, I simply *must* know where—"

Freddie pressed stop and dropped the recorder as if it had shocked him.

"Will this work?" Julie. At his side. Holding a crowbar.

"Uh . . . perfect," he said, baffled. "Where the hell'd you find it?"

"Over there." She pointed back toward the entrance.

On the wall beside the door hung a fire extinguisher, ax, and an empty mounting bracket, all situated above a steel Jobox—the same setup of the kits he'd seen at the guard booths on the way in. It made perfect sense, now that he thought about it.

"Shit." He nodded once. "Good job." He accepted the crowbar then hustled back to the stainless steel squares. To number seven.

The panels were crowded together, maybe a half inch gap between. They were at least two inches thick. This arrangement blocked access to the seam between drawer-face and wall. He jammed the crowbar between seven and eight anyway.

No good. The blade of the tool could find no purchase on the slippery steel.

He tried wedging it into the upper seam. The top of the panel was a little below his collarbone, forcing him to use only his arms, preventing him from throwing his weight into it.

He banged at it several times anyway.

"Freddie?" Julie's haunted voice echoed off the walls.

He halted the crowbar mid-stab and looked over. She stood frozen in place. Three panels down at number four.

"Freddie?" she repeated. Face as white as a winter's moon, her left palm rested lightly on the panel. "Come," she said. "Listen."

His breath was a bellows fanning flames of dread. He set down the crowbar and walked slowly to the panel, eyes locked on Julie's. He had difficulty swallowing around the lump in his throat, tried desperately to ignore the spiders crawling up his spine. She hadn't told him what she'd heard, but he knew what it was. He knew.

He pressed his ear to the panel, still staring at Julie. It was cool in the theater, yet sweat beaded on his forehead. For a moment there was only silence.

Thump.

Impossibly, his heart rate kicked up another notch. He waited, the demons of his mind yanking against the bindings that held them at bay.

Maybe he'd imagined it. Maybe it was just—

Thump . . . thump thump . . .

Then, muffled and faint, a groan.

He tore himself away. "*Jesus!*" He struggled to contain the demons, fought desperately to bind them once more within the chains of sanity.

The lights came on.

Reflexively, he looked up at the fixtures as if to confirm what had just happened, then immediately turned to the observation window.

Doctor Aldus Constantine stood at the very spot he and Julie had only minutes ago. Smiling through the glass, his lab coat like a royal cloak, he held in his left hand a computer tablet. The guy Freddie had pummeled on the elevator sat behind Constantine, leaned back in a swivel chair with an icepack pressed to his jaw.

"Behold." The physicist's voice echoed through the theater. He punched at the tablet.

A loud *clank* from the console startled Freddie.

He gasped, spun on his heel.

Hinged at the bottom, as it turned out, a panel crept open, revealing a gaping hole. Once horizontal, it slowly withdrew into the wall.

From the opening, a mechanical hum. Perhaps the straining circuits of a death row breaker box would sound like this upon the throwing of the fatal switch.

Drawer number seven slowly slid forth.

He approached it, eyes glued thereon, unable to look away. As he'd surmised, it was indeed a morgue drawer. On the flat steel bed, padded by an inch thick black rubber mat, sat a six-foot copper bin—maybe sixteen inches deep and twice that in width.

Though he protested, his feet drew him inexorably forward, revealing inch by inch what lay inside.

A pair of feet. Legs slowly glided from the shadows—then the ghastly torso, shoulders, neck . . .

Then her face. The face in the photo, the face he'd studied a thousand times since Julie had lifted it from the uninvited guest.

"Magnificent, isn't she?" The disembodied voice, omnipotent, all-knowing—malevolent, evil.

She'd indeed once been beautiful, but there was no beauty in the box.

Bile rose in his throat. He choked it back, tried to swallow—couldn't. A hoard of white ants skittered into his periphery and closed his vision to a pinhole.

"Sentenced to death," boomed Constantine like a god. "Treason. But I saved her."

His feet grew icy cold. His hands seemed to float like two balloons. At his sides? Or had they risen, unbidden? He widened his eyes and drew a deep breath in a desperate attempt to maintain consciousness.

She was naked, mired in an amber gelatin that looked like partially congealed chicken fat. Her face was somewhat distorted in the muck, but recognizable, blonde locks plastered out around her head like a malformed halo.

The door to the theater opened. Freddie barely registered it.

All four limbs looked . . . wrong somehow. His breath quickened when he realized why. He'd thought it was an illusion created by the distorting effects of the amber substance. It was no illusion, no hallucination—though he tried in vain to convince himself it was.

She was laid out like a doll staged for assembly, scarlet slivers of space between her trunk and shoulders, pelvis and thighs.

They'd amputated them. All four limbs.

Why the fuck had they cut off her arms and legs?

He felt more than heard Constantine behind him. Without looking up, Freddie asked, "Is she . . ." He was unable to finish.

"Dead? Oh no. I assure you, she's very much alive."

The flesh of her belly had been laid open. Slit in an X, the corners had been peeled back and secured with medical clips. Her insides were revealed, for all to see, study, observe. The backs of the triangular flaps were maroon behind a varicose network of blue.

"In fact," Constantine added from somewhere in a dream, "she'll never die."

Several organs had been removed but remained tethered to her by veiny cords. Like her limbs, a few had been extracted completely, laid aside like spare parts. Of those that remained within the body cavity, all were pierced by the same long needles of various colors he'd seen penetrating the silicon organs back in the lab. To the back of each lance was soldered an insulated cord. Each disappeared beneath the living corpse.

"I've arrived at a theory. You will have the privilege of witnessing my first test."

Freddie didn't respond. He jumped when he felt something crawling up his left arm, then realized it was Julie's hand.

She hugged herself to him. "No wonder she's got amnesia."

Freddie didn't know what she meant, and couldn't seem to focus on processing it.

Constantine typed something onto his tablet then turned to the wall-console. He hovered his finger over a metal toggle labeled *CGA*. "Ready?"

Freddie didn't respond. Her body hopelessly lost, he looked instead to Zoe's eyes. To his horror, he found them locked on his. Through the yellow muck, they widened. She gasped, or maybe cried out, muted by the amber. His despair wrestled with his disgust when a single clear drop formed in the corner of an eye. Rather than spill down her face, the tear broke free and floated slowly through the gelatinous sludge.

When it reached the surface, it formed a tiny puddle. He thought maybe she mouthed his name.

Click

At the tripping of the toggle, the Zoe in the box tilted her head back and twisted her face in silent agony.

"Oh God." Julie's fingers dug into Freddie's arm.

Tiny flashes of light drew his attention to the body cavity, where electric arcs sizzled at the insertion points of the needles into her organs.

Constantine said, "This is called Cerebral Glandular Augmentation. Observe." When Freddie looked up, drunk with shock, he found the doctor's hand gesturing toward the steel tables.

Movement attracted him from that direction. He'd have believed his capacity for further emotion to have been tapped, but his skin tingled when the Styrofoam peanuts scattered as if by a ghostly breath.

"Keep watching . . ."

One of the cell phones vibrated, began flashing, then sounded a ringtone: The instrumental introduction to *Synchronicity.*

Three paper airplanes took flight as if piloted by tiny paper dolls.

Five plastic balls rose of their own accord, floated above the table—then began orbiting.

Julie tightened her grip on Freddie's arm. "What's happening?"

"She's doing it," Constantine explained. "Or rather, we're doing it together. I gave her the power."

The dominoes tumbled with a skeleton clatter, then Freddie shuddered when a chair stuttered across the floor, untouched by any living hand.

"Now to test my theory. When I run the carousel, her psi abilities should multiply tenfold. Yet . . ." Constantine flicked another switch.

Zoe gasped. Not the wretched thing in the bin, but the one standing beside him grasping his arm.

Freddie turned to her.

She was staring down at herself, at her own living cadaver mired in the muck-filled copper coffin. That he could recall, this was the first time he'd ever seen her rendered speechless. Or that she'd trembled. "I remember now." Her hand fell away from his arm. "Everything."

Following her gaze, Freddie saw that the lips of the real Zoe, submerged in amber, moved in perfect synchronization with Julie/Zoe's words. Although the lips moved, the mired countenance remained expressionless as a corpse.

"What the hell!?" From behind them. Colonel Creed. The door to the theater slammed shut.

"Colonel!" Constantine was jubilant. "Come! See my discovery!"

Creed maneuvered blindly through the maze of tables then slowly closed the gap to the drawer. His face clouded with dread as he stared at the scientist, then twisted with horror when his gaze fell to the bin.

"Look!" Constantine shook his finger at Julie/Zoe. "It's her! Decker!" He laughed hysterically. "It's actually *her!*"

"What are you talking about?" Creed wiped his lower lip with his sleeve as if clearing away imagined vomit.

"Don't you see? *That's where she's going when she jumps the carousel!* It's similar to remote viewing, only she's assuming control of the entire brain and body." He paused, trembling. *"Remoting!"*

"Remoting?"

"Yes! She isn't *imitating* Decker, she really *is* Decker! It is as if she's . . . possessing her, if you will." Like a child on Christmas morning, he was unable to contain his glee. "I don't understand why she'd choose a white trash whore, but an explanation shouldn't be difficult to ascertain. Maybe

there's a genetic similarity. Or brainwave synchronization. So much to study; so much to *learn!*"

Freddie realized Zoe, in Julie's body, was seething. Her eyes could have burned holes in Creed's face.

Creed shifted his gaze to her. "Decker?"

"Creed you hypocrite *fuck!*"

"I didn't . . ." His jaw fell open—then snapped shut. He stared back down at the atrocity in the morgue drawer.

Zoe shot behind Freddie and rounded the table. Constantine, realizing the threat he'd posed to himself, shrank from her.

Creed drew his gun. "Stop right there!"

Zoe froze. Hands fisted at her sides. "You're going down, Creed. The world is going to know about this."

Constantine: "I think if we all just—"

She jabbed a finger at him. *"Shut the fuck up!"* Then back to Creed, "You're finished. D-SAlt is *finished!*"

"I won't allow that to happen."

She scoffed. "Just watch me."

The colonel tilted the gun slightly, indicated it with a quick glance.

Constantine: "There's no need for that." He slipped behind Creed to the console and switched off the carousel. "You see?" he assured the colonel. *"We* are in control."

"Are we?" Creed wondered.

Julie flinched, Zoe now back in her box. "Freddie?" She looked about, found his eyes. "What's happenin'?"

Creed: "I'm so sorry, Ms. Ayers."

"For what?"

He shook his head, eyes weary and shoulders slumped. "May God have mercy on our souls."

Creed shot Julie in the stomach.

-Within Your Heart-

Utterly unexpected, the report stole a flinch from Freddie.

A wretched gasp escaped Julie, in morbid harmony with the dying echoes of the gunshot. She doubled over, hands to her belly, eyes wide open—then blinked rapidly in confusion. Still hunched, she examined one trembling hand, then the other.

Both smeared with blood, so much blood—Freddie didn't understand how there could be so much blood. She lowered herself blindly to the floor.

His mind refused to process this. They wouldn't shoot an unarmed civilian, wouldn't murder an innocent girl. Not his mischievous little pickpocket. Not his sweet, innocent, harmless Julie.

He was cast in marble, no longer real.

("You fool! Have you any idea the world of possibilities you just threw away?")

He didn't remember how he got there; just found himself on his knees at her side, cradling her in his left arm.

("Have you *any idea the threat Decker poses? And you went and set her* free?")

Ever the optimist, wild-eyed, she smiled up at Freddie. Her breath came in quick spurts. "Christie . . ." She hummed in pain, lips pursed as if in labor.

"Don't worry, I'll get her." He stroked her hair. "We'll get her."

("I told you I'm in control of it!")

She smiled once more, through eyes that pitied him. She shook her head sorrowfully and raised her hand to his face. "Time for me to travel far—"

"Don't talk that way."

"—though it pains me, to depart." Her eyes clung to Freddie's, taking all she could, offering all she had.

("Control? You've been in over your head since this whole thing started.")

"If it ain't . . . too much to ask?" Her eyes flitted from one of his to the other.

"Anything." He tried to smile, failed.

"Save me—"

He nodded. "I will." A lie.

"—a place . . ."

Freddie watched . . . waited . . .

Her eyes fell out of focus, staring now at another place and time, at something or someone hiding in plain sight, strictly forbidden from the living, visible only to her new sorority of the dead. Her neck relaxed, head askew in his hand.

At peace.

"Julie?" He shook her gently, then urgently. *"Julie!?"*

Face buried in her hair, sobbing, he rocked her as if she were sleeping. Her lifeless arm gently dusted the terrazzo tile.

He turned his anguish to the heavens, but God wasn't there.

Only Creed.

Over the muzzle of a gun.

-Countdown-

"You'll join her now," said Colonel Creed, "in the kingdom of—"

Freddie exploded.

He blocked the gun away, deafened by the blast, blinded by the fire at his face. Something stung his left ear.

He bolted to his feet. Through the ringing in his skull, the whine of a ricochet, the pock-twang of the round careening about the theater.

He slammed his right fist into Creed's face. Twice, then once again. Creed was a nightmare monster, invincible.

He turned his back and looped his right arm over Creed's. Gripped the wrist with all his might. Tore the gun free.

Anticipating the loss of his weapon, the colonel leaped up, snarling, and threw his left arm around Freddie's neck.

Creed was candy. Freddie dropped the gun and seized the choking arm in both hands. Bent double. Sent the colonel sailing over his shoulder.

Creed's ass struck the copper bin. It flipped on top of him like an upturned canoe. Amber gore splashed everywhere.

From within the coffin, Creed's hysterical shrieks. Freddie backed away. Stepped on something that rolled under his foot.

Julie's arm.

He stumbled, kept his balance, straddled the corpse. The gun lay just beside her head. Freddie picked it up then focused on the upturned bin. Creed shoved it upright. Kicked it away. Freddie's stomach heaved. He raised his left forearm to his mouth and bit down.

Still shrieking, Creed rolled the fidgeting torso off of him. She slithered to the floor face up, eyes obscured by the drenched curls clinging to her face. To Freddie's horror, she tossed her head, cleared most of the matted hair away.

Impossibly, her severed limbs writhed on the floor. A bare foot nudged a liver; fingers flicked absently at a spleen. Intestines were tangled with cords and cables.

Creed stood, uniform clinging, drenched in abominable chicken fat. He gawked at one dripping hand, then the other.

Freddie was there, but his mind had departed. Disgust tainted his grief, both exceeded by his rage. His head pounded and his ears rang before he realized he'd fired the first shot. A wet boutonniere flowered on the colonel's chest. Then another, and yet a third as Freddie fired twice more.

Thrice shot, soaked in amber gore now swirled with scarlet, Creed inspected his torso. He didn't fall. He stared up at Freddie, eyes wide . . . waiting . . .

Nothing happened. He turned to Constantine. "What have you *done to me!?*" His voice was garbled, hoarse, blood spattering from his lips at each plosive. He turned on his heel to the wall-console. The exit wounds were a horror show, tendrils of God-knows-what knotted with strips of destroyed uniform. He placed his right palm on a scanner screen. To the left of the screen, a clear plastic box popped open: the cover to a red button about the diameter of a water bottle. Creed slammed it.

A woman's voice echoed over the loudspeakers, calm and dry: "Protocol initiated. 30 minutes to decontamination." She sounded like Susan Bennett, the voice of Siri.

"Turn it off!" Freddie jammed the gun at Creed—then realized it posed no threat.

"It can't be stopped. Mine is the only authorized print, and I'll never scan it." He drew a combat knife from his belt with his left hand and made repeated slices across his right palm. "Neither will you."

"It hurts . . ." Constantine. "It *hurts!*"

Freddie and the colonel looked at him.

"There's no pain if you don't resist." This from Constantine, but not in Constantine's voice.

Freddie looked at the thing on the floor. Eyes dead, her lips moved in perfect sync with the physicist's.

He said (she said), "Get . . . out . . . *(It hurts!)* . . . now!"

The thing on the floor mouthed every word. Chills racked Freddie's spine. He registered a chattering—realized it was his own teeth.

Creed and Freddie locked eyes, Freddie aghast, the colonel desperate.

Creed lunged.

Freddie shot him in the face. Then again, then a third time, each bullet sculpting a horrible new visage.

The thing that was Creed, now a Cyclops, lifted its hands to its destroyed skull. It fell over, kicking and flailing. Something like a scream gurgled from its mouth.

But it did not die.

Constantine: *"GO!"*

Freddie bolted.

-Pressure-

Dr. Aldus Constantine stood stark still, wondering what Creed was going to do. He was sickened by the stink of spilled innards and his own fear sweat, a drop of which fell into his left eye. He dared not wipe it away, dared not even so much as flinch.

Constantine was one of only a handful of people even aware of amber's existence. He'd prided himself on being the sole expert on the substance. But now an unavoidable truth stole the wind from his sails, stung him like a slap in the face.

He reluctantly admitted that what he knew about the material was little more than anyone else. Yes, he'd put that limited knowledge to good use. He clung desperately to that. Still, unwelcome, Percy's warning rang clear in his mind: *"What else might it be doing?"*

He gritted his teeth, resentful of the position in which he'd been put. How alive was Creed? He was not surprised the colonel had survived what should have been three fatal shots to the vital organs. But the man's *brain* was destroyed! How could he have survived *that?* In what capacity could he think now? Much less reason? Constantine had given little thought to the matter but had assumed even amber was incapable of sustaining life through brain death.

Yet there it was, alive and kicking. The Creed Thing.

As it writhed on the floor, its hand fell across a crowbar leaning against the console. For some reason, this seemed to calm him. Calm "it."

Constantine slowly, quietly, tiptoed back a step. He swallowed hard, then immediately regretted it, praying that even these quietest of sounds had not betrayed him.

The thing wrestled itself to kneeling position. Blindly exploring the tool, it craned its neck in an attempt to utilize its one remaining eye—which bulged outside the socket. Apparently, the expanding bullets had exuded enormous pressure within the brain case as they passed through the skull, the point of least resistance the eye socket.

The Creed Thing grasped the crowbar and struggled to its feet. For a moment, it just stood swaying. Dripping with amber and gore. Its skull was an exploded pumpkin. Unspeakable tendrils hung from ragged holes in its torso.

From outside, gunfire.

The Creed Thing snapped its head—or what was left of it—toward the sound. It paused a moment—then lurched away, stumbled into a table, nearly tripped over a chair. Grunting and gurgling, it finally managed to make its way out the door.

-Emergency-

Freddie's thundering footsteps pounded out a polyrhythm with his hammering heart. He slipped on the floor as he cut left, caught himself, then sprinted for the elevator. No more than twenty feet from it, the bell chimed.

He skidded to a stop.

The doors slid open.

Three soldiers came pouring out. The first one spied Freddie and raised his M4. "Halt!"

As the others took up positions covering the hallway, the first soldier crept forward, knees bent. "On the floor. Now!" The muzzle looked like an eyeless socket.

As Freddie knelt and raised his hands, one of the hall sentries screamed. The soldier glanced over his shoulder then cut back to Freddie. "Down!" he repeated.

The sentry: *"It hurts . . ."*

Freddie had thought the report of the .45 was loud. It was but a whisper compared to the M4 in the cramped hallway. One of the sentries went down. Freddie's soldier turned on his heel. A scarlet magnolia blossom sprouted on his back when the sentry's rifle thundered again.

The soldier collapsed. Freddie stood, eyes locked on the corpse. When he looked up, he found himself face to face with the sentry.

"Get out of here, Freddie. You've only got—"

Freddie shot him through the heart.

Amazingly, the sentry tried to smile, shaking his head as he clutched his chest. His words were garbled. "Freddie . . ." His lungs must have been destroyed. "It's me. You need to . . ." His eyes rolled back and he crumpled to the floor.

Freddie bolted for the elevator.

Inside the car, he turned and pressed *B*.

He stepped back. Waited.

He leaned forward and jabbed repeatedly. An admonishing buzz accompanied each press of the button.

Siri pleasantly informed him via the overhead speakers: "Elevator access expires in one minute. Fifty-nine. Fifty-eight. Fifty-seven—"

He placed his palm on the scanner. Surely it would accept any print during a catastrophe.

"Fifty-two. Fifty-one. Fifty—"

Only an extended buzz.

When he pulled away, a red image of his palm pulsed on the scanner, all the loops and whorls of his print. A bold *UN-AUTHORIZED* flashed at the bottom of the screen.

His eyes fell to the dead sentry. He bolted over and dragged the corpse by the arms into the elevator.

"Forty-three. Forty-two. Forty-one—"

He was about to lift the man's hand to the scanner when he thought of something.

He stepped over the body, hurried to the M4. Movement from behind him caught his eye.

"Thirty-five. Thirty-four. Thirty-three—"

He reflexively dove forward as the crowbar came crashing down. The Creed Thing followed him, raised the weapon, then brought it down again. Freddie rolled to safety, pummeled by terrazzo shrapnel.

"Twenty-five. Twenty-four. Twenty-three—"

In a flash, another of Manny Inguanzo's combat lectures ripped through Freddie's mind:

"A meth freak can survive a heart shot, sometimes even a bullet to the brain. They'll die eventually, but I've heard of those guys going nuts on pure adrenaline for close to a minute. That's plenty of time to do a lot of damage. In those cases, you aim for the pelvis. Break the hip and it doesn't matter whether they're alive, because they can't support their own body weight. They go down, and they stay down."

"Fifteen. Fourteen. Thirteen—"

Eyeball like a goiter, the Creed Thing raised the crowbar.

Freddie placed a round right in its left front pocket. He squeezed the trigger a second time, but the slide had locked back.

"Ten. Nine. Eight—"

Nevertheless, as Manny had promised, it went down. Writhing, it stayed down.

"Five. Four. Three—"

Fuck the M4.

He shot to his feet, took a step, slipped in the gore.

Busted his ass.

"Two. One." A pause, then Siri's soothing voice casually informed him, "Elevator access prohibited."

"No!"

The doors slid inward. Foiled by the sentry's body, they hesitated—then opened once more. After a pause, they attempted the process again.

Freddie rose, squeezed through the gap. The buttons, once illuminated, were now dark. He tried the scanner, hoping even for the admonishing buzz.

Nothing.

He bolted from the elevator.

He'd seen no fire escape toward the lab, so he jogged the other way.

Only more offices and supply closets.

He stopped, stood in the hallway. Mind racing. He began pacing in a circle. Gazing at the terrazzo tile. Conventional wisdom struggled to cloud his thinking. *No fire exit means you're stuck.*

He shook his head, gently nudged the thought aside.

"Forget fires, forget emergencies," he muttered.

His subconscious screamed at him: *But this IS an emergency!*

He ignored it. "Think maintenance," he said to the floor. "How would repairmen access different floors if the elevator was out?"

He gasped and stared up at the wall.

He hurried back to the lab. Pushed through the door. Snapped into a fighting stance.

The poor bastard he'd cold-cocked earlier sat trembling in a corner with an ice pack still pressed to his face. He posed no threat, so Freddie ignored him and proceeded.

He hustled back down the hall with a stool. The Creed Thing zeroed on his footfalls, deftly crabbed on its elbows for his feet. Freddie leaped over it, crept to a wall and froze.

The monster glanced blindly around, eyeball bulging, gray matter dangling. Freddie held his breath. Trembling. Gagging.

The Creed Thing locked on something down the hall . . . paused . . . then turned and hitched away.

Freddie quickly positioned the stool against the wall of the elevator, working as quietly as he could. He carefully climbed up. He lifted a ceiling panel and squinted into the shaft.

Illuminated by dim incandescent bulbs mounted in metal cages, he found what he was looking for. He almost climbed up, hesitated . . . then hopped back to the floor. He searched each soldier, careful to avoid attracting the corpse hitching aimlessly down the hall with a trail of gore in its wake.

He collected a combat knife and flashlight. Stuffed them in his cargo pockets. He buckled on a utility belt equipped with a holstered sidearm and spare magazines, then snatched up an M4.

He jumped when one of the radios crackled. A voice spit panicked coded babble. It would be nice to monitor their movements now, wouldn't it? He stepped over, yanked the radio off the corpse and clipped it to the back of his belt. As a last thought, he hefted the crowbar. Eyes locked on the receding Creed Thing.

He climbed the stool and tossed the rifle and crowbar onto the roof of the car. He hoisted himself up, got his bearings, then strapped the M4 over his back. He tested the first steel rung and it held firm.

Until now, he hadn't realized Siri's announcements were also broadcast each minute over the radios. From his belt, she said, "23 minutes to decontamination."

He hefted himself onto the ladder. At some point during the climb, he realized he was crying.

-The Thing-

Every cell of Creed's body and brain were fully alive and would remain so indefinitely. This by no means meant he was the man he'd once been. Normal data processing requires communication between every part of the brain. While the cells of his grey matter remained fully functional, communication between most of them was no longer possible, the physical connections irreparably broken.

There was a part of his mind that was fully aware of who he was, contained memories of all the years of his life from birth to the moment his brain had been scrambled. This portion was completely sealed off from his five senses and thus incapable of forming new memories. It was also incapable of influencing decisions or initiating action based on learned values. The human part of him just "was," lost and alone in the darkness of his thoughts, unaware of the cause of his isolation.

The portion of his brain still connected to physical functions knew only one thing: He was on a mission. Dead set on carrying it out.

Unmoored from all rational thought, this portion was more "It" than "He." It knew only that they must be stopped, and would kill to stop them. Who "they" were, exactly, was beyond it. In fact, it was unaware the issue even needed to be considered.

Had the cells that processed reasoning been able to communicate with those that incited action, "it" would have been "he," Taggart Creed, and would have approached this differently. But the latter was permanently sequestered, the former in full control. It acted only on spontaneous stimuli, with absolute dedication to the mission.

To kill.

The Creed Thing was alerted to a sound on its right. It tried to stand but discovered it could not. It propelled itself along the floor on its elbows, dragging its burdensome legs behind it.

Its progress was stunted by some sort of barrier. The door to the lab—although it had no way of conceiving of anything so complicated. It knew only that sounds beyond the barrier presented a threat. It attempted to push through without success. It tried pounding. Then biting. Then clawing.

The Creed Thing shrieked in rage. It came out only as muted grunts and snarls. It kept clawing, but forgot why it was doing so.

-B-Level-

Freddie wasn't sure what to think of *decontamination*. He got the feeling he himself may be considered one of the contaminates.

On B-level, he hammered the combat knife under the leading edge of one elevator door. Opening it from the inside had not been easy, and he worried how he'd do it on A-level with the girl clinging to his back.

He leaned the crowbar against the wall, strapped the M4 to his back and jogged toward the apartment.

Two soldiers came barreling around the corner. He gasped, almost went for the rifle, but they rocketed past him. He supposed there were more important issues than him to deal with at the moment. Just the same, he switched the rifle to firing position, finger extended on the trigger guard.

This strategy proved wise when a third soldier rounded the corner and skittered to a halt. His body tensed and he went for his sidearm.

"Wait!" Freddie shouted.

Too late.

Before he could be gunned down himself, Freddie squeezed the trigger. Expecting a single shot, the rifle instead spit out a burst of three: *DAT-AT-AT!* The soldier was lifted off his feet and hit the floor like a bag of hammers.

Freddie shook his head. "I told you to wait." He inspected the rifle. The selector switch was set to *burst*.

The most common magazine of an AR-15 held thirty rounds. He didn't own one but had rented them on several occasions at the gun range. The AR was the civilian version of the M4, the rifles indistinguishable save for the bolt and internal parts that enabled automatic fire in the latter. Thus, Freddie assumed the weapon in his hands held thirty rounds.

While bursts would indeed be more deadly, they would also cut the number of shots available to him from thirty to ten. Full auto would deplete the magazine in but a few pulls of the trigger, only one if he held it more than a few seconds.

He set the selector switch to *semi* and hurried down the hall.

As the apartment neared, thumping arose from inside the door. Another few steps and the thumps proved to be accompanied by Christie's high-pitched exclamations. "Hey! *I'm* in here! Let me *out* of here!"

Freddie knocked rapidly. "It's me. Freddie." He spun the rifle to his back, fished the keys from his pocket, fumbled for the Schlage, dropped the damn things, snatched them up, located the key and inserted it into the lock.

Christie slammed into him with a big hug. He twisted sideways just in time to avoid a head-butt where it would hurt most. He patted her back. "Let's move, Sweetie. We're getting out of here."

Christie glanced around him, then stepped into the hall. "Miss Jewels?"

Freddie's heart sank. All the action had mercifully shoved the grief to the back of his mind, but he was well aware he had some pain coming. This was but an appetizer, a nibble before the hearty main course. "She's . . ." his voice cracked.

Christie looked up at him.

"She's somewhere safe," he said—and supposed that was true, or at least part of the terrible truth.

He couldn't do this now. He took a quick breath— "We've got to hurry, Christie." —and grabbed the girl's hand.

Five steps down the hall, she wrenched free. "Betsy!" She bolted back into the apartment.

Siri said, "19 minutes to decontamination."

-Glory-

Gloria sat watching the security monitors. *There!* The little shits were running down the hall, away from the apartment. How the hell had they gotten out? No matter. It was smart of them, using this distraction to make a break for it. She respected that.

The Ayers girl wasn't with them. She didn't know the couple—didn't give a shit about the Shrek—but hoped they could stop them without having to kill anyone. Especially Christie.

But they had to be stopped.

Eyes on the monitor, she drew the Desert Eagle from beneath her desk. With her other hand, she plucked the walkie from the charger and pressed the transmit button. "Anyone on B-level near residence quarters?" She released the button.

After a few seconds, the static broke. *"Martinez."*

She was about to transmit again when the oddest feeling came over her. The back of her neck tingled pleasantly. She felt . . . mischievous. Euphoric. She couldn't decide whether this frightened or comforted her. Shivers overcame her and she allowed herself to just experience it. Indeed it was nice. For a moment.

"What is it? We're a little busy out here."

Gloria, but not Gloria, said, "Creed's office. Stat."

She stood and aimed the iron hog leg at the door.

The guard never saw it coming.

She turned the pistol to the monitors, shattered each in deafening succession. Then she took out the DVR unit.

Finally, she turned the gun on herself.

-Superhero-

Christie was choking the shit out him. He knew if he'd been in front of a mirror, the face therein would have been beet red, veins popping, eyes bulging. He gagged and kept climbing.

The trek from B- to A-level was proving arduous, way more so than he'd expected. With the added weight—and Christie's constant fidgeting—it took much longer than the previous climb. He couldn't seem to get the crowbar adjusted like he'd had it before; his left hand ached.

Freddie breathed a sigh of relief when they finally made it. Panting, he rested his head on a rung.

But he couldn't lean out for the doors with Christie on his back. He shuddered at the thought of plummeting all the way to C-level. Not to mention the Creed Thing, which would no doubt hear them crashing through the roof of the elevator car. It would come for them. Dazed and broken like two bugs that just met a windshield, they'd be defenseless. If they survived the fall in the first place.

He shoved the thoughts from his mind and focused on the next step. "Grab the—" He gagged, took a breath, flexed his neck with all his might. "Christie! Grab the ladder!" It sounded like an Avante Gard Donald Duck impersonation.

She struggled and grunted ... tried again ... then stopped. "I can't reach. Your head's too big."

He resisted a chuckle. "Use my hair."

His head was yanked back when she grasped his mane. He reflexively pulled forward, wincing, thankful he hadn't shaved his head to a bur recently. Little grunts echoed through the shaft as she tugged mightily. Her little feet dug into his sides and back. "Careful," he warned. "Take your time." His scalp was on fire. Tears escaped through sealed eyelids. He was sure the roots would break free, leaving Christie to plummet into the abyss clenching fistfuls of his hair.

The roots held.

Her little hand came into view grasping the rung just above his head. She continued wrestling her way up. A tennis shoe kicked him in the ear then fell on his shoulder. Another chuckle threatened to escape him, but he managed to contain it.

Finally, she was free of him. When he looked up through moist eyes, he found himself staring at her heels, at two little rubber tennis shoe emblems of superhero girls. Caped, each wore a red eye-mask, flying through the air in classic Superman position: extended fist and one knee bent.

It wasn't difficult to visualize them as climbing invisible ladders. Or climbing *him*. The chuckle burst forth, became an outright belly laugh echoing through the shaft.

"What?" Christie asked, giggling herself.

That made him laugh even harder. He realized the clock was ticking. He realized his laughter was a misguided expression of something other than mirth. But he simply couldn't stop.

"What?"

His chin started quivering. When the tears returned, this time not due to the fire in his scalp, he finally composed himself. Took a breath. "Nothing, sweetie. Just silly grown-up stuff. You hold on tight now."

He brought the crowbar into position, leaned out, and rammed it between the doors.

Siri said, "14 minutes to decontamination."

-Silent Screams-

The poor stupid fool—Constantine had tried to warn him through the thick glass. But Percy, drunk with panic, hadn't understood. He'd bolted straight for the exit despite Constantine's wild gesturing against it. The kid was finished the moment he'd opened the lab door.

Like a giant monitor lizard, the Creed Thing snared his pant leg, tripped him, crawled up his thighs and onto his body. With Percy's pathetic squirming, it looked like an x-rated UFC match. Or a rape scene from hell.

Constantine stood vigil over the silent screams, pounding the glass, powerless to help.

The monster at his throat—biting, shaking—Percy's fingers hooked in pain. The Creed Thing yanked its head free, a chunk of gristle clenched in its teeth. A spray of scarlet painted the glass and trickled to the floor.

Constantine turned away and dropped his hands to his knees. He dry-heaved. Tried to think of something else. Took a calming breath.

His eyes watered as his stomach emptied onto the theater floor.

-Stop Look and Listen-

Freddie had nearly shot him on site. But the guard never raised his gun—and in fact had waved them through. *"Go go go!"* he'd shouted. "Take one of the EVs! The blast doors are going to seal any minute!"

They'd bolted past him down the hallway leading to the tunnel.

Freddie slammed the breaker bar then glanced back as he held the door for Christie.

The guard was monitoring their progress. *"Go,* Freddie!"

He took the man's advice, not worrying for the moment about why he was helping them, or how he'd known his name.

Outside the door, he scanned the cavern for a vehicle. A fifty-foot run of chain link fence bordered the sidewalk at which they stood. Beyond that, the road disappeared around a soft curve in the tunnel. To each side of the road, a parking lot. "There!" He pulled Christie into the walkway.

The slapping of shoes on concrete echoed off the cave walls, Christie's in double time, the polyrhythmic ticking of a death clock. They rounded the end of the fence and cut right.

As they arrived at the narrow road across which waited their ride, Christie halted. Freddie released her hand just in time to prevent dragging her off her feet. "What is it?" If he'd been wearing a watch, he'd have glanced pointedly at it.

She beetled her brow. "Stop look and listen, before you cross the street! Use your eyes, use your ears, *then* use your feet!" She peered purposefully in each direction. Satisfied, she ran across, Betsy's head bobbling as she whizzed by.

Siri said, "13 minutes to decontamination."

Freddie found himself grinning as he jogged to catch up. He wondered if this was healthy.

The EV was unlocked. Christie heaved open the back door and climbed aboard one-handed, the other clinging to the doll. Freddie unclipped the radio, set it and the M4 on the passenger's seat and folded inside. "Buckle up," he said over his shoulder . . . then froze.

Oh shit.

Keys.

He had no recollection of the guard fishing in his pocket for them. So maybe they'd already been in the car.

He scanned the seats, leaned over and checked the floor-board.

No keys.

He punched open the glove box.

Nothing but a plastic sheaf of documents.

He slammed it shut. He reached for the sun visor, only to discover it was nonexistent.

When he checked to see if the key was already in it, he scoffed at himself. In place of an ignition slot was a large see-saw switch. When he thumbed it up, it glowed green. He gripped the wheel, punched the accelerator, and the EV surged forward.

They bounced over the curb and swerved onto the road, taking each curve at full speed, Freddie praying they'd meet no oncoming traffic.

The radio crackled. Siri said, "12 minutes to de-contamination."

He stared down at the walkie. When he looked back up, the first set of blast doors appeared about 200 yards ahead.

Rolling shut.

The EV had already reached top speed. He pumped the accelerator, trying to squeeze from the car even a single ounce more juice. His efforts were rewarded with only repeated lurches—seconds lost.

He held the accelerator to the floor, steaming.

Goddamned electric cars . . .

Electricity didn't just make itself. You had to produce it—using fossil fuels, coal-fired power plants, or nuclear energy. Seemed to Freddie that electric vehicles simply exchanged emissions you *could* see for those you couldn't.

The blast doors continued their journey inward.

And what about those 700-pound batteries? Surely the mining for materials to make them destroyed the habitats of untold numbers of species. Then there was disposal of the cells after they died. But what did he know? Maybe electric cars really did somehow have less environmental impact than good old fossil fuel buckets.

With agonizing sluggishness, they crept toward the steadily decreasing gap. He could get out and *run* faster than this!

More likely, people loved envisioning themselves as "Captain Planet," and big corporations were more than willing to help them play out that fantasy. Enter the EV fad.

Emission-free transportation in the complex had nothing to do with saving the environment. Sacrifices were for the little people. Power players lived life in luxury. They would by God drive—or fly—whatever and whenever they damn well pleased, and to hell with the environment and to hell with the little guy.

They weren't going to make it. Freddie threw his head forward in quick thrusts, pressing at the wheel as if he could somehow *shove* the vehicle forward with his body weight.

100 feet.

"Come on . . ."

He aimed the driver's side rearview just inside the spot he thought the edge of the blast door would be when they crossed the threshold—*if* they crossed the threshold.

Fifty feet.

"Hang on, Christie!"

This was it. Freddie made one final adjustment to their trajectory—and braced himself.

He flinched.

They shot through.

Unscathed, they'd passed close enough to discern the machining marks on the massive edges of the steel.

Christie's voice wafted over the seat. "That was a *liiiittle* close, Mr. Freddie."

"You got that right."

But they had a problem. If they'd made it only by the skin of their teeth through this barrier, they'd find the next one sealed shut by the time they reached it.

Siri said, "11 minutes to decontamination."

-Stalking Behavior-

After having studied the Creed Thing through the glass, Constantine felt he understood its behavior enough to survive the task he needed to carry out.

He stood at the lab door, heart pounding. Sweat fogged his glasses. His hands were trembling. He calmed himself, removed his glasses and cleaned them with the tail of his lab coat. He wiped his forehead on his sleeve. Glasses back in place, he was ready—or as ready as he'd ever be.

He slowly turned the knob . . . then cracked the door. He was immediately assaulted by the coppery tang of blood and the reek of body fluids. He choked back nausea, turned his head away and took one final breath of untainted air—then slipped inside.

He'd come up with the brilliant idea of turning off the lights in the theater, making mirrors of the observation windows. The Creed Thing hitched aimlessly along the glass. Biting and clawing at its own reflection. It would crab along slowly—then burst ahead hissing and spitting.

Stalking behavior.

He imagined the creature would remain occupied for a while. Perhaps indefinitely. Dr. Constantine needed only a minute or two.

Carefully monitoring the Creed Thing, he crept as stealthily as he could over to the island. He selected a computer facing the observation windows, the better to keep an eye on the beast as he worked. He forbid his eyes from falling on the bloody heap that had been Lyle Percy.

He lifted a stool and gently *placed* it in position rather than scooting it. He slowly sat down, opened his account, and gingerly entered his password. A smile stole across his face. He was actually going to beat this thing!

After inserting a zip drive, he began downloading his latest files. He needed only the last week's work, and there wasn't much. The rest he'd backed up the week previous—as he had religiously since he'd been here, all saved on a high-security application similar to DropBox. The internet connection had shut down the second the countdown had begun. Otherwise, he'd have simply started the upload and departed.

Constantine was reminded of the joke about a computer contest between Christ and Satan. When the celestial power went out, the former was claimed the victor because . . .

Jesus saves.

He chuckled to himself, wondering if Creed would have found that amusing. He checked the screen, expecting to see the green progress bar nearing its full length. Instead, he discovered an open text document, a single sentenced typed thereon: *What's up, Doc?*

He sat staring at the screen. Flummoxed.

He realized he'd been outfoxed only as the Creed Thing bit down on his left calf.

-Arrive Alive-

Captain Planet surged forward, fluorescents zipping overhead like constellations through the windshield of the Starship Enterprise. Freddie leaned over and dug his cell phone from his pocket. He dared not lighten up on the accelerator, even for an instant. He shivered as he rounded a curve, fully expecting to slam into a forklift or to be crushed by a runaway garbage truck barreling from the opposite direction.

Unslammed and uncrushed, he thumbed the screen.

"Arrive alive! Don't text and drive!"

Freddie shook his head and chuckled. His thumb hovered over Dexter's icon. Then he thought maybe he should dial 911 instead. Not that the police would have any jurisdiction out here. It was a moot point, because a tiny hourglass spun where his signal bars should have been.

He tossed the phone on the seat. "You're right, sweetie. Thanks for reminding me."

The second blast door appeared as they rounded another curve. The good news was, it was still open. He wondered why. Perhaps they closed from the inside out, in order to allow last-minute escapees a fighting chance to exit the complex. Had the threat been from outside, perhaps they'd have rolled shut in the opposite order.

The bad news was, the doors had made much more progress than the first set when they'd been at about this distance.

But maybe they were closer than it seemed.

Maybe by cutting the gentle curves, thereby maintaining a straighter path, they'd pick up the precious microseconds necessary to squeeze by. And of course he would not pump the pedal again.

They weren't going to make it.

"Shit shit *shit!*" He pounded the wheel.

Christie gasped. "You said the *S*-word!" Almost a whisper, seemingly in awe.

He shook his head again and a half grin crept around his ear. "Oops. I sure did, didn't I?" Sweat dripped into his eye. He wiped it away.

"My daddy says using dirty words means you're not smart enough to think up the *right* word."

Seventy-five feet.

"Your daddy's right." Freddie's eyes were glued to the shrinking gap. "Christie, I need you to *really* hang on this time."

"Why?"

Fifty feet.

Why. He recalled how kids were obsessed with the word *why*. "Remember back there how it was a little close?"

"Yeah. It was *vewy* close."

Twenty feet.

"Well, this one's going to be even closer."

"Uh oh."

"HANG ON!"

The wrenching of metal on metal was deafening. From both sides of the car, sparks lit the tunnel as if spit from twin dragons grasping the undercarriage with steel claws. The right rear door was ripped off its hinges like armor from a knight slain by a basilisk.

The cab filled with the acrid stink of searing metal. The gap where the door had been sucked away the fumes in but an instant.

Freddie opened his eyes. He checked the side mirror. Not there. Nor was the other one. In the rearview mounted on the windshield, he spied a hubcap spinning to a stop like a giant coin.

He breathed a sigh of relief and stole a glance over his shoulder. "You okay?"

"I'm good, but Betsy's a little shooked up."

"Well, you just hold her tight and tell her ole Mr. Freddie's got it all under control."

The right front tire blew out.

-Tourniquet-

Doctor Aldus Constantine stood stark still, back glued to the wall. No more than two feet in front of him, the Creed Thing turned its mangled head left . . . then snapped it right.

After a moment, it began dragging itself down the hall, in pursuit of nothing, destination nowhere.

Constantine slid to the floor. Writhing on the terrazzo tile, he pounded his fist. Willing away the pain.

After a minute or so, he sat up and examined his pant leg. Soaked in blood. He could feel it leaching into his sock. A drop formed, then broke free and spattered on the floor. He dared not inspect the damage beneath. Yes, he was a doctor, but this was *his* leg. Treating one's own traumatic wounds was not as easy as they made it look in the movies. Besides, at this point he needed to focus on evacuating.

He sloughed off his lab coat and struggled to rip away a wide swath. His hands shook as he wound the makeshift tourniquet around his calf. He stifled a shriek as he cinched it tight, then lay back on the cool tile. When his head stopped swimming, he sat up, then stood up. Tested the leg. He had quite a limp, but he could walk.

He stuttered down the hall toward the elevator. Seething. If that lumbering oaf hadn't made his way down here, none of this would be happening. Anger was a rat in the pit of his stomach. He clenched his teeth in rage—then thought of something.

He bent to a dead guard and snatched the radio from his belt. He twisted the knob. Depressed the call button. "Uh . . . Somebody help? I'm on C-level. The prisoner has killed Colonel Creed." He released the button.

Now that sounded stupid. He realized the soldiers spoke some sort of code over the radios. *10-4* and all of that. But surely they'd understand plain English.

The hiss of the radio ceased, replaced by noise from the upper levels. A voice barked, *"Who is this? Clear the channel."*

Constantine shook his head and smirked. "This is Doctor Aldus Constantine. Head of research. I'm stuck on C-level." He released the call button.

The voice returned. *"I don't care who you are. Stay off the channel."*

The idiots. The brainless, gun-toting imbeciles. Oh how he longed for the day he'd no longer require military funding to carry out his work.

He thought of another tack, and once again depressed the call button. "In case you haven't noticed, the doomsday clock is ticking. The prisoner is in possession of the only key to shut it down. If you don't find him, we'll all be incinerated and this conversation will be moot." Of course this was a lie. But the centurion nitwits wouldn't have a clue.

Silence . . . then, *"Description?"*

Constantine thought, *He's the only civilian in the complex, you miscreant.* Instead, he replied, "Six-four. Two-hundred-fifty pounds. Disheveled hair, cargo pants, work boots, flannel shirt. Armed and dangerous."

Another pause, then, *"Copy."*

Good. Maybe they'd shoot first and ask questions later.

Now to find a way out. If the oaf had done it, so could Doctor Aldus Constantine. He was a man of science. He'd *think* his way to freedom.

As he arrived at the elevator, he realized this was going to be easier than expected. Difficult, yes, but certainly doable. A stool sat at the wall of the elevator just under an open ceiling panel.

He steeled himself, grimaced as he mounted the stool, and struggled to the roof of the car.

-T-Rex-

The shredded rubber on pavement was a frenzied tribe slapping out a log drum rhythm from hell, the car a crazed warhorse straining to tear free of its rider.

Freddie held the reins in a death drip, teeth gritted, right foot jammed to the floorboard. The wheel pulled stubbornly to the right. He knew better than to overcompensate and cut left, knew to just keep it as straight as he could.

As he'd yet to do, he stole a glance at the speedometer. He was surprised to discover the needle wavering just below fifty miles per hour. He'd have estimated their speed at no more than thirty. The needle was bouncing wildly but didn't seem to be dropping.

Over the deafening rumble of the disintegrating tire, he could just make out Christie comforting her dolly: *"I gotcha, I gotcha."*

Siri said, "9 minutes to decontamination."

The final set of blast doors came into view, rolling inexorably shut, farther away than either of the others had been when they'd first appeared. This time he was *certain* they weren't going to make it. But he had an idea. Desperate, maybe stupid—probably stupid—but their only hope.

"Christie!" he shouted over the din, "I want you to bend down and hug your legs as tight as you can!"

The steel ramparts loomed before him, details emerging with stark clarity.

"But Betsy will . . ."

"Now Christie!"

At the last second, he allowed the car to do as it struggled to do: cut right. The ruined tire ripped loose with a shriek of metal on asphalt.

Although he leaned against it, the devastating forty-five-degree impact jerked him forward and left, *hard*. His head slammed into the door post.

"Hold on, Stevie!"
"Daddy . . ."
"Don't panic, little buddy! Just hold on!"

The evil Harleys circled behind him, closer on each pass. Over the raging engines, the hammering-clinking-grinding of gears and chains, valves and pistons.

The fire raging below leached slick sweat from him. He could only imagine the heat Stevie must be feeling.

"Daddy . . ." The boy glanced down at his own feet, then desperately back up at his father.

Freddie followed his gaze. A length of rebar, maybe six feet long, had skewered his right pant leg like a giant fishhook. The fisher on the other end of the stubborn steel proved to be a trembling slab of concrete as large as any Toyota, tenuously balanced on a pile of rubble.

The chunk dipped, tilted, threatened to pull his son away from him.

"Daddy!"

"Stevie . . . Listen to me! I want you to unbuckle your belt with your free hand!" The pants would easily slide down his skinny legs. But would they slip over his sneakers? Maybe . . .

"Mr. Freddie!"

He was about to repeat his instructions, then puzzled at the strange way his boy had addressed him.

Slipping . . .
"Mr. Freddie?"
Slipping . . .
"Mr. Freddie!"

Betsy whacked him in the face then careened onto the dashboard.

"Hold on!"

No parking garage. No bikers. No Stevie.

"Mr. Freddie?"

At first he mistook the tiny voice as Betsy's, her oversized plastic pigtails jammed against the cracked glass of the windshield. Then he realized it was Christie.

"Hey, sweetie." He groaned, trying not to sound like he felt.

He registered the grinding gears of the blast door machinery.

"We cwashed."

A chuckle escaped him, and flashes of pain hammered his head. "Yes we did." He took a breath, released it. "You okay back there?"

He gingerly touched his left temple and inspected his fingers. As expected, he discovered blood.

"I'm good." Even through the adrenaline, even through the pain, her little voice eased his anguish, inspired him.

The car was shaking rhythmically. Freddie realized why.

Like the jaws of a robot T-rex, the blast doors gnawed away at the left front corner of the EV. Bite release, bite release—in about two-second intervals. With the blind determination of a machine, they chewed.

The whine of the mammoth electric motor revved and eased on each cycle, a demented mechanical brain oblivious to the plights of the living.

On each release, the doors relaxed. Each time it bit down, however, the iron dinosaur made steady progress, the gap narrowing, disintegrating the chassis of the car.

"Mr. Freddie?"

Like giant cat claws, anvil-sized hooked tabs in the leading edge of the right blast door had extended and locked, believing themselves to be embedded in the matching slots of the left. As long as the hooks stayed that way, the doors might remain jammed open should they manage to complete the closing cycle.

"Mr. Freddie, You're not *listening* to meeee."

But maybe they *wouldn't* stay that way. Maybe those iron claws would retract and re-engage somehow. Maybe after all their efforts, he and Christie would end up trapped inside, right at the damned exit.

And "decontaminated."

Now he was just pissed. "Give me a minute, sweetie." He spun in his seat, kicked open the door and strode over to the firefighting equipment. He snatched the ax off the mount, inspecting it as he approached a coupling in the two-inch conduit strapped to the wall. The tube provided power to the blast door motor.

This was by no means the right tool for the job. But it was what he had.

He drew a bead on the most vulnerable point—right where the pipe entered the coupling—and heaved the ax. Teeth gritted, he brought it down with all his might.

The ax bounced harmlessly off the steel pipe.

Undeterred, the Jurassic jaws kept munching.

He realized Christie was shouting something at him. He shut it out.

He spun the ax around to use the pointed end of the head. Snarling, he brought it crashing down again.

Sparks shot from the puncture in the pipe and pelted him with searing droplets.

The T-rex kept crunching.

And the blade was stuck.

Ignoring the blinding molten shower, he slammed his boot against the conduit and wrenched the ax free.

He flipped the tool again and hurled the wide side of the blade.

Still the jaws chewed and the sparks flew—but a gash now breached the pipe.

With a warrior's cry, he swung the ax one last time.

To the final ejections of sparks from the live side of the conduit, the steel beast finally relented. He dropped the ax. Acrid smoke burned his lungs and stung his eyes.

Freddie stumbled back, fanning at the fumes. He made his way to the EV. Christie materialized through the haze, bouncing in the back seat, waving at him through the window.

Smiling.

What the hell did she have to be happy about in all this? Part of her glee was no doubt due to her youth, her naivety. But he understood on a gut level that youth didn't explain all of it, or even most of it. The predominant source of her joy, he suspected, was simply how she chose to process the world around her.

Sooner or later, adversity strikes us all. When life presented lemons, some puckered and grimaced. They hid from the challenge. Or cowered in fear.

Others made lemonade. Undaunted, they drank it up, every last drop, and were nourished by it.

Insanely, he found himself waving back at the girl, a stupid grin plastered to his face.

Lemonade.

Sweet and sour.

Life itself.

"Hop outta there, little bunny," he said as he opened her door.

She bounded out giggling. "Wow, Mr. Freddie. You're *strong!*"

"That's because I eat my vegetables." He bent through the driver's door and grabbed the radio and M4. He stood, strapped the rifle behind him and clipped on the walkie. As he did it, he inspected the blast doors. Just enough gap to squeeze through, even with the anvil-sized hooks.

He also realized it was raining out. Sleepy thunder rumbled in the distance, having exhausted its pre-nap tantrum. Dying flashes from the heavens provided a celestial night-light. The storm probably explained the power outage.

Thunder and lightning.

Lemons and lemonade.

"Up you go." He hefted the girl to the roof of the car. "Mind the busted windshield."

Of course she *leaped* to the hood rather than carefully traversing the cracked glass, stuttered a few steps, then leaped once again to the pavement, to the free side of the barriers. Freddie struggled to the roof himself, then carefully eased one foot onto the hood.

Bullets peppered the blast doors.

A voice boomed over the echo of gunfire. "Halt!"

Judging by the shout, the guard—or guards—were maybe a hundred yards behind them. He wondered whether distance explained the missed shots or they'd been intended only as warnings.

Freddie squeezed through the gap then lowered himself to safety behind the right blast door.

His first inclination was to run for it. However, in his arms or at his side, Christie would render a footrace futile.

He could make a stand at the blast doors, but for how long? And to what end? What, exactly, would happen when Siri's countdown finally reached zero?

He lifted his face to the sky. The rain cleansed his mind, even as the echo of running boots advanced from deep within the tunnel.

Christie gasped. "Betsy!" She looked up at Freddie, hair soaked, face clouded with worry.

Freddie stared down at her. It was just a doll. A piece of plastic.

But it was *Christie's* doll. In the girl's little mind, Betsy was her child.

Her Stevie.

He knew it was irrational, knew it was stupid. And he knew he was going to do it. There seemed to be no clear options here anyway. At least rescuing Betsy offered a call to action, a reason to do *something*.

He'd made Julie a promise *(I'll get her)*. Implicit in that promise was a commitment to care for the kid. So here was an opportunity to express, not in words but in deed, who he was to Christie, or who he was willing to be.

He glared at the gap between the doors, blew away rainwater that had trickled between his lips. Over his shoulder, he said, "Wait here," and approached the gap, examining the rifle.

He set the selector switch to auto.

-Mettle-

Private Dwayne Perkins had been assigned an important task. This was his moment, an opportunity to prove his worth, to demonstrate his mettle. He yanked M4s from the rack and issued one to each employee as they reached him in the line. While only the guards carried these rifles on a daily basis, every staff member had been trained on it.

This was it; this was the big-time. The clock was ticking. The capture of one man stood between victory and death. With everyone armed, their odds of apprehending the fugitive improved dramatically.

Dwayne dropped the rifle he'd been handing over and swatted the back of his neck. Something—maybe a grasshopper or beetle—was clawing at his skin.

"What the hell, Perkins!" The sergeant from the station opposite him.

Wide-eyed, Dwayne froze. Stared back at his superior.

"Perkins?"

He just stood there, shaking, gawking at the sergeant. "It hurts."

"Poor baby. Pick up that rifle and move your ass. *Now!*"

Perkins shook himself out of it. Gritted his teeth. He picked up the rifle. Extracted the magazine and examined it. Fully loaded.

"Perkins?"

He slapped it back in the well. Racked the bolt. "Here's how this works, ass hats."

He killed nine and wounded five before they finally brought him down.

-Betsy-

Under threat, attack what's attacking you. That's what Zoe had said, and that's exactly how Freddie intended to play this. Rather than scanning the cavern for threats, he jammed the M4 around the corner of the blast door and opened up. He kept it brief, fanned the muzzle left to right as quickly as he could. He was rewarded with sudden shouts of panic—and a scream.

He flipped the selector switch to burst. Stock pressed tightly to his shoulder, eyes already peering down the barrel, he rounded the corner, seeking targets over the destroyed EV.

The first guard stood to his left not twenty feet away. Just recovering from the volley. A stitch of .556 rounds cut him from left hip to right shoulder.

The second guard, to his far right, managed to squeeze off a round. Panicked, he hadn't taken time to line up the shot. Freddie calmly moved his sites to the new target and cut him down.

He became aware of a whizzing like bees passing at light speed, accompanied by bursts of flame from deep in the cavern. The back window of the EV blew out. Two rounds slammed into the blast door in quick succession.

Freddie retreated behind the steel barrier, rifle aimed skyward.

"Shit shit *shit!*" He combed his fingers through his mane. Sloughed away the rainwater.

From within the complex, flurries of whispered footsteps. He imagined silent gestures and coordinated maneuvers to advancing points of cover. Aware of the threat now, they would no longer make of themselves easy targets.

Someone loosed a scream. "Get it off me . . . *GET IT OFF ME!*"

Manic shuffling . . . *"It hurts!"*

Boot steps, no longer stealthy. Freddie strained to decipher what was going on over the pattering of rain on the pavement. Thunder rumbled in the distance.

Someone shouted, "Davis. *Davis!*"

A burst of gunfire.

A few potshots, then another scream.

Freddie cocked his head.

A single shot reverberated in the cavern—then another.

Silence.

He drew three quick breaths and again burst around the corner, rifle up and ready. A guard was hitching across the floor. Another stood over him with his pistol drawn. The latter, hugging his left arm to his stomach, shot the former in the head then lowered the gun.

Freddie blindly flipped the selector to semi and drew down on the last man standing. The guard looked up and yelled, "Wait!" But Freddie wasn't taking requests.

He shot him down, one bullet, straight through the heart.

He slung the rifle onto his back and crawled on hands and knees over the crumpled hood. Eyes on the stone gymnasium, he reached blindly through the driver's window and plucked Betsy off the dash.

Back outside, his knees wobbled and his hands shook. He handed Christie the doll. Rather than take it, she nearly knocked him down with a hug. They stood there like that, Betsy drooping in his hand, the rain pummeling them. Freddie closed his eyes, breathed through the adrenaline and patted the kid's back. She pulled away— "Thank you Mr. Freddie." —and finally took custody of her baby. She squeezed it to her face and smiled up at him. "You saved my Betsy."

He ruffled her matted hair.

Her smile faded.

She lowered the doll, holding it by one arm, seemingly forgotten. She scanned the area. Taking in her surroundings.

Her eyes missed nothing.

"The chopper," she said, not looking at him. She blinked, spit rainwater off her lips. "It's our only hope." Her voice was still high-pitched, but she no longer glided her *R*s. In fact, she was suddenly quite articulate. Uncharacteristically bold despite her small stature. Self-assured.

All business.

"We made it out, sweetie." Freddie was uneasy with this transformation. "All we need to do is find a place to hide 'til things die down."

She shook her head. "No good."

"What do you mean?"

"Out is not *out,* Freddie. Not with what's coming." She finally met his eyes. "And don't call me *sweetie.*"

She turned on her heel and hurried through the deluge down the fenced road leading back to the checkpoint. The doll swung from her hand absently. When he didn't immediately follow, she turned, walking backwards now, arms extended. "You coming, nail banger?"

Freddie's jaw dropped.

She stopped and raised her little hands to her hips.

"Wait a minute. Are you telling me—"

"There's no *time* Freddie!" She threw her hands in the air, Betsy swinging wildly.

He stood there gawking, brain in overdrive, the gears of his mind smoking.

"Keep up." She turned on her heel and took off in a sprint toward the checkpoint.

The radio crackled.

Siri said, "6 minutes to decontamination."

Freddie ran.

-|||ogical-

His hands were tiring, and his leg was killing him. He kept his eyes glued to the shaft above. He didn't dare check his progress; he'd been climbing quite a while, had even passed B-level. So peering down into the shaft would serve no purpose. He knew where he was. A-level—and the path to freedom—were just a few rungs higher. There was no need to look down. The door was *right there,* open and waiting for him. Looking down would accomplish nothing. It would be stupid.

Unreasonable.

Illogical.

Doctor Aldus Constantine looked down.

A quiet whimper escaped him. Eyes squeezed shut, he thrust his arms through a rung and hugged himself to it. "Don't look down," he said. Then again, "Don't look down."

He realized he was hyperventilating. He calmed himself, drew slow deep breaths, determined to reason his way through this. He was a man of science. He could do anything.

Tilting his head up before opening his eyes, stubbornly refusing to even think about gazing into the abyss again, he gripped the rungs and took a step up. With his left foot.

Spikes drilled into his calf. He cried out, hugged the rung again. Counseled himself to *stay calm.*

After a full minute, steadier now, he tried again, this time with his right foot.

Except that blood oozing from his left had slopped onto the steel.

Constantine found himself dangling in the gloom, his whimpers echoing around the shaft. Panicked, he pedaled his feet for purchase—for a rung, a crevice in the stone wall, anything. The gyrating loosened his grip. He cried out in terror. Despite his better judgment, knowing it would be his undoing, he pumped his feet all the harder, desperate to find purchase.

His hands slipped farther.

Finally, he froze.

Too late. Because his grip was shot.

Doctor Aldus Constantine was a man of science. Not just an intellect but a *genius*. Certainly no sweaty-armpits *jock* infected with crotch rot. He would never have lowered himself to doing pushups, yoga, or even walking—had never even considered wasting his time on something as stupid as exercise.

He was incapable of even a single pull up.

He hung there. Trying to rest.

He looked down again.

This time, face greasy with sweat, his glasses slipped off. He watched as they faded into the chasm, out of focus, ricocheted off a wall—and finally clattered to the roof of the elevator.

Now that wasn't so bad, was it? Only a few seconds. Not that he was going to fall. But if he did, surely it wouldn't be that bad.

His hands slipped farther.

He resigned himself to the fact he was going to fall.

Okay, think. *Think!*

The glasses careened off the wall. So perhaps I should shove myself away at the last minute so I won't—

Constantine plummeted. He did not shove away.

And he was wrong about the fall.

It seemed to take forever.

Apache

The kid leaped up the door of the chopper, caught the handle and wrenched it down. The door squeaked open. She tossed Betsy inside and scrambled into the cockpit. Freddie was right behind her. "Buckle up," she said over her shoulder as she bounced into the pilot's seat.

"You're a pilot?" Ignoring the elephant in the cramped cabin, he blindly pulled the harness around him. A puddle was already forming on the seat.

"Well . . ." She pushed two buttons, flipped a toggle on the control panel.

"What do you mean, *well?*" He paused with the strap held out in front of him. "Have you flown this thing before or not?"

"Sure I have." She reached for the ceiling, muttered, "shit," then rose to her knees in the seat to throw a switch above her.

"Okay, good." He relaxed a bit and buckled in.

"In a simulator." She pushed and held another button. After a moment, the engine roared to life.

"A *simulator?*"

"Relax. It's just like the real thing."

Through the windshield, Freddie caught glimpses of the rotor blades passing with increasing frequency.

She added, "Almost."

"Al*most?*"

"Freddie." She jutted her chin toward the parking lot.

He followed her gaze. "Oh shit."

Three guards were beating it toward them through the downpour. Freddie threw off the straps, snared the M4 and cracked the door. He knelt, jammed the muzzle through the opening. Bits of pavement erupted around the chopper. Ricochets whizzed through the air. The guards' shots rang out in the distance, a percussive accompaniment to the rising whine of the chopper engine. Ignoring the fusillade, Freddie took careful aim at the man farthest left. Took him down. The report was deafening inside the cabin.

"Jesus!" From behind him, in Christie's voice.

He pulled down on the second guard. Took the shot. The pavement exploded to the left of his target—

and the bolt locked back.

"I'm out!" He tossed the rifle aside. Drew the pistol.

"Don't bother. At this distance you'd have better luck throwing a Frisbee at them." She relaxed into the seat and leaned her head back.

Freddie thought, *What the hell is she doing?* She seemed to be just giving up.

Christie bolted upright, gasped, then smiled broadly. "Hey! We're in a *chopper!*"

Freddie stared at her for a beat, mouth agape, then turned once more to the guards.

"What's this one do?" She was reaching for a glowing switch on the control panel.

Freddie snapped his head around toward the girl— "Don't touch anything!" —then back out to the guards. One of them dropped his rifle and began swatting at the back of his neck. Gyrating like a rain-soaked ballerina on meth. He appeared to be fighting off a swarm of hornets. The other guard, rifle still trained on the chopper, crab-walked through the puddles to assist.

The dancer calmed, stood upright, shook his head. He drew his pistol and gut-shot the approaching guard. The man fell. Rolled in pain on the pavement. The dancer walked calmly over, examined his quarry, then shot him in the head. He stared at the corpse a beat as he lowered the pistol. Satisfied, he looked back toward the chopper. He seemed to be considering something, standing out there in the downpour.

After giving Freddie a distant thumbs up, he turned the gun on himself.

The body had no sooner splashed to the pavement than Christie said, "Secure the door." She did not glide her *R*s.

Freddie knelt there, frozen, staring back at her. "Did you just—"

"Secure the door!" Her voice was high-pitched but nonetheless motivating.

The engine was roaring now, rotors a blur whistling overhead. As Freddie was strapping in, he said, "So, just how far is a safe distance when—"

"Shit."

"What?"

"Can't reach the pedals." She looked back at him, unbuckling her straps. "It's going to have to be you."

"But I've never—"

"Don't worry, I'll help you." She winked, hopped up beside him in the rear seat and jutted her little chin toward the cockpit. "Strap in."

Freddie didn't move. He understood on an academic level what was happening here, but that didn't mean he was able to wrap his head around it. He needed time to ponder, to consider it all—to decide what, exactly, he thought about this. It was uncharted territory. Disturbing. It was—

"Freddie *GO!*"

He shook his head as he wormed into the cockpit. "What was this designed for, midgets?"

"Hurry Freddie!"

Siri said, "4 minutes to decontamination."

"Okay ready." He turned to face the girl. "What do I do first?"

"Just relax." She sat back, took a breath and closed her eyes.

As Freddie watched her, the fine hairs on the back of his neck stood up. A creeping sense of calm came over him—almost euphoria. He ignored the sensation. Thought he was imagining it. Or maybe it was just a post-adrenaline dip, the stress catching up to him.

He resisted it. When it wouldn't let up, he fought it harder.

The feeling became more insistent, like tiny hooks of insectile feet grasping for purchase on his skin. Perhaps a beetle had gotten tangled in his hair.

Or a wasp.

He swatted his neck, brushed frantically at the back of his hair, expecting to discover the crushed exoskeleton of one bug or another, hopefully not one with a stinger.

"Freddie!"

The feeling vanished.

"It won't hurt if you don't resist."

Of its own accord, his chin dropped. He snapped his mouth shut. Started shaking his head. "Uh-uh. *No fuckin' way.*"

"Freddie."

"There's no way I can—"

"Freddie!"

He stopped talking. The rotors churned the air, vibrating the chopper.

"Julie did this for nearly a year," she said softly, "and it never bothered her. She didn't even realize it was happening." After a beat, she added, "I didn't either." Zoe's eyes, through Christie's, fell out of focus, seemingly mesmerized by the engine noise and whistling blades overhead. "That girl . . ." she slowly shook her head. "She just . . . She just accepted life as it came, didn't she?" Her little face darkened. "I had no right . . ."

"Zoe?"

She looked back up at him. "I swear to God, Freddie, I never knew." Her eyes searched his face, seemingly begging forgiveness.

"I understand. *She'd* understand."

She nodded, sniffled, then wiped a rain-soaked wrist under each eye.

Siri said, "3 minutes to decontamination."

"Okay. So help me out here."

She took a deep breath and nodded, all business again. "I know how it works now. The host has to relax. Otherwise, I have to force my way in. That's when it hurts."

Freddie nodded. He heard, he understood, but simply couldn't accept it.

"Worse, I have less control. It takes a lot of effort if I have to force it. I can't hold it for long—and I can't concentrate for shit."

Freddie just looked at her.

"And if I'm going to fly this bird, I need 100%, total, concentration." Her eyes drilled into him.

A loud *pock!* from the starboard window. A split second later, a shot rang out from across the pavement football field.

"Now or never, Freddie."

He stared wide-eyed at the tiny mark on the window, right in line with his head. If the window hadn't been there . . .

"The glass is impervious to small arms fire, but not the motor. Or the swash plate or bearings."

"What are—"

"Freddie!"

He nodded, took one last glance at the pockmark, then relaxed into the seat.

The feeling again. Pleasant, really—indeed quite euphoric. His mind wandered. Thoughts of Big Man's Bar . . . poetry . . . Stevie.

He bolted upright. "I can't."

"Freddie?"

He did not turn to look at her, just stared out the windshield at the downdraft ripples on the pavement. More pocks and twangs riddled the chopper, but he tuned them out.

"Do you trust me?"

He did not reply. Only slowly nodded.

Siri said, "2 minutes to decontamination."

"Then let go, Freddie. Let me in."

A concussion shook the chopper, followed by an orange ball of flame not a hundred feet ahead. Freddie glanced that direction.

"It's got to be now, Freddie."

He nodded again, then leaned back and took a deep breath. Heart slamming in his chest.

"Just let go . . ."

The feeling again. As before, it was nice. He just let it wash over him. When the panic came, he gently eased it away as if guiding a sleepy child to her bedroom. Somewhere in the distance, another concussion. But he no longer cared.

He just let go.

-Spite-

"Something something time to detonation."

Who said that? Where was he? What was happening? He tried to roll over and go back to sleep, then it all came back to him. *Feet dangling . . . hands slipping . . . falling through space . . .*

Constantine bolted awake. The ceiling above him was destroyed. He was lying on the rubble. His head was pounding. His body ached. His left leg felt like it was exploding.

He knew better than to try and stand without assessing his injuries.

The good news was, he was alive. By God, he was *alive!*

Don't pop the champagne corks just yet—you still have to evacuate.

But survival was possible. With possibility came hope.

He wiggled his toes then rotated his ankles. Although the pain was considerable in his left calf, he confirmed his feet were in good working order.

Now his hands.

He slowly lifted his right arm, peered at the fingers, wiggled them. Excellent.

He raised his left hand to examine those fingers. The problem was so obvious, he thought it was an illusion. Maybe because he wasn't wearing his glasses. Perplexed, a half grin twisted his lips.

His ring finger was bent ninety degrees sideways. Right at the middle knuckle. It disappeared behind his pinkie, reappearing on the outside of his hand like a sixth digit. He couldn't believe what he was seeing—except that he could *feel* the numb digit with the back of his pinkie. Strangely, there was no pain.

Completely numb.

He sucked in a breath, then screamed in horror.

Attracted by the noise of the fall, the Creed Thing had crabbed its way down the hall. It had stopped just short of the elevator door, having forgotten where it was and what it was doing. Had Constantine remained silent, the monster may have wandered away.

Not now.

Its cratered head peeked around the corner, eye bulging like a tumor. Scanning for sound or movement. Despite himself, Constantine squirmed, whimpering.

The Creed Thing made a noise like *Ack! AAAack!* and scuttled into the car.

Constantine tried to rise on his left hand. Lightning bolts shot up his arm and he screamed in pain. Fell back in the rubble. Cradled the injured hand.

The Creed Thing zeroed in, grasped Constantine's pant leg, and began its journey upward.

"No! *NOOOO!*"

Constantine hadn't realized how heavy Creed was. He'd been, after all, a muscle-bound soldier. The body weight crushed him. Drove the air from his lungs. Its fetid breath nauseated him. He spied unthinkable fleshy tendrils caught in its teeth as it went for his throat. He ducked his head, tucking his carotid artery between shoulder and chin.

The Creed Thing clamped down on his nose. Shook like a pit bull. Over his own screams, Constantine registered another muted *Aaaack!*

The beast snatched its head away and began clearing its mouth. Its tongue was a bloody bloated slug. The obstruction slipped out but didn't fall free. It dangled there by a thread of gristle.

Constantine thought of the old expression, *Cut off your nose to spite your face.* He screamed again, so hard his head throbbed.

But the Creed Thing wasn't finished. Oh, it had just gotten started.

Ack! AAAAAAACK!

-Escape-

Zoe's eyes snapped open, peering through Freddie's at the control panel.

Siri said, "One minute to decontamination." Then, "Fifty-nine. Fifty-eight—"

With her left hand, she grasped the collective control beside the seat like the handbrake of a car. She twisted the throttle and pulled upwards enough to gain a foot or so of lift. The chopper rocked, swayed—then departed the safety of the earth.

At the same time, with the pedals and cyclic control—a sophisticated version of a joystick—she spun the nose of the chopper toward the squad of D-SAlt soldiers. She turned too far, then overcompensated the other way. She calmed herself, centered her mind, centered the bird. It wavered but maintained position. Now facing her enemies.

The squad knew what was coming. Some scattered like cockroaches in the storm.

"Little late for that, boys," she said under her breath. The deep resonant tone of her voice shocked her. She thumbed a white button on the cyclic control. The chopper jarred with the recoils of finger-sized projectiles fired at 4000 rounds per minute. Twin waterfalls of brass tinkled to the pavement around the chopper as if from a river of frozen metal.

A hundred yards in the distance, a trail of eruptions as tall as a man sprang up from the pavement. As the line crossed any soldier, he was cut down, sometimes in half, in a mist of scarlet.

She moved her right thumb to a plastic cover and flicked it up, exposing a red button. She lined up the crosshairs on the LCD screen and fired.

A pencil trail marked a path from the port side, whistled over the guards' heads and exploded into the mountainside in the distance.

Christie gasped from the back seat. "Fireworks!"

Siri said, "Forty-eight. Forty-seven—"

All but two of the guards got the hint and kept retreating. One of the stubborn two took a knee, hefted a rocket launcher. The other approached from behind him with an RPG.

"You guys are just not getting it, are you?" She moved the LCD crosshairs just in front of the guards—and pressed the button again. Twin rockets were delivered, this time with lethal intent. She didn't stick around to assess the damage.

She cut the chopper sharply left. Swung it into position the opposite direction. She overdid it, forgot to add lift, and the rotor tips spit a shower of sparks from the pavement as if from a welder's torch. She compensated *(Not too much!),* and the bird bobbed and swayed—then stabilized.

Zoe shuddered. Nearly pissed herself.

Christie said, "Mr. Freddie, you're strong, but you're not so good at driving choppers."

She'd come a fraction of an inch from turning the chopper into a five-ton food processor sans giant glass pitcher.

"You got that right, kid." She hefted the collective with her left hand and tested the throttle.

Siri said, "Thirty-six. Thirty-five—"

She tilted the chopper forward and tried to twist the damn throttle off the handle. She overdid it, lost some lift, backed off—then established as much speed as possible while maintaining minimal altitude. "Come on, come *on!*"

Slowly rising, the Apache blazed through the storm.

She was by no means a pilot. Indeed she'd racked up a ton of time in the simulator, even logged a few flying hours during a beginner's course. But she'd never gotten as far as flying solo.

She hadn't understood her motivation at the time, just got the nagging feeling she should do it. Having long since learned to follow her instincts, she'd heeded that mysterious call.

Siri said, "Nineteen. Eighteen—"

She focused on the controls, leaning the Apache forward every inch she could in order to gain every knot she could.

The cockpit was stuffy. Not just from the rain.

"Twelve. Eleven—"

On ten, Christie joined the lifeless voice on the radio.

"Seven! Six! Five!" she cried joyfully, bouncing her heels against the seat bottom on every number.

Zoe switched the LCD monitor source to the rear-mounted camera. Her heart sank at how close the mountain still seemed.

"Three! Two! One!" The radio fell silent, and Christie. The roaring engine and whistling rotor blades seemed suddenly deafening.

Siri said, "Decontamination commencing."

Zoe sacrificed some lift in exchange for more speed, eyes glued to the mountain in the monitor. In her peripheral, through the windshield, she realized the ground was gaining clarity.

For a moment nothing happened.

The mountain seemed to flash yellow. The boulders, trees, the grass and soil, all for an instant yellow—then back to normal. She thought maybe she'd imagined it.

Then the LCD went white, then dead gray, even as the air around the chopper burned a brilliant orange.

"Hold on!"

A shockwave rocked the helicopter; a rumble like bowling balls pummeled the fuselage. The chopper shook violently as if every bolt and rivet was breaking its bonds, mutinying, leaving the bird to tumble through the air in a litter of parts.

The nose dipped farther—*too* far. Zoe's intestines coiled as she found herself staring through the windshield at the ground flashing by. Less than fifty feet below.

They were going to crash.

She was going to puke. She wondered what Freddie had last eaten and whether it would taste as good coming up as it had going down. She wondered if they'd survive.

They were too low but no longer diving. The blast was blowing them forward, she realized, forcing the nose down, the shockwave providing a new gravitational orientation on the rotors. The bird tilted and swayed. The ground whizzed by in a blinding blur. The rotors shredded the top two feet of a passing tree. Christie screamed. Zoe fought for stabilization as best she could, relying more on instinct than her meager training.

Then the sound finally caught up, painful even through the bulletproof glass and insulated walls, all-encompassing, deafening.

They started to dive, thankfully clear of the trees.

That meant the shock wave was dying. She nosed up, achieved some stability. After a full minute plowing steadily forward, she decided they were through it.

She eased off, stabilized . . . then finally hovered. She slowly rotated the Apache to face the complex. Or where it once had been.

Radioactive fog surrounded the blast point. Rain turned to steam hundreds of feet above ground zero, a manmade cancerous cloud. Even at this distance, even through the haze, she could discern the glowing orange flows, blind molten fingers groping the earth.

Legions of souls, malevolent and benign, floated lost on the hill, anguished, oblivious of the searing heat. Surely those ghosts would haunt the mountain, in search of something they'd never find, perhaps for millennia.

Christie piped up from the back seat. "Where are we going?"

"Home."

CHAPTER SEVEN

AFTER

-Swamp-

Zoe stared at the windshield. Freddie stared back. She'd killed the engine, but not right away. Her finger had hovered there for nearly a full minute. Somehow she'd felt that in cutting that switch, she'd be severing all ties with Freddie, with this new life she'd come to love.

Finally, she'd done it.

The rotors were dying. She kissed her fingers, laid them on the cold glass. "You're a good man, ya big oaf."

One moment Freddie was struggling to relax through blasts and bullets, allowing the strange feeling to wash over him. The next he was staring through a ghost of himself into the Florida Everglades. It was dusk, the only illumination provided by a mere reflection of sunlight—smears of lavender on a darkening sky.

The rotors slowed to a stop; the fuselage creaked and groaned.

From outside, crickets were tuning up for an all-night symphony. Somewhere in the distance, an ominous moan arose then died to a resonant cackle. Maybe a frog. Or a night bird.

Maybe a gator.

Silhouettes of sawgrass broke the water's surface, providing cover for countless creatures of the swamp. Shapes of shadowed herons hovered gracefully in the light breeze. An iguana—or perhaps an adolescent crocodile—slipped from a branch into the shallow water no more than twenty feet away.

Although the doors were sealed, he worried about what might seep in. Or come crashing through.

He located the buckles to the harness and released them. Those meager mechanical noises seemed deafening in the stillness.

Christie.

The seat complained as he turned to find the girl seated calmly, staring at him, still strapped in.

"How you doing, Pumpkin?"

"It's me." Her voice was impossibly high-pitched.

"Of course it's you, sweetheart."

"I mean it's me. Zoe."

Freddie searched for something to say but came up dry. He nodded, and his gaze drifted to the floor. He took a breath and let it out, then looked back into her eyes. "So what now?"

She patted the seat beside her.

-Predation-

The cabin had grown murky. Freddie watched as Zoe unbuckled her harness, stood on the seat to snap on an overhead light, then plopped back down next to him. In the dim cone of yellow, he turned his palm up on his thigh. Zoe sighed and placed her little hand in his. She chuckled as she stared at it. "So tiny . . ."

"What happened, Zoe?" He found it awkward addressing a five-year-old as a grown woman. Even more difficult was believing the events of the last hour, despite the fact he'd seen them with his own eyes.

"I was conspiring with a journalist to bring down the agency."

"Why?"

"You saw what they'd been up to back there."

He nodded.

Outside, something heavy plodded placidly through the underbrush, perhaps on cloven hooves, perhaps grazing on grass and tender shoots.

"So what happened?"

Zoe shrugged with Christie's shoulders. "They caught me."

"You?" He scoffed and shook his head. "I find that hard to believe."

Another something, heavier, came crashing through the same underbrush.

"If someone really wants you, they'll get you," Zoe said. "Eventually."

Muffled by the walls of the helicopter, a brief scuffle. Then keening. Growling.

"How'd it happen?"

The brush outside grew still.

"When I found out they were on to me, I took off for Miami, to a safe house I'd arranged personally. Maybe that's why I remoted back there later and somehow chose Julie." She looked up at Freddie. "I felt safe there. That was my mistake. What I didn't know is that they'd been on to me for some time. Knew about my safe house. When they were ready, they just sniped me with a tranquilizer and flew me back to Colorado. By the time I came to, I was already—" She raised her eyebrows. "—incapacitated."

Maybe he imagined it, but he thought he could discern ripping, wet tearing—then grunts of contentment through the smacking of lipless jaws, perhaps under lidless eyes.

"Why not just . . . take you out? Permanently?"

"I'm a black swan." She answered Freddie's unasked question. "They were conducting psi experiments, looking for new weapons our enemies—*their* enemies—had never considered. Telekinesis, ESP, all that. Everyone has at least some latent abilities. In a few, black swans they called them, those skills are much more pronounced. It's still undetectable without close scrutiny.

"I've always had a certain sense about things; I just wrote it off as a matter of—" She shrugged. "—observation."

"Sense about things?"

"I don't know. Like I won at cards, even though I didn't play often. In martial arts, I always seemed to know what was coming in plenty of time to respond."

"The dice?"

"No. Never anything like that. Our Tenzi game happened post-augmentation."

"Is that what the amber did? Augment your . . . abilities?"

She turned her head toward the cockpit. "No. That was Constantine's carousel. From what I was able to gather, psi abilities are kept in check by certain glandular and cerebral functions. It's like nature is holding the skills dormant until we've evolved to the point we're ready to use them. The carousel enhanced and deadened those functions in a specific, intricate sequence." She looked at Freddie. "The problem was, subjects weren't surviving it. Until they discovered the amber."

"What did *that* do?"

She shrugged. "Solved the lethality problem. They hadn't studied it extensively, but one thing it did for certain was sustain the life of any living flesh it came in contact with. *Indefinitely.* Even like—" She grimaced. "—a severed head. If it was already soaked in amber pre-decapitation."

Freddie's face was a mask of horror.

"There were already subjects down there, encased in these strange capsules. One of them was a kid from the 16th century." She let that hang there a moment.

"Good God."

"Yeah."

"Down where?"

"The navy found it in a sunken ETC in the Mariana trench."

"What's that?"

"The deepest known point of the ocean floor."

"No. An ETC."

"Extra-Terrestrial Craft."

"You mean, like a UFO?" His face revealed his skepticism.

"I know," she agreed. "But it was real. I obtained photos. Even a video. I passed them to Brennan Payne, the journalist. Christie's father."

"I never read about it."

"They got to him before he could release it. I was up for sanctioning too, but I was too valuable to just kill. So—" She raised her eyebrows. "—the amber."

He nodded. "So what happens now?" he asked. "With you and me? Christie?"

"She needs you, Freddie."

"Who, Christie?" He was already shaking his head. "No. I couldn't. What happens when Stevie comes home one day? I'll have enough problems just—"

"Freddie?"

His voice trailed off. He looked at the floor.

"About Stevie . . ."

He peered up at the cockpit, studied the back of the seat. "Don't."

"Freddie?"

He shook his head, refused to listen.

"Freddie."

After a pause, he turned to her, eyes pleading.

"Stevie is already home, Freddie."

"Please, Zoe . . ."

"Not at your house."

He laced his fingers in his hair and propped his elbows on his knees.

"You know that."

He shook his head. His breath quickened.

"How could he return to your house when he never left there?"

Freddie's lips trembled. He closed his eyes and whispered, "Please stop."

"In fact, he never left that parking garage, did he Freddie?"

"Gotcha!"

"Dad!"

"Hold on, son!"

"Don't drop me! Please, Daddy. Don't drop me!"

"Who's the strongest man in the world, little buddy? Huh?" He did his best not only to reassure the boy, but to distract him, keep him calm.

"You are," Stevie said, half crying half laughing.

"Alright then. Just you hang on, and ole Dad'll have you out of there in a jiffy." He winked down at his son. "We'll be riding bikes before you know it."

The boy didn't answer, but his eyes trusted.

Freddie crawled backwards. Refused to think of Stephanie's charred corpse. He lost sight of his son but heaved with all his might. He was making progress, dragging the boy up the wall of rubble, almost there . . .

The boy hung on something. Stuck. Immovable.

"Wait!" Stevie yelled.

Indeed he could go no farther, could pull no harder without yanking the bony arm right off the shoulder.

"Dad?" the boy whimpered. "My leg."

Freddie held his grip and looked back over the edge. He could see only Stevie's face. No farther. The boy peered down toward his own feet, then desperately back up at his father.

Freddie scooted farther out.

Hooked in the boy's pant leg like a cruel claw, a vicious finger of rebar.

Sirens in the distance. Had they just shown up, or had he been too distracted to notice them until now? Maybe rescue personnel were already on the scene.

Freddie studied the rebar-pinned pant leg. His stomach dropped when he realized the other end of the steel was firmly embedded in a slab of concrete the size of a small car. Bal-

anced precariously on the rubble. Swaying, ever so gently. Or maybe it was just his imagination.

Both their hands were sweaty. Bloody.

Slippery.

Freddie tightened his grip. Blocked out the throbbing in his forearm. "Help! Up here! SOMEBODY HELP US!"

Stevie joined in. "Help!" He'd raised his free hand to his mouth to focus the shout, jostling himself.

"No, Stevie! Don't move!"

But he had *moved.*

Freddie denied it, tried to convince himself he hadn't felt it.

The slab had shifted.

No. Not that. Please, God, not that.

"Stevie listen to me! I want you to unbuckle your belt with your free hand. Slowly!" Muscle spasms. Pain. In his arm and in his heart.

"HEEEELP!" Freddie screamed. His lips were trembling, his body numb. Under his breath, he whispered, "Please, God . . ."

The kid was making progress with the belt . . . then the concrete rocked. Slipped another inch.

Stevie stared up at him, buckle forgotten. "Daddy?"

"Stevie . . . " This time it was a whimper.

The boulder tilted.

Their hands slipped farther, only fingers on bloody fingers now.

"I love you, little buddy."

"I couldn't . . ." Freddie looked at his hands. He didn't recognize them. "I couldn't . . ."

"Freddie?"

He looked up at her. "It was just . . . buried." He stared up into the glow of the dim fixture, as if looking into the eyes of God. "I was . . . crushed. Terrified. I hid it from myself somehow. I mean, I knew, but yet . . . I just couldn't . . ." he lowered his eyes from God's to Zoe's.

"Couldn't let him go?"

He nodded absently, then looked away.

"I know." She shook her head slowly. "I know, Freddie."

He said to the floor, "Stevie blames me."

"He *doesn't!*" She shook his arm. "You blame *yourself,* Freddie. I guess that's your prerogative, although I think it's bullshit, but *Stevie* doesn't blame you."

"You can't know that."

"He told me," she said. "Stephanie doesn't blame you either. You did all you could that day. More than anyone else could have done—or would have even thought to do. Your family was proud of you."

He looked back at her, eyes accusing. "How could you say that?" He shook his head. "Not cool, Zoe. Not cool at all."

"No one ever really dies, Freddie."

"Yeah, that's what they say." His voice was laced with bitterness. "But you don't know. No one does."

"The last thing you said to Stevie was, 'I love you little buddy.'"

Freddie's brow furled, looking from one of the girl's eyes to the other.

"The day Stevie was born, Stephanie said, 'Look at that cute little big head. Definitely a Schaeffer.'"

He shifted his gaze to the cockpit.

"They loved you, Freddie." She gripped his hand tighter. "They still do."

The tears came in a torrent, shaking him to the core. She sat with him. Held him. Her arms lacked the reach to make it around his chest, but she clung fiercely to his shirt with her tiny fists. Sometime as he wept, she whispered, *"You can let go now."*

After a full minute, he looked up, nodded, then wiped his face with his sleeve. "Okay." He sucked in a breath, blew it out through pursed lips. "Okay, okay . . ."

"There's someone else who needs you now. In *this* world."

"Christie."

"Yes."

"What about her father?"

"That was Brennan Payne. The journalist, remember?"

"Mother?"

"Dead."

"Relatives?"

Zoe just shook her head.

"I mean, even if I were to take her in, how would it ever work? What about her birth certificate? School records? Hell, the agency?"

"Leave all that to me."

"How would you—"

She raised her eyebrows, tilted her head toward him.

"Yeah okay," he said, and couldn't resist a pained smile. "So, what happened to Christie's family?"

"Payne and his wife adopted her. Then the wife died when Christie was two. You know what happened to her father."

Freddie nodded.

"She doesn't know it yet, but she's all alone now." She smirked. "Of course, good old Uncle Sam would make sure she got fed and didn't die of pneumonia." She shook her head. "That's not good enough, Freddie. A child needs someone she can count on. Someone to take her side, right or wrong. She needs a home, a place that's hers and no one else's. Drop her at a fire station, she'll be shuffled between institutions until her eighteenth birthday. Orphanages. Foster homes. Lot of those kids wind up in jail. No one would ever really give a shit. No one would think *her* coloring page was the best, even if another kid's was better. No one would call her 'their special angel.' Absent that kind of love, her little spirit would shrivel and die—or grow too hard and cold to ever hold anyone closer than arm's length." She studied her lap, picked at her pant leg. "Trust me. That's no way to grow up."

Freddie asked the question he dreaded most. "And what about you?"

"Oh, I'll be around. For a while. There's a bureaucrat somewhere who's going to delete some files. Create some new ones. Forms will be signed, personal recommendations submitted. Post-dated adoption papers will be delivered to your house one day in the name of Christie Schaeffer. Complete with a birth certificate and adoption agency records to back it all up. I'll figure it out."

"Will I see you again?" That's what he'd really meant.

"See me?" She shrugged. "Maybe. But Freddie, what right do I have to do this?" She air-brushed her little fingers over her body. "Even briefly? Right at this moment, I'm robbing Christie of precious life minutes."

"I don't know. Maybe . . . a criminal?"

"A blonde bank robber with legs up to her neck and a double-D cup? That what you're thinking?"

Freddie chuckled, shrugged. "Well . . ."

"No, Freddie. It wouldn't be right. Even with a criminal. People can change, you know."

"Can they?" He genuinely wondered.

"I did. You helped me, hammer head. I'd have never trusted anyone again if I hadn't met you. I'd sure as hell never have loved—or been loved." She stroked his face with her tiny hand. "Julie changed too, didn't she? And Dexter?"

Freddie slowly nodded.

"But they can't change if they never get the chance, if they're crammed back into their subconscious, unable to think and reason and decide and *act*."

Freddie sighed and raised his eyebrows in reluctant agreement.

"By the way," Zoe said, "Julie says to tell you, 'this is totally freaking her out, man.'"

An unexpected laugh burst forth from him. Zoe joined in,
and they laughed together, one step from crying, this one last
time.

After they settled down, Freddie asked, "So, where *are*
you, Zoe? I mean, when you're not . . . remoting."

"The same place Stevie is. And Stephanie. And Julie and
Johnny and everyone who's ever passed along this way."

Freddie nodded.

"I am nowhere." She paused, bore deep into Freddie's
eyes.

"I am everywhere."

-After-

They'd spent the night in the Apache, Christie sleeping
peacefully, Freddie starting at every howl croak and crackle
from the Everglades. Early the next morning, he'd located a
backpack and loaded it with what provisions he could
scrounge: MRE's, full canteen, compass, a flashlight and other supplies.

He'd expected a long and arduous journey through the
swamp. The first mile or so, he'd kept the pistol cocked and
locked, out and up, raised and ready. But it was as if during
the wee hours, a crew of Disney animals had struck the stage
of nature's violence and replaced the set with her beauty for
the morning performance. He'd seen signs of neither the cloven grazer nor the stalker, nor the slightest evidence a struggle had occurred. Rather, colorful birds sang cheerily, seemingly leading them to safety. Frogs leaped gracefully from
their path and splashed into the water. Christie's constant

banter had kept him distracted and delighted. Other than fending off clouds of mosquitoes, it hadn't been so bad.

A trucker had picked them up a half mile down the Okee-chobee freeway.

The TV provided background noise as Freddie prepared breakfast for two.

They'd mourned together, and the experience bound them as one, father and daughter.

During the first several months, his grief had been spiked with fear, certain another Bill Vargas would appear at his door, this time with pistol drawn, sans pretenses. Or that they'd be torn to bits when a blast, ground zero Old Mable's starter coil, tore through his neighborhood.

Over the next year, their grief had descended like the setting sun, a new dawn on the horizon. His fear had eased to worry, his worry to concern. Now he simply maintained a prudent caution. Monitored the news. Kept himself informed.

Just in case.

Through the television speakers, Raven Stryker, aka The Voice, revealed the latest tragedy through tight lips and tart beard. Freddie sighed.

"Yet another mass shooting rocked Washington today when General Adam Kinsley, director of the DSA reconstruction panel, opened fire with an assault rifle on various members of the board he himself had gathered. From the capitol, here's F. Schmitt Walker. Schmitt?"

Freddie called out, "Rise n Shine, Bunny Butt!"

"Raven, investigators are still trying to piece together a motive for the slaughter. According to one survivor, a stenographer whose name is being withheld for security purposes, Kinsley had apparently hidden the assault rifle in the board-room ahead of time. He pulled it from behind a cabinet, stood on a chair and shouted—now keep in mind, these are his words, not ours—he shouted, and I quote, 'Here's how this works, you shit-wings,' unquote. That's, 'Here's how this works, you shit-wings.' Again, the LLM broadcast network does not condone the use of such language, but our goal here is to provide the most accurate news available."

Then why did you say it twice, 'shit-wing?' Freddie slid the eggs smoothly from pan to platter. Pouring himself a cup of brew, he yelled, "Hey! Princess Pretty Pants! Time for breakfast!"

"Schmitt, was there anything else? Anything that might give any indication as to why Kinsley opened fire with the as-sault rifle?"

The repeated use of *assault rifle* was not lost on Freddie.

"Well, Raven, another survivor, Kentucky senator Chuck Hasher, said Kinsley seemed to have chosen specific targets. Like the senator, a few were passed over, even politely asked to step aside. This according to Hasher. Strangely, Kinsley targeted only those sympathetic to his DSA expansion pro-posal. Finished with his bloodbath, Kinsley tossed aside the assault rifle, drew his sidearm and turned it on himself."

"But did he *say* anything else, Schmitt?"

You mean like another shocking profanity? Freddie car-ried their plates to the table.

"In fact he did, Raven. His final words, just before taking his own life, were apparently an expression of the remorse and mental anguish this tortured man was feeling."

"What did he say, Schmitt?"

"He said simply, 'It hurts.' That was all. 'It hurts.' And it does, Raven. It hurts us all. This is F. Schmitt Walker, reporting."

Stryker, limelight all to himself now, launched into a diatribe. He asked how we as a nation could sleep with ourselves when we allowed the legal sale of assault weapons. How did we let a mentally disturbed individual get his hands on a firearm? When would we wake up? When would we finally get every single gun off the street for good? It was long past time we melted them down, every single one, and sank the whole molten blob to the bottom of the sea. It was time we voted for change, time for . . .

Freddie located the remote and clicked off the Voice Chamber. He strode back to Christie's room, the old electronics room. He knocked respectfully—waited—then cracked the door. Lavender walls and purple painted furniture brightened the room, and his heart.

"Hey kid, I hope you're dressed and ready for school."

Olaf fidgeted when a lump wiggled beneath the *Frozen* bed cover.

Freddie smiled and shook his head. "Hmmm. Now I wonder where that Christie could be?" He opened the closet door. "Nope. Not in here."

A giggle rose from beneath Olaf.

He opened a dresser drawer. "Not in here either."

"I'm too big to fit in tharr," said the lump. Christie had been working diligently on her *R*s. Now, rather than gliding them, she exaggerated them. Instead of Freddie's little "British Princess," she'd become his "Irish Angel." He knew she'd eventually get it right, but he hoped it wouldn't happen any time soon.

Freddie gasped. "Who said that?"

More giggling . . .

"Hmmm . . . Did it come from this little lump under Olaf?" He poked his finger into the snowman's nose, found the girl's ribs on the first try. Christie shrieked with laughter, threw back the covers and squirmed off the bed. As she bounded for the door, Freddie realized she'd indeed dressed herself. In a Queen Elsa gown, complete with crooked ice-tiara and over-sized bunny slippers.

They were going to be late for school—again.

That night, Freddie pushed through the door with the red fox.

"Freddie the Fixer!" Big Man's booming voice easily dominated the jukebox, where John Waite was pining, *I ain't missin' you.*

By the time Freddie pulled up a bar stool, a frosty mug was waiting for him.

Big Man propped his elbows on the bar. "See that thing about that general?"

Freddie finished his first sip, then nodded in way of an answer as he set down the mug. Still nodding, he wiped foam from his lips with his sleeve.

"Manners," Dexter teased. A stack of napkins appeared on the bar. "Wonder how long she'll keep it up?"

"Who knows?"

They shook their heads, wondering.

"Where little Irish Angel tonight?" Big Man pushed up from the bar, crossed his massive arms and grinned. "You didn't forget and leave her at school, did you?"

"Nah, she's at the Zaydon's. Princess dress-up sleepover."

They both chuckled. Freddie took another pull from his Amber Boch. This time, he used a napkin.

Christie had decided she wanted to be a poet, "just like Miss Jewels." Freddie made sure they documented every verse. She wrote it down, he scanned it.

Her first had been about a storm they'd survived together.

The wind goes fast,
The wind goes past.
Just like a hurricane,
The wind goes all around.

The verse was etched in Freddie's heart. "So, you and Shirley got any plans for a little prince or princess? Need me to draw you up instructions on how to make that happen?"

Dexter threw his head back and boomed with laughter. He'd met Shirley a week or two after Freddie had returned from hell with Christie in tow. After a few months, they'd thrown a small intimate wedding in Freddie's back yard. "Just so happens, I got some news for you."

"Get the hell out of here." Freddie's grin practically lit up the bar.

"Yep, yep. Five months in. It's a girl."

"Hey!" Freddie's smile faded. "Five *months?* Why the secrecy? Why didn't you tell me the day you found out?"

"Well, Shirley, she didn't want to say nothing 'til we knew everything's gonna be okay. Didn't want all the attention if, you know . . ."

"Yeah, I get it. But my feelings are still hurt."

"Just got clearance to talk about it today. You the first to know."

Freddie nodded, took another swig. "Congratulations, Dexter." He held out his fist. Big Man bumped it, then plucked a rag from his belt and began wiping the already spotless bar.

"So, you gonna name her after where she was conceived? Like maybe, 'Caprice?'"

Big Man belted out more garrulous laughter, tucked the rag away and lowered himself to his elbows again. He looked into his best friend's eyes. They stared at one another, waiting.

Their smiles faded.

"Julie," said Big Man. "We namin' her Julie."

NOTES FROM THE AUTHOR

I sincerely hope you enjoyed *Drawer #7*. A book lives and dies based on reviews, especially at Amazon. I would very much appreciate it if you could spare the time to leave one.

Thanks in advance!

The idea for this story was sparked by the disturbing experience of seeing someone else staring back at me in a mirror. Of course, an instant later, I realized the mirror was an interior-wall window, the face on the other side my brother Chuck's. We look similar enough that it really freaked me out for a second. That was all it took; my imagination was off and running.

But for the longest time, all I had was a character seeing a stranger's face in the mirror. Great but . . . it ain't a story. Then as I was rummaging through some old boxes in the attic, I came across a dusty booklet of poetry, written and staple-bound by a friend of mine from ages past. The real Julie V. Ayers—though not her real name. She really could spin a poem out of thin air, about anything you pleased. And she really used to say, "Go on, name somethin'!"

I thought, *What an interesting character.*

DING!

The entire novel came spooling into my head.

As you may have noticed, DN7 is peppered with alliteration and rhymes, a tribute to Julie, and to my long lost friend.

Fox's was a real place here in Miami. We used to come pouring in there, hot off the mat, like a swarm of beer-starved locusts. Though its history in DN7 was from my imagination, it really did shut down. And it really was a sad day for the dojo, and everyone in the area.

I had my own barstool and my own drink, the "Goldilocks." A shot of Jack and a Corona with a lime. Big Man is based on Fox's cook, a cordial, soft-spoken giant who showed himself only rarely, and whose name I never learned.

Christie is a carbon copy of my caprice, perpetually happy daughter Ezra. Ezi really did used to glide her *R*s. As of the publishing of this story, she has reverted to exaggerating them. My little Irish Princess. Like Freddie, I know she'll eventually get it right, but I really do hope it's not too soon. The poem about the storm, *The Wind,* is all Ezi, exactly as she wrote it.

Stevie is based on my son Seven, who holds the Guinness world record for speed-clapping as of the publishing of this book. We really do rehabilitate and ride bikes together. He has created a comic strip, *Punky the Monkey,* which we'll be publishing soon. He is alive and well, never fell into a fiery abyss. That I know of.

There is no Jongo's, but I sure wish there was.

Freddie is based on my dear friend Kristin Mertz. The guy really is a creative genius. And he really is enormous. Unlike Freddie, Kristin practices martial arts and holds a black belt in Aikido. He carved his own bokken, which we affectionately dubbed, "The Telephone Pole."

Though dear friends have done exhaustive editing and proofing as beta readers, I haven't the budget for a professional. The other day, my four kids plowed through an entire dozen eggs for breakfast.

Then asked for more.

Like that.

So if you find errors in this book, I humbly ask your assistance in ferreting them out. Just email me and I'll fix them. And thanks in advance!

Thanks for reading,

Jeff

More by Jeff Wade

Dread (A short story. Free on Amazon!)
Finding Nowhere
Drawer #7
The Good Father

As a "thank-you-for-reading" gift, please enjoy free of charge my novella *Finding Nowhere*. Just sign up for my New Release mailing list at **JeffWade.com.** Don't worry; I'm no SPAMmer. I only reach out occasionally with free deleted chapters, discounts, new releases and other goodies.

Correspondence:
Grandmaster Jeff Wade, 7th dan, owner
South Miami Martial Arts
4542-B SW 75th Ave
Miami, FL 33155
305-265-7404
786-290-4603
Jeff@JeffWade.com

Manufactured by Amazon.ca
Bolton, ON

31218932R00269